"What's the CIA's real int
Marina Alexan
"So what's really going on here?

"It's possible—in fact, probable—your father has knowledge of confidential information, some of which is not outdated," Bergstrom said. "We have recent data that indicates the Skaladeskas could be a potential threat to this country and others. And if indeed they have taken your father back, his knowledge could put our nation at risk. We need to locate him and bring him back."

At last: the meat of the matter. "You want me to help you find him," said Marina.

No effing way.

They nodded together: MacNeil, with his short, quick affirmation, and Bergstrom with a more vigorous, energetic bobbing. "Yes, Dr. Alexander—because other than your father, you appear to be the only other expert on the Skaladeska clan here in the Western world—and perhaps anywhere outside of Taymyria. We want you to join our team—to find your father, and to find out everything we can about the Skaladeskas."

"No."

"You know of other experts who could assist us?" Bergstrom's congenial smile told her he'd purposely misunderstood.

"I'm not going to help you find my father." Marina was no longer hungry. They couldn't be serious about trying to recruit her. Sydney Bristow she was not. "I'm not joining your team. That's ridiculous. I'm not a spy. I'm an historian."

"And a caver, a pilot, a rescue worker, and an expert on human subcultures. And you bear the mark of the Skaladeskas. You don't need to be a spy, Dr. Alexander. But we need you."

Other Books by Colleen Gleason

The Draculia Trilogy
Lucifer's Rogue
Lucifer's Saint
Lucifer's Warrior

The Medieval Herb Garden Series
Lavender Vows
A Whisper of Rosemary
Sanctuary of Roses
A Lily on the Heath

Modern Gothic Romance
The Shop of Shades & Secrets
The Cards of Life & Death

The Stoker & Holmes Series
(for teens and adults)
The Clockwork Scarab
The Spiritglass Charade
The Chess Queen Enigma (forthcoming)

SIBERIAN TREASURE

A MARINA ALEXANDER ADVENTURE

C.M. GLEASON

AVID PRESS

Siberian Treasure
Second Edition, updated and revised
© 2010, 2015 Colleen Gleason

Cover photography: Tim Gleason
Cover design: Kim Killion
Interior design: Dan Keilen

ISBN: 978-1-931419-83-3

1044823

To Larry Yuhasz:
the one who suggested it all.

PRELUDE

Through the pain that never seemed to leave her, Anastasia Romanovna, wife of Tsar Ivan Vasiljevich, the Fourth, heard her nurses muttering.

"The tsarina grows weaker with each moment. She will not live another night."

"When she goes, the tsar will go mad!"

"How will we cope? What will they do to him?"

Anastasia didn't want to hear more, for her caregivers spoke the truth.

She was dying, and her husband's hold on sanity was tenuous at the best of times. The boyars and peasants alike called him Ivan *Grozny*—Ivan Awesome, Ivan Terrible.

Anastasia's death would leave him alone and vulnerable to his bouts of rage, his madness, and his rampages of violence, for she was the one who helped him control them. She was the one on whom he relied.

Gathering all of her strength, she called for one of the nurses, one of the few members of her husband's court that they trusted. "Adejana." The nurse she'd named came to her bedside. "My husband...please find him for me."

"I will call for him." The nurse bobbed a bow and dashed from the room, but not before Anastasia saw pity in her face—and then fear.

Indeed, the nurse should fear. When Anastasia was gone, there would be no one to hold her husband's rages in check. Ivan would have the heads of the men who poisoned his wife, who now waited gleefully in the wings for her to die. Theirs would not be a simple, nor a quick, death.

She felt no pity for those men, devout Christian though she might be. They were stealing her life at the age of twenty-six. And for no reason other than to destroy Ivan.

Anastasia's pain blended into sleep, then back into wakening. She sipped from something when it was brought to her swollen, cracked lips. It felt cool and smooth sliding down her throat.

Then he was there. Ivan.

His large, warm hands grasped hers and she forced her eyes open to look at him. Pain and anger lined his face.

Anastasia could not save herself, nor could she save him from the madness in his eyes. But she could save something.

"Ivan. The books."

"Yes, yes, the books. I will care for them. Rest. Do not speak; you will get better."

She rolled her head on the pillow in negation. It took too much effort, but she opened her mouth to speak. "They will destroy them."

"My grandfather's books?"

"I have heard it is their plan. My spies…tell me." She paused to catch her breath, and Ivan leaned toward her, bringing his familiar scent of cinnamon and clove. He trembled, for though he spoke otherwise, surely he knew it was too late for her.

But the books. They must be saved. She would make him understand that he must protect their secrets.

There were hundreds, perhaps a thousand of them. The volumes filled three vaults that were specially made to protect them from the fires that tore much too often through the wooden buildings in Moscow. Brought from Byzantium by the bride of Ivan's grandfather, Sophia Palaeologa, and hidden away beneath the Kremlin, the tomes and scrolls and papers surely bore untold information. Much of it was as yet undiscovered, unread, unstudied. No one knew all that was there—even her husband.

Ivan, with his insatiable love of reading, had visited the library countless times during his youth. He'd pored over the books, and later shared them with Anastasia. The two could read very few of them; they were written in ancient Greek and Roman and other unfamiliar archaic languages.

At Anastasia's urgings, Ivan had selected a few trustworthy scholars and set them to work in secrecy, translating the works. But there were so many, and the pages were old, delicate, and faded. They had barely begun their daunting task

"The library must be saved," she managed. "Promise me."

"I do promise, my love. I do." And beyond the unhealthy glint in his eyes, she recognized determination. He would see to it.

And she could die now, for there was nothing else she could do. She could not save either of them.

Only the books.

Four months after his wife's death, just as the heavy snows of winter began to descend upon Moscow, Tsar Ivan Vasiljevich emerged briefly from his despair and grief to fulfill the vow to his wife.

He had kept other promises he'd made to himself upon Anastasia's death, including torturing and killing the boyars he knew were responsible for poisoning her with mercury. Though he knew they were guilty, he had no proof. But he didn't care whether there was proof. God knew the truth, and that was all that mattered to Ivan.

And then there were the writings. The ancient library.

It took him weeks to make the arrangements; even longer than it should have, because when the rages and madness overtook him, he lost all reason. His forehead, scarred from the splits and cuts from when he smashed it against the floor in agony and fury, still throbbed and bruised, and caused him to fade in and out of lucidity.

But the books.

Knowing his own time on earth was limited, he'd worked quickly to have them carefully crated up. He executed or exiled some of the men after they had done this work, for he couldn't allow the boyars to learn what he planned. He dared not allow the traitors to discover the priceless library.

The men Ivan had not killed numbered four scholars and twenty soldiers, and he ordered them aboard a ship with the crates. His only concession was in selecting good, loyal men who had no family to leave behind, for he knew the depths of grief. The man to whom he gave complete and utter responsibility for the library the journey was his wife's cousin, Leonid Aleksandrov. A good man. One Ivan trusted as had his beloved Anastasia.

Under the instruction of Aleksandrov, the captain would sail the men and the library north along the wintry waters of Moskva River, into the Barents Sea. Then they would travel far east to the lands of mountains and long winters.

To a land remote and safe. A land newly conquered by Ivan: Siberia. It was place unexplored and thus protected from the murderous hands of the boyars, who'd threatened Ivan from the day he'd become Russia's ruler at the age of three.

Someday, God willing, he would leave the madness that was his life and go to the wilderness, and to his books.

Away from the ugly memories and violence of his youth.

Perhaps then he would be at peace.

PRELUDE II

September 15, 1942
Somewhere over Siberia

Irina Marina Yusovsky slipped her arms into the military-issue parachute as she struggled to maintain control of the tossing plane.

Icy air permeated the cockpit, and frost fringed her eyelashes. The temperature had dropped below minus thirty Celsius and she could barely move her fingers from their grip on the controls. The radio had long since died. The fuel was nearly gone.

Since she'd lost her way from the rest of the 73rd Guards Stalingrad-Vienna Fighter Regiment four hours ago, Irina had had no contact with the outside world.

She'd been forced from an air battle near Stalingrad by three Ju-88s—enemy aircraft determined to shoot her down. Her guns had failed, and Irina banked the plane and zoomed away from the battle.

A sudden storm had taken her by surprise, and she became lost in the buffeting winds. Ice formed on the inside and outside of her YaK-1, causing the radio and navigation devices to fail. The sky was dark with grey snow clouds, and she couldn't elevate the plane high enough to rise above them and navigate by the stars.

Now, four hours or more from home, lost in the mountains of Siberia, her only choice was to abandon the aircraft.

Fuel was low. She could barely move in her seat, and her only chance of surviving was to eject from the plane.

Irina tried one last time to radio for navigation, for help, to hear any human voice. But the only sound was the blast of wind and the sputtering of the engine as it tried to go on.

She guessed her altitude must be over 7500 feet. It was a long way to drop onto unknown terrain. She nosed the plane into a descent to help bring her closer to the ground.

Tightening the straps, Irina took one last breath and peered into the darkness surrounding the aircraft. If only she could see something below. For all she knew, jagged, icy mountains rose beneath her, ready to catch her fall and slice her to pieces.

When the time came, she moved quickly. Out of her seat, after checking the supplies strapped to her body and the parachute to her back, she reached for the hatch. One quick prayer followed by a flip of the lock, and a blast of air burst into the cabin.

She jumped.

The wind whistled along her, and the roar of the plane above careened off to the side as she plummeted toward the ground. Irina's chute expanded with a whoosh above her, and her free-fall stopped abruptly, then began to ease down.

She flexed her fingers, moved her ankles, rubbed her arms. It seemed forever that she fell, in the dark and silent world of billowing snow and gusting wind.

She thought about her companions and hoped that they, at least, would survive the fighting. They were tenacious and skillful flyers. Only two days ago, her comrade Lilya Litvyak had become the first woman to shoot down an enemy aircraft. She had shot down not one, but two Ju-88s.

As she descended, Irina thought only of Lilya, and her other comrades—not of her parents, or her sisters, or especially Kostya, her lover. If Marina Raskova, Irina's mentor and the woman who had commandeered the all-female fighter regiments, had survived in the rugged mountains by living on berries and chocolate bars for ten days, Irina could do the same. She was, after all, descended from the branches of a great and royal line—the Aleksandrovs, who were cousins to none other than Ivan the Fourth's tsarina: Anastasia Romanovna.

She would live.

She *would*.

Her feet slammed into ground, one after the other, catching her by surprise. Her knees buckled as she landed on them, her hands following to press palm-flat on the swampy earth. It was still dark, but as she struggled to her feet, she stripped off the parachute's silk and fumbled for the flashlight strapped to her waist.

Irina pulled it free, her frozen fingers still aching with every movement, and fought with the switch. A beam of yellow glowed in the darkness and she turned in a circle to survey her surroundings.

Her light cut through the dimness and suddenly illuminated three tall figures. They stood, wrapped in furs that covered their faces and arms and legs so that Irina couldn't even guess at their gender.

One of them brandished a gun.

Anything she might have said died in her mouth.

Another of them stepped forward to snag her arm, yanking her toward the group. Alarmed by his sudden movement, Irina stumbled and tried to pull away, losing the flashlight. But the grip on her fatigued muscles was too firm. He pulled her after him as they started to trudge silently into the darkness.

The third figure picked up Irina's flashlight from the ground and led the way.

They did not speak, even to each other, as they prodded her through the darkness. The flashlight had been turned off. They needed no illumination to find their way. Irina stumbled along in their midst. They hadn't left her for dead and they hadn't used the gun. Perhaps they meant her no harm.

She tripped over tree roots and stones while the men around her walked smoothly and carefully. At last, they came to darkness that loomed in front of them. The base of a mountain.

Before she knew what was happening, Irina was shoved through a small crevice in the wake of the leader and found herself inside: safe from the elements, but in darkness and closeness and in the presence of strangers.

They hustled her between them deeper into the mountain, down into the darkness of the earth.

ONE

June 30, 2007
Allentown, Pennsylvania

Police Chief Vince Bruger launched his fishing line with a smooth, practiced stroke. The baited hook plopped into the water with a satisfied sound and he sent two more lines sailing into the water. Then, after settling the last of the three rods in its propped holder, he relaxed against a fallen log.

Other than the constant movement of the river water, and the occasional birdsong, silence reigned. Just the way he liked it on a Friday afternoon. Maureen had the kids down to Philadelphia for the day, shopping and visiting with her mother, and Vince had been glad for the excuse of not joining them.

Not that he didn't like his mother-in-law. She was fine as they went, but he'd wanted to finish staining the woodwork around the living room. It was a lot easier to do that when two kids and a wife weren't underfoot, wanting to help and wondering when he was going to be done so she could find something else for him to do. On his day off.

It had taken all of thirty minutes for him to finish that task (not that he'd ever admit it to Maureen) and now he could kick back and relax.

It had been one hell of a week at police headquarters in Allentown. Not anything as bad as a homicide, or even any major accidents or fires. But with the new computer system upgrade, the move to a new building, and the Fourth of July coming up next week…Vince'd had enough on his hands to just want a day of peace by the river.

After all, next week they'd be managing all kinds of amateurs with their fireworks, as well as bonfires and picnics and parades. Celebrating the independence of his country was important, but one hell of a lot of work went into it for him and his law enforcement team. And there was a full moon coming. He'd been in law enforcement for twenty years, give or take, and call him loony, but a full moon always meant more trouble, more fires, more accidents and injuries. More crazy things happening.

He reached for the cold beer nestled in the small cooler. And he felt the ground tremor.

One of his fishing poles fell from its perch, and a few leaves fell from the trees above. Then the earth was still again. Strange.

He gulped down a couple swigs of Rolling Rock, then set the green bottle back in the cooler. As he shifted forward to readjust the pole that had fallen over, the earth rumbled beneath him again.

What the hell? An earthquake in Allentown?

The shifting and trembling became stronger, and he could hear the heavy, deep roll of the earth moving beneath him. Or something.

All of his poles clattered to the stone-strewn beach, and the rumbling got louder, and stronger. Vince was on his feet by now, and good thing, too, for a large branch crashed to the ground where he'd been sitting.

The river water churned and sprayed, more branches fell, and, to his horror, Vince saw cracks appearing in the earth beneath his feet.

He bolted away from the crevices and dashed toward his black F-150 parked a hundred yards away, digging in his jeans pocket for its key. Forget the fishing poles, the cooler. He needed to get his ass into town and find out what damage was happening there.

So much for a relaxing Friday afternoon.

Sirens wailed and disaster warnings blared. The earthquake had ended, but left the town center buildings in shambles, and people acting hysterical. Trees and buildings were ruined; rubble, branches, spikes of metal, and concrete littered the city center.

He didn't even try to get to his office. Instead, he headed for the city's disaster command center that had been created in the wake of 9/11. It was underground near the outskirts of the city off Route 145.

Inside, the trained staff was calm and organized, hectic and determined. Since all appearances indicated it was an earthquake, they could at least rule out terrorists. So, despite the disaster and its consequences, an earthquake was preferable to believing the town was under attack by some suicidal terrorist group.

A quick meeting with Mayor Fullton, a touch-base with his team, and then Vince was back out into the center of the furor. He'd learned the new chemical plant on the outskirts of town was completely leveled, and that was where most of the rescue efforts had, of necessity, been focused. Assistance was coming from Philadelphia and Princeton, and other places as well. Interestingly enough, no other communities had felt more than slight tremors during the disaster. It was all contained in the fulcrum of Allentown, and the epicenter appeared to be directly beneath that new chemical plant.

It was an odd-looking mess for an earthquake, Bruger thought. He'd seen pictures on television; never seen one in person before, of course, because they didn't have earthquakes on the East Coast. It looked like a whole island of ground had erupted from the earth, as high as ten feet in some places. And in the perimeter around it, ground had sort of fallen away. Deep, rugged crevices and chunks of earth, some fifteen, sixteen feet deep. The buildings and vehicles around the area had tumbled to the ground, crashing on top of each other and into the deep pits and cracks, making more of a mess.

The plant hadn't had a chance.

Three fire trucks, four ambulances, and five cop cars crowded the rubble, mingling with the vehicles of the overtime shift workers. At least it was late Friday, and not as many employees were within the plant. Still.

"Thirty-five people missing," Officer Melanie Grant told Vince as he rushed up to the property guard's office, which had been turned into a temporary command post. "Lots of them had left for the long weekend by the time this hit, thank God. We've had a couple calls from cell phones, several trapped under the rubble, but as for the rest—it's going to be a long haul."

"We've got rescue teams coming up from Philly," Vince told her, strapping on a protective helmet and lifting a radio to his ear to listen to a broadcast from Command Central. "Another team coming from Jersey. They should be in here in an hour or so." He shook his head. "We're gonna need dogs, and more heavy equipment to move this shit."

"Not to mention a lot of prayers," Grant told him. "If one of those drums with the chemicals collapses, it could ignite and add explosions to our mess here."

"Holy shit." He snapped his attention to Grant, a tall blonde woman who, from the look of the streaks on her face, had already been digging through the rubble. "What's the chances of that?"

"The plant manager, who was off-site today, says the nitrotuolene is highly flammable and compressed in the drums. If the area of those metal drums is compromised, or the area compresses any further, they'll ignite. We were able to find three under some concrete and steel beams. So far, they seem to be holding up, but if anything shifts, we're dead meat."

Vince swore. "We'll just have to work fast and easy." As he spoke, a paper fluttered across the empty parking lot and tumbled at his feet. He would have kicked it away, but Grant bent down to pick it up.

"Another one," she murmured, and stared at it for a moment.

"What?" Vince snatched it from her hand. "What do you mean another one?" He looked at the plain white paper with the strange image printed on it.

"There're a bunch of these papers blowing around," she told him, resting her hands on her hips. "Do you have any idea what it is?"

Vince shook his head. "Probably some kid's drawing for a club or something. Or maybe a new icon for a gang. That's the least of my worries right now." He crumpled the paper and pitched it toward a heavy metal trash can. "Let's get to work."

TWO

June 30, 2007
Princeton University, New Jersey

The United States Geological Survey records over fifty earthquakes a day in an average year." Professor Paul Everett brushed chalk-dusty hands over the seat of his dark trousers before he realized what he was doing. "Most of them can't even be felt by the average human. About eighteen earthquakes a year measure in at 7.0 on the Richter scale, and perhaps one or two at 8.0 or higher. Those are the ones we hear about in places like Bam, Iran."

Darlene was going to read him the riot act if he came home with powdery streaks on his dark pants again. He could never remember to use his handkerchief when he was in the middle of a lecture. Maybe he ought to just wear white pants.

"At this time, there isn't any accurate way to predict earthquakes," he continued, glancing at the clock at the back of the classroom. Five minutes and he was on vacation with Darlene, heading to the Shore.

And if he so much as stopped for a cup of coffee on the way home, delaying their Friday afternoon start time, she'd know— and he would hear about it. Focusing back on the lecture, Paul continued, "We can *anticipate* that one will strike in places like Hawaii, where the magma moving underground causes some extra activity prior to a quake, but in other areas where the earth shift is caused by pressure along fault lines, there is no accurate prediction method. Which is why I don't live in California." A soft murmur of laughter acknowledged his comment, but he knew his audience was about ready to check out.

"Scientists are collecting data using Global Positioning Systems to find where the major faults and fault lines are and combining that with statistical analysis. They hope to use that data to try and predict quakes.

"And recently, there was a study in Iceland that measured water chemistry—the levels of certain chemicals in the water before and after a large quake there. Scientists hope to be able to use that information to begin a data warehouse, which may also help predict future quakes."

About three minutes left, and then the class would slam their laptops, AlphaSmarts, or notebooks closed and shove them into their backpacks while streaming out of the geology lab. They were just as eager to start their weekend as he was.

Paul gestured to the university's seismograph mounted directly on the ground outside of the lab. "Many people confuse the purpose of the seismograph and believe it can be used to help predict earthquakes. And while this machine can record even the most sensitive of ground movements, it can only do so after the fact.

"As you can see, it's placed directly on the ground, and if the earth shifts, the needle will record even the slightest of the earth's movement. We'll talk more about what normal seismic activity looks like next week."

Most of the students had little real interest in the studies. They elected the class during the summer term as a last-ditch effort to fulfill a science credit in the liberal arts program at Princeton. He tried not to let the apathy bother him. After all, he taught three other, more advanced, classes for geology or biology majors. They not only looked at the seismograph readings, they had a clue what the readings meant.

"I'll cover Chapter Ten in next week's lecture. Come with questions, because that will be the last class before the exam." His last few words were lost as they rose en masse to sling backpacks over shoulders and stampede out of the room.

He turned to switch off his laptop, hoping to get out and on the road in time to beat the weekend traffic, and noticed one of his students standing next to the seismograph. The young woman was actually *looking* at it.

"Professor Everett, what is that?" She pointed to the paper roll that showed a series of red markings. Etched with gentle peaks and valleys was the activity in a fifty-mile radius around Princeton.

And there, on the seismograph, were big spikes coming from an area in the middle of low hills and valleys.

Big damn red spikes.

Paul swallowed the words he'd planned to give: a quick answer, before he'd seen what she was pointing at. He looked at it again.

Big damn spikes right in the middle of nowhere.

Paul frowned and peered at the little needle radiating up and down with its etchings. It appeared to be working.

"Shouldn't there have been some kind of warning before such big spikes? And what would cause something like that? There aren't any earthquakes around here, are there?"

Apparently someone *had* been listening, even though she'd spent half the class flirting with a young man across the room.

Paul adjusted his trifocals. Damn glasses; couldn't trust them to see when he needed to without having to move them around to get the right lens.

But, yes, the spikes were still there, like upside-down icicles. And as he watched, several smaller peaks jumped up—little aftershocks, they would be, if indeed it was an earthquake.

But an earthquake—of maybe seven or eight on the Richter scale, he guessed—in eastern Pennsylvania?

Incredible.

"Professor Everett?" She was staring at him.

He realized he'd never answered her question. "If I didn't know better, I'd think it was an earthquake. But there aren't any major fault lines in this area that would cause such a large response." He shook his head, scratching at the flimsy wisps covering the top of his scalp. "I don't know what else would create a graph like that."

Then he froze. He *did* know of something else.

Paul frowned, his brows drawing together. The last time he'd seen something like this, it was decades ago. Hundreds of miles away.

He'd have to find his old papers, his old records of seismic activity from thirty years ago.

Because if it was what he thought it was, he was going to be on the phone to the USGS and not heading for the Poconos.

Darlene was going to kill him.

Baltimore, Maryland

Barbara Melton, PhD, president and chief executive officer of AvaChem, had just sunk a beautiful putt when her brand new iPhone vibrated against her hip.

"Perfect timing," she muttered, glad it hadn't come moments before. The birdie put her two strokes ahead of her partner and lover, and that much closer to the wager they had riding on today's game: who was going to be the submissive during their sex play that night.

Tempted to ignore the insistent buzz, she nevertheless pulled the phone from its clip and noted the number of the incoming call. Theo Meadows, the COO of AvaChem, wouldn't call during her Friday golf time unless there was something important going on.

"Nice shot," her partner, Roger Brady, complimented as he dropped the pin flag back into the hole. "Haven't you trained your husband not to call you when you're on the course?" he joked. "Of course, if he'd called sooner, during your shot, I might be the one handling the handcuffs tonight." His eyes gleamed wickedly.

"It's Meadows. I'd better answer it," Barbara replied. "Melton."

"Jesus, Barb, have you heard?"

Barbara's heart stuttered as she slid her putter back into her custom tooled-leather bag. The last time Meadows had started a conversation with that question, the news AvaChem was dumping toxic chemicals into the Delaware River had just hit the press. "I've heard nothing. I'm on the fifteenth hole. What is it?" she snapped, nervous and impatient.

"Allentown, Terre Haute, and Hays—the plants are gone."

"Gone? What the hell do you mean, gone? In flames?" She leaned against the golf cart and began to fumble for her nitroglycerine tablets. There was always the risk at a chemical plant for an accident to occur, but three of them at once...?

"Bombs?" Barbara heard the squeak in her voice that made her sound like a teenybopper.

"You won't believe it. Earthquakes!"

She paused, her hand inside her pocketbook. "You're joking." She started to laugh, strained, but feeling the relief that trickled through her.

"Turn on the fucking news, Melton! It's all over the country! Three earthquakes, all of them where our buildings are located. They're completely destroyed. Everything's gone." Meadows' voice spiraled into a hysterical wail. "The IPO's shot, and we're *fucked*. We're *fucked*, Barb, do you hear me? And those federal fines— they're coming out of your pocket and mine, now, do you hear me?"

Barbara heard him, but she didn't believe him. Three plants, leveled by earthquakes—in the most unlikely places all over the country? All on a Friday afternoon?

All at once?

It couldn't be a coincidence, or pure, unadulterated bad luck.

It had to be those damn Greenies.

And there was no way Barbara was going to be stuck for two mil because of their tree-hugging antics.

She snagged her driver out of the bag and turned to the sixteenth tee.

Riyadh, Saudi Arabia

Dannen Fridkov had always heard Riyadh described as an island, a refuge, in the center of barren desert, and indeed, the Saudi Arabian capital was exactly that.

Located in the middle of the Kingdom, the city sported an eclectic combination of mud-dabbed buildings and fortresses, courtyards with palm-tree-trunk pillars, and modern white spires. And the only greenery to be spotted for hundreds of miles.

Doors to traditional and modern buildings alike were ornate, with Islamic art and designs in colorful geometric and organic shapes, often repetitious in their patterns. The streets were generously wide and busy, thronged with pedestrians, limousines, and the brown and yellow commuter buses available to women and those with limited funds.

Fridkov had visited the city only once before, briefly and at night, so this mid-day visit in the cloak of desert heat was quite a different experience. He would have preferred time to wander a bit—perhaps shopping for rugs on Talateen Street—but his mission was clear, and, of necessity, must be quick. He settled back into the seat of his chauffeured car, adjusting the unfamiliar skirts of the *thobe* he had donned in an effort to blend in as a native rather than a Western businessman.

The Lincoln Town Car moved smoothly through the streets, and Fridkov eyed Riyadh's water tower looming above the city. It rose like a flower toward the sun, with a long stem and a flat, fan-like top, glowing dirty yellow in the radiating heat. It was ironic that one of the most prominent landmarks in a city made from oil wealth was a water tower.

The industrialized world might be dependent upon oil, but in the end, water was the greater need—and something the earth gave more freely.

The minarets of the Great Mosque speared the sky, and Fridkov mused to himself that the devotion of the Arabians to their daily scheduled prayers was akin to that of the Americans to their television and French fries. He identified several members of the *muttawa* patrolling the streets, screening for violators of Islamic fundamentals.

Fridkov realized he was not so unlike the *muttawa* himself. However, he would draw the line at removing the nipples from the mannequins in a women's clothing store. Fridkov's style was much more subtle—yet direct.

The car turned onto Al Matar, and now he must focus on the task at hand—-the meeting with Israt Medivir, the president of Medivir Petroleum. The Medivir Building, though not nearly as tall and grand as the Ministry of Petroleum, still displayed the great wealth and success of the company. Success and wealth that had come purely by happenstance and not because of any great effort or planning on the part of Israt Medivir.

It was only his name that Medivir had given the company. The rest of his good fortune had come to him as nothing less than a gift—a gift that had now turned into a threat.

Looking in a well-positioned mirror, Fridkov arranged the traditional headscarf, *ghuttera*, over his dark hair so it framed the sides of his face like a curtain. He placed the *aqal* around the crown of his head to hold it in place and adjusted the mustache and goatee he'd donned on the airplane. With his naturally swarthy skin, dark eyes, and thick brows, Fridkov would blend in perfectly.

His briefcase rested comfortably against his calf, not so heavy, for it didn't even contain a laptop. No. What Fridkov needed for his meeting wasn't any burden to bear.

At last, the car eased to a halt in front of the Medivir Building. A tall, glistening glass spear, the offices of one of Saudi Arabia's largest petroleum companies clearly bespoke its prestige. Fridkov paid his driver with riyals and stepped from the cool comfort of the Lincoln into a wall of heat that made him gasp audibly.

A burst of air from the revolving door rustled his *ghuttera*, and then he was once again in cool comfort. How did people live in this forty-five-degree Celsius heat, day after day?

The Arabians have a love for their desert, despite the barrenness and aridity of the waves of sand. Fridkov could not imagine feeling anything but dislike for the dust and grit and skin-tugging dryness—not to mention the thirst and boredom.

The floor of the main lobby boasted an intricate granite and marble design, and it gleamed like the glass of the building's exterior. It was quiet and empty but for the fifteen or so live date trees that grew from holes in the floor, surrounded by round metal grates. The ceiling of the lobby rose high above, curving gently to meet at the top. No security guards, just a desk with two young men, who looked up as he approached. Fridkov flashed the counterfeit Medivir employee badge as he walked on past.

Continuing his stride without waiting for acknowledgement, he made his way to the elevators that nestled in a small alcove to the north side of the building. The buttons were labeled in both Arabic and English, of course, and he pressed the one that said 35. The top floor, where Medivir's office overlooked the city.

Medivir wasn't expecting him, but Fridkov had no qualms about appearing without warning. He knew for certain the man was not traveling and would be in the office today. Once Fridkov's presence was announced, Medivir would not dare deny him entrance. Even if Fridkov had made an appointment, or attempted to make one, the casualness of the business culture would not guarantee that he would see him today. And he must see him today, before another—Fridkov pulled back the sleeve of his robe to glance at his watch—four hours had passed.

The elevator doors opened to display a small, rounded greeting area. A gentleman sat behind the reception desk, his black hair combed back and gleaming as if it were wet. Instead of the traditional *thobe* and *ghuttera*, he wore a Western business suit, white shirt, and subtly patterned blue and black tie. He looked up and offered a polite greeting. "*As-salam alaikum.*"

"*Wa alaikum as-salam,*" Fridkov responded appropriately in Arabic, telling the receptionist that God's peace should also be with him, then he switched to English. Although he spoke a myriad of languages, Arabic was not one of them. His best choice was English, the most common second language spoken in Arabia. "Please give this to Mr. Medivir. I need a moment of his time."

He slid a small white card across the desk to the receptionist. The younger man picked it up, looked at the front in confusion, then turned it over to find a blank side. He looked at Fridkov, who merely smiled. "Mr. Medivir will understand. You need give it to no one but him, if you would. I will be happy to wait."

The young man hesitated, then, apparently recognizing the unyielding determination in Fridkov's eyes, rose from his seat and hurried out of the room.

Moments later, he returned with a much more relaxed expression on his face. "Sir, you may please have a seat for only a moment. Mr. Medivir will shortly finish his telephone conference and will then see you immediately. May I offer you some coffee? Or tea, perhaps? Fizzy water?"

"A coffee would be most welcome," Fridkov told him with gratitude. It had been more than twelve hours since he'd been sent to Riyadh from Amsterdam, and between the planning, traveling, and off and on sat-phone conversations—plus the jet lag—he could use a bit of a boost.

Fridkov had just added pinches of cardamom and cinnamon to his steely black coffee when an unobtrusive door near the reception desk clicked and opened. A tall, slim man in a Hugo Boss suit and Armani tie stepped through. At forty, Israt Medivir was younger than his photos made him appear, and with his olive complexion, hooked nose, and tiny black patch on his chin, he looked more like an Italian businessman than an Arabian oil sheik.

He made a direct line to Fridkov, who stood immediately, choosing to show the man deference while under the observation of others. With a slight bow, and then an extended hand, Medivir offered the same greeting of peace Fridkov had shared with the receptionist.

Again Fridkov replied appropriately, and when his host asked him to follow, he fell into step behind him. They passed no one during their walk down a short hallway illuminated with soft yellow lights and then into an expansive room. Medivir's private office.

Fridkov strolled into the room, and continued walking across until he reached the ceiling-to-floor windows along one wall. Amazing to be this high, overlooking the city, nearly eye to eye with the Faisalia Tower, with its odd spherical cap—and then to see the vast expanse of flat brown desert in the distance.

"I am most honored at your presence," Medivir said from behind him. "Your people have not visited the Kingdom for many years."

"Ten years, I believe it has been. Your dealings were with Roman?"

Medivir nodded. Fridkov had a moment to wonder what that meeting would have been like: the controlling, precise Roman striking a deal with the younger, staid Medivir. A deal that would make Medivir, who had been, at that time, a tradesman dealing in coffee, wealthy beyond his imagination, and forever beholden to Roman and his people. Rather like Daniel Webster selling his soul to the devil.

"Yes, Roman and I have continued our business dealings through videoconferencing, telephone, and email, but he has not returned to the Kingdom since our initial meeting."

Fridkov would have liked to learn more about how Medivir had been chosen. How Roman had met him and selected him to be the bearer of his people's product. But that was immaterial now.

He glanced at his watch. Three and a half more hours. He must finish the meeting successfully and be back at King Khalid for his flight.

Silence stretched for a moment, and then, as if remembering himself, Medivir offered his visitor a seat. Fridkov sat across the desk from his host, noting the way the man's hands trembled while he kept his fingers busy arranging pens and papers. He was, and should be, uneasy at the surprise visit by Roman Aleksandrov's representative.

"The latest news of the *Crimson Shell* reached Roman yesterday," Fridkov said. He held his flat black briefcase on his lap, pulled up against his abdomen. "He was not pleased, as you can imagine."

Medivir shot to his feet. Agitation played over his face and through his nerves as his fingers moved in an erratic dance over the desk. "Tragic. Very tragic. We—"

"A Tier Three oil spill is not acceptable." Fridkov opened his case with a snap sounding like a gunshot.

"We have already called in the containment specialists. They have been working around the clock since the spill. It is not—"

"But, yes, it *is*. It is unacceptable. The damage will be horrific, both biologically and economically. I have been authorized to advise you that our partnership will cease as of"—he looked at his watch for effect—"twelve minutes from now. Noon today." He slid his hand into the leather envelope and pulled out a small pen.

Medivir's dark face took on a greenish cast. "No! No, there must be—we will take complete responsibility—"

It was pathetic. But then, perhaps if he were in Israt Medivir's shoes, just on the verge of losing his fortune and power, Fridkov would be tempted to plead as well. He fingered the metal pen, considering.

No. No, he would not. He would face his defeat, his mistakes gracefully.

He pushed the clip on the pen, and the tiny ping was barely audible over Medivir's fumbling apologies. The dart found its mark and the man across the desk abruptly stopped speaking. Eyes and mouth open in astonishment, he froze, then pitched forward.

Fridkov was already moving, and caught the man before he made a thump that might be heard outside the room. He laid him on the floor behind the desk and hurried over to lock the door.

Fifteen minutes, no more than twenty, and he would be finished.

He pulled a small syringe from his case, followed by a plastic bag of dark liquid that sloshed as he moved it. Five of his fifteen minutes later, Fridkov had finished with Medivir and took the man's seat at his desk.

Clicking effortlessly on the computer keys, he made his way through Medivir's confidential files and into Medivir Petroleum's main database. As he quickly and efficiently erased every file that contained details that would identify their arrangement, the only other Arabic phrase he knew slipped into his mind: "*In shallah.*"

As God wills it.

And so it would be.

THREE

June 30, 2007
Allentown, Pennsylvania

Oh my God! It's going to blow!"
     "Get back!"
     Vince Bruger grabbed the uniform sleeve of whoever happened to be standing next to him, slamming him to the ground as he dove behind a large pile of rubble. Pain fired along his shoulder, jarring his teeth and snatching away his breath. The other guy, an EMT, tumbled on top of him just as the ground erupted into flames only yards away. The shattering boom left his ears hollow and ringing.
     The explosion sent debris crashing around them, raining cinder blocks, bricks, glass, and rock. Something hit Vince's helmet, slamming his face into the ground, while another weighty object smashed into the back of his leg. Intense heat scored the air and seared his lungs. Damn lucky he wasn't any closer, or his hair would be singed.
     Spitting sand and glass from his mouth, Vince slowly got up, though the pain down his leg made him wince. He looked at the spot where the plant had once stood—tall, with iron-grey walls and a glassed-in front entrance that jutted out like an arrowhead.

Now it was a mass of black smoke, a jumble of rock and steel and concrete that roared with deep, angry flames. Good God. Anyone left in the plant was toast. Jesus H. Christ.

Reminded him too much of 9/11. Vince's stomach felt like he'd drunk a whole case of beer with a plateful of tacos. He wiped a hand over his lips. Bits of glass and dirt ground into them and he spat again, tasting blood and pebbles.

He checked his waist but the radio was gone. Probably went flying when he crashed to the ground, now a melted glob of metal and plastic. Someone bumped into him and Vince turned to see Darrel Blake, the fire chief, covering his eye with a hand.

"You okay?" Vince asked.

"Got hit in the eye. Jesus, God, will you look at that?"

The inferno reached into the air like brilliant orange claws against the blue sky of early evening, and a tower of black smoke ribboned toward the puffy white clouds. They had to crane their heads back to get a good look at it.

"Any of your men in there?" Vince asked, dreading the answer.

Blake shook his head. "By some blessing, no, none of 'em."

"One thing to be thankful for."

"Yeah. But there's at least five people still unaccounted for, last report I had. I hope to God they were either found or beyond help before that."

Before Vince could reply, the renewed wail of sirens drowned out any further conversation. The fire truck that had been parked at the back of the parking lot trundled toward them as fast as its bulk would carry it. He nearly smiled, but couldn't quite get his lips to move in that direction. Good guys, Blake's men. Already on the scene.

Shit. He shook his head, that urge to smile evaporating. How many lives gone?

Someone handed him a cell phone, warm from overuse. "Someone from the USGS on the phone for you, Chief Bruger."

"The who?" He took the phone. "Vince Bruger."

"Charlotte Messing, US Geological Survey, Earthquake Hazards. Chief Bruger, I understand there's a report of an earthquake in your area."

Vince tore the phone away from his ear to stare at it. Was this some kind of fucking joke? He was about to slam the phone back into the hand of whoever'd given it to him, but figured he'd at least better find out what the lady wanted. "By the looks of the city center, and the way one of our manufacturing plants has collapsed, it sure as hell looks like you're right. And, oh, the crevices in the ground too. Yep, looked and felt like an earthquake to me." Jesus Christ.

"I'm calling you, Chief Bruger," the woman continued, and she had that same tone in her voice the wife had when she was about to lecture him about something stupid he'd done, "because we have no report of any true seismic activity in the vicinity of Allentown, and—"

"Well, I don't know what the hell we felt here if it wasn't seismic activity. Look, I have a fire to put out, a town to clean up, and a whole fucking crew of television and news reporters waiting for me to tell them why we just had an explosion on the top of everything else—plus a whole slew of families who are wondering where the hell their husbands and wives are. I don't have time to talk with you. Watch the news, and in the meantime, maybe you better check your equipment to make sure you didn't miss it, because we sure as hell felt genuine *seismic activity* here." With that, he did jam the phone into the abdomen of the guy standing next to him, who had been barking orders into another cell phone.

Vince stormed off, not waiting to see what happened to the phone. Crazy scientist. What the hell did she mean there wasn't any real seismic activity? It sure had felt real to him.

He tramped over to the team of rescue workers who stood watching the blaze as the fire crew blasted it with streams of water. It occurred to him, briefly, that he ought to call Maureen and let her know he was all right, but then he figured the statement he'd given the press about an hour ago would tell her he was alive and well—and busy. He was just glad she and the kids hadn't been around when this all happened.

"We got one over here!"

Vince turned as a shout of triumph came from a cluster of workers on the other side of the rubble. It would be nice if he had some good news when he gave the press an update in about—he looked at his chipped, scratched wristwatch—ten minutes.

Sure enough. A bloody, dirty figure lay on a stretcher, but the man was breathing. Thank God. One down, four to go, if Blake's last report was still right. Maybe even less.

"Where'd you find him?" he asked one of the doctors. Couldn't remember the doc's name—he wasn't from around there.

"Behind where the plant stood," the man replied in precise syllables. His green eyes were piercing and serious. Man, Vince'd never seen eyes that green before. Maybe he hadn't met him. "Down inside a big gap in the earth. He must have fallen in when it shifted. We got him out before it all blew."

"Great news." Vince nodded. "Any chance there's anyone else down there, doc?"

The man shook his head. "I don't believe so. However, it's far enough away from the fire that we could look. By the way, my name's Varden." He had a faint accent that sounded European, but he spoke English fluently and easily. Must have studied here or in Britain.

"Dr. Varden, pleasure. Vince Bruger, chief of police." Vince shook his hand. He guessed he hadn't met the guy after all. He'd have remembered those eyes and that accent.

"People here are lucky. The death toll could have been a lot worse," Varden commented, peering toward the mess.

"Yep, coulda been." He was stating the obvious, and the conversation was superficial, but Bruger didn't care. Lord-a-Moses, he was tired. It crashed into him all of a sudden, kind of like it did after he'd had one beer too many. As soon as he stood, he felt the results. His legs would hardly move. His brain's function had fizzled. He didn't want to have to think.

"But the plant itself. I heard it was a big pollutant, wasn't it? They'd been fined. For environmental violations. Good thing—if this dust-up had to happen, it happened on a Friday afternoon when so few people were there."

Vince smashed his hand over his eyes and rubbed like hell. It eased a little of the tension. But not nearly enough. "Er…yeah, I guess that's a way to look at it. But one life lost is more than I'd like."

"And I as well. But it is the way of the world—nature takes its toll, goes its course. And earthquakes—they are a natural event. They can't be tracked, or prevented, can they? It's almost as if it was a sign, do you think?"

"A sign?" Vince knew he was at the end of his brainpower now. The doctor's conversation wasn't making any sense, and he couldn't form the words to reply coherently. He'd best get some sleep before getting back to this hellhole tomorrow. "Listen, doctor, it was my pleasure. I've got to finish a report and get home for some rest. I'll be back tomorrow." It was an effort just to get those words out, but he did.

And as he walked away, still rubbing his dry, creaking eyelids, the image of Dr. Varden's intense green gaze stayed in his mind.

Riyadh, Saudi Arabia

It was nearly two hours after Israt Medivir and his guest had disappeared into his office that Konal, secretary to the company president himself, took it upon himself to interrupt them.

It wasn't that Medivir was late for a meeting, or that there was some urgent matter that must be addressed. Nothing like that. It was just that Konal had a feeling. An odd, squirrelly feeling that he should knock on the door.

It had been so quiet. No voices. No laughter. No orders for food or drink or copies or reports or files.

So he knocked and there was no answer.

He waited and then five minutes later knocked again, louder. A warm rivulet of sweat rolled down his back. Did he dare open the door?

Fifteen minutes later, he could no longer contain his curiosity and the odd nervousness worming itself around in his belly.

Konal knocked one more time, and then turned the knob slowly, oh so slowly, so that if he heard the sound of voices, he could stop, pull the door back, and be satisfied and protected at the same time.

There was no sound of voices, and Konal became bolder. He turned the knob and pushed the door open three centimeters. And was greeted by silence.

"Mr. Medivir—" His hesitant greeting slapped to a stop when Konal saw the toe of a shiny black shoe protruding from the side of the desk that belonged to Israt Medivir.

Konal flung the door wide, dashing to the side of his employer. He did not need to touch the clammy, cold skin to know he was dead.

Working quickly, he scrabbled through the pockets of his inert employer and found the cash he always carried there. Only after stuffing the wad of riyals into his pockets did Konal run screaming from the office to alert security.

Under the circumstances, it did not bother him one bit that his scream sounded like that of a woman.

Hamid al-Jubeir did not wear the traditional red beret that many of his colleagues in the *Muhabith*, the secret police, sported. He preferred, when conducting his criminal investigations, not to call attention to himself.

He almost regretted that decision to be unexceptional when he reached the Medivir Building and was nearly trod upon by a collection of reporters and photographers. The word that Riyadh's most successful rags to riches story had been found dead in his office had spread more quickly than the assignment to Hamid had been given. Not that that was saying much, for Hamid's superior, Tirat al-Haebir, who was the director of the General Directorate of Investigation, was known for crossing every *t* and dotting every *i*—as the Americans would say—when he made his assignments.

It was fortunate for the GDI's slow and deliberate director that his staff was quick and efficient, most particularly Hamid al-Jubeir. Which was, of course, the reason he'd been assigned to this most unsettling task.

Hamid had never met Israt Medivir, but of course he knew as much about the self-made petroleum magnate as anyone else—including the fact that the dead man was younger than the investigator by more than ten years. And that he'd been a coffee importer before moving into oil and making billions of riyals in less than ten years.

Hamid had always wondered about the correlation between coffee beans and black gold.

The body was sprawled on the floor of his expansive office, ostensibly as he had been found. But from the unblinking, overly innocent expression and the shiny, damp forehead of the man who'd found the body, Hamid had reason to question that assumption. But later. First, the victim.

The reason Tirat al-Haebir had crossed so many *t*'s and dotted extra *i*'s on this case was because it wasn't immediately evident that Israt Medivir was a victim of anything other than a bad heart or a faulty brain. So setting the GDI's top homicide investigator on the case was a risk in itself for the Ministry of the Interior. The ministry wouldn't want rumors that the oil magnate had died from foul play until and unless it was to its benefit to have that be common knowledge.

Hamid stood with pursed lips, the thumb and forefinger of his right hand rubbing against each other in quick, small circles, as he stared down at the body. The medical examiner would determine the cause of death, and other members of his team would be collecting forensic evidence, but Hamid liked to have several moments of getting the feel for the scene first.

Whatever the case—foul play or natural death—Israt Medivir looked exceedingly comfortable. No protruding tongue or bugging eyes. Nothing to indicate spasms or pain before death. No pooling or stench of bodily fluids having been released. No blood.

But the man had been young.

Hamid crouched at last beside the body, and one of his associates, who'd been engaged in gathering fibers from the ground beneath the victim as if it were most definitely a crime scene, moved aside.

He snapped on gloves, then lifted Medivir's head and gently rolled it from side to side. He paused. A tiny mark near the chin caught his attention. It was too perfect and round to be a shaving nick. It could be something, or it could be nothing more than a bite from a tsetse fly or mosquito.

But Hamid noted it, and then moved to the man's trunk. Raising the left arm, he tried to push the Western jacket and shirtsleeve away, but it was too tight. Another investigator might have moved on, but Hamid was thorough. He found the buttons at the cuffs of the shirt and flipped them open, crinkling the crisp white cloth as he pushed it away.

When he saw the bare wrist and forearm, and the markings there, Hamid hissed a long breath between his teeth. Yes.

And then…odd, very odd. The blood, dried and ringing the small mark at the center of Medivir's inner elbow. Curious. That spot where a phlebotomist might draw blood if he needed to… the blood there was dark. Not brown and rust-colored as blood dries, but dark. Black.

Almost oily.

Hamid snatched in his breath. He bent to Medivir's limp arm and sniffed at the markings there. And when he smelled it, and touched it, he settled back on to his heels, still crouched next to the dead man.

Oil had been pumped into the veins of the oil magnate.

FOUR

July 1, 2007
AvaChem Corporate Offices
Baltimore, Maryland

Special Agent Helen Darrow took an instant, inexplicable dislike to Dr. Barbara Melton. This, despite the fact that it was due to Dr. Melton that Helen's acrylic nails no longer smothered her natural ones, and that she could wear them indefinitely without worrying that fungus or germs would grow under the fake nails.

AvaChem's advances in the health and beauty industry had made the company an overnight success. It was only four years ago that Barbara Melton had unveiled her special formulas for acrylic nails, odorless nail polish, and permanent mascara. Her little company's sales had skyrocketed once they landed supplier contracts with marquee companies like L'Oréal, Estée Lauder, and Avon.

Helen knew all of this because as soon as she'd been called to the site of the earthquake at Terre Haute, she'd started getting information from the web. It had come as a surprise to her that she was actually wearing a product made with AvaChem formulas. Pink Clamshell nail polish, courtesy L'Oréal.

Barbara Melton's own fingernails were French-tipped, with about three centimeters of opaque pearlescent white. She was an attractive woman, if one thought that a rail-thin, tanned-to-mahogany body and hair highlighted with every shade of blonde from platinum to honey was attractive. She wore elegance with an edge. A harsh one.

Helen could be just as harsh; she just hoped she'd never look that brittle. Though there'd been a time after David when she felt as though she was ready to crack. "Who do you suspect would sabotage AvaChem's plants, Dr. Melton?"

"We have any number of enemies," she replied, opening a fluorescent pink iPhone. Without looking up, she began tapping quickly around on its small keyboard. Helen wasn't sure if she was pulling up a list, or whether the woman was multitasking.

From what Helen had learned, Barbara Melton was the kind of person who wouldn't be above a little sabotage herself. The company was run with an iron fist, and every iota of profit eked from it. Additionally, and of particular interest to Helen, a public offering was scheduled for September. If something kept that from happening, not only was Dr. Melton going to be paying an awful lot of money to the EPA for some major environmental protection violations, she was also going to lose the chance to make billions more.

Unfortunately, it appeared that Barbara Melton, while working to provide better and healthier cosmetics to the women of the US, didn't care much about the health of the world in which they lived.

"Some of those Greenies or fanatics from the Sierra Club, of course. We've had threats from every group imaginable." Melton looked up briefly, then returned to tapping. "I will have my assistant provide you with a list of organizations and individuals before you leave."

"That would be helpful." Helen jotted a few lines in her spiral notebook, feeling quite the Neanderthal with her handwritten notes and penciled-in calendar. She'd never even graduated to a Franklin Planner, let alone coveted a pink iPhone. She hadn't even known they made pink ones. Maybe Melton was a breast cancer survivor. "I realize that it seems implausible to you that three plants should be leveled by earthquakes in one day, but at this time, we have no indication of how any group could have engineered such a thing."

That stopped Melton's tapping. "Nature may be erratic, Agent Darrow, but it's impossible for any logical being to believe that the devastation of my company was an act of nature."

Helen happened to agree, but she felt herself bristling at the woman's tone. The truth was, the Bureau had been working with the US Geological Society to try and determine whether the quakes were random or prompted by some unknown force. Before they struck, there hadn't been any unusual seismic activity in those areas, as would happen with a natural earthquake.

The only sensible theory thus far was that some entity had somehow caused three underground explosions, which created the quakes.

But that was where the logic ended. The size of equipment needed to drill deeply enough to cause such an explosion would never have gone unnoticed. In short, the theory was plausible but the execution was impossible to comprehend.

So Helen, as special agent in charge, and her team were back at square one.

"We continue to explore all avenues, Dr. Melton," Helen said briskly. "But there aren't any environmentalist groups in the country that have the money or technology to produce earthquakes."

Melton put down her iPhone. "Perhaps they've tired of protest marches and pipe bombs and have allied themselves with al Qaeda." Little lines radiated upward from her lips like stitches, as if she'd held that position often. "Regardless, I expect that the FBI will find who destroyed my company. My assistant has your list of potential suspects."

She stood, and Helen joined her, glad for the excuse to get out of the office and back into the investigation. Interviews could be tedious and a waste of time in the best of circumstances, but when they were with individuals who rubbed her the wrong way from the first moment, she found them even more excruciating.

In the interest of leaving, Helen forbore pointing out to Barbara Melton that it wasn't the Greenies who'd been known to use pipe bombs or threats of harm to get their way.

It had been their opponents.

July 1, 2007
Somewhere in Siberia

Impossible.

How could such a breach of security happen?

Roman Aleksandrov, wearing reindeer-suede shoes, strode along the hallway carpeted with sheepskin. The walls, smooth and sloping into an arch above his head, were bare and white. Small lights hung at intervals along the way, illuminating the darker tunnels that did not have access to the sunlight that burned even in the early hours of morning this time of year.

From the outside, the world Roman had designed for his people appeared to be nothing more than a blue-white mountain of ice. But the gleaming, jagged mountainside was a dome of solar panels, designed and created to harness the energy of the sun, enclose the small city in which they lived, and provide year-round protection from the elements—as well as repel any radar that might attempt to sense the living, breathing community. Roman had first envisioned the concept over three decades earlier when he visited the Kimball Conservatory, a massive, greenhouse-like structure that contained several different habitats all within one compound.

It was only one of the many improvements Roman had implemented over the years. He'd brought bursts of technology and science to his people and had helped the small cluster create a comfortable, luxurious world hidden in the mountains of Siberia, as well as in other secret pockets on other continents.

And now it was all in jeopardy.

It was eight minutes of solid, rhythmic striding through the hallway before he reached the end of the Aleksandrov family's Segment. When he came to the sliding door that led from their collection of living spaces to the main courtyard under a high-reaching solar-paneled dome, he pulled a small wooden tab, the size of an American dime, from a case by the door. He dampened it on his tongue, then fed it into the small slot of the identification tube.

The machine, created by Roman's confidante and lover, Stegnora, read the DNA in his saliva and allowed the door to slide open.

Normally, Roman would stride through the entryway after this procedure with very little thought, but this morning, after learning of the breach of security in Allentown, Roman felt particularly grateful for the expertise and knowledge Stegnora brought to the Skaladeskas. A brilliant physicist and inventor, she was the woman who implemented and managed all of Roman's ideas and operations. She gave birth to his concepts.

Roman insisted she come "home" with him for a visit while they attended university together in London—even though she was engaged to another man. But Roman was a persuasive and skilled lover, and she had fallen madly for him. Yet, to his shock and devastation, she returned to her American fiancé, married him, and even bore him a child in the mid-seventies. Yet they remained in touch, meeting at numerous locations in Europe and America. Then, nearly thirty years ago, Nora came back to Roman—leaving behind a promising career as one of the few females in nuclear physics, along with her family.

He wasn't sure which loss had been more difficult for her.

Yet, despite her sacrifices, she would never leave him again. Not only did she believe in their work, she was also implicated in all of their plans and initiatives. She'd been his partner for decades, and had loved him since Oxford.

In fact, she'd been the one who suggested the bargain with his brother, those many years ago.

"Nora!" Roman burst into the lab she called her own.

Looking up from a flat-screened computer monitor, Stegnora removed black-rimmed glasses and made to rise. "Roman. What is it?"

Shooting his gaze onto the two other men in the room, Roman said, "Leave us."

Brilliant men they were, in more ways than one. They stood and hurried from the room, one pausing just long enough to snatch up a small, hand-held device so he could finish his work elsewhere.

Roman shut the door behind them to ensure privacy and stalked across the room, turned, and stalked back. "An incredible breach of security at one of the test sites. It's put the whole operation in jeopardy; in fact, our whole existence."

Stegnora remained silent, but she came from around the ovary-shaped table to stand closer to him.

"I just received communication from Varden, in which he reported that shortly after the detonation in Allentown, during the first wave of response to the destruction, a number of papers were found blowing about the site, all with the symbol of Gaia on them."

"How—how could that be?" Approaching sixty, Stegnora was still a beautiful woman. Although her figure was not as slender as it had been when they met at university more than four decades ago, she was still fit and in shape. Her unlined face and startling blue eyes made her look much younger than her years. Her eyelashes were still thick and full and her mouth wide and sensual. She wore her wavy hair cropped short. Over the years it had faded from a chestnut brown to a silvery gold that, although natural, looked as though it had been created by a talented hair colorist.

"It must be Hedron. He'll do anything to undermine me, and I've long suspected he somehow plans to sabotage this operation. He will bring all of us down and destroy all our plans with his power-hungry ways."

"Were the papers found? Is there any indication the authorities—"

"Varden handled it. He destroyed all the ones he could find and believes there is no danger of connection between us and the detonation at this time. The authorities assume the symbol belongs to a local group of troublemakers. The Out-Worlders haven't any indication it was our prompting that caused the earthquake. Yet."

"It was very prudent of you to send Varden to the test sites, then. As much as you needed him here."

"He's the only one I can trust completely. And Fridkov, of course. It's Hedron's sons who concern me. Surely they're involved in this at some level—I am certain of it." His brows drew together much too tightly, and he took a deep breath, forcing himself to relax. "The Out-Worlders could never make the connection of us to the symbol of Gaia. With the elimination of Medivir, there is no one who even knows of our existence."

But even as he spoke those words, he knew them to be untrue. One look at Nora, their eyes locking in sudden understanding, and he felt another surge of tension settling at his temples.

"Mariska is marked with the symbol. Surely Viktor has told her what it means. And she is not the only one who would know. Or who might remember."

"Fridkov has been charged to bring her to us. He will." Roman wheeled and stalked toward the shaded window on one of the few exterior walls in the compound. Yanking on the white cord, he pulled the shade up and looked out on the grey water tossing white caps and pointed waves in rhythm with the wind. Cold and furious was the lake today. "As for the other… No one will ever find us unless we choose to be found. And the time is not yet right for that, Nora."

"I don't disagree. Roman—"

"This is confidential information—regarding the breach. You will share it with no one. Varden has done what they call damage control, and I don't expect any problems to come of it. But I will take no chances. We can't undo the problem. If a connection is to be made, we must be prepared."

"No one can find us, Roman, you've made certain of that."

"That is true. It's impossible. But a counterpoint must be made. I'll not sit here and wait. We will move up the timeframe for Phase Two. Fifteen days, Nora. We will execute in fifteen days."

"Fifteen days? Roman—"

"Fifteen days. If you can't handle this, I'll find someone who can. Varden."

"I'll manage it," she said quickly.

"Of course you will. And by then, Mariska Aleksandrov will be reunited with her father and there will be no one to stop us."

July 5, 2007
Ann Arbor, Michigan

Marina Alexander stumbled through her front door, arms laden and aching. She was exhausted, dirty, and sore, but the trip had been a success.

Her team of dogs and their handlers had located and helped pull five live finds from the earthquake in Terre Haute. On the fifth day after the quake, when they were forced to shift the search-and-rescue effort into a search-and-find operation, only one person out of two hundred had remained unaccounted for.

Marina dropped her duffel, backpack, and cooler on the floor and bent to accept Boris's ecstatic kisses. His tail beat wildly against the wall in the narrow entryway, and though he was too well trained to jump up on her, the German Shepherd's wriggling dance made it clear it was only with the greatest of efforts that he curbed his enthusiasm.

"Settle down, Boris," she said, laughing as he finally succeeded in upsetting her balance, dumping her butt-first onto the tiled foyer. "You're going to rip your stitches!" He would have accompanied her on the search-and-rescue operation if he hadn't been recovering from minor surgery.

Marina pulled back to her feet and, after gathering up the stack of mail that consisted of at least five catalogs, jabbed a finger onto the blinking light on her answering machine. Probably a solicitor. Everyone important knew to use her cell number, because she never knew when she might be called to a rescue.

She'd left for Terre Haute on Saturday morning, less than twenty-four hours after the quake had struck, demolishing the AvaChem plant. She had arrived on-site in Indiana by early afternoon. From then on, it had been four days of climbing, clambering, shifting, and stumbling through the ruins of the plant, searching for anyone who might be alive. Her own technique was hampered by the absence of Boris, but she'd worked with another canine whose handler had been injured on the first day. Now, home at last early on Thursday morning, all she wanted was a hot bath, a glass of wine, and something substantial to eat, and then sleep. On a real mattress.

Oh, please, sleep!

"Marina, this is Manjiri Prikash speaking." The cultured, feminine voice blared through the answering machine, grabbing Marina's attention from her half-baked perusal of the latest Pottery Barn catalog. Manjiri was a colleague who lived and worked in various locations of India, Pakistan, and Myanmar, and while they regularly communicated by email and instant messaging, they rarely spoke on the telephone. "I hope you are well, and I am sorry to call you on your home telephone, but I have some difficult news. The Royal Cambodian Government has issued a statement that the Lam Pao Archive must be returned to them by the 15th of July. This means we have less than two weeks to examine the manuscript and validate its historical accuracy before it is gone."

"Ten days!" No way. Not now. She was teaching the summer half-term in two weeks. Blasted governments and their politics. This could only be a reaction to the little tussle between the University of Chicago and Yangon last year.

She and Manjiri had expected to have at least six months before Cambodia started making a fuss about wanting the ancient Buddhist manuscript—the one that had been missing for two centuries, the one that Marina and Manjiri had helped Myanmar archaeologists locate—back in their control.

Ten days to finalize the greatest achievement of her career? In the best of circumstances, it would take a month of study to complete the project.

And now she would have, at the most, barely a week.

Forgetting her exhaustion, she dropped the catalog and snatched up the phone, dialing the familiar number of her favorite airline. She'd just have to get herself to Mandalay as soon as possible and finish what she could.

Damn.

Just as she was making her selection—"For international travel, press three"—her cell phone rang. Marina tucked the landline phone between her ear and shoulder and grabbed the small one with the tinny ring.

"This is Marina."

"It's Bruce. Marina, we need you over here in PA. We've got a missing caver in the Allegheny North Coal Mine. Can you come?"

"I thought they closed it to cavers last summer," she said, dropping the landline phone onto its cradle and launching to her feet. She could call the airline later, once she figured out how long this rescue was going to take. Adrenaline rushed through her as she grabbed her still-packed gear and started for the door. On the way to the airport, she'd call her dog-sitter Dawn to come back and take care of Boris again.

"They did. But somehow these two guys got in here, and one of them's been missing for five hours. How soon can you get up here?"

"Already on my way out the door—I just got back from that quake site in Indiana and still have my gear packed up. Boris can't come, though. He's still recovering."

"Aw, shit, Marina, I didn't know you were down there, though I should have expected it. But it's a nine-hour drive over here—"

"And a ninety-minute flight in my P210 from Ann Arbor to State College. I'll be there by lunch if all goes well."

"Marina, you must be exhausted—"

"Maybe, but at least I'm not lost or injured in some cold, dark cave. I'll be there, Bruce, don't you worry."

FIVE

Langley, Virginia

Colin Bergstrom didn't consider himself a particularly lucky man.

In fact, he'd had enough unfortunate and downright bad things happen in his life that he figured Lady Luck wasn't on his side in any way, shape, or form.

But today, something beyond his comprehension of "coincidence" and "luck" occurred, and gave him an opportunity he never dreamed he'd have.

A second chance.

His first day back at the office in Langley after a week's vacation for the Independence Day holiday, and he was going through the piles that had accumulated on his desk and the emails that had stacked up in his virtual inbox.

Later, he never could say what drew his attention to the bulletin that came in on email regarding the earthquakes in Allentown, Terre Haute, and Hays, Kansas; they weren't a CIA investigation. The Bureau was on it. But nevertheless, something drew his attention, and he perused the bulletin with close interest.

Interesting, intriguing, but nothing that pertained to him or his counterterrorism team.

Yet something gnawed at him in the back of his mind, something told him he needed more information, and he logged on to the database that linked all the branches of Homeland Security to read more. There were photos, and he skimmed through each one, trying to determine what it was that caught his attention.

Bergstrom hadn't worked with spooks for thirty years without trusting his instincts.

And they didn't fail him this time, because on the sixth page of images, one of them caused him to freeze and gape. His fingers curled around the computer mouse so tightly he accidentally pushed one of the buttons, and had to jerk the mouse, clicking and dragging to get that image back on the screen and make sure he hadn't imagined it.

But no.

It was there.

By God, it was there.

He stared at it, and felt the way his breathing worked his lungs, quickly and shallowly.

The chance he'd been waiting for.

Dr. Paul Everett, a retired geologist who taught part-time at Princeton, had left a message for Helen Darrow two days ago.

"I'm sorry it's taken me so long to return your call, but I've had to personally visit all three of the locations of the earthquakes," she explained, readying her pencil and narrow-lined notepad. She'd been glad to return to her office in Chicago after traveling around half the Midwest in the last three days. "Pennsylvania, Indiana, and Kansas. There aren't supposed to be earthquakes in those areas, are there?"

"Not ones like those." Dr. Everett's voice came through the phone ringed with politeness and a formality that reminded Helen of her grandmother's new boyfriend, who always tried to make a good impression on the family. "That's the reason for my call. I saw the seismogram of the quake, and actually put off a vacation in order to travel to the site in Allentown, because it's not so far from where I live in Princeton.

"I'm not sure if you are aware that the site itself, at least in Allentown, has a unique formation to it."

"You mean under the ground?" Helen asked. "Is that what caused the quake?"

"No, what I meant to say was that the result of the quake was a very unusual surface deformation. Agent Darrow, perhaps you are already very knowledgeable about how earthquakes are caused, but if you would indulge me for one moment just so that we may be on the same wavelength, I might be able to clear up some of your questions. And help with your investigation."

Despite her liberal arts degree from Northwestern, Helen was fairly comfortable with the concepts of faults and shifting plates. She figured she could check her email while he talked—and it wouldn't be a bad thing to have a refresher. "Sure. Go ahead." The USGS hadn't done so; they'd just told her it wasn't a normal earthquake and they didn't know how to explain it.

If this man had some ideas, she was all ears.

"As you may know," he was saying—and she recognized that he'd slipped into lecture tone, "the layer of ground we walk on is the earth's crust. It extends about thirty miles deep to the mantle, which is filled with hot magma. Below the mantle, at the very center of the earth, is the core—which is solid, due to enormous pressure.

"Most earthquakes happen when pieces of the crust floating on that mantle, or lava, bump into each other, or one tries to slip under the other. It causes the ground to shake, as you know.

"I believe what happened in Allentown, at least, was not an earthquake caused by that normal kind of movement. Based on the unusual activity seen on the seismogram—the record produced by the seismograph activity—and the unusual surface deformations above the site, I am fairly certain it was not a natural earthquake but an underground explosion."

Those last two words snagged her attention firmly. "An underground explosion. How?"

"Let me first begin by telling you that I've seen this kind of activity, and its seismological effect, only once before. This was in the late sixties in Nevada—perhaps you heard of the Faultless Project?"

"Sounds like a government program to me."

"Right you are. They were testing the atom bomb in Nevada, under the ground, where it was believed the damage would be minimal. Faultless, as you might say.

"It didn't happen that way—instead, there was massive destruction in the area despite the fact that there weren't any fault lines. Windows were shattered over eighty miles away. Needless to say, Faultless didn't go any further, but I was working with the USGS at that time. I saw the seismograms of the activity. What happened in Allentown is nearly identical to the activity that happened when the atom bomb was detonated underground."

"You're not suggesting that someone detonated atom bombs beneath these three plants?"

Everett sighed. "I'm not sure what I'm suggesting. An atom bomb, not likely. But something, yes."

"But couldn't something else have caused that kind of seismogram?"

"There is other evidence too, Agent Darrow, as I mentioned. For example, the surface deformation left by the quake.

"You see, during the familiar type of earthquake activity, the ground shifts in a random pattern. As the plates crash against each other, the disruption creates shifts and makes crevices in the ground—you've seen the pictures.

"But in the case of Allentown, and perhaps the other places, I'm not sure—the formation was not random. An entire area of approximately a mile's radius from the center of the quake looks like it was shoved up, like a massive stage or dais. The entire ground, like an island, looks as though it was displaced from beneath."

Helen's mind was racing. "Yes, I see. If it were an explosion, the force of the explosion would have blasted a whole chunk of the ground up. Like an abrupt elevator."

"Indeed. And, if you notice, all around that area, in the last few days, the ground has fallen away, down, sixteen, seventeen feet. Almost like a moat. That is identical to what happened during the Faultless Test."

"My God." Helen breathed. Until he said that, until he painted that picture, the possibility that the quakes had been man-made had been farfetched. Like something out of a thriller novel. But now, she could picture exactly how it had happened.

And in the other locations... "They're all like that. I've seen every one of them and they all have that kind of island of ground thrust up from the rest of the land, and then the crevice around it." She sat back in her chair, pencil dangling from her fingers. "But how?"

SIX

Langley, Virginia

"Dr. Sayed said you should take at least another two months, Gabe."

"Dr. Sayed's just worried about his reputation. I'm damned ready to be back. Three months to lick my wounds is plenty long enough, don't you think?" Despite his irritable words, Gabe MacNeil's voice was colored with the faint lilt of a West Virginian accent.

Colin Bergstrom settled back in his chair. The man across from him could have been his son if one were considering age and level of intelligence. But where Bergstrom's Matthew was short like his father, MacNeil was tall and rangy, with close-cropped dark hair that had more than its share of grey edging the sideburns and along the front of his hairline.

Bergstrom guessed he must be considered good-looking, if the way all the female admins constantly mooned over him was any indication. And there was, of course, the incident with Rebecca Yves. She hadn't flickered an eyelash at any of her colleagues until MacNeil came along.

In his mid-thirties, single, dedicated, and sharp as they came, MacNeil was just what Bergstrom needed for this gig. And, since he insisted on returning prematurely from a medical leave of absence, and was thus currently unassigned, he needed an operation he could sink his teeth into while easing back into fieldwork.

Bergstrom wasn't above keeping this early return a fact between himself, HR, and MacNeil—for the time being. He wasn't going to miss the golden opportunity that had just landed in his lap.

He'd been telling him about the three coincidental earthquakes before he'd looked at the report regarding MacNeil's return to work, and noticed that the recommendation from Dr. Sayed was that he take another two months. At least. Sayed had put him at approximately seventy-five percent physical capacity, and eighty-five percent mental readiness.

But this little project Bergstrom had in mind was not a demanding operation. And with MacNeil still officially on leave, he could utilize him without digging too deeply into tight, well-managed resources.

The fact that he would be putting one of his best agents on the project, under the blind noses of the Powers That Be, gave him only the slightest of hesitations. Doing it this way would ensure that if the project came to nothing, no one need know MacNeil was back to work early—and that Bergstrom had laid his ass on the line on a hunch.

"Everything related to those three earthquakes is being investigated. Even a mass of flyers that were found blowing about the site in Allentown. You know how it is now—everything out of the ordinary is a potential terrorist attack until proven otherwise nowadays."

"I hardly think an earthquake, or even a series of them, could be considered a terrorist attack. As we know, subtlety is not one of their trademarks."

"The theory is that it was some kind of underground explosion. Some professor at Princeton who was watching the seismograph at the time recognized the unusual activity—which consisted of several large spikes out of the blue, with no other activity before."

"An underground explosion." MacNeil's wheels were obviously turning. His hands were clasped on his chest, the left thumb tapping on top of the right as if in rhythm of his thoughts.

"Certainly is a consideration, but how in the hell a bomb was placed twenty feet—or however deep—under these sites, in solid rock, is impossible to fathom."

"You're right, of course, but the team, led by SA Helen Darrow, has been combing the areas, looking for anything that might indicate that's what happened—but it'd have to be a cave or some other underground passage that gave them access. And there's nothing like that in any of these places."

"Darrow? She's never handled anything this big before. She's sharp, but if this is really a terror operation, she might be in over her head. Still. She's no dumb blonde."

"I didn't realize you knew her that well," Colin said.

The other man gave a short nod. "You could say that."

"Well, you're right—she's sharp. Darrow did find something. And I've offered to put you on it."

The spark of interest was back in MacNeil's grey eyes. Whether it was due to the lovely and intelligent Ms. Darrow or the case wasn't clear. But it didn't matter. In a few more moments, MacNeil would be fully engaged. Bergstrom slid a photograph across the desk. "Take a look at this. There were about twenty papers blowing around the Allentown site with this symbol on them."

MacNeil took the photo. "It's an odd-looking symbol. There were three other earthquake sites too, right? Were any found there?"

"No. Only Allentown. And that's the crux of the matter—Darrow doesn't have the manpower with her own team to follow up on something like this that's likely unrelated. Yet she's smart enough to know she can't take the chance on something slipping through. The police chief told her he thought it was a gang symbol. Guess they've been having lots of problems with that in the local high schools."

"So you got involved how? And you're putting me on it—why? Because I've been away for a few months and I need to be eased back in, chasing around monkey clues? If this is a counterterrorism investigation, a whole helluva lot has changed in the last few months."

"This isn't a Mickey Mouse operation. I happened to see the symbol, just by accident, and I contacted Darrow and told her I had someone who could do the follow-up. Actually, I seized the opportunity. Purposely."

"You know what it is, then."

"Yes."

Bergstrom opened his mouth to continue, but MacNeil beat him to it. "If this was found at the scene of the quakes, how can you horn in? It's a Bureau investigation. They're still pretty touchy about domestic investigations, and I can't see Darrow bowing out of the way for us."

"Homeland Security's all over the Feds' asses on this. Darrow's resources are tight, and if we can continue to collaborate with HSA, the Feds, and the NSA in cases like this, then we have a better leg to stand on when we ask for budget increases. The biggest argument is that there's no indication whatsoever that it's related to the quakes. So she doesn't want to waste her resources, but if I'm willing to provide free manpower, well, she's on it like frosting on a wedding cake."

He looked at MacNeil with a sharp gaze to ensure that the weight of his next words was clear. "This is an assignment that is extremely important to me, Gabe, in a personal nature, and that's why I'm placing you on it. Even though Sayed says you're not quite ready to come back."

In Gabe's opinion, Dr. Sayed was too damned conservative. And besides, he was going crazy at home every day with nothing to do but think about what a fool he'd been. His leg still hurt a little from the car wreck—not nearly as much as his ego—but a little pain wasn't going to stop him. He was ready to be back, and though he'd rather something a little more challenging, this would do. It might be interesting to see Helen again.

Or it might not.

Regardless, there was something more going on here than met the eye.

He looked at his director and waited for him to continue.

Bergstrom's sharp, intelligent eyes were framed by thick glasses that sank deeply into the sides of his nose. Whenever he removed them, two dark red ovals decorated either side of the bridge of his nose and he rubbed them harshly.

He wasn't rubbing the red marks today. Instead, he watched Gabe steadily, as if to gauge his interest. He seemed more intense than usual. Or maybe it was just that Gabe had been away for long enough to forget. He shifted his aching leg to a more comfortable position.

Apparently satisfied he had the appropriate level of attention from his agent, Bergstrom leaned forward and rested his elbows on the desk, one on a stack of files and one on the smooth mahogany, and steepled his fingers.

"The symbol is from an ancient tribe in Siberia that still exists and continues to live in the mountains of that region. The Skaladeskas, they're called. In the early seventies, there were some incidents with their only known external member, who had expatriated himself to England. He was ostensibly studying there at Oxford, and—well, I happened to be there as well. I got to know him as much as anyone else did. He had some crazy ideas that weren't well received—along the lines of using crystals as an energy source. And he was more than a bit fanatical about environmental policies—even back then. A real Rachel Carson kind of guy."

"What kind of incidents?"

"Some research went missing out of an engineering lab dealing with nuclear physics, and a man by the name of Victor Alexander—formerly Viktor Aleksandrov—was believed to have taken it. However, it was never found and never proven he took it. In fact, another young scientist who had disappeared during the same time period was also accused. It was said she had been close to Alexander. She was never found. Later, Alexander gained entrance to the US and is the only known member of this tribe who lives here in the States.

"As I've moved through the ranks here at the Agency, I've taken it upon myself to keep a sort of eye on him, and his people. Initially because he was Russian, and this was during the Cold War. And also because I knew him when I was at Oxford. I just wanted to make certain nothing untoward was to happen." He looked at Gabe. "You know as well as I do that there are *Aum Shinrikyos* and *Kuala Pohrs* perking out there—acting like harmless cults, but waiting for their opportunity to make a violent political statement."

Gabe had first-hand experience with the clan that had called themselves *Kuala Pohr*—a seemingly innocuous group who followed a belief system around a leader startlingly similar to David Koresh. That alone should have put the CIA and FBI on alert, but they ignored the group until they were forced otherwise by a subway bombing on Washington DC's Metro system in late 2004. His uncle, a national security officer, had been killed during the attack, and Colin Bergstrom's peer, Manning Browne, had been caught with his pants down.

More often than not when he reflected on the *Kuala Pohr* incident, Gabe wondered just how Browne felt nowadays when he looked at himself in the mirror. Did the dead bodies of burned women and children haunt him? Did he relive and re-review every decision he'd made—every command, every order—and wonder if he could have saved the lives of those thirty people if he'd been a little more diligent, a little more suspicious?

Gabe didn't want to have to interrogate himself in the mirror, and neither, he was certain, did his director.

"All has been quiet until now—this incident with the earthquakes. The flyers being found there may mean something, it may mean nothing. They could simply be the symbol of a gang—maybe someone saw it somewhere and chose to borrow it for that purpose. But it's your job to find out—and do it quickly and quietly, because I haven't any authorization from my superiors to use resources for this. I'm afraid this administration's attention is focused more on threats from fundamental Muslims and narco-terrorists than indigenous tribes in Siberia."

Gabe took the photo again and stared at it, giving himself the opportunity to consider the situation. Bergstrom was being deliberately vague. No dates or reports or photos, or any of the other collateral he usually received when put on an operation. Perhaps there wasn't anything to give.

But Gabe knew better.

He'd worked for Bergstrom for eight years; he knew he was holding something back.

He'd said it was personal.

"If it's not officially approved, then what kind of resources can I count on?"

"You'll have whatever you need. I'll see to it."

Gabe placed the photograph on the desk and looked at his boss. "What else is there, Colin? What aren't you telling me?"

"There's nothing else I can tell you at this time."

His words were carefully chosen. Not a lie. Not an admission that Gabe was right. Nearly an acknowledgement, in fact. Seriousness and some other emotion swam in his unwavering gaze as he stared back at Gabe.

It was almost as if he were asking him for a favor. Pleading silently, but proudly.

Gabe had never met anyone he'd respected more than Colin Bergstrom. If the man needed him, he'd do it. "All right. So I need to find Victor Alexander."

Bergstrom's lips twitched into a half-smile as he handed Gabe a folded yellow paper. "He's already found. You just need to bring him to me. Him, or his daughter Marina."

SEVEN

July 6, 2007
The Mountains of Central Pennsylvania

Marina watched as Dennis Strand's prone body hung suspended in the cavern of the twenty-foot shaft. The trick was to keep him from brushing against the walls. If the hole had been wide enough, Marina would have been lifted along with him to keep that from happening. But as it was, she could only watch from below as he rose, legs hanging uselessly, bent at the knees.

Her radio beeped and she snatched it from the clip at her waist. "Ready?" came Bruce's voice.

"Ready." Marina moved gingerly against one of the walls, splashing in about ten centimeters of cold water as the rope for her own lift tumbled down. She clipped it to her belt and slipped her foot in the noose, then stood straight and slender. Two sharp tugs on the rope to signal that she was ready, and she braced herself.

Slowly, just as they'd done with Strand, they lifted her from the deep, dank winze. By the time she reached the top, the other half of the team had begun to move Dennis Strand across the chamber toward the tunnels that would take them out.

"Good job, Marina." Bruce clamped her shoulder. "Perfect setup, and—"

A sound that sent prickles over the back of Marina's neck stopped his words. As one person, she and Bruce dashed over to the vertical shaft from which she'd just arisen and looked down. Their lights mingled together, down into the blackness, to illuminate a swell of water swirling inside. A helluva lot more water than Marina had been splashing around in.

"Jesus Christ," Bruce breathed. "It's coming fast."

Marina spun away from the shaft. "Go! Now! Fast!" she screamed after the team that had already started through the tunnel that led to the larger passages, and then to the exterior chamber. "Leave him and get out of here!"

She turned and ran into Bruce. It was as if he read her mind. "You're not doing it alone," he said. "I'm with you."

"You've got two daughters and a wife. Get your ass out of here. I'll get him out." She shoved him toward the tunnel and followed behind.

They had thirty minutes, maybe forty-five if they were lucky. She resisted the urge to dash back over and check to see how fast the water was rising; refused to think about how quickly it could fill that shaft and rush in to fill the tunnels they had to negotiate to get out.

Tunnels they had to crawl through.

Tunnels they might, if they were lucky, only have to swim through.

Bruce hesitated for a moment as Marina bent over the stretcher to rearrange Strand's limbs. She didn't look up at her colleague because she didn't want to see the look on his face. Though he'd tried to hide it, he was in love with her. She'd known it for some time. It happened, she supposed, when you worked in life-and-death situations with another person you admired. Or, at least, for some people.

Even if she cared about Bruce the same way he obviously did for her, she would never act on it, or even allow him to acknowledge it. And the last thing she wanted, or needed, was to have him do something stupid like risk his life for hers, and not make it out of here. He had daughters, and a wife she knew he loved.

Swiftly, aware that the water was bubbling up rapidly in the tunnel, she buckled Strand's legs and arms so that they wouldn't catch on the walls of the tunnel and made him a more compact burden. His tall shadow loomed over her as he shouted to the others to make their way out. As she finished the last buckle, she said, "Bruce, go. I will not have Anna and Olivia and Maria's grief on my conscience."

She stood and he grabbed one end of the stretcher, leaving her to pick up the other. "I'll help you get to the Close, at least," he said. This part of the tunnel was tall enough to run through, although he, with his above-average height, needed to bow his head.

Marina could fit easily at this stage, and with the two of them carrying the stretcher, they'd make it much more quickly. But after this, she'd drag Dennis Strand's stretcher by herself if she had to. She wasn't going to leave the man behind.

A hundred meters into the tunnel they reached Close Knocks. It wasn't called Close Knocks for nothing. It was tight and twisty, and the only way one could fit through it was to duck-walk the first thirty feet, then crawl and twist through the rest.

Marina and Bruce dragged Strand's stretcher through the tunnel as quickly as they could. The rest of the team was far ahead of them; reluctant though they'd been, they'd followed her instructions and run as far as they could. Now she could hear them as they made their way through the Close. The water sound was getting closer, and Marina knew it would be much sooner than later before it came surging through the tunnels.

"Go," she told Bruce, shoving him with as much force as she could toward the narrow entrance. Since he was over six feet by at least three inches, and muscular enough to carry that height, her prod was about as effectual as it would have been against an elephant. "Please, Bruce. Go. I'm right behind you. This was my rescue plan, and I'm not taking you down with it. You know how hard it is to get through here, and how fast the water's coming."

They couldn't push the stretcher between them through the narrow tunnels, for if something happened and the stretcher became wedged, the one behind wouldn't be able to crawl through.

He looked down at her, and for a moment, she thought he was going to say something they'd both regret. "Bruce, go on," she said quietly. "You have to go. I'll do this."

At last he turned away, stooping to crawl through the tunnel, leaving her alone with Strand. Fear rose inside her, just like, she imagined, the water was bubbling and swirling in that pit behind. She could hear the sound of pouring echoing through the cave, and knew that it was only a matter of time.

Water. Her hands grew icy in her gloves, unrelated to the chill and dampness of the cave. She was well beyond that now. Air and land—they held no fear for her. But water clogging her nostrils, blanketing her like some smooth, heavy cloak, tangling her limbs…

Marina had to shake her head, hard, to pull herself from her reverie. A near-drowning when she was ten had given her a healthy respect for lakes and seas. She'd tried to conquer that fear, to take hold of it and manage it by learning to scuba dive, but in raw situations like this, all of her forced training disintegrated.

Bruce was gone. He'd heeded her warning and moved ahead, and at least she'd not die with his two daughters on her conscience.

Die?

Marina moved toward the tunnel of Close Knocks. Where had that morbidity come from? She wanted to get the hell out of there, and get to Myanmar.

The thought of actually getting her hands on the archive gave her a slam of adrenaline. Poring over the dusky brown papers, the fading ink. She focused on that, on discovering something new, something that had been lost for centuries. Strength flushed through her, and she made a massive effort, dragging, tugging, shimmying that stretcher with Dennis Strand still buckled on, his legs and arms crossed over his trunk to make him as short as possible.

She made it through the "easy" part of Close Knocks, and felt her breath going short and her gasps for air covering any sound of rising water behind her. But she knew it was there; only a matter of time.

She thought she heard her name once, far ahead, but she didn't respond. No need to have someone come back for them.

Marina pulled the stretcher into the narrowest part of the Knocks and maneuvered it through the passage she had traversed four times already that day. As she moved through, backward, feet first, so that she could pull Dennis behind her, she heard a low noise. It sounded like steam, hissing from a whistling teapot.

Good God. It wasn't steam. It was water.

And it was coming up fast.

Terror zipped through her, red and numbing.

She was trapped, nowhere to go, nowhere but into Close Knocks. Further in, tighter and smaller, but she knew she could get Dennis around those corners if she had enough time.

If she only had time, a way to slow that water.

She moved three feet, three excruciating feet.

Another two more.

Then she came to a curve, a hairpin bend, and felt the stream of sweat trickle down the side of her face as she strained to tip the inert body to the side, along the wall, and pull it through and around. Like getting a sofa up a narrow two-flight staircase that turned, but much more precarious. And impossible. She tugged and shimmied and jerked at her burden, aware that the greater the movement, the worse it could be for Strand…but it would be even worse if she couldn't get him out. The stretcher wedged; it was too wide to get around the corner.

It was stuck.

Smothering a shout of frustration and fear, acutely aware of the rush of water in the distance, Marina realized what she had to do. Frantically, in the closeness of the tunnel, she flipped and pulled and tugged until she freed Dennis Strand from his moorings on the stretcher.

She was going to endanger his injuries further by pulling him through, but she had to take the chance—or he wouldn't have any chance at all.

And neither would she.

She inched them three more feet.

It was a little easier now that she didn't have to contend with the board. She pulled and twisted, and felt him groan against her once, in pain, and she gritted her teeth and kept moving, feet first, belly-crawling; backward, backward, scooting, scooting, pulling, *pulling*... She focused on the rhythm, because that was all she had.

The sound was loud now, she could feel the shift in the close air and her heart rammed in her throat. Her knees screamed in pain and her back ached.

How much further?

Too far. Much too far.

The Western Coast of Ireland

When Junie Peters finally dragged herself out of bed, it was still dark. Four thirty in the a.m. She'd had a total of three hours of sleep since tumbling into the bed inside a church that had been reorganized as a base for the crew. It was really only a cot, but it was better than one of those inflatable mattresses on the ground, where she'd slept more than once during a cleanup.

She'd dreamed of oil slickening her hands and her body, smothering her as it did the loons that tried to clean it from their feathers, clogging her breathing as it did the whales that needed to swim in it, blinding and suffocating her as it did to the crabs and lobsters that lived near the oil-drenched shores. Twisting through her hair like evil black braids, liquid ones that closed around her neck and arms and into her nostrils.

It was always like this. She had the nightmares and dreams during the cleanup, and for months after, with decreasing frequency, until they finally went away…until she was called to the next one.

She'd worked on ten different spills over her career as a marine biologist, and each one seemed to affect her more deeply. The dreams and images hung in her consciousness longer each time, and her despair with the carelessness of a world so dependent upon oil worried deep in her stomach. She swore she was developing an ulcer.

Her jeans and waders were slung over a chair next to her cot, and she tried to be silent as she reached for them. The others were still sleeping, and if they were anything like her, they would need it. Too bad she couldn't keep her eyes closed.

Once she dressed, Junie slipped into the church's toilet to relieve herself and wash up. Trying to keep her wellies from clumping too loudly, she made her way out of the building into the early morning.

Pulling her grey sweatshirt closer, she zipped it and yanked the hood up to cover her ears. Impossible thing about short hair—it provided no warmth, and it was always cold near the ocean at night. She beamed her torch around, but she'd made the trek to and from the workstation so many times in the last twenty hours that Junie knew she didn't really need it.

The walk to the site of the beach where the cleanup crew had been stationed took only ten minutes. Junie moved quickly, as much to keep warm as to get to the area and get to work again. Saving the life of even one more salmon or trout, or using dishwashing detergent to clean the oil off the feathers of one more seabird, would help to ease that tension gathering in the base of her spine.

A Tier Three oil spill was the worst of its kind. It would be millions of euros in damage, and decades before the wildlife in the region would completely recover from the infestation of its habitat. A tragedy to this habitat…and yet the rest of the world went on.

She sniffed the air, drawing in a deep breath of salty sea tang. Junie had loved the ocean since she was a little girl growing up on the western coast of England, and she was fortunate she'd found her life's calling studying something she loved.

She sniffed again. Fresh, cold, crisp. Familiar.

Then she realized she smelled only the ocean, its natural smell. The ooze of oil that usually tainted the air at one of the cleanups wasn't so strong.

She walked faster. She must not be as close to the beach as she'd thought.

The sun had begun to faintly light the sky, and Junie saw that, no, she was wrong—she was right at the beach.

Odd. The oil smell wasn't strong. In fact, she couldn't smell it at all.

Maybe her olfactory nerves were getting used to it, and so didn't sense it any longer.

Junie strode down to the beach where only hours ago black oil had swept onto the sand or crashed onto the rocks, mingled with the foamy waves. It would splash onto the boulders or shore, then the water would pull back, leaving slimy black residue to seep into the sand.

Only, the sand wasn't black.

And the water…

Junie stared, flashing her light around. It was dim and grey in the early morning, but she could see well enough with her flash that the water was just water.

Junie dashed toward the wave crashing at her feet, and knelt in the sand in her rubber waders. She pulled off a glove and reached for the water and sand, sifting it through her fingers. No oily residue. Nothing.

Was she dreaming?

Her head felt light all of a sudden, and she tilted to one side, her hand bracing herself in the damp sand.

Suddenly dizzy, Junie pulled to her feet, beaming her light along the shore. The shore that, only hours ago, had been thronged with workers and animals they'd pulled from the oiled water.

The oil was gone. Miraculously disappeared.

And that was her last thought before the ground raced up to slam into her face.

EIGHT

Central Pennsylvania

The rush of water was coming closer, and Marina felt her adrenaline spike and a welcome wave of energy surge through her limbs.

Leveraging her toes, bent and aching inside her sturdy boots, she scooted backward. Knees, hipbones, elbows; shimmying, zigzagging, squirming through the narrow passageway, canting from side to side, half rolling, grunting and groaning, she worked them back through the tunnel.

A fear that had never been with her before, a tense closeness from confinement, worked into her consciousness. Marina shook her head suddenly as if to throw it off, and her helmet banged against the side of the tunnel. She heard a *pop!* and everything went horribly black.

Not dark, not the darkness of the middle of the night, where, if you stared long enough, shadows began to form. No. This was true, ink-black nothingness.

No daylight, no illumination, however faint, to allow her eyes to adjust to the light.

Just black. Like someone had wrapped her head to toe in black construction paper.

Cold swept over her. Pitch darkness, in a cave. Water rushing in.

She had to ignore the chill that came from the inside out. Marina took the chance and let go of one of Dennis's hands. Gingerly, she pulled her own hand toward her body, barely able to bend her elbow in the narrow space to bring her arm back to her side, where she needed to pull her extra light from her ride-side belt clip.

That move wasted precious seconds, and was nearly as difficult as bringing Strand through the tunnel. At last, she grasped the light, pulled it from her belt, and switched it on. With that in her hand, she could only hold on to one of Dennis's hands now, unless she continued to move in solid darkness.

Solid darkness. She could do that. There wasn't anywhere to go but through the tunnel.

Marina crabbed herself backward, craning half around on her side, curling back to spear the light through the tunnel behind her, just to see where she was going to be navigating in the pitch dark—and suddenly she saw it.

She'd forgotten!

The one part of Close Knocks that could save them!

Marina gauged the distance, feeling her breath slow. She could do it. She would do it.

And she had to, for that steaming sound of water pouring through the area was filling her ears. Getting louder. Soon it would fill this small tunnel, smashing them against the walls, slamming them into the low ceiling, carrying their bodies.

Clipping the waterproof flashlight, still lit, to her belt, she grasped Dennis's other hand and reached for her extra line, wrapped it around the only part of his body she could reach, his wrists, then tied it to her belt. At least she wouldn't lose him in the rush of water. Then, with renewed strength and purpose, she began to move backward quickly and painfully. She had to get them a little further before the water came blasting in.

Six inches. Twelve. A yard.

And then the wash of water spewed around a curve in the tunnel, smashing suddenly onto the inert body in front of her, slamming into her face. She let it come. It picked her up, and she allowed it to, holding on to Dennis's bound hands with one hand, and reaching out, grasping above her head, and—yes!

She caught it!

A heavy ledge, the only part of Close Knocks that actually branched off onto a second level. She caught it, grabbed the armlike formation she'd targeted with her light only moments before, and pulled up above the rush of water.

Her weight was dragged by Dennis Strand, but Marina was able to use her feet on the bottom of the low tunnel to push herself half upright. As she came up, she wrapped an arm around Dennis's waist and shoved him onto the ledge, only shoulder height from the ground.

But high enough, she thought—she hoped—to be safe from the swell of water in the narrow tunnel.

It was the only chance, and they'd only find out after waiting.

The water bubbled and swirled against her as she scrambled up after him, again using the force of her legs to launch up from the bottom of the tunnel. She barely made it onto the ledge; another few inches and she would have missed it. At last, she collapsed on the narrow space at Strand's feet, and gasped for breath as the water rose and fell and swirled below. Marina didn't watch it; instead, she tried to see what condition Dennis was in.

The ceiling bumping against her helmet, she struggled closer to him. The ledge was long but narrow, and the ceiling low, and she had move alongside his limp body. It took some effort to tip him to the side, and then she lay next to him, pinching his nose and blowing into his mouth. Only two breaths, and he jerked, coughing. She tipped him to the side to let the water pour out.

In the narrow space, she counted his faint pulse, and the labored breathing after his coughing told her he was holding on, but for how much longer? The rescue operation had been going on for hours; it was well past midnight and he'd been in the bottom of that winze for at least five before.

Marina shined her light to the right, into the area that branched off from her ledge. Did she dare try to follow that course if the water continued to rise?

It was brushing the top of her ledge, spilling water over her feet, lapping at them like a tease.

She watched it, watched it, terror numbing her more than the chill as she stared at the pool of golden light while the cold black liquid splashed over, surging over her shoes, ebbing back, and surging again.

And then, suddenly, it wasn't pooling over the top any more.

Marina looked again. It did look lower.

And it seemed to be moving slower.

She took a deep breath, closed her eyes, and then opened them again. Yes. It was lower.

It was lower. She'd done it.

As she watched, the water slowly receded. Minute by minute, centimeter by centimeter, it ebbed back, slowed, sank.

Now it was just a matter of time until someone came in after them.

It was later, three hours after the water in the tunnel began to recede, that Marina helped ease Dennis Strand through the last narrow passage into the main cavern of the old mine to cheers and applause.

She was freezing, exhausted, filthy, and screamingly sore.

But she'd never been more exhilarated.

Darin McCarty, an EMT who had remained in the main cavern waiting for the injured man, helped to lower Strand's body onto a full litter. The lines of concern in McCarty's face etched deep, and Marina quashed a pang of regret. She'd done what she had to do to get Strand out. At least he was alive.

Bruce pushed his way through the crowd and slung an arm around her shoulder, crushing her against him. Their helmets clunked like two dull marbles. "Thank God," he muttered near her ear. "Thank God."

At that moment, flush with adrenaline, exhausted beyond measure, Marina wanted nothing more than to sink fully into his embrace, to sag against him and let it all go. She wanted to respond to the bald need in his eyes, to see what he would taste like. She wanted comfort. She wanted someone.

Drawing a deep breath, she pulled back, because if she didn't...

"God, I need a shower—no, a hot bath," she said with a laugh, looking away from Bruce and smiling at McCarty and the others. "With a glass of wine. And something to eat."

And then, bed. Alone.

Unfortunately.

"Marina Alexander?"

An unfamiliar voice dragged her attention from the rescue team, and she turned to see two men standing near the mouth of the cave.

They weren't rescue workers, or EMTs, or even journalists. The pair looked cold and out of place in their dark suits and thin leather shoes, standing close to a heater running on a generator, and holding matching BlackBerrys.

"They've been here for hours," Bruce murmured. "Wouldn't tell us who they were or what they wanted. Just waited for you. Darin said they looked like Men in Black."

"No sunglasses." Feeling curiosity, apprehension, and some kind of dread, she kept her expression cool as she turned toward them.

One of the men looked about sixty. He wore glasses, and his top-thinning hair was brushed neatly over his scalp. Even from a distance, she noticed the sharpness in his eyes, and the air of authority emanating from him. He was handsome for his age, but his belly puckered out beneath the open buttons of his suit coat, giving him a gentle pear shape.

He was above average height, but his shoulders slumped in toward his chest, making him appear less imposing than the average man of over six feet. Shorter and slighter than the tall, sturdy man next to him, he gave her the impression of an easygoing, fatherly persona. Except for those penetrating eyes.

The other man, younger by perhaps half his age, and closer to Marina's own thirty-two, had short-cropped dark hair going prematurely grey. His body was tall and rangy, like a soccer player. His good-looking face was just as serious as his colleague's, but unrelieved by even the slightest hint of good humor. In fact, he looked outright annoyed.

Flipping open her chin strap, Marina sighed with relief as her jaw released. It was like taking out a tight ponytail, or removing a well-anchored hairpin: you didn't notice how painful it was until you removed it.

"Tammy," she called over her shoulder as she walked toward the two men, who'd simultaneously shoved their cell phones into matching belt cases. "I'll need you and Ken to manage the de-rigging—tomorrow, when the water has subsided all the way. I'm sure we've lost some of the equipment, but a good portion of it should still be at the top of the winze."

Satisfied that everything was as under control as possible—McCarty had Strand on the way to the hospital and Bruce was debriefing with the rest of the rescue team—Marina turned to her uninvited guests. "I'm Marina Alexander."

"We gathered that," the younger man said dryly, and she noticed that the bottom half of his trousers were soaked. Probably from standing too close to the mine entrance during the pounding rain.

He gave her what was probably supposed to be a disarming smile, but it had an edge to it that told her his patience was about at its limit.

So was hers. After all, she was the one who was bruised, sweaty, dirty, and physically and emotionally exhausted. She was the one who'd been crawling through a cave for ten hours.

She was the one who'd almost died.

"This is Gabe MacNeil and I'm Colin Bergstrom," the older man said. "CIA."

MacNeil flipped open a battered leather case to show the glint of a badge. She looked down at it, her helmet tipping awkwardly because she'd released the chin strap.

CIA. An officer in the Directorate of Operations, whatever that was.

But why…

Dad?

Absurd for that to be her first thought.

Talk about out of the blue. A *non sequitur*. And a place she didn't want to go even if it was the topic of conversation.

It couldn't be about Dad. Why would it be?

The Lam Pao Archive, then. She relaxed a bit. That, she could handle.

Whatever it was, she wasn't in any mood to be hassled. "Am I under arrest?" That, at least, was pertinent to the situation.

"No, Dr. Alexander, you aren't—"

"Good." Suddenly, her limbs felt like lead. She needed food and a shower. In whatever order they came. "Then it can wait until I've cleaned up. I'm out of here."

"Shouldn't you get checked out first?" Bergstrom asked.

She felt the crusted mud crack above her eyebrows. "At the hospital? I'm fine. Nothing wrong with me a hot shower and a glass of Cabernet won't cure. You're welcome to follow me back to State College to find a hotel, but I'm not going anywhere else until I clean up. I'll drive my own car. Wouldn't want to get your government-issued vehicles all dusty with bat dung."

Bergstrom laughed like a dog barked. At least one of them had a sense of humor.

He'd probably been playing Brick Breaker on his BlackBerry while MacNeil worked. Then she remembered his eyes, behind those thick glasses. No, probably not. He was the kind of guy who only looked harmless. "We appreciate that, since we spend an awful lot of time in them. Blood's not a problem, but we really like to stay away from guano. We'll follow you back to your hotel, then."

"You want to tell me what this is about before we get there? I thought it only happened in movies where the spooks played their hand close to the vest, with cryptic comments and vague explanations." She was too tired to spar for much longer, but damned if she was going to let them noodle around without at least a token fight.

Gabe MacNeil was obviously resigned to playing bad spook to Bergstrom's good spook, because his reply was short and snapping: "The Skaladeskas."

The Skaladeskas?

Damn. This *was* about Dad.

NINE

July 7, 2007
Dublin, Ireland

Junie Peters woke in darkness.

At least, it appeared to be dark until her eyes adjusted to the faint light and she realized she was in a hospital room. The telly mounted on the wall in front of her, near the ceiling, and the tubes attached to her wrist were the first indications. Something protruded from her nostrils, too. She reached up to touch it gingerly and found a small plastic curl attached to a long tube that fell away into the nothing next to her narrow bed.

The faint *bong* from the other side of the wall sounded like the subtle cue for a nurse or physician to attend to a patient's call. The crack of her door allowed the low light to come in. The windows were shaded, but even so, it was clear it was night.

Junie frowned, trying to recall how she'd come to be here. She blinked, trying to shake off weariness and a fog of confusion.

And just as memory flirted with the edge of her mind, a shadow in the corner of the room moved.

She gasped only because the sudden movement startled her, but the face that came close was appallingly handsome and even in the grey light shone with concern. And relief.

"You are awake." His voice, smooth, carried a breath of an accent that she couldn't place. It wasn't American, yet he spoke English perfectly. "I can remove this now."

Listing to one side, he bent down next to her bed. Junie became aware of the soft rumbling sound only when it stopped. Then the man reached over and gently plucked the curving plastic from her nose. His face was illuminated for one instant and she saw strong brows and intense green eyes.

"Who are you?" Junie was surprised that her voice came out easily.

"The only person who could help you. And now you will recover completely." He wrapped the long, slim plastic cord around his wrist and tucked it into his pocket. He bent, and when he rose, he held a small machine.

"I don't remember what happened—the oil spill." Suddenly, she did remember, and the impossibility of it shocked her anew. "It...disappeared."

"It did indeed. You happened upon the scene too soon after the cure was applied. I am sorry for that; but you will recover completely now."

"But...how? And who are you?"

He didn't answer. Instead, he turned and slipped out the door. And Junie slid back into a restful sleep.

Central Pennsylvania

Marina's hot shower would have been heavenly if Bergstrom and MacNeil hadn't been hovering just outside the bathroom door. Talk about intense.

"Could you order up some food for me? And a glass of red wine?" she called loudly. There weren't too many hotels in State College that offered the amenities of room service, but the CIA had managed to find one.

And since Marina had gone directly from the airport to the mine over twelve hours ago, she hadn't given lodgings any thought at all. She'd figured she'd crash wherever Bruce was staying.

Which was why she was showering in Colin Bergstrom's hotel room.

She heard the door open and she peeked around the opaque, heavy-duty standard hotel shower curtain to see the CIA team peering into the room. "What? You're going to interview me while I'm showering? Can't you give me five minutes?"

"It's a matter of efficiency," MacNeil replied, but she saw the glint of humor in his eyes. "Government cutbacks and all that." Despite his initial annoyance, he was beginning to enjoy this. She had half a mind to invite him to join her—for efficiency's sake. From the looks of the way his suit fit, and the breadth of his shoulders, it wouldn't be a hardship at all.

"If we'd been able to talk to you six hours ago, we would have. We haven't a lot of time for delays," Bergstrom told her. Despite words that could have been harsh or accusing, he exuded a friendly, almost chagrined attitude—as if he reluctantly respected her making her point, like a parent who had lost a logical argument with a very young child.

"The short-term discomfort of you two gentlemen was nothing compared to the condition of the man at the bottom of a winze, and I was the one who devised the rescue plan. So I had to be there to execute it. I'll be out in five." Marina ducked back into her shower.

There was something about Bergstrom that she connected with, and she realized he was a man she would like. Respect.

Unlike her father.

And she didn't give a rip if they wanted to stand outside her door as long as she could stay under that hot, pulsing water as long as she wanted to. And they had food waiting when she got out.

"Execute, and also risk your own life in an against-the-odds situation? Above and beyond the call of duty, Dr. Alexander. I am exceedingly impressed and deeply touched by your commitment."

Bergstrom's voice carried through the cracked door, over the hum of the shower.

"It's not in my nature to walk away from someone who needs my help."

"Then I'm sure your accommodating nature will include assisting the CIA." MacNeil's deep voice filled the room. She noticed he had the flavor of the South in his tones—an anomaly in an otherwise sharp, solid persona. "I hope you like your steak medium rare."

"That'll do," she replied, letting the water pound on the back of her shoulders. "And, to answer your question, it might. Depends what the CIA wants. I'm scheduled to fly to Myanmar on Saturday evening—oh crap! That's tomorrow!" It was indeed Friday morning. "How did you get them to make steak first thing in the morning?" she asked, pitching her voice over the noise of the rushing water.

"It was on the breakfast menu. Steak and eggs. But the wine was a bit of a problem."

"When was the last time you spoke with your father?" That was Bergstrom.

The change of topic might have been meant to disarm her, but Marina didn't care. This whole situation was bizarre.

"I have a feeling you already know the answer to that," she replied carefully, smoothly, soaping her hair. It would take at least two wash-rinse-repeats to get all the sweat and dirt caked up there, even though she'd worn her helmet, and by now she was resigned to the fact that they weren't going to allow her to shower in peace. "But I'll tell you anyway—about three weeks ago, I spoke with my father by phone. It was Father's Day." And she'd made her dutiful call to wish him felicitations, speaking with him for all of three minutes, twenty seconds. She knew because the time flashed on her cell phone for fifteen seconds after the call ended.

"And you haven't had contact with him since?" That was MacNeil again. His voice was a bit louder now, and when she looked up over the shower curtain, she saw the door had opened a bit more.

"I didn't say that." She looked out to clarify. "I had an email from him about a week after that." Of course, the email was a generic announcement about an article that was to appear in a professional journal, but Marina didn't feel the need to supply that detail.

"So are you going to tell me what's going on, or keep asking me questions when you already know the answers?"

"We're trying to locate your father. He's disappeared. Do you know where he is?" Bergstrom's voice came out like a flat slap.

He had intoned his announcement like a death knell, and for the first time, Marina felt nervous. Something odd was going on. Something she knew she wanted to stay far away from.

"Why?" she asked. Should she care? She should. She didn't want to. "How do you know? Even I know the CIA can't spy on Americans on American soil."

"Special Task Team G can, because we're part of the Counterterrorism Unit," MacNeil interjected smoothly. "But that's beside the point."

"Do you know where he is?" Bergstrom asked again.

"I have no idea."

"He's not been at his home in Northern Michigan for over two weeks."

Was all this because Dad was a former Russian? From well before the Cold War? That didn't make any sense. "He could be anywhere. Traveling anywhere. When he's not teaching a class at Michigan Tech, he travels quite a bit around the country." As far as she knew, anyway. She didn't really keep track.

"He's not. We can't find him. Would your mother know?"

"No. They've been divorced for more than fifteen years, and it wasn't amicable. She's remarried."

Marina buried her head under the full force of water, letting it fill her ears and drown them out. This wasn't something she wanted to be involved in. Her life was a lot easier, smoother without Victor Alexander playing any kind of role.

But here she was, trapped in a hotel room with a couple of CIA agents. And they expected her to tell them about her dad.

"You said you wanted my help. What is it you need?" Her voice remained cool, but had a sharper edge than before. They were the CIA, sure, but they needed her or they wouldn't have waited six hours in a flooding, forty-degree cave to talk to her.

Although…she was planning to fly to the Far East tomorrow. There was always the chance if she didn't cooperate they could make it difficult for her to get out of the country.

Dammit. Damn Dad! Even when she had nothing to do with him, he creeped into her business.

The sooner she answered their questions, the sooner she could return home to her regularly scheduled life. She was going to have to be polite and brush these guys off quickly and permanently. Without pissing them off. "I thought you wanted to speak with me about the Skaladeskas," she said, turning off the water. "You can shut the door now."

She heard the dull thud as the door closed. While she was toweling off, Bergstrom pitched his voice so she could hear it through the door. "Yes, the Skaladeskas. Tell us what you know about them, please, Dr. Alexander, and then we'll try to answer some of your questions—as well as we're able, and when I don't have to shout. Some of what we know is confidential."

As if she'd forced him to raise his voice loud enough to be heard in the next room. Marina had never been interviewed by the CIA before, but for some reason, she was pretty certain they didn't usually go about doing so in such an unusual way.

She stepped out of the bathroom. "The Skaladeska people were a small tribe in Taymyria—northeastern Siberia. My father was with the Skaladeskas until he came to the US to study. He met my mother and they married."

"The US?" MacNeil asked from his stance at the window. "Did he spend any time in England?"

"Not that I'm aware of. What else do you want to know?"

"Are you familiar with any of their culture or language? Did your father teach you any of it?"

"Language? Well, maybe a little. I don't know if I would remember any of it, it was so long ago." Before her father started drinking, and turned into a pathetic, foggy-minded, weak man she hardly knew. "I don't have any reason to use it. I know a bit about their culture, and I have their symbol—the one they used to identify themselves—tattooed on the heel of my foot. My father had it done when I was a baby." She'd never gotten a clear answer from him as to why he'd marked her body that way. Long ago she'd concluded he must have been drunk. She was relieved he hadn't chosen to put it somewhere visible, like her arm or ankle.

Bergstrom had practically bolted from his seat and now hung, suspended halfway between sitting and standing, by hands braced on either arm of the chair. "You have the marking of the Skaladeskas on you?" His voice quivered with some suppressed energy—not exactly enthusiastic excitement, but something more intense and sure. It was as if his brain had clicked into gear, and now the whirring inside what must be a brilliant mind—for why else would such an unexceptional man be running a team of intelligence agents?—raced at top speed.

"Yes. But it doesn't mean anything. The tribe died out decades ago. My father and two other children were the only survivors, and those other two died shortly after they were rescued from an avalanche in the mountains. Their village had been destroyed. My father is the only one left."

She read their faces. Wrong.

Dammit again. "There's more to this than I know, isn't there?"

It was Bergstrom who spoke. "The tribe is alive and well, Dr. Alexander. As far as we have been able to glean, they may still live in a remote region of Taymyria, deep in the mountains. Or somewhere else just as remote. One thing is sure: the tribe never died out. Your father escaped—defected—from them thirty-one years ago when he left to study abroad in Oxford, England."

Dad had lied to her. It should bother her. It would bother most people. But it didn't. She'd stopped caring about his lies, as well as his promises, long ago. About when she was sixteen and he'd promised to quit drinking and buy her a little Mercury Capri if she got straight A's. She got the straight A's and the Capri, but kept the drunkard for a father. "So what does this mean?"

"As I said earlier, your father has disappeared. Because of some recent events, we believe the Skaladeskas have—er—retrieved him and taken him back to Taymyria. He could be in danger."

"As I *asked* earlier," she said, "what is the CIA's interest in him? You obviously didn't travel all the way here to tell me you believe he's disappeared and been forcibly returned to Siberia."

MacNeil took up the tale. "During the time your father studied in England, some important research data was taken from a nuclear physics lab at Oxford, and he was suspect. It was never proven that he'd taken the information, nor was it ever found, but due to the sensitivity of the Cold War, and the fact that he was originally from Russia…well, the CIA has kept an eye on him and his whereabouts for the last several decades."

"So, what, you think he has some thirty-year-old data he's going to use—to do what?" They must think she was born yesterday. And where was the food?

That question, at least, was answered by a knock at the door. Marina hurried to answer it and welcomed in the room service waiter with such alacrity that he nearly forgot to have her sign the bill. She signed Bergstrom's name and gave the man a twenty-five-percent tip.

MacNeil pulled away from the window to join her as she began selecting her meal and piling it on her plate. Steak, pineapple, toast, fried potatoes with cheese, and a few tomato slices. She had to give him credit for good taste in food. "You going to eat all that?" he asked.

"Yes." She slanted a smile at him. "I'm starving." Then she turned back to Bergstrom. "It would seem that you have more pressing matters than to keep such close tabs on a former Russian geologist. There are radical Islamic fundamentalists calling for a *jihad* against the US, along with nuclear weapons testing in Asia, and a whole lot of other threats to be investigated. So what's really going on?" she asked.

"It's possible—in fact, probable—that he has knowledge of confidential information, some of which is not outdated," Bergstrom said. "We have recent data that indicates the Skaladeskas could be a potential threat to this country and others. And if indeed they have taken your father back, his knowledge could put our nation at risk. We need to locate him and bring him back."

At last: the meat of the matter. "You want me to help you find him."

No effing way.

They nodded together: MacNeil, with his short, quick affirmation, and Bergstrom with a more vigorous, energetic bobbing. "Yes, Dr. Alexander—because other than your father, you appear to be the only other expert on the Skaladeskas here in the Western world—and perhaps anywhere outside of Taymyria. We want you to join our team—to find your father, and to find out everything we can about the Skaladeskas."

"No."

"You know of other experts who could assist us?" Bergstrom's congenial smile told her he'd purposely misunderstood.

"I'm not going to help you find my father." Marina was no longer hungry. They couldn't be serious about trying to recruit her. Sydney Bristow she was not. "I'm not joining your team. That's ridiculous. I'm not a spy. I'm a linguistic historian."

"And a caver, a pilot, a rescue worker, and an expert on human subcultures. And you bear the mark of the Skaladeskas. You don't need to be a spy, Dr. Alexander. But we need you." Bergstrom remained calm and soothing. Assuming he would have his way.

"I'll tell you what I know about the Skalas—which isn't all that much, thanks to Dad. And I'll be available from Myanmar— by phone or email—if you want me to answer questions about my father, if you feel that will help. But I'm not getting any more involved than that, in any aspect of this so-called investigation." She had to keep every bit of it at arm's length—physically and emotionally. Anything related to her father.

"Why not?"

"Because I like my life the way it is. I have a great job, I have my rescue work where I help save lives—not so different from what you do, I guess, but on a smaller, more personal scale—and I don't have any desire to disrupt or change or compromise it. Plus,

I'm about to complete the coup of my career. I don't have the time or the desire to stray from that project. Whatever you think you can get from me, I'm sure you can get somewhere else."

She stood. "I'm ready to end this meeting now. I'm tired, and sore, and I helped drag a bloody, broken man out of a cave this morning. I'm finding a bed and going to sleep. And tomorrow I'm leaving for Myanmar. I'm not going to do anything that will jeopardize that opportunity."

Colin Bergstrom didn't look like an indulgent parent any longer. "Dr. Alexander, clearly you don't understand the severity of the situation. We need your cooperation and your assistance. Unless you provide us your support, I'm afraid you won't be going to Myanmar after all."

TEN

Hamid al-Jubeir normally preferred to keep his investigations civilized. He didn't stoop to the fright tactics of some of his peers by threatening bodily harm or worse to people he believed could assist him in his work as an inducement for their cooperation.

But the assistant to Israt Medivir challenged Hamid's lofty ideals.

The man was dumb as a roach, ready to slip with his fogged brain into a dark corner at the earliest opportunity. Hamid had had him into his office twice since discovering Medivir's oil-infested body. And each time, he was certain that the man, Konal, had something to hide.

And perhaps something to share.

Finally, frustrated beyond courtesy, Hamid gave up all pretense of civility and rounded on the slender man.

"I do not care if you took riyals from the dead man's pocket, or if you stole his business secrets! You must have something more you can tell me about your master's visitor."

Konal's eyes popped wide in his stolid face. Hamid realized he'd struck the nerve he'd been hoping for, and he lowered his voice into one that hinted of menace. "If you do not recall what it is I know you are hiding, I will set my colleagues of the *Muhabith* on you to find out where and how you came into a sudden fortune."

The man's Adam's apple bobbed in a long, slender throat the color of mahogany. "I have already told you what the man looked like. Your artist drew a picture that looked very like him."

"Yes, but I know there is more. Did he…" Hamid trailed off as a thought struck him. "He did not give his name, nor did he have an appointment. Did he perhaps have any identification on him? Or provide a calling card of some type?"

The wary look disappeared from Konal's face. "A card. He did have a card."

"And what happened to that card? What did it say on it?"

"I didn't think anything of it, for it had no writing on it. Just a symbol. An odd symbol that I had not ever seen before."

At last. "What did it look like? Can you draw it? Where is the card?"

"I may still have it."

Hamid resisted the urge to throttle the man in front of him. The Qur'an made it clear violence was not a solution. Still. "Where might it be if you still had it?" He forced his voice to be slow and low and calm, and tried not to think that nearly a week had passed since he'd found Medivir's body, and that this *balid* had sat on important information through two other interviews.

Thank Allah that Hamid knew how to read people, knew when something was missing, and knew when to push.

To his complete astonishment, Konal reached into his thobe and pulled out a flat black billfold, opened it, and thumbed out a card.

A business card.

It was blank on one side and on the other, just as Konal had described, was a black symbol. Nothing else.

Hamid had never seen anything like it before.

But he was certain that somewhere in the world, someone had. Where one murder happened, another followed, and may just as likely have been after a previous one.

He snatched the card from Konal and called for his assistant to take the absurd, thieving man from his office. Before he strangled him.

And then he got on his computer and started emailing every contact he had in every law enforcement precinct around the world.

Someone would know something about that symbol.

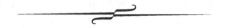

Ann Arbor, Michigan

"Bergstrom isn't one to make idle threats, but he's also not one to make any threats at all if he doesn't need to," Gabe MacNeil said to Marina as he eased the government-issue Taurus down Main Street in Ann Arbor, the city where she lived. He'd never been to the university town himself, but had heard enough about it, and was enough of a Big Ten fan, to want to take a spin past Michigan Stadium. The Big House. It almost made it worth having to bring her home, if only temporarily.

"Idle threat or not, he made it. He's eliminated any voluntary help I might have provided now or in the future. I'm not going to be going out of my way for Colin Bergstrom."

Marina's short, messy hair tossed in the breeze of the open window. She flattened it with the palm of her hand, smashing it down, apparently heedless of any formal style. Despite her black expression, she was a good-looking package: with her pointed chin and wide, sensual mouth, round, apple-sized breasts, and long, slender legs. Her features had a trace of the exotic, with almond-shaped eyes, high, slicing cheekbones, and dusky olive skin. More than once, he'd found his thoughts wandering to that shower she'd taken in the hotel room, and he had to catch himself and refocus—which pissed him the hell off. Even when he was on a case with Rebecca Ives, he'd been more focused.

Of course, they had been sleeping together at that point, so the curiosity had been sated.

Irritation with himself came out in his response. "You won't help Bergstrom even if it's regarding a threat to our national security? That's big of you."

"I'm here, aren't I? The CIA's got me for eighteen hours, and I'll do what I can during that time, clearly under duress." She returned her attention to the pedestrian-clogged thoroughfare. Friday night on Main Street. It was hot in Ann Arbor, and it showed in the tank tops and short skirts clinging to the college kids that had stayed on for the summer.

Antipathy burned off Marina in the same way the sun beat down on the tall, awning-less buildings. It was too bad, because, as annoyed as he might be with the way Bergstrom had set this whole thing up, Gabe also recognized that the man didn't make mistakes. His instinct was usually dead-on. Obviously, this operation was important enough to him to go out on a limb with not only a civilian, but also with Gabe, while working around the Agency's protocols. Gabe trusted and respected his director. He didn't always agree with him and his methods, but he trusted him.

"Why are you so sure my father's in danger?"

He'd never said that Alexander was in danger. Instead, he turned her question back around. "What do you think? You know more about the Skaladeskas than any of us—which isn't saying much, because we know very little. If he left them against their will years ago, why would they want him back? Are they such a close-knit group that they insist no one venture to the outside? And if they do—are there consequences?"

Of course, the guy could be dead somewhere too, which would put a whole different spin on this situation.

The reality was, the Agency crowded too many other issues on its plate to be concerned about a tiny little tribe in the snowy mountains of Siberia. He and Bergstrom and their intelligence reports about Taymyria would never make it into the daily briefing for the president. In fact, this data was barely reviewed. If it didn't have anything to do with al Qaeda, nuclear weapons, or drug trafficking, they were pretty much left alone.

That was good and bad. Good because Colin and Gabe would have little interference. Bad because they had fewer resources. Which was, of course, one of the reasons Bergstrom wanted a free ride with Marina Alexander. She could help, and she would be a cheap resource. Free.

One thing was sure: unlike Manning Browne, whose team had been taken unawares before the *Kuala Pohr* incident, Gabe was not about to be caught picking up the soap in the case of the Skaladeskas.

He didn't care if he came across as hyper-vigilant or overly suspicious. He wasn't going to have the deaths of innocent people on his conscience.

"So why would the Skaladeskas want your father back?" he asked again.

Marina shrugged. Despite her long legs, she had a small frame that made her appear delicate. Though from what he'd learned from his background check, she was anything but. The woman flew planes, explored caves, traveled to unsafe regions of Asia and parts of the Middle East to see first-hand the art treasures she taught about, and was training a rescue dog. She'd even made a trip down the Amazon in a little skiff for the pure adventure of it. And in her free time, she volunteered for cave rescues.

No wonder she thought she was in charge.

"Until this morning, I believed my father and I were the last of the Skaladeskas, and that the line would end with me. I had no clue any others existed at all anymore, so I don't have any idea what to think. I tend to wonder if your team hasn't jumped to conclusions that these people have taken my father. Maybe he just took a vacation."

Gabe turned down the tree-lined street she indicated. He could already feel that it was cooler here. The houses were brick, the street curved, and the sidewalks were well kept there under the shade of tall oaks and maples. Saabs, Volvos, and BMWs of various ages and conditions sat in many drives, and more than half the houses sported mailboxes or garage doors with the big M for Michigan on them.

As he pulled into the driveway of her home, his attention focused on the tidy brick Cape Cod, the shady, lush green lot, the well-tended flower gardens. When did she have time to do that, if she was always running off on rescue missions? "You ever fire a gun?"

"A gun? No, I'm generally trying to save lives, not take them. Why?"

"Just curious. You might have to someday."

"I doubt that very much."

He followed her up the brick walkway lined by some frilly pink flowers, listening for the rapturous barks of the dog he knew she had. When he heard nothing but the distant sound of cars, and the shift of wind, his instincts went on alert. "Wait a sec."

"What is it? You think there's a bomb waiting on the other side for us? It must be difficult living a life of suspicion."

"I don't hear Boris," he replied. She had no idea what they might be dealing with, and he hoped she was able to keep herself out of it.

"He's not here. He's with my neighbor." She turned back to inserting the key into the lock, and Gabe didn't try to stop her.

Inside, her home was stuffy from being closed up. He found it casually neat. Not pristine, *House Beautiful* neat like his mother-kept house, but organized and cluttered in a charming way. There were stacks of catalogs on a square coffee table and a haphazard row of shoes and boots lining the floor in the foyer. Lived in. Not so different from his own condo, with his paints and canvases tucked into the same corner as the kitchen stuff his mother kept buying for him. He still had no idea what to do with a lemon zester.

From his research, Gabe got the impression Marina moved around and in and out so quickly and so often that she didn't spend what would be a waste of time to her arranging and moving things, and the soft clutter of her home bore that out. The interior was not well lit unless the lamps were on, due to the thick green trees that hugged the house, but once she flipped on the switches, a soft glow filled the room, illuminating what looked like an original movie poster for *The Man Who Knew Too Much*.

Catalogs from Pottery Barn, Hammacher Schlemmer, Anthropologie, Sundance—but no Victoria's Secret—and a whole slew of other places he'd never heard of were piled on the center table, next to a group of crystals: amethyst, ruby, an opaque green one that could be jade. So she was a New-Ager.

He reached to pick up the palm-sized amethyst crystal.

"Good choice," Marina said, eyeing him as she placed a stack of mail on a credenza.

"What do you mean? It matches my eyes?" Strangely enough, the crystal actually felt warm to the touch.

"Mmm…no. Hold on to it long enough, and it will help take the edge off your impatience. Maybe ease your anger a little, too." She surprised him with the first sign of a sense of humor as she bent to drop three more catalogs on the table with a loud *thwack*.

"What's this one for, then?" He picked up the small blood-colored one that sat next to it.

"Ruby? That's for impotence. Among other things."

Gabe chuckled. He didn't know if she was saying that to needle him, or because it was true, but either way, he appreciated her wry tone. "I didn't peg you for the kind of person who believes in crystal healing."

"I take aspirin for a headache, or I hold my amethyst. Either one works for me. There are a lot of natural healing methods that have been passed down through the ages. If they work, I use the ones from the earth. No side effects."

Time to get back to business. "I'd like to check through all the rooms, if that's all right with you."

"Knock yourself out, MacNeil. I'm heading upstairs first. If you want to follow me, you can lug that up." Marina pointed to a hefty suitcase—the one he'd carried for her before.

She might not be thrilled about his presence, but she was an opportunist. That was one quality she and Bergstrom shared. He grabbed the handle and followed her up the stairs, equally opportunistic as he noticed an excellent ass and toned legs.

"That was one of the benefits I gave up when I got divorced," she was saying as he stepped from the top stair directly into her attic-like bedroom. "Someone to help me drag my luggage through the airports. Not that I can't manage it myself, of course," she continued, gesturing for him to put the suitcase on the bed, "but if help's to be had, it's welcome."

He knew about her divorce, of course. Nearly three years ago, from an engineering professor at the University of Michigan named James Zelder. They'd been married for three years. No children. He'd since remarried and had a three-year-old child with his new wife—likely a contributing factor to their marriage breaking up.

Gabe tossed the case onto her sapphire, topaz, and ruby colored bed, a design reminiscent of traditional Islamic art, and noted another movie poster, this one for *To Catch a Thief*. Definitely a Hitchcock fan. And more crystals—small ice-colored ones, three of them of different shapes—on the table next to her bed.

He scanned the room, walked into the adjoining bath area, looking and sensing and listening. It smelled like something pleasant in here, not like cleaning supplies. And not too many bottles lined up on the counter. Very low maintenance.

Nothing felt out of place in the upstairs, so he decided to finish scoping the rest of the property.

Marina watched as he disappeared down the stairs, leaving her alone for the first time in twenty-four hours. And it would be another day or two before she was really left alone. Hell.

She was furious Colin Bergstrom had made such a threat.

And even angrier that she'd had no choice but to succumb to it.

She really had no choice. The CIA could easily stop her from leaving the country, and despite Bergstrom's power play, Marina believed him when he agreed she could leave tomorrow evening as planned if she gave them her full assistance until then. He'd had to fly back to Langley from Pennsylvania, but he would be meeting them at the airport the next morning.

She closed her eyes. She might as well stop stewing about it, because there was nothing she could do. She had to play along with the Good Old Boys. Not something unfamiliar to her. After all, she was in academia.

Marina relaxed, tipping onto her side and resting her head on a pillow.

Good grief, she was tired! And sore. She was actually looking forward to her flight to Myanmar. She'd be able to relax a bit. Catch up on some sleep.

Twenty-four hours and she'd be on her way. Twenty-four hours of playing along with the spooks. She could do that.

She just had to get through this little glitch first. Get Gabe MacNeil and his boss off her back.

Get Dad out of her mind.

But first, she was going to travel with the CIA team up to Michigan's Upper Peninsula to her father's house west of Marquette, just, as Bergstrom had put it, for one day, for her to look around and see if there might be any clue to Dad's whereabouts. As if she would recognize anything out of the ordinary anyway. The last time she'd been to his house was, what, seven years ago?

But she could do that, placate the CIA, and then she could get to Myanmar on time. She'd have a little less opportunity to get organized or prepared, but at least she would have done her duty. The bare minimum. Against her will.

And wasn't that all she'd ever gotten from Dad anyway?

At least MacNeil seemed to be as eager for them to part ways as she was.

Her eyelids drooped. It was surreal to even consider that her father was involved in some kind of international intrigue. That she or Dad might somehow touch the world of James Bond or Sydney Bristow.

No effing way.

She liked her life just the way it was—danger and adventure limited to that of her own choosing, thank you very much. And as fatherless as it could be with her guilt forcing her to make Father's Day and birthday phone calls on schedule. Thank God they were six months apart.

Though she wanted nothing more than to doze off, Marina forced herself to climb off the bed and change her clothes. Good grief. She'd have a ton of laundry when she got back from Myanmar, with all these back-to-back trips.

When she came downstairs with her small bag, repacked, she found MacNeil on the sofa, flipping between several news channels and occasionally touching base with the All-Star Game. "Everything in order?"

"Far as I can tell. Let me know when you're ready."

"I need to take care of a few other things. And then we can get something to eat on our way out of town." Marina swept through the small room and headed for the adjacent office, where she fired up her laptop to check email for the first time in a week. They didn't have Wi-Fi at the Betty Lou's Beds motel she'd used as her home base for the last week in Terre Haute. Great cinnamon rolls with thick, heavy icing and gravy-laden meatloaf, but no internet access.

"What's good to eat around here?" called MacNeil from the living room. She heard him shift the volume lower on the television. Apparently his hunger overrode news and sports at this juncture.

Her laptop whirred smoothly as she logged in to her email. While she was waiting for them to download, Marina wandered back into the living room to answer his question. "Just about anything you might want. You name it. I've eaten everything from python to mopanē worms during my travels, so I'm not fussy at all."

"Mopanē worms?"

"Cheap food in Zimbabwe. They look like large green and blue caterpillars and taste like wooden cardboard. I prefer them fried and served with peanut sauce."

MacNeil's expression spoke volumes. "I think I'd rather have something like steak or fish."

Marina strode back into her office, smothering a grin. Not that mopanē worms had been exactly high on her menu selection, but at least she'd tried them.

Her email box had 1300 messages, 1245 of which were spam. She rued the day she'd filled out surveys on a few websites a decade ago when spam was unheard of. Thus her email address had long been added to the spammers' lists. Good grief, she was still getting advertisements for the Iraq Top-50 Deck. Not to mention suggestions regarding improving her sex life (increasing the size of her penis and strengthening her endurance) as well as suggesting that she could get Cialis for cheap.

No blind dates. *Delete.* No Top-50 cards. *Delete.* No need to improve her sex life. (What sex life?) *Delete.*

The rest of her messages were legitimate—from former students, colleagues, friends, and…Dad?

Marina's fingers froze on the mouse, then she clicked rapidly, clumsily, in her haste to open the email. *Mina*, the message read, *Trust no one. Do not get involved. Stay away from this. Stay away from anyone who wants your help. Dad.*

She stared at the message. Then she clicked the screen closed, but not before she felt MacNeil behind her. Her reaction had been a split second too late, apparently, for he said, "'Mina'?"

"He's the only one who calls me that." She stood, pushing her chair back with enough force that it bumped into his legs. Probably even ran over his foot. Good. Served him right for peering over her shoulder.

"Or it's from someone who wants you to believe it's him."

"That's already occurred to me. Anyone could hack into his account, or even force him to write it. But then again, he could have written it himself. I don't have any way of knowing. Except that not many people would know he calls me 'Mina.'" She stepped away, around MacNeil, out of the office, into the kitchen, walking as quickly as she could in the small space. She had to get away. She had to think.

"I know what you're thinking," came MacNeil's smooth voice behind her. She'd already taken note in the less than a day since she'd met him that it was always like that: low, cool, unruffled, steady. Really annoying.

"I'm sure you do. You know pretty much everything about me, my life, and my family, don't you?" More, it seemed, than she did. Marina pushed past him, stalking back toward the living room toward the front door.

She opened it. "I've changed my mind. I'm not leaving with you—at least not right now. I want some time to myself to figure this out without you shadowing me and popping up behind me every two minutes. My house is secure—you've already checked that out—so why don't you go get something to eat. Come back in a little while. A few hours. Tomorrow. Better yet, next week when I'm gone."

To her astonishment, he complied. He walked past her—his blue eyes glinted with annoyance, but he did leave. And it sounded like he muttered something about why didn't she hold on to the amethyst for a while.

He'd be back, no doubt about that, but at least she had a private moment to catch her breath.

Now that she'd received the email purportedly from Dad, though, Marina had to think about the situation more realistically. Was she putting him in danger by working with the CIA? Was he even in danger?

Or had someone else written the message to warn her off?

Of course, they could try and track the email. In fact, Gabe was probably already on his BlackBerry calling Langley to get that process started.

The fact remained, however, that she'd received an email date-stamped only thirty-six hours earlier, telling her not to work with anyone. So someone knew that his disappearance had been noted and quite possibly that the CIA—or someone—would come to Marina.

Thus, there was something about Dad's disappearance that was cause for concern to more than the CIA.

The knock on her front door deepened her annoyance. Back already. It figured.

Marina pulled the heavy door open and found herself looking up into a shadowed male face she did not recognize.

Instincts took over and she reacted blindly, whipping the door shut with a force that jolted the painting on the wall next to it. Her door was still locked, so when she closed it, it couldn't be opened from the outside without a key. Thank God.

She started to turn, to run, then stopped. Her nerves were dancing, but the man at the door hadn't done anything threatening.

He'd just knocked, and she'd opened to someone she didn't expect to see, and because of Gabe MacNeil, she'd reacted from her gut. Not a very auspicious action. Another skill she would have to hone.

Feeling sheepish, Marina returned to the front door and peeped out of the curtain sidelight.

The man still stood there, but now he was holding a gun.

ELEVEN

Marina turned just as the gun butt smashed through the glass of the sidelight.

The stairs in front of her beckoned, and she pounded up them as she heard more sounds of breaking glass and dull thuds against the metal of the door. When the door below flew open and crashed into the wall, she felt the whole house shake.

Dashing on light feet into the bathroom, she shut the door quietly and locked it. Not that it would hold for long, but long enough for her to get out the window and down the tree outside. He wouldn't expect her to go upstairs. He'd expect her to try and run outside.

The only problem was that the window in her bathroom was very small.

Marina hesitated only a moment, gauging the situation, then, standing on the toilet, she yanked the sliding window open. The heavy metal frame made a loud, sucking, rolling sound she hoped couldn't be heard below. In the midst of her adrenaline rush, heart pounding in her ears, Marina paused for a half-second to listen. She heard nothing: nothing from below, nothing from upstairs.

Then the unmistakable thudding of heavy, fast feet on the stairs.

Galvanized back into action, she rammed her elbow into the flimsy screen so that it caved, then pushed it all the way out. She was right behind it—up onto the toilet tank and then, just like in Close Knocks, shimmying her body through the slim opening just as she heard the deep thud at the door behind her.

She wriggled with frantic movements, not the careful, measured ones she'd used in the cave. And this time, it was the metal ridges of the windowsill that bit into her abdomen and thighs instead of rock. She grasped for the rough branch of the tree, clawing with her fingernails to drag herself closer as she heard the door splinter.

Marina kicked off from the toilet, leaping through the opening and taking hold of the branch as she was airborne, swinging free from the window just as the door slammed open. Her legs dangled before they crashed into the trunk of the tree, sending shudders through her body.

Frantic inside, but moving with measured actions, she ducked around the tree, launching herself from one branch to another, so that the trunk was between her and the window, and she climbed to a higher level.

Could bullets go all the way through a twenty-four-inch tree trunk?

She clutched the uneven bark, her legs spread in a triangle between two branches, her arms tucked around another large one at shoulder height. There was silence except for the breeze tickling through the maple leaves that sheltered her. The man couldn't fit through the window, so he'd have to go downstairs if he wanted to catch her. Unless he planned to shoot her.

She could either double back through the house and hide somewhere inside, or climb down and try to run away. Or stay in the tree.

A door slammed below. He'd come out the back door. Any moment now, he'd fire up into the leaves.

Marina shifted to look behind her. A few feet above, the branches of another tree clashed with her tree's. She could climb to the next one, and then maybe to another, and onto the roof of the Tibbetts' house.

Something from below whistled past her and the bullet *pinged* into the flesh of the tree.

Marina moved. She scrambled up the branches until she could hoist herself to the other tree, then, arms and legs wrapped around the branch, she scooted down the sloping branch toward the trunk.

When she moved, she could see down to the ground and the figure below in her fenced-in backyard. There would be no help from the neighbors, thanks to the privacy fence she'd had installed for Boris.

The intruder looked up into the greenery that surrounded her, and although Marina was sure he couldn't spy her, her heart kicked up a notch when he raised the gun. His aim was far off, still toward the other tree, but she didn't waste any further time. She moved, and made her way carefully to another tree, this one on the other side of the fence, in the Tibbetts' yard. One more shift and she landed flat-footed on the sandpaper-rough shingles.

Deep breaths.

He couldn't get to her now. And he couldn't know where she was. Yet.

Marina clawed her way along the slanted roof, using her toes and flat-palmed hands to go up and over the peak, onto the other side. The Tibbetts had an attached garage, and Marina slid down onto its roof, then flattened herself. Peeping over the top of the garage angle, she looked out at the silent street. How could it be so quiet and empty on a Friday night?

She watched and waited to see if he would reappear somewhere below. Once she was sure she was safe and wouldn't be overheard, she'd call MacNeil and tell him to get his ass back here. This was not part of the deal.

Marina remained on the Tibbetts' garage roof for an hour before she felt safe enough to find another tree to use as a ladder. Nevertheless, when she dropped to the soft, sound-deafening grass, she slid along the side of the brick cottage, pressing back against the solid wall for support and protection.

Curving around the corner, she looked toward the street, alternately thankful and regretful that Dr. and Dr. Tibbetts were on an archeological dig in Peru instead of being here to see her slink through their cotoneasters and azaleas.

She dug the cell phone out of her jeans pocket and dialed MacNeil's number. When she'd programmed it in at his insistence the day before, she had no idea she'd ever have to use it.

"Gabe, it's Marina," she said as soon as he answered. From the sounds in the background, she figured he was probably sitting outside at one of the bars on Main Street. "Someone just tried to break in my house. I'm guessing it has to do with this mess you've dragged me into, so I suggest you get me out of it and on my way to Myanmar."

"Where are you now?"

She told him. "The guy's gone, I think, but I'm going to cut through a few backyards and I'll meet you two blocks away. I'm not going back to the house." She gave him specific directions and hung up.

Fifteen minutes later, MacNeil pulled up at their meeting place, and as Marina yanked the car door open, she noticed he already had a weapon in his hand.

"You seen anyone?" he asked as she slammed the door. He was peering into the darkening street as if looking for the intruder.

"No. I'm sure he's gone, but I didn't want to take any chances. You've got that." She eyed the gun.

"You could have one if you want."

"No thanks. I'm going to be on my way and out of this mess before I could learn how to load it."

"Well, obviously you're unhurt and escaped unscathed. What happened?" He was talking to her, but looking around as he continued to crawl the Taurus down the street, turning the corner back onto her road.

Marina told him, and had the satisfaction of seeing approval on his face when she described her escape route. Maybe now he'd stop looking at her like she was a bimbo. And she wasn't even blonde or stacked.

"Did you get a good look at the guy? Anything familiar about him?"

"Nothing discriminating that would help identify him. He was about forty, I'd say, dark hair, olive complexion, nice face, no facial hair—average height. Like I said, nothing discriminating. I'm sure I could give enough info to an artist for them to do a mockup. I could pick him out in a lineup, or from a photo, probably, but I was moving pretty quickly."

"Out the bathroom window and through the trees like Tarzan. Good thing you listened to your instincts and slammed the door on him right away, or it would have been a different story."

"The question is—was he trying to kill me or kidnap me? Or was he looking for something?"

"That is the question." MacNeil pulled the car into the driveway of Marina's home, his weapon at the ready and his eyes dark and sharp. "Stay here. I'll go check things out."

Marina hesitated, but decided that prudence was the best choice at this point. She wasn't armed, she didn't know how to shoot a gun, and there was no sense in being one of those silly females who ignore the suggestion of the cop to stay put when it made sense to stay put. It wasn't as if she hadn't just saved her own skin and needed to prove something. Nor was she Buffy Summers or Ellen Ripley. Not by a long shot.

She did lock the doors, however, and slid over to the driver's side of the car, where MacNeil had left the keys, just in case they—or she—needed to make a fast getaway.

He returned a few minutes later and gestured for her to get out of the car. With trepidation for what kind of condition her little house might be in, Marina followed him up the walk and into the foyer, which was littered with glass. Other than that, a quick perusal of the house showed no other damage. Clearly, the man wasn't looking for anything other than Marina, or if he had been, he didn't take the time to do a thorough search.

Marina felt the presence of the invasion like a pervading smell. She was more than ready to get on that plane and leave this mess behind.

The only place things looked out of order was her office, and that was where Marina found a small card printed with an odd-looking symbol. It was lying on her chair, and it wasn't hers.

Well, maybe it was. Her hands were cold. "Gabe."

"This is what you have on your foot?" he asked, taking the card. The symbol was printed on one side, like a business card.

"Yes. My father has one too."

"Do you know what it stands for—what it means? Did your father ever tell you?"

"Yes, he had one too. On his ankle. It represents something central to the people—their culture revolves around the worship of the entire earth as a whole being, a goddess. Gaia. It's an image that represents her and her favor." At least, that was how she remembered what Dad had told her.

"Earth worshippers?"

"Their view is that every natural being on this earth is part of one living, breathing thing: Gaia, or Mother Earth. Every tree, every animal, even every rock. The concept was actually quite publicly promoted by a group of scientists in the seventies. Have you ever heard of the Gaia hypothesis?"

"No."

Marina closed her laptop as she explained, shoving it into its case, coiling the power cord to follow. "A scientific theory based on that concept that the earth is one living organism—that it's actually alive. And every part of it contributes, or detracts, from its health as a whole. The theory touts that Gaia, the earth, will correct itself as a bio-entity if it gets thrown out of balance; if something begins to skew its homeostasis."

"I can see why I haven't heard of that theory. It sounds like someone would have been laughed off the podium if they'd presented that theory at a lecture."

"Actually, there is quite a bit of scientific evidence that supports the hypothesis. For example, the fact that plankton in the ocean has the ability to affect the temperature of the earth by producing clouds. When it's sunny, the plankton grow faster, producing the chemicals that create clouds—which, in turn, help block the heat from the sun, thus lowering the temperature. In other words, the organism is correcting extremes by itself."

"You sound more like a scientist than a historian," MacNeil commented, but she noticed he looked thoughtful. "So do the Skaladeskas actually worship the earth? Like a religion?"

"I'd say, from what I remember—and this is from years ago, you have to understand—that it was more of a respectful relationship, rather than a worship. But, again, my memory is fuzzy because my father—well, after I was about nine or ten, we didn't talk much about it." Because that was when he started putting his face in the bottle.

MacNeil tucked the card into his inner jacket pocket. "Do you have your things together? I'd like to get up north to L'Anse tonight. The sooner you can look over your father's house, the warmer the trail of his disappearance will be."

"Yes. But I want Boris to come too."

"All right. I won't argue with that. Is he trained as an attack dog?"

"Boris is just over a year old, and I've begun *Schutzhund* training for him—a combination of tracking, obedience and protection—"

"I'm familiar with *Schutzhund*," he interrupted. "He's just a year old?"

"Yes, he's still young, but he's doing very well."

"And you're working on rescue training as well?" He slung up her suitcase and she grabbed her duffel and laptop case.

Marina locked her door, although what good that would do she wasn't sure. "I'll need to get someone over here to fix this," she said, gesturing to the smashed sidelight. "And, to answer your question, yes, the rescue training is just an expansion of the tracking in *Schutzhund*. Boris is going to be very good at it."

They walked down the sidewalk and stowed her luggage in the trunk.

Marina looked at her house, shaded by the trees that had saved her life earlier that day, and felt a sudden sense of loss.

As if something brutal had changed.

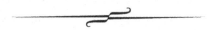

Being in the company of an elite team of CIA agents had its benefits when traveling, Marina learned. Of course, they could also put a damper on travel plans as well, but since she was cooperating for the time, it wasn't an issue.

A Cessna Skylane transported herself, Bergstrom, MacNeil, and Boris to the airport just outside Marquette, Michigan, late Friday night. And early the next morning, they reassembled from outside their hotel rooms to climb into a large and comfortable Explorer, in deference to Boris.

His tongue hanging to his collar, shaking and surging with excitement, Boris steamed up the windows as he looked outside from the cargo area in the back. Slender in the flanks, but wide across the shoulders, he was a perfect specimen of the German-bred German Shepherd.

In fact, his parents had been born and raised in Germany and brought to the US, where Marina had picked from their first litter on this side of the Atlantic Ocean. She'd continued the tradition by teaching him his commands in both German and English, with an emphasis on the former.

He had the saddlelike markings on his back of a true Shepherd, and his coloring was black, tan, and a shiny copper color—brighter than Marina's own dark auburn swag. And with his gleaming brown eyes and dark swatches of black over their lids that looked like eyebrows, he had a human, expressive face.

"At Dad's house, I'll be looking for anything that might give an indication of where he's been taken, or anything that appears to be out of the ordinary. Not a small task, considering that I haven't been there for over seven years." She had to speak loudly, because the two men were in the front, and she was near Boris.

MacNeil, who Bergstrom had asked to drive so he could work, wheeled the SUV onto the curved, paved road. It would take them forty miles into the little town of L'Anse, ten miles south of where Victor's cabin was built onto the east shore of Keweenaw Bay. "Why is that? Too busy?"

Even the CIA wouldn't be able to understand all the nuances of her relationship with Dad. Marina sure as hell didn't. And she preferred not to try.

"Let's just say that we're not close. I talk to him occasionally on the phone—Father's Day was the last time I spoke with him, as I mentioned to you. I didn't have any reason to visit, and he traveled so much, he rarely had time to visit me." Time to change the subject. "So how'd you get into the CIA? I suppose you were a big James Bond fan."

"Oh, yeah. All those women walking out of oceans in bikinis. That did it for me."

"So was it Barbara Bach or Ursula Andress who clinched it for you?" Marina asked as the pine trees flew by on either side of the road.

State Highway 43 from Marquette to L'Anse was two-laned, curved then straight in long stretches, and cut through the deep Hiawatha State Forest. No one ever traveled the speed limit of sixty-five, except for the semi-trucks that the locals deplored getting behind, and MacNeil seemed to be just as comfortable managing the SUV along the road as a local would. His wrist rested casually on the top of the steering wheel, and the corner of his mouth quirked with humor.

"Neither, actually. I graduated with a degree in art. It was those nude models in Drawing 102 that got me hooked on art classes. After I graduated, I started with the Agency in the Disguise and Documents Division, making fake passports and other documents, and designing disguises for our officers and agents." He looked into the rearview mirror and his easy expression tightened. "Hang tight."

The Explorer leapt forward. MacNeil kept his eyes focused on the view behind him, his mouth a tense line. "I think we've got company."

Marina craned her neck to look around as Bergstrom shifted in the front seat. She saw the flash of cold black metal in his hand, then turned her attention to the large rear window. A black Cherokee raced along behind them on the two-lane, S-curved road.

MacNeil slowed the Explorer and made a quick turn down an even narrower county road that headed off into a thickly forested area. The black SUV screeched around behind them, barreling in their wake on the tree-canopied road.

"Sonofabitch." MacNeil's knee disappeared as he jammed his foot onto the accelerator. The SUV cranked up faster, bumping along the road and jolting Boris to the floor. He whined and tried to pull to his feet, but the racing truck kept him off balance.

Marina tightened her seatbelt and stared into the side-view mirror as the Cherokee roared closer behind them. The asphalt road curved wickedly, and, covered with towering trees whose branches reached across it, was more like a tunnel than a road. The early morning sun was fairly blotted out, leaving a cold, dark eeriness surrounding them.

"Hang on," Gabe spat, as tense as the fingers Marina had clutching the door handle. "I'm going to try something."

She listened to him, bracing herself, and was glad she did, but sorry for poor Boris, who, though he was lying down, slammed against the side of the cargo area as MacNeil wheeled the truck around a sharp bend, then swerved around off the road so the truck careened to one side, up onto two tires, then slammed back down to the ground as he finished a 180-degree turn. It was a miracle that they hadn't crashed to the ground.

The truck blazing behind them came along the blacktopped road, peeling and spitting rocks under its wheels. Marina caught sight of the driver's intense face as they blared past, then registered the stopped vehicle.

While Gabe accelerated, sending the Explorer leaping back onto the road in the same direction from which they'd come, the other vehicle careened backward, in reverse, as the driver spun the wheel. Marina watched behind them in fascination as the pursuing Cherokee rose up on two wheels just as they had, hung balanced in the air for a moment, then crashed to its side.

"They're over!" Bergstrom said in a calm voice. "Let's go."

To Marina's shock, MacNeil slammed on the brakes and jammed the SUV into neutral. "Stay here with Boris," he ordered, and suddenly had a weapon in his hand. He didn't need to tell her to lock the doors, or to move to the driver's seat.

The two men vaulted from the vehicle and dashed toward the fallen truck as Marina watched out the rear window. Her heart jammed in her chest, and the pathetic whines of Boris, who had struggled to his feet, set her nerves on edge.

"Boris, *platz*," she told the dog, the only command that made sense and meant "everything's all right." She wanted to be able to hear gunshots if there were any. But once Boris settled down into his supine pose, there was nothing to hear.

Marina watched out the window, itching to know what was happening. The last she'd seen of MacNeil and Bergstrom, they'd slipped into some brush, melding with the shadows of the deep forest. It was silent and dark and cool.

Boris, who was too well trained to do anything but obey, had lain down, but his head still cocked up and his ears snapped to attention. He sensed something happening, but remained in his position, quivering with interest.

Marina itched to open the door and peer out of the truck, but she knew it would be a foolhardy move. She was unarmed and had no idea where MacNeil and Bergstrom were and what they were doing. Still, the feeling of being helpless and waiting did not appeal to her. It was not in her nature to sit and do nothing.

Then a huge, rolling boom erupted from the upended vehicle and made it impossible for her to sit.

Marina wrenched the key in the ignition, grinding the engine, and slammed the truck into reverse. Whipping the wheel around, she floored the accelerator and blasted toward the billowing inky smoke. The stench told her it was a gas fire. The tipped Cherokee had somehow ignited.

Her only thought was to find MacNeil and Bergstrom, praying that what she would find was not charred remains. Only a few meters from where she'd been parked, around the corner, was the tipped, blackened truck with flames shooting everywhere and the fogging smoke turning the already-dark road into a hot, smothering mess.

Marina threw the truck door open and called for Boris. He bounded out in her tracks as she dashed toward the choking smoke, calling for her companions.

As she drew in a deep breath to yell again, the nasty black air clogged her lungs, sending her into coughing spasms. Still, she ran around to the other side of the burning vehicle, staggering in the smoke and tripping over roots and bushes as she searched for Bergstrom and MacNeil. There was no sign of any humans in the area, and Marina was beginning to fear they'd all gone up in smoke when Boris gave a sharp yip.

She recognized the bark as one of recognition, and released Boris to go find them with the command "*Fass!*"

He dashed off through the woods and Marina started to follow, picking her way through the brush.

Suddenly, something dropped to the ground behind her with a heavy thud. Before she could whirl, strong arms grabbed her, clapping over her mouth and wrenching her arms up behind her back. Marina barely registered that her assailant had taken a page from her book and used the trees above as an escape route before she was yanked toward the SUV which sat, key in the ignition, motor running, just as she'd left it.

Knowing MacNeil and/or Bergstrom had to be nearby, since Boris had recognized them, Marina struggled with every bit of energy she had. Once she was in the truck, she'd be cooked.

Feigning a trip, she lurched to one side to throw her attacker off balance and simultaneously hooked a foot around his leg behind her. With a smooth movement, she wrenched and turned and extricated herself from his grip. As he fell, he pulled her with him, and they tumbled to the rough ground, smashing into a sturdy bush. She lashed out, the solid part of her palm striking him in the cheek hard enough to jolt his head.

But now they were face to face, and Marina got a close look at him as he whipped her around, slamming her back onto the ground under his considerable weight. It was not the same man who'd invaded her home, and in the midst of their tussle, Marina felt a stab of renewed anger that there was yet another man who wished her harm. She thrust at him with a knee, catching him in the side of the thigh as he struggled to force her wrists to the ground.

Before Marina could land another blow, he twisted expertly so she rolled to the side and he had her hands imprisoned at the base of her waist. But this left her head free, and she reared up and slammed her forehead into his face. *Crunch!* She connected with nose cartilage and teeth, and her assailant roared with pain and anger. She took the opportunity to wrench her hands away and struck out at his ear, connecting sharply with a palm.

Marina heard Boris before he leapt, bounding through the brush, and felt his weight as he landed on the back of her assailant. She pushed him off as the man shrieked, turning to attempt to fend off the dog, which had turned from a docile, happy pooch to a feral, red-eyed, snarling mass of anger.

As she scrambled to her feet, panting, Marina heard the shouts from MacNeil and Bergstrom as they crashed back through the underbrush. "Boris, *aus!*" She commanded him to release the man while readying a heavy stick in her grip, just in case he tried to dash away.

"Marina!" MacNeil limped up, then stomped to a halt between her and her attacker. He brandished his weapon, but one look at Boris crouching and snarling over the bloodied assailant, and his stance relaxed. "Well, I guess you've got everything under control." His glance brushed over her, certainly noticing the leaves and twigs that clung to her clothing and hair, and the scratches along the side of her face, but he made no further comment.

Bergstrom, who was obviously not as used to being on field operations, arrived in MacNeil's wake, and pulled a pair of handcuffs from the glove compartment of the Explorer. He started toward the dog and his prey, but stopped when Boris whipped his face up to glare at him. Just one corner of his lip lifted, but that was enough.

"Boris, *hier*," Marina commanded, and the Shepherd immediately trotted to her side, leaving Bergstrom free to restrain the assailant. She crouched to lather affection and praise on her dog, realizing yet again the value in having him with her.

Bergstrom recognized it as well, and, moments later, commented as he slid into the passenger's seat, "One of them got away, but thanks to Boris, we've got one—and you're still in one piece. Good call on bringing him along."

Marina throbbed all along her left side, where she'd thudded to the ground, the soft side of her abdomen landing squarely over a protruding tree root. She was going to have black and blue all along there; worse than the time she'd become twisted in a tight passageway in a remote cave in North Carolina and had to be pulled out. Her forehead pounded—there'd be bruising there too. Hope she didn't have to wear a caving helmet anytime soon. "Boris will get a special treat tonight."

"We'll drop our friend here off at the local police station, and then continue our way to your father's home in Pointe Abbeye. They may be able to wring some information out of him before we return."

Marina rather doubted that, but she kept her opinion to herself. "How did they know we were coming along here?" she asked, more interested in preventing another attack. Two in less than twenty-four hours, thanks to her father and the CIA.

"Logic, I suppose. When you foiled your visitor's attempts to kidnap you yesterday, they probably figured our next move would be a return to the scene of the other crime. Yesterday. They're pretty blasted determined. You've already been attacked twice—in less than twenty-four hours."

"Yes, I'm quite aware of that. I'd like to thank you once again for dragging me into this."

At that, Bergstrom turned to look back at her. "You're wrong. If it weren't for us, Dr. Alexander, you'd have no idea what was going on and you'd probably have opened the door to that guy yesterday."

"I have better instincts than that. I do know one thing. If it weren't for the CIA, I'd still be in Ann Arbor packing for my trip." She settled back in her seat, folding her arms over her middle. Took a deep breath. She'd be on a plane to Mandalay in less than twelve hours. "And why are you so sure they were after kidnapping me and not plugging me with a bullet?"

"Rubber bullets." MacNeil glanced at her in the rearview mirror. "I examined the ones outside your house. They weren't meant to kill you. Just slow you down a little."

"I feel so much better now."

Marina felt the tension that had gathered in the back of her shoulders and neck, and wished for the hundredth time she'd already been on her way to the Far East before the CIA found her.

Was even Myanmar far enough away?

She was being shot at and assaulted, and she was going to have to visit Dad's house and search through everything. She'd done such a good job of moving on, dealing with having a non-father in her life, putting away all those horrible memories…and now she was going to have to immerse herself in those banned emotions. Her stomach hurt.

The sooner she got it over, the better.

Another fifteen minutes and they were on their way back on track to Victor Alexander's small log cabin nestled deep in the woods, on a bluff overlooking Lake Superior. When the truck eased to a halt at the end of the curving drive, Marina hesitated before stepping down from the running board.

The hair at the back of her neck prickled, and she felt her pulse kick up. Either she was inexplicably nervous about what secrets she might find inside her father's home, or her instincts were at work, warning her to be cautious. Or, perhaps, to turn tail and run.

Of course, that wasn't an option, so Marina called for Boris to come, and watched the dog as he dropped to the ground at her feet. Instantly, Boris came to attention, his ears straight up—not pointed forward, which was a good sign—and his tail raised but still.

MacNeil watched in open curiosity, obviously respectful of the dog's non-human instincts. He slid the handgun from his holster and met Marina's eyes, giving her the wordless signal to let the canine assess the situation.

It was a damn good thing they hesitated, for Boris suddenly froze and his ears snapped forward, then lay back flat and he whined, ramming his nose into his mistress's leg, then dashing toward the open door of the SUV.

"Get in the truck!" Marina yelled, a split second before Boris moved. She vaulted herself back into the vehicle in Boris's wake. Bergstrom hadn't climbed out, and MacNeil was already moving. Their doors slammed shut in perfect unison.

Fast with the keys, MacNeil had the engine turning over before he'd even settled in his seat, but he didn't have enough time to even shift the truck into gear before the little log cabin exploded into a rolling inferno.

TWELVE

July 8, 2007
Siberia

"The test phase of the operation *Ypila* has concluded satisfactorily," Roman told the *Naslegi*, the advisory council of his clan. "The events occurred at three sites as planned. Today we will finalize the details for the second phase, and I will work with Stegnora to implement the plan."

The *Naslegi* had been meeting in the same room for centuries, but it was only due to Roman's influence over the last three decades that its furnishings had become more comfortable and technologically updated. Running on massive amounts of stored solar power and crystal energy, the lights, computers, and flat screens completed the chamber's amenities.

"Shall we not first give thanks to Gaia?" asked Hedron in a pompous voice. Several others slid sidewise glances at him, as if appalled he would interrupt or divert Roman. "It is only because we act in her name that our mission can be accomplished."

"Indeed." Roman turned frigid blue eyes toward the second brother of Nila, his wife. Her first brother, Brimar, was a much more pleasant man—this one made it his business to combat Roman at every turn. Perhaps Hedron was envious because it was the dead Brimar's son Varden who was Roman's favorite, and none of his own. "Hedron, I trust no one needs to be reminded that our very actions are for Her glory and protection." His stare lingered on his brother by marriage for another moment, and then shifted to the opposite end of the elongated triangular table. "That is the reason I named this mission 'Praise.'"

Opposite Roman, at the point of the triangle and just above the height of the table, was a crystal orb. It was large enough that a man would need two hands to cup it in his palms, and even then would not be able to wrap his fingers completely around it. The orb emanated a faint incandescent glow of brilliant greens slowly fogging into deep azures and disintegrating into aqua, teal, indigo, and moss in turn. Warm to the touch, as many members of the *Naslegi* had occasion to know, the crystal was much too heavy to hold comfortably. A single column of clear crystal acted as a throne for the orb, and lent the impression that it floated in midair. Just as Gaia herself did.

"Let us then turn ourselves to praise for our Oneness with Gaia," Roman said.

The others joined him with a low rumble murmuring the wake of his words: "Oh Gaia, Mother, Source of Plant and Rock and Mortal; Abundant, Loving, Devastating… One in All… Maid who links eternity in our own world, Immortal, Blessed, crowned with every grace, Draw near, and bless your children…"

When he was finished, Roman placed his palms on the smooth table before pushing himself upright with his splayed hands. When he removed them from the crystal slab to clasp them at his waist, they left moist fingerprints near the table's edge. A flaw on the otherwise smooth, clear expanse.

"With Gaia's grace, we now consider the next phase in her *Ypila* by focusing on the greatest threat to her well-being.

"As you well know, the rape of Gaia and the destruction of her being comes from every direction, affecting all aspects of her entity: fossil fuels plunged relentlessly from her depths. Smoke and chemicals belched into the very breath of her air, and the razing of natural habitats and landscapes to make way for concrete roads and steel skyscrapers. Unceasing noise shatters the stillness of our world, scattering our wild brothers and sisters, and the unnatural blare of light shattering the midnight darkness that should be broken only by the stars and moon.

"Our work in Her name will send a message to those Out-World that they must change their ways, or Gaia—through our actions—will destroy them." Roman looked over the room, his gaze resting on each of the nine men, and finally, Stegnora, who sat next to him.

"How many targets will be identified?" one of the elders asked.

"Three is the optimal number. And unlike our test phase, we will be targeting an industry, rather than one particular pollutant. The devastation will be immense."

"Perhaps now that the test phase was completed, a second phase will not need to be executed," suggested Hedron with a sly look. "Surely the Out-Worlders will listen to us now."

Roman's fingers went back onto the crystal table, adding twin images to the already marred surface. "I have lived among the Out-Worlders, Hedron, and you have not. They are foolish capitalists and ignore even the warnings of their own scientists in favor of their financial gain. They build more buildings, drive more cars, manufacture more and more unnecessary machines, annihilate more resources. And they continue to stuff Gaia with their waste."

"We have only your word that you attempted to turn the Out-Worlders to our perspective, Roman," Hedron continued, undeterred. "And that was over thirty years ago. Perhaps—"

"Your own sons have only lived Out-World for a short time, Hedron. Eight years, perhaps ten. But our nephew Varden agrees with me—the Out-World is not yet ready to listen to reason. They are stubborn and live only for the moment, not for the future."

Varden had studied Western medicine and lived Out nearly as much as he lived among the Skaladeskas. It was a particularly tender point to Hedron that Varden, who was estranged from his uncle, was the confidant and heir apparent to the childless Roman and his aunt Nila.

This was a point Roman never failed to drive home when confronted by Hedron.

Having garnered the attention of those gathered around the table once more, he continued, with rapid-fire words shooting from his mouth like staccato notes, "Anyone who is foolish enough to believe the Out-World will listen to reason when they have not truly been threatened does not belong as part of the *Naslegi*. I was not accepted by the Out-Worlders when I moved among them. And anyone who leaves here will not be accepted by them. That is the reason Varden and the others continue to return to our world. They know they cannot have a place outside of this."

"Indeed." Hedron stared back at Roman, his eyes burning angrily, but said nothing further.

"Now." Roman scanned his attention over the room. "I have a recommendation that I hope the *Naslegi* will accept, regarding the industry we will target. Through the reporting of Varden, and my dear brother Viktor, we have concluded that the businesses that promote the burning of gasoline and the use of oil be our first targets. We shall start with one industry, though there are many. But the Out-World cannot do without its modes of transport— two and three cars for every family in America, one person per vehicle to commute to their places of business, yet many travel to the same place from the same cities."

"But we have the solution to the oil problem," said a younger member of the council, a man named Stanley. Despite the cloistered settlement of the clan, influences from the Out-World colored everything from entertainment to names and technological developments—hence his untraditional moniker. "Why do we not simply bring it to the world leaders and share it with them? Then we do not have to take such measures."

"If it were that simple, Bruce, that would have already occurred. Three decades ago. At that time, I attempted to bring a solution to the Out-World, and not only were they disinclined to listen to my suggestion, they found the concept of crystal energy as a replacement for electricity laughable. The capitalists wanted to sell oil, and weren't interested in any other options, for fear it would destroy their profits. A grievous mistake on their part, and one that has become our strength."

Once again, he scanned the room, making certain he had the attention of the entire group. Even Hedron was attentive. Even Stegnora, though she knew all of his stories and had lived Out-World herself for many years, was watching with rapt attention.

"Thirty-some years ago, I returned here to the Skaladeskas, and vowed to lead our people in Gaia's name, ignoring the closed-mindedness of the Out-World. As you know, we have done so until now, allowing them to continue to violate our mother. And now, Gaia has called us to act in her name. You know She has spoken through our holy chief and shaman, *Sama* Lev. We dare not insult him or our Mother by questioning or challenging this commune. She has named this the ideal time. We will not fail Her. She has been angered, and She is not helpless.

"In her name, it is our duty to destroy that which is bent on destroying her."

July 8, 2007
Point Abbeye, Upper Peninsula of Michigan

"The explosive appears to have detonated here." Gabe pointed to a concave black hole in what had been the kitchen of Victor Alexander's house. "Could be professional grade, or a simple fertilizer bomb. We won't know that for a few days. I'm guessing it was a plastic bomb."

The remains of the simple log cabin smoldered around them. The last breaths of wispy smoke spiraled into the air, still managing to annoy Marina's nose. Grit from ash and soot irritated her face and darkened the coppery fur of Boris's neck hair. Waterlogged cushions of Dad's once cranberry and gold sofa littered the ground, along with the charred remains of his books. Some were nearly whole and untouched, others no more than piles of fragile, curling ashes.

Marina half expected to find a few blackened bottles of Stoli amid the ruins.

The firefighters had just rolled back down the narrow drive, their job finished, and she, Gabe, and Bergstrom had been picking through the smoldering logs, crumbled walls, and charred furnishings.

Dammit.

Things were just getting worse.

Marina was getting in deeper and deeper, and she was finding it harder to blame the CIA.

Her father, yes; the CIA, not so much.

Bergstrom had had a point when he said if it weren't for the CIA she wouldn't have had a clue what was going on.

She'd probably be dead or kidnapped by now.

And aside from the physical danger, this whole situation made her want to break out in a cold sweat. Because now she had to let all those buried emotions bubble to the surface.

It was so much easier to ignore them.

The problem was, she couldn't ignore it. Dad was involved in something serious—and he had somehow involved her, the dutiful daughter, who couldn't walk away knowing he could be in danger. Where had she learned this dedication, this devotion? Certainly not from him!

Going home, or even going to Myanmar, wouldn't solve anything. It wasn't going to keep her safe, keep her away from the shootings and the car chases and the break-ins and the explosions.

Going home and ignoring all of this was likely to get her killed.

But what if helping the CIA meant she lost her only chance to see the Lam Pao Archive?

That was not a thought that bore contemplation now. She focused on the real question: how was she going get out of this mess?

Forget doing her duty, giving only the bare minimum. She was going to have to jump in as deeply as Gabe MacNeil and Colin Bergstrom if she was going to climb back out.

And if that jeopardized the Lam Pao Archive validation, she would have to live with it. As she had with all of the other ways Dad had impacted her life.

She picked her way through the rubble to where Bergstrom and MacNeil crouched in the ruins. They wore gloves to protect their hands from smoldering embers and clinging ash. MacNeil appeared to be rummaging through a blackened file cabinet. The open drawer sported an awkward vent, as if it had been pried open. It probably had, if the metal rod lying in the rubble next to it was any indication. Bergstrom looked up from his handful of half-burned papers.

She spoke without preamble. "I'm going to delay my trip to Myanmar and do whatever I can to find Dad and stop whatever's going on here."

"Welcome aboard." Bergstrom nodded once, but there was a satisfied gleam in his eye.

"I don't think I'm going to be much help wandering through the mess here, but I'll give it a shot," she added.

"Right. Thanks." Bergstrom continued to flip through charred papers that looked like nothing more than old phone bills and Sears credit card statements. "Why don't you wander over there and see if anything strikes you as being out of place."

She turned to walk toward what had been the back of the house, the side facing the bluffs of Lake Superior. If she focused and worked hard, they'd find Dad all the more quickly, and she'd be back to life as she knew it.

A large, black, molten mass caught her attention, and she stumbled over a charred two-by-four as she made her way toward it. It looked like a melted tub of sorts...on a cedar-planked dais.

In fact, it looked like a hot tub.

Weird. Dad hated hot tubs. He said the chlorine was a terrible pollutant and awful for the body. Marina, too, avoided chlorine-laden pools and tubs in favor of clean lakes, natural hot springs, and baths scented with essential oils instead of stinging chemicals. It made her shudder to think of how those unnatural compounds affected the skin, eyes, and nose.

A hot tub.

It was wrong.

There was no way Dad would have one.

She clambered gingerly to the other side of the tub, which had melted in the heat and now looked like some oversized plastic black ashtray from the seventies. As she touched the shiny plastic in one of the indentations that would hold a giant cigarette, she suddenly realized why her father had a hot tub in his house.

"Yo! MacNeil!" she called as she began to dig away the rubble near the ground around the cedar stage. The hidden door was there, easy to find now that the tub had melted and become deformed.

It was a door, a cellar door, not unlike the one Dorothy's Aunt Em ducked into when the tornado was bearing down upon them. Hidden under the hot tub's base, the door flipped up to reveal a ladder, then dropped into nothingness.

"I'm thinking there might be some clues down here that weren't burned to a crisp." Marina gestured to the hole as Gabe jogged up, leaving the slower Bergstrom scrambling through the rubble behind him.

"Well, screw me blind." Gabe pulled a flashlight from the clip at his waist and beamed it into the darkness.

Excitement and apprehension pumped through her veins. "You can follow me down," Marina told him, moving purposely past him to step onto the first rung.

"Wait. You don't know what's down there."

"I'm going." Marina gently but firmly pulled away and descended into the darkness.

He grumbled, but kept the light trained so she could see where she was going while he clanged down the metal rungs. As she disappeared, Gabe wedged the flash under his arm and slipped his Smith & Wesson from its holster.

But when he got to the bottom, he saw no threat and slipped the gun back into its place. Marina had already found a light, and fluorescent bulbs hummed white noise, then sputtered into full illumination.

Gabe looked around the small room. The space was blinding with its white-painted concrete block walls and floor. No more than ten by ten feet.

And *damn*. The hidden cellar was rigged with more communication equipment than an air traffic control tower: two computers with flat-panel monitors, a satellite radio, a printer, a satphone, and another radio. Plus some other equipment Gabe didn't immediately recognize. Boxes that looked like electronic components, and a six-foot machine that resembled a massive metal detector. Wires and boxes with buttons and lights. It was a regular command central.

Marina had already begun to move through the room, touching the computers, turning them on, resting her hands on every item as if to prove to herself they were real. Gabe figured she must be in some kind of shock, finding out that her father had a secret life.

At least, he assumed that was the reason for the blank expression on her face.

Marina didn't speak. She pulled open drawers and flipped through files. Gabe should have sat down at one of the machines to see if there was anything helpful, but he watched her instead, for she paused at a drawer.

Sinking onto a nearby chair, she pulled what looked like a loosely bound book from its depths. Gabe stepped closer to look over her shoulder.

It was an odd book —if you could call it a book. It was more like plastic pages tied together. About six by six inches, the pages had a dull plastic sheen to them. But it wasn't until Marina opened the book that he realized it wasn't going to be found in just any library.

The pages had writing on them—writing he didn't recognize and definitely couldn't translate. The Skaladeska language. It had to be. And the pages looked like the homemade paper arts-and-crafts types made using wood pulp and twine and fibers, yet they were shiny, and looked laminated. Translucent. Each page looked like a textured shower curtain liner with writing on it.

He reached over Marina's shoulder to touch the book. The ridges of swirling texture, like heavy linen, felt smooth and cool. It was dull cream color, definitely looking homemade. Thick but translucent.

"Can you read it?" Gabe asked, watching the way she stared down at the page.

"It's in Skaladeska."

"Can you read it?"

She hesitated, closed the book. "Maybe. It might come back to me. I knew a little…when I was younger." Then she pointed across the room. "I bet there's another passageway over there."

Gabe saw nothing to indicate a door or opening, but suspected she was right. An expanse of empty wall, when the rest of the place was covered by shelves and cabinets? Definitely.

Marina rose, tucking the book under her arm, and moved toward that side of the chamber.

"There's got to be a door here. If you help me, we can find it." She was moving up and down and around, running her fingers all along the wall like some kind of expert at finding hidden doorways. It hadn't slipped past him that she'd been vague about her ability to read the book. She certainly appeared to be reading it. Why would she lie?

In the end, it was a small hidden panel that tripped the switch. A door slid open, revealing a yawning tunnel of metal. Dim recessed lights studded the ceiling in a line disappearing out of sight. Marina was already moving down the hallway, and Gabe didn't bother to warn her about potential hazards. But he did pull his weapon from its holster once again.

Although he'd guessed the tunnel was heading toward Lake Superior, when it finally ended, a surprise awaited. Another door slid open, and he and Marina stepped into what could only be called a fish bowl. He and Marina being the fish.

All three sides of the chamber were made of glass, or some heavy-duty plastic. The dark green waters of the depths of Lake Superior surged against the walls, covering them to the ceiling, and, as Gabe realized, likely well above the ceiling. They were in an underwater chamber with one wall outfitted with a specialized opening.

It was clearly an antechamber for some type of underwater craft...and the vehicle was missing.

THIRTEEN

July 8, 2007
Allentown, Pennsylvania

What the hell is this?" Vince Bruger snapped, looking at
a lump of black metal sitting on his desk. A long metal
rod crossed over a messy stack of files. Dirt clung to each end. A
young woman dressed in blues, with a shiny badge and a name-
plate that read BURNETT, startled to her feet.

"All right, Dr. Everett. I should be at your house in less than
an hour." Walking in Bruger's footsteps, Helen Darrow flipped
her cell phone shut with a flick of her thumb as she entered the
chief's office. She glanced at wide-eyed Officer Burnett, who
looked like she'd just gotten out of the academy. Yesterday. Maybe
even this morning.

"We found this approximately five miles from the epicenter
of the earthquake," Burnett explained. "Knew Agent Darrow was
going to be here and figured she'd want to see it."

"On my desk?"

Helen had to give the newbie credit. Even though Bruger
looked like he wanted to jump down her throat, Burnett's response
came out smooth and steady. And loud enough to be heard.

Helen stepped toward the desk, her fingers tingling—a sure
sign something was about to give. The last time she'd had that
powerful feeling, that singing, twitching in her fingertips, she'd

apprehended Mad Melia, a nurse who liked to help her patients into their afterlife earlier than their maker intended, after nearly missing her hiding in the back of a Jeep Cherokee. A woman's instinct, she had learned, was never to be ignored.

Now she looked at the metal rod with interest, and that tingling spiking through her.

At last. Something.

Just the kind of thing she'd been hoping for.

During her conversation two days earlier with Dr. Everett, Helen had become convinced he was right—the earthquakes were not quakes at all, but underground explosions. So she'd had to turn her team's attention to finding out how they'd been caused.

She and Bruger poked at the box and the long rod. A small screen and two dials were the only break on the smooth metal surface of the box. She noticed no other markings or identification at first glance.

"This could be a drill of some kind. Like they use for oil." She looked at her watch. "I'm going to have to leave for my meeting with Everett right now. I'll have Mingo start looking at these in the meantime, but I'll also see if Everett will take a look and confirm whether they'd be used for this kind of operation."

Bruger growled his agreement. The poor man looked like she felt: dead tired and stressed. But Helen at least had the advantage of makeup to hide her secrets.

Moments later she was off on the highway, heading northeast from Allentown over the state border into Jersey.

When she reached his home, Dr. Everett was pruning his rosebushes. Helen had only spoken to the man twice, but each time he'd managed to mention two topics unrelated to the geological discussion at hand: his wife Darlene, who obviously ran the roost, and his fifty-three rose bushes. And their fifty different hues. She wondered which ones were duplicates, but decided to keep that thought to herself.

"Agent Darrow! It's a pleasure to see you again." He put the clippers down and gestured to a round table and a set of wicker chairs under a tilted umbrella. The fragrance of rose was in the air;—not surprising, because the bushes created a half-circle of pink, magenta, yellow, and crimson around the patio.

"Dr. Everett. Thank you for meeting with me. I had originally intended to talk with you in more detail about your experience in Nevada, as you'd mentioned it, but now I have even more specific questions. And something to show you."

"Please. Ask away. Darlene will be bringing some lemonade and iced tea—she was peering out the window when you drove up."

It was almost too quaint, too cute, Helen thought. The half-retired geology professor and his love of gardening, and the bustling, grandmotherly wife who would bring them lemonade, iced tea, and, if the cliché was fully formed, a plate of cookies. Helen was hoping for oatmeal raisin.

But before she had the chance to tell Dr. Everett what they'd found, the screen door slammed and a tall, slender, gorgeous woman of no more than forty hurried down the steps. No grandmotherly type here.

"Hi, you must be Agent Darrow. I've got something to drink for you, but I can't stay and chat because I've got to run to the store. I just ran out of blue paint!" The youngish woman, only a few years older than Helen, had pale dots of blue all over her hands and bare legs. She dropped the tray quickly and none too gently on the table in front of them, planted a kiss on her husband's bare forehead, and hurried off, keys jangling.

"What was that?" Helen couldn't help but say, reaching for a glass filled with ice. Lemonade and iced tea, combined, was one of her weaknesses.

Dr. Everett laughed. "She never stops. She was one of my students, way back when, and—well, you can imagine the problems we had, especially twenty years ago. But it was just one of those things... Anyway, Agent Darrow, I know you must be very busy. Please, tell me what you've found."

"Well, you'd told me that in order to create an underground explosion, somehow the explosive needed to be put under the area."

He was nodding as he gulped half a glass of lemonade. When he took the glass away from his mouth, he said, "Yes, and that was the problem. Any equipment that could be used to dig under the ground, or drill, as we would say, would be so large as to be noticeable. In fact, we often use directional drilling when digging for oil, and those rigs are even larger. Just to be certain we're on the same page, allow me to explain the specifics of directional drilling.

"There's a bit on the end of a long string of pipe that drills the hole. Once they reach the desired depth, the drillers use pressure to direct the angle of the hole horizontally. So they drill down, and then over to the location they need to be.

"But as I told you on the phone, these are large machines, and the rigs certainly couldn't be carted into an area and used without being noticed."

Helen's hopes fell. The metal rod they'd found couldn't have been used for something so heavy-duty. "So these machines can drill at an angle, underground. And they could drill deep. How far away from the site could they be?"

"Definitely, they can drill deep. And with present technology, the bottom hole location could be several hundred feet, or even up to a couple of miles, away from the surface location. But what have you found?"

"I thought we might have found the drill, but it's very small."

"Excellent!"

"It's extremely small, though. Too small. It's only six inches in diameter. And eight feet long." She waited. Was her theory possible?

"Yes, I would say...that's too small. A drill of that size couldn't—well, I should not say couldn't, should I? I suppose it's conceivable, if the material was right. But..." He shook his head almost sorrowfully. "Well, I suppose it isn't completely impossible. Tell me more."

"Right. And this is the best part. We think the machine was remotely controlled by someone on the surface. The box was set into the ground with this directional rod on it to dig, and it was controlled as it burrowed into the ground, through miles of earth—or maybe just a mile or so—to where the explosive detonated. We have a box that could be the controller."

"Incredible. Impossibly incredible! Could I see it? I would love to see it and examine it."

"Yes. I'd like your opinion as to whether my theory is plausible, and whether the equipment we found is capable of digging down through the earth's crust at that distance."

Everett had drained a second glass of lemonade, and now he muffled a gentle belch. "Excuse me." He rubbed his hands gleefully. "When can we go? But wait. The size of the explosives. In order to create an earthquake of that magnitude, it would have to be a very powerful explosive. Based on what occurred during the experiments in Nevada, the explosive would have to be huge."

"Yes, indeed. That's the next phase. We think we know how they got it down there, but how they made the explosives so powerful in such a small package we'll need to further investigate. Is there any way we could get to the explosion site, there underground, to see what actually happened?"

"I don't think so, my dear. If any caves or caverns exist at that depth, which I doubt, they would have been destroyed by the explosion.

"But there is one other consideration." Dr. Everett's face settled into serious lines. "There would have to be very loud noises during the drilling. People would hear it. We'd see it. Unless, well, perhaps if the drill is small enough to do what we think it did, perhaps—perhaps they had a way to drill without causing loud noises. If this is the case, then whoever did this is far advanced in directional drilling. Much farther advanced than any oil company I know of."

Just then, Helen's cell phone buzzed against her thigh. She snapped it off its holder and checked the number. "Excuse me, Dr. Everett. This is my boss and I need to take it." She opened the phone. "Darrow."

"Helen. New development on the AvaChem case: Barbara Melton was just found dead at her home in Baltimore."

"Dead? How?"

"The local authorities have started the investigation, but since you're handling the earthquake case, I believe you should be called in on it as well." He rattled off the address of the home in Baltimore.

"Do they know anything?" Helen asked as she rummaged for a pen to jot down the information. "Can you give that location to me again?" The pen didn't work, and Helen cursed her distaste for technology. A PDA stylus never ran out of ink. "One more time, please," she said, finally getting a pen that worked.

He obliged, then continued, "She was found dead on the floor in her home and the autopsy was performed early this morning. The local authorities didn't realize they had to notify us until the results came in. Then I guess they figured out that you might need to know, since you're on a related case." Sarcasm wove through his words.

"Well?"

"Best as they can tell, it was some kind of poison, but they haven't been able to identify it. But here's the weirdest thing. After, or as part of her death, she was injected with a chemical."

"What?" Helen frowned, her brows knitting together in a way that did not bode well for keeping her forehead wrinkle-free.

"They found a chemical composition in her veins. She was injected with one of her own chemical compounds."

FOURTEEN

Siberia

Lev was too old to feel such biting anger. It wearied him. Depressed him.

He already felt his age in the deepest marrow of his bones, in the brooding aches and pains that accompanied every breath. The slightest movement of his fingers, or the basic act of blinking his eyes—eyes clouded with cataracts so he could hardly see from them anyway—caused ripples of discomfort. The lashes that should have protected his vision had long since fallen out, so the dust and particles in the air gritted his dry eyeballs, grinding into them as he blinked.

He was ninety-nine years old. Perhaps it was to be expected.

He was more than ready to die, but the fury of betrayal simmered deep inside, fueling his ebbing energy.

Roman might be his son, but Lev was still Gaia's Chosen. And Roman still answered to him.

Lev's life had been long, full of purpose, and successful, by his measure. He had few regrets—some, true, but they were few. One deeply buried, one in particular he fought to forget.

Yes, they were painful, but they were few. He hadn't many things to finish before he left this world, and returned to the ground, from which he'd come. What did the Christian Bible say? "Ashes to ashes, dust to dust."

He ached for that moment of dust even while he knew his time separate from the Earth was not finished, and would not be until Roman was fully prepared to lead.

Or if not him, then Varden. Perhaps it would be better off if it were he, despite the fact that Rue Varden was not of the direct line.

There was no hope for Viktor.

And there was no other hope, for the line of the Aleksandrovs had ended with Lev's twin sons. Neither Roman nor Viktor had seen fit to procreate.

The pages of an ancient tome crinkled under Lev's hands while the soft pads of his fingers brushed over sacred words. He turned his attention back to the faded, angular scratchings of the archaic language of the Skaladeskas.

"*As Gaia lives, She breathes. As She breathes, She creates life: in every living creature, in every struggling plant, in every solid rock as One in Her.*"

He'd read those words many times over his life. They'd never meant more to him than they did now.

The time had come.

Yesterday, he'd ventured out of the compound for the first time in months, now that the fierce winter had subsided, and his joints did not ache so much. He needed to visit the outdoor world and draw in the clean air. To breathe of Gaia and calm the ache of anger.

Air. Blessed air.

Grass. Sky. Trees.

Gaia…she was beautiful.

Lev had not gone far, true—for to do so, he would need to clamber up from the small courtyard carved on the side of the mountain. But this was enough for an old man, who'd spent too many days lying on his bed and remembering the beauty of the Earth.

The crisp air bit at his face. He stood, breathed deeply, and was filled with the beauty of the moment. Grey-green grass straggled about, tufting in clumps amid the stony ground. Four pines marked the edge of the steppe there on the edge of the mountain.

Four pines: one for each of Gaia's elements. Mineral, animal, vegetable, water. The four elements that melded and meshed and threaded together to create the Earth herself: a living, breathing One.

From here, Lev had seen the greenish outlines of smaller mountains—hills, really—studded with more pines, and other trees…and the far grey sharpness of true mountains, jutting in the distance. Below the steppe, the dark grey waters of the river below, tussling Roman's small boat against its moorings. And far to the northeast, where the river dumped into the fog-frosted steel-blue waters of Kara Sea.

His world.

A world more threatened each day.

The air dirtied. The glaciers melting because of holes in the atmosphere. The earth stuffed with chemicals and unnatural waste. The trees sliced from their roots, and grasses and brush and earth torn up and tossed about.

He had not seen it himself, not in person. He'd never ventured beyond the mountains as his sons had; he'd never wanted to or needed to. But the images, film footage—those he'd seen. The rape of the land, the natural resources scraped and mined and sucked from Earth. Devastation. Waste. Death.

Here, they were far from the destruction. Near the top of the earth, in the barren, cold mountains of Siberia, the destruction of the rest of the world hardly touched them. Once Lev had believed they were far enough away that it would never touch them.

But he was terribly wrong. And now it fell to him to correct it. To save Her.

For they were all One, all part of Gaia. What one animal, rock, plant, or stream did in one corner of the Earth affected Her throughout, just as one lesion on Lev's body or one scar on his skin could cause infection that would stream through his own blood, poisoning the whole. Or as one cancerous cell grew, it would weaken his very constitution.

If one fed oneself vile fare, it permeated the body and polluted it. Weakened it. Eventually, destroyed it.

So it was with Gaia.

The lesions, the cancer, the poison…it grew everywhere within Her.

And She could no longer fight it herself. Powerful She was, indeed, but She could not battle it alone.

And that was why he had not yet been called back to Her. He'd not yet been allowed to melt back into Her dust.

She had brought him here. She was not yet finished with him.

Now, his fingers spasmed over the aged book in front of him. The delicate pages had long been protected. At first by a glass case, and then more recently by flimsy, clear coating over each page to keep away the dust and the oils of his fingers, but also allowed for his studies to continue.

Just as he closed the heavy cloth cover, a faint whirring sound came from the door, and it slid open to reveal his son. Lev drew in a deep breath to clear his mind and shake off the heavy mantle of grief that weighted him more often each day.

He was still Gaia's Chosen, and he would not disappoint Her. He would be strong.

"I thought perhaps I'd find you here, *Sama* Father," Roman told him as he strode into the room. Despite the fact that he was alone, he approached Lev and sank into a brief bow at his slippered feet.

"Have you anything new to report?" Lev gestured to a chair opposite his, and Roman settled into it. His attention was sharp and ready, his pulse quickening. Now he would see how truthful his son would be.

Roman was a handsome man, and in many ways Lev could not be more proud of him. His head, clean-shaven by choice rather than chance, was a perfect oval, and his scalp smooth and unmarked. Dark, neat brows, a mixture of grey, black, and brown, framed intelligent brown eyes that reminded Lev so very sharply of his Irina. At sixty-three, Roman still had a remarkably unlined face with a solid, square chin. He stood much taller than his father, topping him by half a meter, and carried an abundance of confidence and charm that he used to his advantage at all times.

Now, settled in his chair, he looked around the room for a moment as if needing to choose his words. How much it would cost Roman, how much would he struggle, to tell Lev what he already knew?

Would he be brave enough to do so?

As the silence simmered, Lev declined the urge to follow his son's attention as it scored the chamber littered with books and scrolls borrowed from the Sacred. Several chairs, used only when other Shamans were present during study or their spiritual journeys, clustered one corner of the room. His shamanic drum hung from the wall above one of the chairs.

The walls were the same smooth plasterlike material as the other buildings in their settlement, but instead of the blinding white of the hallways that led from Segment to Segment, the walls in this room had a soft yellow-gold tone, sloping gently from floor to ceiling. Inset lights provided illumination over two large tables made from slabs of pine and the gently crossing antlers of the Great Elk. Crystals of various shapes, sizes, and characteristics were piled in the center of the table closest to Lev. And in the corner were three ceremonial drums.

Lev waited until Roman spoke.

"The test phase has been completed to our satisfaction. We continue preparations for Phase Two, and have identified the three targets. They will be in the city of Detroit."

"Three?" Lev pulled himself upright in his chair, ignoring the creak of his right elbow.

"We believe three will produce the optimal effect. There are the three major automobile manufacturers. It is fitting."

"Did we not determine two would have the appropriate strength and decrease the potential destruction?"

"I believe it must be three targets, Father," Roman replied. "One can be considered nothing but a coincidence; two will not prove our seriousness. Three is a sacred number and will display the level of our commitment. One for each of the three elements affected by those targets: air, earth, and water."

Lev reached for the oval-shaped carnelian stone next to him. He knew his place in the world. And he had made certain his sons knew their places as well. Indeed, one of them had put his own dreams and desires aside to meet the demands of his father. He'd come home and stayed...

And one of them had not.

"You make a weak argument, Roman, for the third target. I do not approve of it—for it means more destruction—but I will commune with Gaia and meditate on whether we should proceed with your plans. I will be journeying to the Upper World tomorrow. That will be soon enough, I trust." His last journey— not a physical one, of course, but in the trance brought about by the traditional, fast-paced rhythm of the drums—had cost him greatly. But Lev knew his duty to Gaia, and his son would learn it too.

As he smoothed the scarlet crystal over his right elbow, Lev watched Roman as he struggled to subdue the rash, angry response he wanted, but feared, to make. It was almost as if he was chewing on his tongue.

"I didn't realize you would be undertaking a journey again so soon. But of course, *Sama* Father. We are prepared to proceed as you direct."

Despite the fact that Roman was a grown adult, and had taken over the full leadership of the clan a quarter of a century before, he still feared his father's power. And rightly so. For though he coveted it, Roman was not yet ready to take on that role of patriarch, of leader. Of Shaman. He had much more to learn: restraint, gratitude, forgiveness.

Roman might have the sharp, bright intelligence that had bettered their clandestine world through his initiatives and inventions, but he did not connect with the spiritual world as readily or as easily as one must to be the same powerful Shaman that Lev was. That lack would be a weakness as he continued to build his levy of supporters and his government, for there were two critical aspects to leading the Skaladeska clan: intelligence and strategic leadership, and spiritual communion with Gaia.

Feeling the healing warmth from the crystal soothe his arthritic joint, Lev said, mildly but firmly, "I will journey again tomorrow. Then we will talk again. Make no further arrangements until we have discussed it."

Roman nodded in acquiescence, and gave a short bow, as if preparing to leave.

But there was more to be said, and Lev would have it from his own son's mouth. He was tired of waiting. "When will Viktor arrive?"

Roman froze.

"Viktor?" Roman repeated. Then he recovered. "Ah. I should have guessed you would learn of his imminent arrival through your communion with Gaia."

"You kept this information from me, and I am severely displeased."

"Father, I was not sure how you would respond, knowing what happened and the history between you. I felt it was the right time to bring him back as we move into our second initiative, but I meant to speak with you about it first."

"For what purpose have you invited him to return?" At one time, Lev did not think he would ever desire to see his son again. But now, with age, perhaps he could consider forgiveness.

Perhaps.

"As we implement Phase Two, I intended there to be no one in the Out-World who might be traced back to us. Safety for us, and for him as well."

Lev nodded. His son's explanation made sense, and he accepted it. "Indeed. I will not argue that Viktor could be a weak link in our chain. You will notify me when he has arrived, then."

"I will."

"Now then, what else have you to report from Out-World? It has been several days since you have deigned to visit me alone."

"That is true, but I meant only to give you time for your meditations and journeys. And I bear not the best of tidings."

Lev felt the darkness in his son's mind, and he knew there was indeed bad news. "What is it, then?"

"An oil spill."

Not what he had expected. That was a tragedy, not merely bad tidings.

He lurched from the chair to his knees, brushing his hand over the covering on the floor, sending his energy through to the rock and soil beneath—to soothe and comfort her. "Where?" he whispered as pain radiated through him.

Oh, Gaia.

The horrific images from past oil spills assailed him. Seabirds, loons, eagles swallowed in thick black grease, so filthy their feathers turned blue black and grey, and the dainty nostrils in their beaks clogged and dripping. Helpless salmon, herring, even killer whales, gasping for breath in the oil-slick water, washed onto the beach, their scales slick and black, flopping helplessly in the sand. He felt their helplessness, breathed their demise, felt Gaia shuddering with them.

Crude pools and puddles shining on top of the water, winking with rainbow streaks in the sun. Gaia did not deserve this smothering of her oceans. Turtles, sea otters, penguins; all of them destroyed, starved, swamped with the greasiness of man's carelessness.

"It is not as bad as it could be," his son told him. "It was the *Crimson Shell*. Our oil. She ran abreast of a sea rock, and spilled off the northwest coast of Ireland."

No, not as bad as the *Valdez* or the Jessica Spill in the Galapagos, but bad enough. And dangerous for the Skaladeskas for different reasons. Any investigation into this particular spill could lead the Out-World back to them.

"I have already given the directive," Roman told him. "The Kamut antidote was applied within twenty hours of the report of the spill. And Fridkov has severed our ties with Medivir. Permanently."

Lev nodded, his worry ebbing. Not so bad as it could have been, thank the gods. Despite his other failings, Roman was more than capable when it came to operations and management. "Excellent. That was a dangerous mistake—one we cannot afford at this time. And the Kamut?"

Roman appeared to relax for the first time since joining his father's presence. He settled back in his chair as he had when he first sat down and allowed his hands to move in graceful gestures. "It was applied via aircraft, as planned. It was in the early morning hours when the rescue workers had returned to their camp, and no one would have thought it anything more than a random rainstorm. However, there was one human casualty—a rescue worker who apparently woke early and returned on her own just after the antidote was applied—but it is likely she will recover. Varden has traveled to Dublin to see to it."

"Have you ordered Varden to return here? He must be by your side when the second phase is executed. There must be no chance he could be apprehended or injured during the events." Varden was very wise in the ways of the Out-World—more so than Roman, although Lev's son believed otherwise.

Additionally, Rue Varden brought with him a more purposeful, tempered view than Roman had. He was a needed foil and trusted confidant for Lev's linear-minded Roman.

"Yes, of course. I have commanded him to return within three days."

Lev waited for a moment, watching Roman closely. There was more. He would wait, for here was the test.

His son shifted on his chair, and Lev sensed him curtaining his mind, obscuring something he preferred not to discuss.

But discuss they would. He had moved beyond his pain, his desire to seep back into the ground and to give up. It was not yet time for him, and while he walked the earth, he would command and lead with the strength he always had. Though his son might not wish to acknowledge it, Roman still answered to him—and, through Lev, to Gaia Herself.

Lev considered his son. There was something else Roman was not telling him. Rather than draw it forth at this time, he would wait.

He had other ways to learn what happened beyond these walls.

After ninety-nine years, he had learned the patience of nature. After all, had it not taken Gaia aeons to evolve?

FIFTEEN

July 8, 2007
L'Anse, Upper Peninsula of Michigan

Marina sat on the edge of the bed, the rickety table in MacNeil's hotel room positioned in front of her.

Because the Best Western was booked, they'd resorted to taking rooms in the simple, outdated, but clean Lake View Motel. Since the busiest season for motels in the Upper Peninsula of Michigan was not during the summer, but during hunting season, Boris was welcomed as well. He wasn't the first dog to stay in the log cabin inn. In fact, the front desk boasted a sign offering dog dishes upon request. The room smelled like Pine-Sol and smoked whitefish, and its solitary double bed was draped in red plaid flannel—even now, in the middle of summer.

The owners of the motel were so welcoming to Boris, in fact, that their preteen son had asked if he could take the dog for a walk along the lake. Marina agreed, knowing Boris needed some time out of the small motel room.

On the low table in front of her rested the book they'd found in Dad's hidden cellar. Marina turned the brittle pages and scanned each one, looking for something she could translate. Or at least something familiar.

The inscriptions were handwritten in some kind of brushed ink. The characters flowed with ornate curlicues and sweeping serifs on the first line of every page, but the rest of the text showed more restraint. The ink was a dark green color, and the fancy letters decorated with blue, red, yellow, and violet were not unlike the scripts written by Christian monks in the Middle Ages of Europe.

How old was this manuscript? What did she hold in her hands? Something more important than the Lam Pao Archive?

The key to an entire world she hadn't known about, or had merely forgotten?

Or had she simply blocked whatever she knew about the Skaladeskas from her mind?

Diagrams appeared throughout the text, often taking up a whole page. The same symbol of the Skaladeskas left on the paper in Marina's office also littered the text and diagrams.

Marina smoothed her hand over the crinkling, textured pages, staring at words and characters she knew she'd seen before, struggling to read them, but managing only a word or phrase per page.

But it was there. The words and meanings were there, swimming at the edge of her consciousness, ready to burst forth. Sometime.

MacNeil sat on the bed behind her, long legs extended and ankles crossed. He was finishing the last piece from the pizza they'd shared for a late dinner and, she was sure, was waiting impatiently for her to translate the book while he flipped through the news channels. She couldn't help that her attention kept wandering toward him instead of being focused on the pages in front of her. Gabe had seemed to warm considerably toward her since they'd left Ann Arbor.

Bergstrom had returned to Langley, leaving the two of them to spend another day at the ruins of her father's house. If only Gabe would leave to get some air, instead of alternately glowering impatiently or checking her out when he thought she didn't notice. It was the latter that befuddled her more than the impatience. His restlessness she could handle. But the other, the subtle awareness of her...well, that was unsettling.

Not necessarily in a bad way.

"Are you getting anywhere?" he finally asked. He walked over to the small wastebasket, already overflowing with the pizza box his boss had tried to jam in there, and shoved in the wad of paper towels he'd been using as a plate. "I'd like to give Bergstrom something when I call."

"I think I recognize a few words, articles and pronouns mostly. The word 'Gaia' appears quite often—the goddess of the earth."

"Isn't Gaia a Greek word?" MacNeil asked, surprising her.

"Yes. I always wondered about that. How did a small tribe in Siberia come to use a Greek name for their goddess?"

Marina smoothed her hand over the rippled, translucent paper. "I wonder what this is made of, if it's some kind of special text…or just the way they make books in Skala Land."

"Aren't you supposed to be an expert in ancient texts—oghams, epigraphs, and hieroglyphs?"

Marina blinked. "Someone's been doing his research." She smothered a smile, wondering if he knew the difference between the three terms he'd spouted. She looked up and saw the touch of a smile on his lips.

"Damn straight. So, you can't read anything else?"

"Not now. Maybe later it will come back to me. It's familiar, but I can't read it now. Though I feel as if I'm on the verge of the language flooding back into my memory."

Perhaps if she took a break and let her mind wander, it might shift into place. Maybe she should meditate—but that would mean getting rid of MacNeil, and he didn't seem inclined to leave.

A change of topic might help. "You agreed to tell me what you know about this whole mess. Now would be a good time to tell me why you think a small tribe of earth worshippers in Siberia are a threat to the US. Or my dad. They are his people, after all."

MacNeil sank onto the only chair in the room, which was next to the wastebasket. His blue eyes became sharp as he settled wide, tanned hands over his belt. "Do you remember the sarin gas attack on the Japanese subway in 1995?"

"Of course. It was conducted by a small religious cult. Oh, I see where you're going with this…"

"*Aum Shinrikyo.* Yes, they were a relatively unknown religious cult that had been overlooked by Japanese intelligence until their leader, Shoko Asahara, induced them to execute the attack. Five thousand people were injured, and the Japanese were taken completely by surprise. They knew practically nothing about the group, and certainly didn't consider it any kind of threat—until it was much too late."

"But *Aum* is a doomsday cult, and they conducted the attack because they believed it would help bring on the Apocalypse. There's absolutely nothing to indicate that the Skaladeskas are violent, or preaching the end of the world as *Aum* was. They're simply a small religious cult that worships the earth. Harmless."

"The fact is, any religion can go bad. When there are fundamentalists of any faith or cult, we see it happen. They make absolute truth claims, require blind obedience from their followers—and, most dangerously, declare their version of a holy war. It's true the Skaladeskas may be harmless, as you say. But Bergstrom and I aren't going to be looking in the mirror at our guilty faces the day after the shit hits the fan if they aren't. There will be no *Aum Shinrikyo* on my watch. No horrific surprises."

"Does the CIA expend this much energy and expense to investigate every small, insignificant religious cult?"

"Since 9/11, since the sarin gas attack, since *Kuala Pohr*—remember them?—no one in national security is insane enough to take the chance on letting something slip by. Believe it or not, we're serious about proactively saving lives."

Marina looked at him. He'd become intense and irritated. She wondered if he and Bergstrom had been touched by the great ball-dropping between the CIA, the Feds, and the NSA that had resulted in 9/11.

"I see your point in that you have to keep an eye on things," she said. After all, that was part of the reason she'd agreed to help. If something happened to Dad, it'd be on her conscience—along with all the other baggage he'd already burdened her with over the years.

Like she needed anything else weighing her down.

"But I can't believe my father would be involved in something like that. And I can't believe a small band of earth worshippers would pose a threat to the any of us. They probably live in caves or huts and live off the land."

"But if they subscribe to the Gaia hypothesis, which says, according to you, that the earth moves to correct anything that threatens it, perhaps they might find a reason to correct something they perceive as a threat to their goddess. Think of the fundamentalist Muslims—part of the reason we don't get along is because they believe we are controlled by money, capitalism. And, in fact, there is an indication that the Skaladeskas might not be as harmless as you think."

"Ah. Now we come to the crux of the matter," Marina replied. "There's something you've held back. Why didn't you tell me this from the beginning, instead of blathering on about Dad's disappearance and the whole story you gave me about protecting him?"

"That's Colin's story. There are some things he hasn't told me, and I haven't pushed him because I know he has his reasons. But I think you should know the real reason we're looking for your father. It's because there's a possibility those earthquakes last Friday were man-made. Caused by the Skaladeskas."

Marina stared at him. "What? How is that possible? And how could you connect them to it?"

But before he could respond, something snagged her attention. A sharp prickle across her shoulders sent her leaping to her feet. She banged against the rickety table and knocked the book to the floor just as something crashed through the window.

"Get down!" MacNeil yelled, already slamming himself to the floor. Marina dove, and he yanked her down the rest of the way, her head thumping onto the thin rug. Pain smacked into her temple just as she smelled a puff of sweet-smelling smoke.

She dragged her hand over her mouth, and grabbed at the flannel bedspread that hung next to her face to cover her nose and eyes.

It was too late. The sickening, sweet gas worked quickly, and Marina's eyes spouted tears that streamed down her face. Her head felt like it was in a pool of Jell-O, sluggish and clogged, and before she could turn to look for MacNeil, she lost the battle.

When Marina regained awareness, it was in a dark, close place. Something warm and solid pressed against her back, crushing her fingers between them. She was sitting, and her arms and legs were immobile. The pain cutting into her wrists was unforgiving metal, but it was tightly tied rope that confined her ankles together. A rumble under her indicated she was in some kind of vehicle that was not only running, but moving.

The sudden jounce of what must have been a pothole shoved her against something warm and solid. MacNeil.

She attempted to uncurl her fingers, and they brushed against rough flesh that moved, tickling against her. "Gabe?" Her voice came out in a soft croak, barely audible above the rumble of the engine.

"You hurt?" His words weren't much louder.

"No. You?"

"No."

They both fell silent. It wasn't necessary to speak the obvious. They didn't know where they were, where they were going, and what was going to happen. The only thing that was fairly certain was that they had been snatched by the Skaladeskas—or some entity that didn't want them to find them.

"Can you move at all?" He shifted against her back as he proved that he, at least, was slightly mobile. The warmth went away, then returned in awkward bumps as he tested his mobility, brushing against her.

By now, she'd figured out that they were in the back of a truck, about the size of a UPS delivery truck, she guessed, based on the air space and the fact that she could only touch two walls.

"I've got a"—she grunted as she tried to scoot back toward the sound of scrabbling—"small light in my pocket."

"Here." His voice was closer than she'd expected.

Marina scooted toward him and found that her feet, which were tied together at the ankles, were also tied to something else heavy. Perhaps the wall. "I can't move any closer. I can lie down so you can get at it. The light's in my front pocket, left side. If they didn't frisk me."

"Okay, lie down."

She let herself fall backward, expecting the back of her head to slam onto the floor, but it landed on something warm and solid. His leg. Marina shifted again, and rolled so her head fell the short distance to the floor with a dull thud. Then he moved, and after much scooting and grunting, she felt him back up to her hip and feel around with his fingers.

Then another grunt, and he pulled his hand out. "Got it."

"It's one of those little micro-lights you squeeze to illuminate," she explained. "I got it from a catalog that claimed they're used by the FBI."

"At least one of us was prepared. Now let's see how we can get out of here."

Suddenly, the light came on and Marina found herself looking into MacNeil's dark blue eyes. They were close enough that she could see his lashes and feel the warmth of his breath. He was smiling a little, only inches away, and Marina thought for a moment that he might take advantage of their proximity and lean closer.

Just then, the truck slammed to a halt. The impact threw both of them to the floor, and the light went out, followed by MacNeil's curse. "Dammit. Dropped it."

"Well, at least we got to see for a minute. How about getting my feet untied and I'll work on yours."

"Nice idea but—" He stopped just as the sound of metal scraping against metal grated at the back of the truck. "Play dead!"

They fell against each other as they slumped to the floor, and Marina felt something hard and irregular jamming into the underside of her wrist. She curled her fingers around the small, flat light MacNeil had dropped, and managed to shove it into her back pocket.

Then she waited.

The doors opened, and through slitted eyes, Marina saw very little illumination. In other words, it was still night. Or they were in a garage or cave.

And their captors numbered two.

If these were the same guys who'd given them chase in the SUVs, and one of them was in custody, where had the third one been during the car chase?

Setting off a bomb, most likely. Attempting to destroy any evidence at Dad's house.

They yanked Marina out first after unlocking the padlock that held her legs attached to a hook on the wall with a bicycle chain. MacNeil wouldn't have been able to free her anyway, unless he carried lock picks. Someone dragged her out of the truck, banging her hands on the edge before she was thrown over her captor's shoulder.

Continuing to feign a faint, Marina kept the exclamation of pain deep inside her chest, even though it hurt like hell when her curled fingers clanged into cold metal. She did open her eyes as she was being carried and confirmed that if it wasn't the dead of night, at least it was just before dawn.

It was night. It was cool. The wide white swath of moonbeam cut across the pathway below her bobbing head.

Then she heard the sound of water. Waves, lapping and rushing against a dock or shore.

Terror surged through her. Marina caught her breath, blinking fast, trying to focus. Trying to keep her mind clear, to open options, to relax so she could plan—

Water. Closer. Rough, cold, angry…

"No." She couldn't help it; she started to buck and twist.

Her sudden moves must have surprised her captor, for he lost his grip and she tumbled to the ground. She crashed hip-first onto something hard that knocked the breath out of her and shot pain into her side. Even that didn't slow her. She rolled as fast as she could toward the looming trees.

Shouts of exclamation punctuated tramping feet and activity from the two men, and Marina experienced only a moment of reprieve before someone snatched her up again. He tossed her over his shoulder again with enough force that the edge of his shoulder knocked what little breath she had left out of her.

And he trotted along the path. Closer to the sound of waves splashing onto some shoreline.

Marina took a deep breath. Tried to focus. Paralysis threatened to seize her again, but she forced herself to drag in her breath, and send it out…drag it in, send it out.

She tried to talk herself into the fact that this was an abduction, not a murder. It had to be. Surely if they'd wanted to kill her and Gabe, they'd have done it by—

And then the shift of her captor's walking rhythm changed. She looked wildly around and saw him step up onto a metal stair that clanged under his shoes. A dock.

Then, suddenly, she was falling. White terror colored her vision. She stifled a scream and instinctively held her breath. But, blessedly, instead of a splash, she made a dull thud as she hit the ground, shoulder first. A fish-scented floor of rough plastic carpet scraped her cheek.

A series of thuds told her MacNeil had met the same fate, and in the dim light, she saw the lump of his foot next to her.

The low rumble of a motor broke the silence, and a rocking motion told her they were about to set off in a boat.

The chill breeze became stronger as the boat set into motion, thumping over the waves. Her bare arms were cold and numb, and spray from the water splashed over the side of the boat and made the wind feel even colder.

Based on the cool temperatures and healthy waves, Marina assumed they were speeding over Lake Superior. And she had a terrible feeling they were either going to be visiting the bottom of the lake, or their captors were taking them to Canada.

"Marina." MacNeil's voice barely reached her over the roar of the motor.

"Yeah."

"Just wanted to make sure you weren't hurt. Nice try back there."

Marina wanted to laugh at the irony of it. She hadn't "tried" anything. That had been pure self-preservation. But she wasn't about to tell MacNeil that. "I'm fine. They're probably taking us to Canada."

She hoped they were only taking them to Canada.

They must have driven east from the motel where they'd been kidnapped—only four hours from L'Anse would have put them near Sault Sainte Marie, which was on the border of the US and Canada. Transferring them to a boat to go a short distance across Lake Superior would preclude them from having to go through customs, despite the fact that it was one of the easiest border crossings in the world, and possibly allow them to dock at a private location in Canada.

Frightening how easy it was to take someone out of the country.

A shiver overtook her, and without warning, she was trembling violently on the wet floor. Her teeth chattered and Marina tried to think of the hot sun, the white beaches of Grand Cayman, a roaring fire, a strong, warm body lined up next to hers—anything to push away the chill that seemed to permeate her body.

The ride was interminable, but it did, at last, end. The rumble of the motor slowed to a purr, the jouncing of the waves became less pronounced, and their captors began to move around.

The boat jolted against the dock, and suddenly the night air emptied of sound as the motor was cut.

A hand closed around one icy arm and yanked Marina to her feet. With a few slashes near her ankles, they were released from their bonds. Her captor shoved her forward and she stumbled on numb feet, falling once more to the rough ground.

He dragged her upright again with a mutter under his breath, but this time he waited until she got her balance before prodding her along.

She could see. The sun was beginning to glow at the edge of the earth, and the black of night was giving away to the greys and blues of shapes and shadows.

They walked from the boat onto a wooden dock, then along a narrow path in a thickly wooded forest. The silence was unnerving.

"What do you want?" Marina finally asked, pausing on the path. They hadn't dumped their bodies in the lake, they hadn't shot them or hurt them, so she figured she had a right to ask.

"Keep moving. We will talk soon." An unfamiliar accent tinged the words of the man behind her.

"Where's my father?"

"Keep moving. There will be time for talk later." And this time, a flash of metal appeared in his hand.

Marina didn't budge. Guns no longer frightened her. Much. "You can un-manacle me. Where am I going to go in the middle of the woods at night? And it's easier to walk. I'll be able to move more quickly." She stood in the middle of the pathway, facing the man who wanted her to move along.

This was her first glimpse of his features, and despite the fact they were by moonlight, she could see well enough to recognize that he was not the same man who'd broken into her house. He was perhaps six feet tall, dark hair (the color was indeterminable in the low light), and an angry mouth. His nose had a generous hump in on its bridge, and he was clean-shaven.

"Move." He brandished the gun.

"Marina." MacNeil's voice from back along the path carried a note of warning.

Looking deep into the eyes of her captor with the humped nose, Marina scored her gaze into his. Something almost palpable crackled in the air, and she felt rather than saw his indecision. She felt as if she knew what he was thinking, and spoke instinctively. "My father will have their heads if they harm me."

Those words surprised her nearly as much as they surprised the man in front of her, if the rapid blinking of his eyes and the blanch of his mouth was any indication. "Now, why don't you make this easier on all of us, and unlock my handcuffs. And his too."

"There are bears and wolves here. You do not dare to run away," her captor told her, as if to excuse his compliance with her demands. "Bran." He snapped his finger at the other man, who apparently went by the name of a cereal. His companion, who appeared to be as taken aback by the turn of events, urged MacNeil forward so that the group of four stood in a small circle on the pathway.

He dug in his pocket and withdrew a small ring of keys, and shortly MacNeil and Marina were un-cuffed.

She'd probably have to answer just as many questions from MacNeil later as she would for her kidnappers.

"Thank you."

With that, she turned to continue along the path, sensing she'd pushed her advantage just as far as it needed to be pushed for the moment.

They walked for over an hour, Marina judged by the position of the waning moon and the faint lightening of the sky to her right. Her chilled skin warmed slightly from the hike, but by the time they reached the paved road that appeared in the middle of the forest, she had resorted to rubbing her hands up and down her bare arms in an effort to warm them. Even in the middle of summer, the temperatures rarely reached above eighty degrees. And most often fell to the forties or lower at night.

The paved road turned out to be not just a road, but a private runway, if the small plane on one end was any indication.

Marina slowed her pace as she realized they were headed for the Piper Mirage, and looked back to catch MacNeil's eye. Damn. Taking them across the border into Canada wasn't so bad. They couldn't be more than a few hours from the US border. But factoring in a plane flight put a whole new spin on things.

"Keep moving or I'll cuff you again," growled Bran's accomplice, whose name Marina had yet to learn. He carried a gun, and, as emboldened as she'd been earlier, she wasn't foolish enough to push his frayed nerves. She'd seen the panic in his eyes when she mentioned Dad.

So Marina led the way to the Mirage that sat like a gleaming white moth at one end of the runway. There wasn't another building, plane, or hangar in sight. It was as if the plane and its private takeoff path had been plopped down in the middle of a forest.

A private plane and its private airstrip. Just dandy.

"Who's going to fly that plane?" she asked, eyeing it with a combination of apprehension and enthusiasm.

"You are."

SIXTEEN

July 9, 2007
Siberia

Lev's frail hands shook as he faced Roman.

Less than twenty-four hours ago, he'd confronted him about Viktor's arrival. Now, he had been made aware of another incident of which Roman had again neglected to apprise him. He thrust his fingers into his lap to hide the emotion he needed to suppress.

"Is there nothing else you wish to tell me? No other reports? Nothing untoward that occurred during the test phase?" Lev was gratified to see the faint red that mottled his son's forehead. No, Roman would keep no secrets from him.

"There was one small mishap. An unexpected glitch at one of the test locations."

"I am fully aware of the papers that were released with our—Gaia's—mark on them. *How did that occur?*"

Roman's throat constricted, then stopped as if stuck, then constricted again. Lev heard the friction in his son's dry swallow. "I do not know. Varden reported it to me immediately. He managed to gather them up before they were noticed. Even pulled them out of the trash and destroyed them."

Lev felt only faint surprise that Roman did not ask how he knew of the problem. It was never prudent to rely on someone else for critical information, and much as he loved his son, Lev did not fully trust anyone—including his own flesh and blood. He'd learned the depth of betrayal from one closest to him.

From his own son, Viktor.

"And you did not intend to inform me of that occurrence? What right do you have to keep such information to yourself? It could have jeopardized our cause, Roman. You are not foolish enough to believe I would not want to know. And would not want you to locate and disable those responsible."

"Varden collected all of the papers. No one gave them any attention. They were too busy pulling people out of the rubble to notice or care about some papers."

"But if someone should recognize the mark of Gaia, Roman, if someone *should*, then we will be in jeopardy. And that is not acceptable."

"No, it is not. I should have told you, Father, but I hoped to spare you needless worry. Varden has assured me no one has given any thought to the papers. He has been intimately involved in the rescue operations in order to ascertain what investigations are occurring. And who even knows of Gaia's Mark—except for us?"

Lev stared at him for a long moment, allowing disappointment and warning to flare in his eyes. "You will not withhold any information from me for any reason again. Regardless of your opinion of its triviality. Do not forget, I am the one who speaks for Gaia. You and Varden—you do not."

"Of course, *Sama* Father."

"And when you have determined which of our people allowed such a thing to happen, you will handle it with the same finality with which you handled Israt Medivir."

"Of course, *Sama* Father. I have no qualms about dealing with those who fail or who do not follow orders. Only last week, Igor Minofsky was reprimanded publicly when he called into question the direction I gave him. He wanted a more definite sign from Gaia that this was the perfect time; he dared to question you and your knowledge—but, of course, not to your face. Stegnora believes Hedron may have been involved in this challenge, stirring up enmity among some of the tribe. Hedron's sons Bran and George have been out of contact for more than a week now, and we have been searching for them."

Lev nodded. This, he hadn't known—about Bran and George, who were currently living in the United States—but he was fully aware of Hedron's belligerence. Lev suspected he would risk upheaval in the clan in order to remove Roman from his ruling position, despite the spiritual power still retained by Lev himself. For, to Lev's surprise and Roman's acute dismay, Hedron had proven his ability to commune with the spiritual world in a way that eluded Roman.

Lev spoke smoothly. "I presume you will locate the two young men? And what of Fridkov?"

"Of course, Father. Fridkov arrived Stateside and has been reassigned to conduct his own investigation on the whereabouts of Hedron's sons. And appropriate steps will be taken."

"I would expect nothing less, Roman. Do not disappoint me again."

Langley, Virginia

Gabe MacNeil was missing.

With a civilian.

Colin fumbled for a capsule of Prilosec then downed it with four slugs of coffee. Black. And strong enough to remove rust stains.

He had a feeling it wouldn't help.

For twenty years, he'd walked the straight and narrow. Always following the rules. Always getting expenses approved before utilizing them. Always clearing investigations as needed. Always being completely forthcoming with his team.

Always justifying his work for the Agency.

And the one blasted time he didn't, this had to happen.

With a civilian.

Bergstrom was going to have to do something. MacNeil's satellite phone wasn't working, and he'd heard nothing from him since he'd left Marquette yesterday afternoon.

He'd allowed his past and his personal prejudices to lead him and now he was going to have to face the consequences.

Damn. It had been a simple assignment: bring Victor Alexander to him so he could find a way to hold him. Simple.

But, like the time he'd decided to install a new light in the dining room, what had seemed an elementary, straightforward task had turned into an abominable mess.

He'd lied to his officer, withheld information, and misled him. Endangered a civilian. Utilized unauthorized Agency resources during a time when budget cuts required accounting for everything.

All because he saw the opportunity for revenge.

And now he was going to have to pay the piper, and hope it wouldn't result in the loss of his job. Because if he lost that, he lost everything.

His attention bounced around his office, unsure where to focus. Onto the stack of files that needed to be dealt with.

Onto the laptop screen, which, behind its screen saver, held nearly a hundred emails.

Onto the minutes from, ironically, the budget meeting he'd attended yesterday.

And, finally, irrevocably, onto the old photo of his wife.

He flipped listlessly through a file while his mind worked. How could he get a team up to Northern Michigan to track down Gabe? Would Darrow agree to it?

Why the hell didn't Gabe call?

He had a satphone.

But Bergstrom knew Gabe would have called if he could have. Which meant that he was in trouble.

That assumption was a light at the end of the tunnel of his own making. Because if Gabe was in trouble, that meant there was trouble to be had. And if there was trouble, it would justify his actions.

Before he could stew on it any longer, his desk phone rang. "Bergstrom here."

The voice that came through sounded far away and tinny. At first, his heart leapt. Gabe? But no.

"This is Director Colin Bergstrom?" came the precise, clipped voice that Colin recognized as someone who'd learned English as a second or other language. He spoke his first name "Cole-in."

"Speaking. Who is calling?"

"This is Inspector Hamid al-Jubeir of the GDI in Riyadh, Saudi Arabia."

"Yes? How may I help you?"

"I am involved in an investigation related to the murder of a wealthy oil producer here in Riyadh. The man who killed him left a calling card with a black drawing on it. A symbol."

"Yes?"

"Through the Interpol database, I found that you have been investigating such a symbol in relation to some activity in the United States. Yours is the only identifier I could find for this drawing. I hoped you might have some information that could help me."

"Indeed. Indeed!" Perhaps the sun would shine. "Can you fax me a copy of the symbol? Do you have any other information?"

"The assistant of the man who was killed met the suspected murderer. I have a composite drawing of that man. Would that be of interest to you? And have you anything to share with me?"

"Yes, to both. Perhaps you can email them to me?" At the very least, Colin would run the photo of the murderer through the database in Langley, unless by some odd break of fortune he recognized it as Victor Alexander. Identifying another Skaladeska—especially one who was a suspect in murder—would immediately support his questionable investigation. And then he could use more resources to track down Gabe.

Colin gave Hamid his email address, and while the investigator was preparing the attachments, Bergstrom gave him a sketchy outline of who the Skaladeskas were. "At this time, we haven't any reason to believe they are a danger to anyone. However, with this new development—and if it is indeed a Skaladeska who is suspected in the murder of…Israt Medivir"—he had to look at his notes to make sure he had the name right—"it will give credence to our decision to continue monitoring those people."

Perhaps, perhaps his personal feelings had not been skewed too far from professional after all.

His instincts had never been wrong yet.

Somewhere in Canada

Marina looked at the Mirage sitting on the end of the runway. She'd flown one twice, and although it was bigger than the SR-22 with which she had logged more than a thousand hours, it had more than a few advantages over that. It could fly higher and carry more weight, to name a couple.

And they wanted her to fly it.

Her kidnappers wanted her to fly a plane.

Why?

Marina didn't remember the question coming out of her mouth, but she must have spoken it, because her captor replied, "You have the skill, and I am most certain you will do your best to ensure we have a safe trip. I will be watching you very closely."

Ah yes. The very same tactic employed by bank robbers and other felons: have the hostage drive the car while they keep a gun on him. It provided for fewer distractions and better security, from the felon's point of view.

"Where are we going? Do you have a flight plan?"

"You will find all you need inside."

By now, they had reached the plane. A shadow moved inside the little craft, shifting into the shape of a man, who yawned and stretched before he opened the plane door. It opened toward the ground to display built-in steps.

"Is he your guard dog?" Marina asked, and suddenly she thought of Boris. The canine would be frantic when he returned to the motel room to find her gone. The sense of struggle in the air would be evident to him and he would know she'd left under duress.

"Inside." She felt a jab at the base of her back, and it brought her back to the matter at hand. Boris would be fine. The boy who'd taken him for a walk would take care of him.

She, on the other hand, was going to be in a bit of a mess for the foreseeable future.

Glancing back at MacNeil, Marina gave a little smile and was rewarded with a wry expression in return. They were in this together, and they hadn't been hurt or killed yet, he seemed to say. Onward and upward.

Literally.

Inside the Mirage, she slid into one of the pilot seats and began reviewing the flight plan, which had been on the small console between the two seats. Someone knew what they were doing.

The plan was a visual one, which meant it wasn't filed with air traffic control and she wouldn't be relying on instruments during flight. They would also be flying at a lower altitude than what the Mirage was capable of—a precaution, she assumed, on the part of whoever had planned it, because if they flew at a high enough altitude—say, over 18,000 feet—they'd have to file the plan with ATC. Which meant that they'd get a four-digit Squawk code—something she could potentially use to alert ATC that they were being hijacked or kidnapped. So using a code to notify the ATC wasn't going to work. She'd have to think of something else.

Marina wondered if it was either of these gentlemen, or if someone else had prepared their route. If they hadn't prepared the flight plan, that could mean neither of them were skilled pilots. Which left some room for her to get creative.

Marina turned her mind from questions she couldn't answer, and focused on refamiliarizing herself with the plane, which was a

2004 model and the newest, most feature-laden aircraft she'd ever flown. Despite the fact that they were being abducted, it was going to be a rush to fly it. The flight plan indicated they were going to be flying at about 14,500, and heading northeast of James Bay.

She checked all the gauges and controls on the digital screen, confirmed the aircraft was fueled, and finally settled in her seat.

"Where exactly are we going? I need to know if I'm going to fly this thing."

"Our final destination is near the Arctic Circle."

"The Arctic Circle? That's going to take at least two days!" she said, looking at the man who had taken the seat next to her. "We're going to have to stop to refuel at least three times. And—"

"We will not fly so far. You will follow the plan and land where you are directed."

"What, are we taking dog sleds from there? And don't you think we're going to be a little cold?" Marina asked, gesturing to her bare arms. At least the plane had the comforts of heat, as well as a pressurized cabin.

He shoved a heavy hooded coat at her as he replied in annoyance, "Your duty is to fly this plane. Your questions will be answered at the appropriate time. You have no choice but to cooperate."

She didn't, did she?

Marina set her jaw and draped the coat over the chair behind her back. She found a pair of warm gloves in one pocket, and a hat in the other. At least she wouldn't freeze when they landed.

At least, not right away.

Her mind raced as she settled back in her seat. As the CIA had learned, she didn't embrace dictatorial orders without a fight, or without considering all the alternatives.

Based on the way her so-called copilot was looking at the array of controls, she wagered she knew more about the plane than her companions. He appeared to be trying to hide his fascination and awe of the dash that was crammed full of dials, gauges, and buttons.

She had more than a hunch he knew next to nothing about flying. So they'd see whether she had a choice to cooperate or not.

Marina carefully chose the time to make her move.

They'd been in flight for well over an hour, having reached their altitude. The sun had begun to rise, and they were just below the clouds so she could see the terrain below: vast, empty, no mountains or hills in sight. Very few signs of civilization. No large cities. Some small towns, but nothing to worry about.

They were near Elsas, Ontario.

Removing her hands from the yoke, under the guise of a stretch—which was not all that difficult to fake, considering the only sleep she'd had was when she was out cold in the back of the truck—Marina craned her neck to look at the rest of the cabin. It was laid out just like a six-seat limo, with four seats facing each other in the back.

MacNeil was sitting in the facing seat to her right, with Bran directly in back of Marina's seat, which made it easy for her to catch MacNeil's eye without Bran noticing. It was a swift-moving, sliding glance, but their gazes snagged. She made sure hers was full of meaning.

As she settled back in her seat, Marina heard MacNeil cough. It was the first time he'd done so, and she knew that was his response that he'd read her signal. Good. She might have to drag him off the plane, but at least he wouldn't be panicked.

Of course, she didn't expect a guy like MacNeil would panic about much anyway.

She allowed the Mirage to fly along for another fifteen or twenty minutes before slipping it out of autopilot and putting her plan into motion.

A quick in-drawn breath was enough to catch the attention of George, the previously unnamed kidnapper who sat next to her. But Marina knew well enough not to overplay. Just that in-drawn breath, and an adjustment to an instrument that looked like she'd had to react quickly…and then nothing. Studied casualness.

She felt George's eyes on her. He'd turned toward her, but said nothing. She could tell he wondered, so she took care to tighten her mouth and add a little frown between her brows.

A few more minutes, and she changed her facial expression as she stabbed quickly at a different instrument and at the same time banked the plane quickly to the left, then righted it, all so quickly that it appeared she was correcting the sudden swoop and not causing it.

"What is it?" George asked.

"Nothing. I thought…I am not familiar with this plane, and I thought for a minute there was a problem with the vacuum pump." She made her words light, but kept that little tension in the top of her forehead. "There's no—"

She did it again while George was distracted by her speech: pitched the plane downward and then leveled it off quickly, causing her captor to fly forward, then back into his seat. She tried to keep the smile from twitching the corners of her mouth at the expression on his face.

Marina had learned to fly aerobatics, and preferred that kind of thrill to any roller coaster Cedar Point might ever conceive. She was fully aware, having experienced it herself, that motion sickness was common among aerobatic pilots in training. In fact, it was so common and fairly expected that when Air Force pilots trained, they were not allowed to clean up if they vomited. Nor were they relieved of duty.

Those who continued flying despite being ill were lauded and kept on, but those who were not able to continue were discharged.

Marina herself had flown enough aerobatics that she was immune to the motion sickness problem, and found that as long as she flew a few hours regularly, she kept that immunity up.

She was counting on George and Bran—and, unfortunately, MacNeil—to be on the other end of the spectrum, and hoped neither of the kidnappers would have had the fortitude to make it through the Air Force training.

If Marina felt any regret for putting MacNeil through the same, she didn't dwell on it. If it didn't kill him, it'd make him stronger. Besides, it would give her a good sense of just what he was made of.

She banked the plane to the left, and then to the right, in quick succession, ignoring George's frantic demands to know what was wrong. Instead, she kept her face tight and her eyes focused outside the windshield as if she was just as terrified as he was. That in itself was a battle, to keep the exhilaration from showing in her face.

After leveling the plane for about three minutes, during which time she responded to George with a clenched-jaw, "Be quiet! I'm just trying to keep us in the air!" she slipped the plane into one of the aerobatic routines she'd learned.

It was fifteen minutes of loops, banks, and steep turns, and it was certain to turn the stomachs inside out of every man on the plane.

She bit the inside of her cheek to keep from grinning in delight when George finally succumbed, bending forward to rest his head against the other yoke. That was the worst thing to do, but she wasn't about to share that little tidbit with him.

Marina settled for bumping the plane up and down as if it were going over the moguls in the snow below so she could take a good look at the man sitting next to her. Yes, the gun butt was sticking up between George's bottom and the seat, forgotten.

A quick look toward the back told Marina that MacNeil wasn't doing much better than George. She couldn't see Bran. But she managed to catch MacNeil's attention again and give a quick nod. He coughed, but she wasn't sure if that was his signal or a precursor to him retching all over the floor.

Someone puked as she turned back quickly. A quick glance told her it was Bran. And that pushed the beleaguered George over the edge.

Marina did another loop for good measure, then made her next move. With a measured shift, she twisted the yoke to the right, and as George flew up off his seat in the same direction, she snagged the gun from under his rear and dropped it on the left side of her chair in one motion as smooth as the plane's loop.

"Marina." She heard a choked voice from behind. Gabe. She righted the plane and cast a quick look back. He caught her eyes, then, holding his hand over his mouth, he flipped open his seatbelt and lurched across the small cabin toward Bran.

She couldn't see what happened next, but Marina assumed Gabe was relieving Bran of his weapon, so she kept the plane steady for a moment so as not to jar him out of his calculated move.

When she glanced back around, she saw Gabe back in his seat, fumbling with his seatbelt with one hand, clutching the gun in the other, and retching over the side of the armrest.

The plane was going to be hell to clean up.

Once the plane was flying level for more than five minutes, Gabe recovered from his bout of motion sickness. Now that he and Marina had the weapons, it was short work for him to take control of George and Bran, who hadn't realized they'd lost their guns along with their dinner until it was too late.

Marina kept the plane straight and level as easily as if they were out for a Sunday jaunt while training one of the guns on George. She appeared to have gotten over her reluctance to hold a weapon. When she turned toward the back as if to see what he was doing, Gabe assumed she'd put the plane on autopilot.

Still a bit queasy, he assisted Bran in moving the handcuffs from his pocket to his wrists. Bran barely resisted. He was covered with vomit and his face was speckled with tiny red dots from the force of his puking. Gabe was thankful for the fact that he hadn't had anything to eat since that long-ago piece of pizza in the hotel room, and had therefore been content with little more than dry heaves.

After Bran was cuffed with his wrists behind the seat so there would be no unexpected distractions, Gabe made his way to

George and half dragged, half pulled him from the front seat to a back seat and cuffed him in a similar manner.

"Sorry, guys. We're not going to be as accommodating as you were for us."

Once he was sure they were immobilized, Gabe dropped into the seat next to Marina, taking care not to step in George's vomit.

"That was some fucking ride."

"I'm sorry." She didn't sound the least bit remorseful.

He couldn't decide whether to be pissed off and tear a verbal chunk out of that shapely ass, or kiss the hell out of her for her quick—and creative—thinking. Annoyance finally won out—the kissing could come later—for it was obvious she'd loved every minute of the discomfort she'd inflicted on them. Including him.

"Couldn't you have faked something else?" he asked. "Like low fuel?"

"Then I would have had to land, and we might not have been able to disarm them. I thought it would be better to disable them first."

Couldn't fault that logic. "Speaking of landing…"

"I'm going to try and contact a nearby airport and see if we can land there. We can get something to eat and clean up and maybe rest."

"I'll let Bergstrom know where we are so we can get these guys into custody."

"Yes. But I want to get some info from them if we can, because I think we ought to finish the flight and go to wherever they were taking us. It's the only way to find out what's going on."

"What about your career?" Admittedly, he had to work to keep the sarcasm from his voice. Hard.

She didn't appear to notice, but a grim smile tilted her lips. "I missed my flight ten hours ago. And these guys aren't going to be the last of my problems—so I'm in. All the way until the end."

SEVENTEEN

July 10, 2007
Siberia

Victor Alexander never expected that he would set foot in the world of the Skaladeskas again.

But Roman had called him home. Insisted he rejoin the family. The ideal time was at hand, he'd said. *The ideal time.*

An event that Victor had not expected to occur during his lifetime.

And since he'd arrived, he'd been treated like an honored prisoner. Not a guest. Not the welcomed prodigal son of the Bible's New Testament. But as a hostage. A prisoner of sorts.

Yet his conscience questioned him, deep in the recesses of his mind: *Do you deserve anything different?*

If his father knew the truth about him and Roman—about what they'd done—Lev would likely order him banished into the wilds of the rough mountains to meet his fate at the paws of the wolves and mountain lions, or have him executed.

It was only by Roman's grace that Victor remained alive. Roman had had use for him over the decades. But Victor greatly feared his summons home portended the end of his usefulness. The thought nauseated him.

He knew how ruthless his twin could be.

It had been the method of his travel that gave Victor the first indication all was not as simple as it appeared when he was ushered from what had been a neutral meeting place into a waiting car.

It wasn't that the rooms here in the compound (there were three of them in his suite) were uncomfortable or lacking in anything. No, Roman would not go so far as to keep his prisoner in physical discomfort. His style of manipulation was much more subtle. And there was always the chance Lev might learn of his presence and perhaps be willing, at his late age, to listen to Victor's story. Perhaps he would forgive him for the accident.

No. He would never forgive him. Lev had loved Irina almost as much as Gaia Herself. Perhaps more.

Victor swallowed the bile that burned his throat. He would not think of it.

He forced himself to look around the room again, as if there might be something he'd missed noticing over the last fifteen days.

There was plenty of space, plenty of entertainment options, including a slew of Broadway musical DVDs, food, even women sent to him for massages or anything else he might wish. It was the women and the DVD selection that had Roman's fingerprints all over them.

Amazing how Roman disdained the Out-World, yet embraced certain aspects of its culture. Just one of the amazing inconsistencies in his "younger" brother that others failed to see.

He'd been in his suite of rooms for nearly two weeks and hadn't heard from Roman at all.

The only people Victor had seen was a maid, who came to clean every other day, and the women who brought in food twice daily and offered massages and more.

One thing that was lacking in his accommodations was a replacement for the bottle of Stolichnaya he'd found and finished off by the second night. The bottle had been replenished four times since, but not since he finished that fifth one more than three days ago. The trembling of his fingers and the raging headaches told him his body missed it as much as his psyche did.

What bothered him most was that he wasn't exactly sure where he was. Was Roman even here? Could Victor possibly be in Siberia?

He'd left his home in the northernmost part of Michigan via the small submarine late in the evening. He'd traveled under the lake toward the Canadian shore, and three hours after leaving home, he beached in a thick forest along the Canadian side. The spot was a rendezvous site where someone was to escort him back to Siberia and the Skaladeskas. Having been gone for more than thirty years, and well aware of Roman's penchant for technology and secrecy, Victor knew he would never find the place himself.

No one could, unless they were Skaladeska. Roman had made certain of that. Even with their fancy radar and the satellite scopes, the Out-World couldn't locate them.

Victor's wariness had not been ill-founded. Once he met Bran and his companion, they pulled guns and urged him into a car. The fact that they carried firearms shocked Victor, for that couldn't be on Roman's order. Unless he'd somehow overcome his deep-seated fear of guns—or unless he permitted his men to use them outside of the Skaladeska world.

They drove for well over an hour, then they flew in a small plane for another four or five hours and landed in a remote area of northern Canada. Surely they were well into the Arctic Circle, but he couldn't be certain.

Victor had been taken deep into a cave and escorted onto a small, egg-like vehicle that fit perfectly in a cylindrical tunnel that ran underground.

He'd fallen asleep—or been drugged—and awakened several hours later to be escorted once again out of the train and into these scalding white rooms that had been his home and prison for the last fifteen days.

Surely he wasn't in Siberia.

"They've *what*?" Roman did not succeed in keeping the shock from his voice.

"We believe the plane might have landed off schedule—crashed, perhaps, or made an emergency landing. We're not able to raise them through normal communications." Shyna looked at him as if waiting for the axe to fall.

And well it should, but not on her.

"Is it possible—no, I'll not even consider that. Give it another five hours, and if we haven't been able to raise them on satellite radio, I authorize you to send someone up there to investigate."

"Of course." She gave a formal nod and turned, hurrying out of the room as if to escape before he changed his mind and lowered that axe.

Roman's control was leaking. Everything was shattering, out of control. Failing.

First, the oil spill from the *Crimson Shell* and the necessary steps that had required.

And somehow papers with the sacred symbol had been released at the test site.

Next, the reports from Stateside that one of the boxes and drills was missing. Lev wasn't aware of that bit of information yet, and Roman prayed to Gaia that he wouldn't learn of it. He couldn't afford for him to find out.

And now Bran and George, missing somewhere in Canada with Marina Alexander and a man named MacNeil.

The only thing that could make the situation more dangerous would be news of Fridkov being identified or apprehended. If that happened—no, no. Fridkov was too good.

Nearly as good as Roman himself.

But now Roman could put it off no longer.

He would speak with Viktor.

Langley, Virginia

Helen Darrow's heels clicked like a countdown as she approached Colin's office. He could hear her drumming down the hallway, in time for the urgent meeting she'd called only thirty minutes earlier. She'd been en route in a helo, insisting that he clear his calendar for an update on the earthquake investigation. He'd had no qualms about obliging.

"Come on in," he said unnecessarily, rising as she opened the door ahead of his assistant. Carol Mueller, his iron-haired and iron-fisted admin, probably wouldn't like being left in the dust.

But Helen Darrow, it appeared, cared little for niceties. A fact that was neatly confirmed by her first words.

"I need to know what your team's got, Colin," Darrow announced as she hurried in past him in a gust of some kind of perfume, towing a box on a luggage cart. She slid the strap from her briefcase from her shoulder and let it gently thud to the floor. Her heels clicked purposefully, annoying at this close range, as she walked back to the door and closed it. "We've got evidence the Skaladeskas caused those earthquakes, and I need to figure out how to nail them. You're the only person who knows anything about these people, so I hope you have some updates for me."

Colin could have been offended or irked by her presumptive attitude, but sharp women didn't threaten him. In fact, he enjoyed watching them work. And, of course, there was the fact that he'd married one.

The pang of pain surprised him, and he firmly directed his thoughts away from the past.

He knew his job and did it well, even when he went out on a limb like he had with this one. Thank God that limb had begun to sprout some leaves.

"So far our best connection is between the Skalas and a murder suspect in Riyadh," he told Darrow. "And as soon as I reach Marina Alexander, who is with my officer investigating the Skaladeskas, I'll see if she can identify the composite of the murder suspect. That might be a connection, as we know her home was broken into by a man who left a card identifying himself as a Skaladeska."

"When did you learn this? What kind of murder?"

"Only hours ago. In Riyadh, a Saudi oil baron was found murdered. He'd been injected with a kind of oil." Colin explained about Hamid al-Jubeir's phone call and the murder of Israt Medivir.

"Injected? Barbara Melton was injected with her own chemicals—she was the CEO of AvaChem. Same MO. There's a connection with the symbol?"

"So they were both injected with a poison of sorts." He smiled grimly. This was it. The connection they needed.

"The Skaladeskas, based on what your initial report said— thank you, by the way—they're earth worshippers," Helen said slowly, putting into words the same thoughts that had gelled in his mind. Her heels clacked again as she stalked over to the box on the table. "Oil and chemicals…injected. AvaChem was known for its environmental violations. Chemicals…there's the connection. The Skaladeskas would see those chemicals as a poison to their beloved earth. They killed their victims in the same manner in which they believe we're killing the earth. *And* they're creating natural events for large-scale destruction. Earthquakes. Using the earth to fight back?"

They stared at each other, each mind nipping along to assimilate this possibility.

And who could say, Bergstrom considered, that the Skaladeskas were completely out of line in their beliefs? That the earth wasn't being destroyed, little by little, day after day, policy after policy?

Global warming. Waste and usage of natural resources. The pollution of the ground, water, and air. Deforestation.

Who could argue those practices didn't damage the environment? That something had to change? And that governments and policymakers hadn't listened?

This wasn't about a difference in religious opinions, or societal or economic practices.

This was about something that affected every living being on the earth. How could they be on opposite sides when it came to protecting the planet that hosted all of them?

Yet to the Skaladeskas, it was more. It was their religion. From what he knew, it was the essence of their beliefs: to protect their goddess at all cost.

"A new kind of holy war," he breathed.

For the health of the earth.

Darrow nodded. Then she moved over to the cart she'd pulled in.

"That's the *why*. And now we've figured out the *how*. How they caused the earthquakes." She summarized the situation as she unhooked the straps on the luggage cart and hefted the box onto Colin's conference table.

"What is this?" He had risen from his desk and came around to help her, but by then, she was already standing back, gesturing to the box.

"It's got the symbol on it—see." She flipped over the box. It was heavy and clunked onto the table with a sharp thud. On the bottom, she showed him the faint etching that was the now-familiar symbol of the Skaladeskas. "But what I can't figure out is why would they put their symbol on it? They'd know it would implicate them immediately. Why do that?"

"Holy Christ." He stared at the box. The tension that had settled between his shoulders, which had been there since he secretly sent Gabe off to find Alexander, began to lessen. At last. "What is it?"

"This, best as we can determine, is a controller that served two functions that ultimately caused the earthquake in Allentown. I have teams searching the other sites for similar equipment, but as of now, this is the only one we've found. The ballistics team believes it was used to control and direct a small, extremely powerful drill that dug diagonally through the earth's crust several miles away to under the site of the earthquake's epicenter.

"Once under the epicenter, the drill deposited a very powerful explosive of a very small size—only a foot or so in diameter. And then the controller detonated the explosive."

"And that caused the earthquakes."

"That caused them, without a doubt."

Colin rubbed his thumb over the symbol etched on the box. "You asked why they would put their sign on it? The sign of Gaia, their goddess—that's what Dr. Alexander told me. It represents the deity of the earth. Perhaps as a form of blessing? As if to confirm their actions were being made in her name? For her?" He looked up, and Helen was nodding in agreement.

"Yes, that could be. And, if it weren't for you, we would have no way of assigning this symbol to the Skaladeskas anyway. They wouldn't expect us to make the correlation—even if we happened to *find* this box. Which we would have had no reason to look for, to believe existed. And even so, there's nothing in our database with this symbol on it. You're the only connection. How fortunate for us."

Colin chose not to meet her eyes. "I would never have guessed. They'll do it again. Of course."

"Yes. They haven't claimed responsibility for the events yet, but they will. They'll want to. If they're acting in the name of their deity, if they want some response from us, they'll be happy to admit responsibility."

She paced again, somehow having acquired a pen that she slapped rhythmically against her palm. "Given the right kind of leader, any religion can turn evil—we've seen it happen since the beginning of organized worship. When a holy war is declared, the end justifies any means to those crusaders. We need to be ten steps ahead of them, Colin.

"If we can't penetrate their shell, then we'll have to wait for their warnings, their claims of responsibility, and their implicit hints and threats. I'm not willing to wait. You came to me with your background knowledge about these people—your team needs to get in there and find out what's going on, who the leader is, and how we can stop their next threat. You know as well as I do there will be one."

And another.

And another.

EIGHTEEN

Northern Ontario

As it turned out, by the time Marina and Gabe landed with their prisoners and contacted Colin Bergstrom, everything had blown wide open. There was no question about them proceeding as Marina had suggested.

Especially since when they swept the plane, they'd found a map and documentation that appeared to outline the remainder of the journey.

"We can finish the flight plan and follow this map to the meeting point," Marina said. Her reluctance to follow through on this mission had evaporated. Now determination burned as strongly in her as it did in Gabe. She had come this far, through this much danger. Though she'd lost her chance to see the Lam Pao Archive, she would resolve this mess and find her father. If he was still alive.

"If we wait too long, whoever's at the other end will get suspicious and we'll lose our chance to find out where we're going," she told Gabe.

"You just want to fly that plane again." Another dry comment she hadn't expected from the sarcastic spook, but she didn't deny it. She loved her P210, but the Mirage was an awesome plane.

When MacNeil finally made contact with Colin Bergstrom, the CIA director was overwhelmingly relieved to hear from them.

After listening to his operative's debrief, he shared news of his own, his voice blaring over the speakerphone at the local police station.

"I've been contacted by an inspector in Saudi Arabia. A man was murdered there, and a business card was left with the Skaladeska symbol on it. That alone indicates there is something brewing, and that we are not just following a hunch. There's more, but first I am going to fax you a drawing of the man who is believed to be the murderer. Dr. Alexander, if you would please examine the drawing and give me your opinion, it would be appreciated."

While Marina waited for the fax to come in, she called back to the Lake Side Motel to check on Boris. Meanwhile, Gabe took Bergstrom off speaker and got a further confidential debrief from his director.

"We've made the connection between the Skalas and the earthquake in Allentown. Helen Darrow's team found the controller that detonated an underground bomb and controlled the drill. It has the Skaladeska symbol on it. They caused those earthquakes, they're implicated in at least two murders—"

"Your fax just arrived, and Marina has identified that photo as the man who broke into her home."

"So we can add attempted kidnapping to the list. Unnecessary at this point, but I'll let Darrow know. I agree with Dr. Alexander— you need to follow up on this map and travel route and see if you can locate some of these people. They've got to be planning something else—why would they stop at one incident? And not even take credit for it?"

"They wouldn't. We'll go on and see what we can find out. You need to get me a satphone and a weapon stat."

"I want to send up some backup personnel, too, but it's going to take at least twenty-four hours to get them approved and up there."

"We can't wait," Gabe said. "Get me the phone and the gun. Marina is insistent that we keep the trail hot, and I'm afraid I agree with her, despite the risk of involving a civilian. We might lose our chance of meeting whoever we were supposed to meet up with if we're delayed. Or they might hear about the capture of their colleagues. And we're more likely to be successful with just the two of us than some big team, if we get into Skaladeska territory.

"Marina's hot to go, and I'm afraid if we don't manage the investigation, she'll do it on her own."

Bergstrom spoke abruptly: "Taking a civilian isn't the most optimal of plans, but I'm not going to miss this opportunity. We brought Marina Alexander into this because of who she is, and who she knows. And what she might know but doesn't yet remember.

"She has the mark of the Skaladeskas on her—that could be invaluable to us. Even though she may not realize it, whatever she knows about them is more than anyone else does. She's been in dangerous situations before. She knows how to handle herself. And you've convinced me—a small team makes better sense in this case. Hold on, let me see about your phone and gun. I should be able to get them to you pretty quick."

Gabe stood at the desk in the police chief's office, thankful for the privacy, and shuffled his feet. He could hear Bergstrom's movements in the background over the phone, and his low-toned voice rumbling as he spoke and, likely, manipulated, begged, borrowed, and stole. He wondered if Helen was there, and whether she knew Gabe was on the other end of this case.

"Okay, Gabe, you have thirty hours on your own." Colin came back on the line, breathless but firm. "And I don't want Dr. Alexander running the operation, so you'll have to keep a rein on her. Darrow wants to send her team up there too, but I've managed to convince her to hold off for thirty hours. Get me what you can in that time."

Nearly twenty hours later, after a stop for refueling and a generous nap, Marina landed the Mirage at an airport near Waswanipi, Quebec. It was midmorning, but since they were in the Land of the Midnight Sun, the sun had been shining like it was noon for hours. It was surprisingly chilly—near forty degrees, though Marina had expected it to be closer to sixty since it was July. The gloves and hat would come in handy.

Gabe had arranged for a rental car when they stopped for fuel, and it was waiting in the parking lot.

"The old key under the mat trick, eh?" Marina commented as she climbed into the Land Rover. "Somehow I expected the CIA to be a little less obvious."

Gabe started the engine. "You watch too many spy movies."

"Watch them? I'm in one! That tunnel from Dad's cellar under the lake was too much like Dr. No's underwater room. And I like Hitchcock better than Bond anyway."

"Better than Bond?" Gabe pulled the Land Rover out of the airport parking lot and flipped the switch to turn on the heater. A blast of welcome, warm air burst into the vehicle.

"Much better than Bond. At least Hitchcock's films are somewhat believable."

"Well, we'll see if you still think Bond is unbelievable when we're done with this op." He cast her a grin as they sped along the road. "You and your father aren't close."

Gabe's understated comment drew Marina's attention from the passing scenery of scrubby brown grass and rolling hills.

"No. Not at all." Talking—or even thinking—about her relationship with her father wasn't something she indulged in often. It was too messy. Easier left alone.

"Why is that?"

"You trying to make conversation or are you just being nosy?" But her voice wasn't angry.

"Both. You fought getting involved in this with both arms flailing, and now you're trying to lead the charge. That kind of change of heart makes me curious. It didn't seem like concern for Victor was the driving force behind your change, either."

Perhaps she owed it to Gabe, who was accompanying her on this journey, some explanation. "I didn't want to get involved because I've spent my adult life, and much of my adolescence, trying to get past him, to forget about him. He was never a father to me in any way that mattered—except that he gave me physical life. I dealt with it. Grew up without him, without Daddy-Daughter Dances and a cheering father at my sporting events, and without the glowering, dominant figure sizing up my dates when they came to pick me up. I had no male mentor, no father figure, no one to look up to in that way.

"But I handled it. I put it away. Lived with it, and grew into a normal person. Put him out of my mind. And preferred to leave him there, except when I had to do my duty on Father's Day. His birthday. You know."

"Then we showed up."

"Yeah. At that point, I lost control of my life—the one I'd tried so hard to manage and keep normal. The one I'd kept him out of. So, at first, I did the least intrusive thing I could: I talked to you and Bergstrom. And then all hell broke loose."

"Normal? You call your life normal?" The corners of his eyes crinkled when he laughed.

She also appreciated his gracious change of subject. "It's normal to me. Did I mention that I'm stubborn, and once I get started on something—thrown full-force into it—there's no stopping me?"

"You didn't have to." He glanced at her. "So why do you do all those things?"

"You mean, why is a nice girl like me not settling down with a regular job, a husband, and a couple kids?" The little bit of attraction she might have felt waned.

"No," he said. "I mean why do you fly and cave and go down the Amazon and eat mopané worms? If you'd knock the chip off your shoulder, you'd probably stop reading between the lines and hearing things that aren't there."

Marina's fingers uncurled and she found herself giving him a genuine smile. "Sorry." She glanced out the window, formulating her thoughts before responding. "I want to make a difference in the world. I want to live life to the fullest and experience everything I can, and if I can help people at the same time, I will. I have nothing to lose."

"Except your life. You told me the other day you weren't a spy, a Sydney Bristow. But you do things that are even more dangerous sometimes. That cave rescue in Pennsylvania wasn't a cakewalk."

"No. But it had to be done, and since I don't have a family waiting for me, I take the risks so that others don't have to."

"So," he said casually, his wrist leveraging the steering wheel, "what's with you and the tall guy—Bruce?"

Marina looked at him, and when she didn't respond right away, he looked over at her. Challenging, brows raised, a tiny smirk at the corner of a wide, sexy mouth. He needed a shave.

"What's with you and Helen Darrow?" she countered, thinking how that stubble would scrape against her skin.

"Well…" He gave a short laugh, returning his attention to the road. "You're either sharper than I gave you credit for, or you're damned lucky."

Marina shrugged, pleased her guess had been confirmed. "I notice things."

"It's been almost five years," he told her, his voice nonchalant. "Just before she transferred to Chicago. Haven't seen her since. So how about the tall guy—Bruce?"

"He's married."

"I saw the ring. But I also saw the way he looked at you." He jabbed a finger in the air. "I notice things too."

"Like I said, he's married. Looks don't mean a thing." She turned to gaze out the window, effectively ending the conversation, suddenly feeling as lonely as the flatlands that stretched alongside the highway.

They stopped only for lunch, eating beef-and-gravy-laden pasties that Gabe, who was from West Virginia, had never had before, and then continued their journey. Between the map and the directions printed on the sheet of paper, they easily found their way to…

"This is it?" Gabe turned to stare at Marina, his hands poised on the wheel as if ready to yank it into a turnabout. His weapon rested in his lap, slipping into the space between his jeans-clad thighs.

"This is it. A patch of grass in the middle of nowhere. Hills to the north, trees to the west. No sign of life or a place to meet."

Marina craned her neck to look around. It wasn't as if anyone could be waiting in ambush—there was nowhere to hide.

"Remind me what we're supposed to be doing here."

Marina chose not to respond. Since she'd gotten them here in one piece, she was of the opinion he should keep any comments to himself.

With a snap, she unbuckled her seatbelt and yanked the handle to open the door.

The air was warmer than it had been when they left the airport, but still cool enough she needed the coat. Tucking the gloves into her pocket, she strolled away from the Land Rover as much to give her legs a stretch as to clear her mind.

There had to be a reason they were led to this place. The directions had been in a bag kept by Bran and George. Despite the fact that they were in English, the information had to be legitimate.

She stood in the middle of the field. It wasn't so very large, maybe ten or twelve acres of scraggly brownish-green grass. A firm breeze dashed over the small meadow, tufting and shifting the taller grasses, and she inhaled deeply. Beautiful. Clean and fresh.

Nothing like the polluted oxygen she and the majority of Americans ingested.

Despite her Russian roots and the numerous travels she'd done for her work, Marina had never been to the country of her blood—or even as far north as she was now. Perhaps she'd been wary of getting too close to her lost family. But now, as she looked around at the world under the startling blue sky and the brilliant sun that would barely sleep that night, she recognized a unique beauty in the Arctic.

Yet another facet of Gaia's magnificence.

Gaia.

Just for a moment, she felt a kinship, a oneness with the world around her. Nature, raw and untouched, and alive. And she remembered that it was threatened, every day. That places like this remote area, virginal and new, were disappearing.

And she started to understand what her people felt. The greatness, the majesty of their planet. Its incredible, irreplaceable variety, strength, and beauty.

The earth *was* one with them. And in order to survive, they had to protect Her.

"Ready to head back?"

Marina jolted. She hadn't heard Gabe approach from behind; hadn't even heard him slam the truck door. "Not yet. No. Let's walk over there." She pointed to the low hills studded with pines.

"Marina—"

"It's the closest thing to mountains around, and that's where the Skalas live. In Taymyria, anyway. It's worth checking it out."

"Something wrong?" Gabe looked at her with shrewd eyes.

"It's beautiful here. I was just appreciating her. Nature."

"Yes." He drew in a deep breath, then exhaled. "All right, sixty minutes to check out the hills, then we head back and check in with Bergstrom. I'll call him on the satphone when we leave."

By that time Marina was already several yards away. Gabe jammed the weapon into the waistband of his jeans and watched her go, thoughtful and focused.

The look on her face when he approached had been one of intensity and concentration. She was standing there like she owned the world. Her hands thrust into the pockets of her jacket, eyes clear and bright, and her long, slim nose tipped red by the chill breeze.

And here he was, following the damn woman for a hike around some hills when he should be calling Bergstrom. Maybe they'd cracked Bran and George by now and there were some facts to go on.

He looked toward where he'd last seen Marina, and she was gone. He stepped up the pace and approached the base of one of the small hills.

"Tire tracks," he heard her call, and indeed, there were the two narrow strips of pressed-down grass that indicated a vehicle's passage. The tracks were on the far end of the field from where their Land Rover was parked, explaining why they hadn't noticed them.

The direction of the trail was easy to follow, and they hurried along between the two tire lines as they wound around one of the hills.

The far sides of the hills were rocky and jagged with shale; more like small mountains than the hillocks cupping the meadow. The tire tracks led right into a throng of trees that grew between the vee of two hills.

Marina looked at Gabe and put her hands on her hips. "I'll bet you the entire Bond DVD collection there's a cave in there."

He looked toward the low-growing, scrubby pines. "This is your thing, so I'm not betting. You're right." He resisted the urge to pull her back and allow him to go first, but somehow they'd evolved from an expert protecting a civilian to equal partners. Besides, she wouldn't go for it anyway.

Marina found the narrow passageway through which the vehicle had traveled. They followed the trail, stepping on a mat of rust-colored pine needles that had probably been collecting there for centuries—perhaps even millennia. Only yards beyond the trees, a crust of grey rock jagged from the hill, and as they approached, Marina edged up next to it.

Gabe read her intent and sidled up behind her, against the rock, and she felt his fingers touch her wrist as she began to peer around the corner. She peered around the outcropping of rock and found exactly what she'd expected. Although every instinct in her body wanted to hurry into the cave, she paused—and not just because Gabe tightened his fingers in warning.

They waited and silence continued to reign. Even the sound of the breeze rushing through the tree branches made little noise. Finally, she felt Gabe move behind her, loosening his grip. He pushed past her and she let him go. After all, he had the gun.

Close behind, she followed him into the tall, narrow crevice, one that would have been hard for a vehicle to enter, but was more than generous for the two of them. The cave opening was nearly ten feet high and about six feet wide. Grass grew right up to the entrance, then straggled off as the dirt and rocks took over from the eruption of the small mountain.

Inside, it was black and silent, as caves are wont to be, and Marina pulled her flashlight from the clip at her waist. Cupping her hand over to dim it, she turned it on. The bare glow did little to illuminate the room, but burned an eerie reddish-orange cast on her fingers and palm.

Cautiously, she opened her hand and allowed more light to spill in. When Gabe gave the short jerk of a nod, she released the light completely and spanned it around. They were in a cave, one similar to the hundreds she'd explored. Damp and cold, dark, rough, and musty-smelling.

The chamber elongated near the left side of the back, and as Marina stepped closer, she saw it angled off into blackness. Gabe followed as she started that way—the only option for exploration, unless they wanted to go back out the way they came.

"We don't have the right equipment," she said in a low voice, "but we can explore a little ways."

"You mean all those caves I explored in my backyard when I was growing up—I did it all wrong because I didn't have the equipment?"

They walked along the slightly downward passage. Marina felt inclined to take her time, noticing the character of the cave: its texture and scent, its dampness, the jagged edges, and how the space made her feel. All the while, she felt Gabe practically breathing down her neck. He was in a hurry to get back to the Land Rover, but she was enjoying the heck out of this and refused to be hurried.

Besides. Her instincts told her they were on the right path of something.

That is, until the tunnel narrowed and shortened, then narrowed and shortened more until they were nearly crouching.

"Okay, game's over, let's go," Gabe said. A combination of irritation and smugness tinged his voice. "Can't go any further."

Damn.

She stopped. He was right. There was nowhere else to go.

"All right. Let's go call Bergstrom." She turned and gave him the flashlight so he could lead the way out, and started after him. Marina had taken two steps when she stopped and whirled around. There *had* to be something there. She *felt* it. She could nearly reach out and touch it.

Gabe kept going, his shadow falling back from the beam of light, but she didn't call after him. He'd only grunt and grumble, and if she didn't find anything, she wouldn't have to listen to it. If she did—well, he'd come back after her.

She dug into the depths of her front jeans pocket and pulled out that handy little squeeze light she'd recovered from the truck when George and Bran had first kidnapped them.

Good grief—was it two days ago? It seemed like forever.

She beamed the powerful light around and shimmied herself into the narrowing end of the tunnel, feeling blindly with her hands. If this really was a James Bond movie, she'd find a passageway, or a hidden panel that opened a door further into the cave.

But nothing. Absolutely nothing.

She was just about to call out to Gabe when she heard him coming back down the passage. He must have realized she wasn't behind him. He came around the corner and she opened her mouth to make the first wry comment that came to mind, but he lunged, and clapped a hand over her lips. His large body pushed her back, away from the corner, and she dropped her squeeze light. It bumped against her shoe when it fell.

His words, barely discernible, fed into her ear. "Someone's out there."

She froze, closing her mouth under his fingers, her hand caught against his chest. She stepped back as if she could merge into the stones.

"How many?" she breathed in a barely audible voice. "Who?"

She felt him shake his head against her hair. They pressed back against the wall and listened, but Marina couldn't hear anything. She could feel the outline of his belt buckle against her hip, and the angle of a shoulder against her ear when Gabe shifted. He bumped into her again as he reached to the back of his waistband, and she felt him pull his gun out.

Silent, hardly daring to breathe, she bent her legs, lowered herself to the ground, scrabbling silently for that little light.

After brushing over small pebbles and the damp cave floor, her fingers closed over the micro-light, just as Gabe grasped her arm to yank her upright. "Follow me." His words puffed hot into her ear, and Marina had to tuck back an exclamation of surprise that he hadn't told her to stay put like a good little civilian.

She followed. Listening.

His weapon leading the way, Gabe moved like a wraith, silently and swiftly. Marina stayed close enough to touch his shirt, but far enough back that if he turned suddenly, she'd be spared the black eye. They traveled quickly back through the tunnel, and just before they reached the larger chamber, both of them paused.

It was dark; nothing to indicate anyone was in the large chamber. No voices, no noises. Just silence.

"They're gone."

"Did you see them? What did you hear? Were they Skalas?"

"I don't know if they were Skalas, but I do know they didn't come from outside."

So she'd been right. "You watch the entrance. I'm going to search this chamber. There must be some other entrance or passage that we missed." She felt Gabe ready to protest, but she drowned out anything he might have said with a low-voiced comment: "You're the one with the gun and the good aim."

She thought he might have muttered something mildly unflattering about her, or about women in general, but Marina chose to ignore it.

It wasn't long before she discovered her error. If she'd paid closer attention when they first entered the large chamber, she would have seen it right off. Instead, she'd followed the tunnel leading out of the main chamber—it had worked perfectly as a decoy for any curious party that might have visited the cave.

But, knowing there was another way in, Marina quickly found it: the raised pattern on the wall, cleverly designed to blend into the water-drip stains and striations in a massive rock—too big for a human to move alone. Or, at least, that was how it appeared. She touched the boulder, and it shifted at her barest movement.

"Gabe!" she called, still quiet.

He dashed a glance back out into the sunlight, then loped over to her.

She didn't have to explain. A simple gesture, and he understood immediately. But before she moved the false rock again, she asked, "You're certain they've gone?"

"Yes. They were talking about getting something to eat. And something about getting to Detroit."

"Detroit?"

"Yes, I'll be passing that tidbit on to Bergstrom ASAP."

"Let's go." Marina pushed the lightweight stone and it slid away, rolling as smoothly as if it were a horizontal elevator. "Holy shit. This *is* James Bond," she breathed.

The comparison of the rock door to an elevator was so accurate, Marina laughed as she stepped into a world of sleek metal and low, glowing lights. Everything reflected silvery and metallic, and looked as pristine as the inside of a new car engine.

"What in the world is this?" She stepped toward a bubble sort of object that looked like a metal egg protruding from the stone wall.

The egg was approximately ten feet in radius, and appeared to be wedged into the cave wall itself. But when Marina squeezed her little light and shined it onto the egg, they saw the opening in the stone wall was rimmed with metal. Looking down, she expected to see train tracks, for the egg reminded her of a round mining car.

But no tracks on the ground. Just damp, glistening metal on what had been the cave floor.

"There's a door, or a hatch, it looks like." Gabe had stuffed the gun back into his waistband, and was smoothing his hands over the pod. Just as he spoke, a soft click sounded in the room, and a door popped away from its moorings and slid open—like the side door of a minivan.

Marina didn't hesitate. She followed him through the door and they found themselves in a small chamber with seats arranged in facing rows. The hair on the back of her neck lifted.

"It's like a plane. Or a limo."

"The only thing it's missing is a wet bar," Gabe commented. "Or a bed." He sat in one of the seats and flipped open a small door on the console next to it. "Here are the controls. Want to take it for a spin?"

"I'm game. Even if you can't offer me any champagne." She closed the door, and found the lock to secure it. Selecting a seat across from Gabe, she sat down and looked at him.

"We could end up anywhere," he said. "There doesn't appear to be much in the way of navigation. It looks like it's just red for stop, green to go, and nothing else. You still on?"

"Yep."

He began flipping switches. Lights dimmed, then courtesy lights flared near the floor. The only illumination was inside the console with the controls, and which was obviously meant for only one person to manage.

The egg, for lack of a better term, shifted and rumbled beneath their seats. The hum and initial slight jerk reminded her of an elevator. Then the pod stopped, and they heard the sounds of metal moving, gliding. And then, with a dull thud, the last parts slammed into stillness.

The noise sounded like a heavy, electronic door closing, and it came from behind Marina's seat—from the direction in which the large chamber sat. She guessed the pod had somehow moved out of the main large chamber and they were now in some other passage or channel.

There were no windows in their vehicle, so they couldn't know for sure. All was still.

Then…a roar, muffled by the metal surrounding them, and the pod began to shimmy slightly. A soft hissing sound filled the air and Marina drew herself up sharply. Gas? Were they going to be poisoned? Drugged?

She started to unbuckle her seatbelt, then realized what it was. She'd heard it, experienced it often enough. It was oxygen pressurizing the cabin, just like in an airplane.

Suddenly, the shimmying settled into a smooth, dull rhythm, and without warning, the pod began to move. Fast.

Smooth, but fast and surrounded by the dull roar. Though Marina had no idea where she was going, or whether she would make it there alive, she sat still and silent, intrigued and energized. This was terrifying, fascinating, and dangerous all at once. She found the experience exhilarating.

They rode for some time. Perhaps thirty minutes; perhaps longer. Marina wasn't sure, as her watch didn't seem to be keeping time any longer.

"Should you stop this thing at some point?" she asked.

"There doesn't appear to be any way to do so." Gabe sounded grim.

"I thought you said there was red to stop and green to go."

"I misspoke."

"What happened to the red button?"

"It's not red anymore. It's off. I don't think there's any way to stop this thing until it gets to wherever it's going. Like an elevator."

"In the elevators I'm used to, there are always emergency stop buttons." Marina frowned. "Is there a fuel gauge? Something to indicate how long we might be zipping along here in limbo?"

"The only gauge shows something called pressure. And the dial jumped from the red to the green, which is the far side, as soon as we started moving. It hasn't budged since."

"Well, let's hope we don't need to stop suddenly." Perhaps she should be more worried, but Marina easily talked herself out of it. Obviously this was some sort of transport that had been used by the men who exited the cave—likely Skaladeskas or someone related to them. It seemed safe, smooth, and mechanically perfect—wherever it was going.

Gabe seemed to read her mind. "Might as well get some sleep. Wake me when we stop." He yawned, and led his head drop back onto the headrest of his chair. Then he opened one dark blue eye. "Unless you can think of something better to do."

She rolled her eyes.

He smirked, and closed his.

Come to think of it, the chairs were pretty comfortable—and designed for sleeping, if the tilt of the headrest was any indication.

She let her head tip back and felt the curve of the headrest cup her skull. He was right—might as well get some rest. Who knew what they would be up against when they finally stopped.

And if they didn't stop, well, then she'd go to her death without even knowing it.

They did stop, finally, and Marina came awake as the low rumble beneath her ebbed into stillness. The console lights dimmed and overhead lights came on. Gabe was awake too, and they looked at each other across the way. Marina unsnapped her seatbelt.

"Please remain in your seats until the aircraft has come to a complete stop."

Marina ignored Gabe's attempt at humor, but she didn't miss the edge in his voice—nor the spare, smooth action when he picked up his firearm and hefted it in his hand.

"What time is it? How long have we been traveling?" she asked, knowing his satphone would be the best measure of accurate time.

Gabe flipped it open. "About three hours, total. It's about four p.m."

The pod jerked more harshly than it had at the beginning of the journey, signaling it wasn't finished with its trip. Marina felt another, more minor jolt and heard a low *snick* as something clicked into place, and then everything was deathly silent.

Marina flipped the seatbelt straps away and stood as they clattered against the sides of her seat. The palms of her hands felt slick and her throat dry. Gabe, on the other hand, was already fiddling with the lock on the door as if he was a prisoner finally finding his escape.

The door slid open suddenly. Marina tucked herself back inside across from Gabe, leaving the opening clear in case someone or something was waiting.

But the area beyond the open door was still and empty, and appeared similar to the cavern they'd left behind hours before. Gabe stepped down from the pod onto a smooth floor, and that was when Marina noticed it wasn't rock, but tile. Metal tiles, glowing cool silver in the well-lit room.

The lighting wasn't harsh in the metal and rock chamber. It could have blared like a spotlight, but instead it was welcoming and just bright enough that she could see the entire interior of the chamber and a doorway that was surely an exit.

Gabe had stepped a few paces away, and she noticed that he was pushing buttons on his satellite phone.

"Calling Bergstrom?" she asked, stepping near him.

"I will as soon as I figure out where we are."

"You have GPS on there. Great!" Marina was wondering if they'd traveled within Canada during their three-hour journey, or whether they'd strayed into Alaska.

Gabe was frowning, and the expression on his face changed as she watched. "Don't tell me we traveled back down to Michigan," she said.

"There's no way." He was staring at the numbers. Then he punched some more, and stared at them again. "Impossible."

Marina felt odd. In her experience, stoic Gabe did not often have moments where he showed such pure astonishment. "Where are we, then?"

"It appears that in three hours, we've traveled—been sucked over—from Canada to Siberia."

NINETEEN

Siberia

"The prodigal son…at last."

Roman chose the most comfortable seat in Viktor's spacious apartments. "I presume you've been well cared for during your stay?"

"The vodka dried up a week ago," Viktor snapped. "Other than that, I have few complaints. Brother dear."

"Ah. The vodka. I would have thought you'd tired of it by now." Roman swept his gaze over his twin. "You look well."

Or he would, if he were two decades older than he was. Viktor's sallow skin hugged hollow cheekbones, and his hair, still thick but now a metallic grey, needed a trim. The same dark blue eyes set in Roman's own face stared back at him, foggy but still glinting with life. Perhaps the vodka hadn't numbed Viktor enough. Serious tremors shook his thin hand as he reached for a glass of water. If he'd shaved his head, he'd still look enough like Roman to be mistaken for an ill, thinner version. Perhaps if Roman had been the one to live Out-World, he would look the same.

Perhaps not.

"I never thought I would see you again," Viktor told him, surprising Roman with his frankness.

"I did not intend for you to do so. Our agreement was such. But as time has evolved, things have changed, and I chose to call you back."

"Does Lev know?"

Roman knew there were several layers to that question, and he thought about which levels to answer. He chose the simple one that answered them all: "He is aware that you are expected."

"All these years…" Viktor shifted, his bony wrists knocking the table with the clumsiness of someone much older than he actually was.

"I hope you had a good life. Got all that you wished." And for that brief moment, Roman meant the words. His envy of Viktor had nearly ruined him, and would have negated all that he had accomplished. It had been long years before he accepted how things had turned out. It took him a decade to realize that, in the end, he would have it all. That the sacrifice of living in here, cloistered away, pretending to be someone he wasn't, would yield all he'd ever wanted.

Viktor believed he'd walked away the winner of their deal: independent and free.

But he was wrong.

Yes, Roman had lost those years. But soon—oh, very soon; he could *feel* it—he would have all he desired, while his brother would remain this shell of a man. And would carry, he hoped, the guilt and their secrets to the grave.

"And Mariska?" Roman demanded softly. "What does she know about this? About us?"

"Nothing! Of course, Mina knows nothing!" Fear leapt into Viktor's eyes. Good. His daughter meant something to him. "I've told her nothing."

"That is well. She will be joining us soon, Viktor. I prefer to be the one to educate her, if you don't mind. For obvious reasons." His smile turned cooler. "And my brain is not sodden with—is it Stoli you prefer?—and I wager I'll do a better job."

"Don't involve her in this, Roman. What good will it do?" Viktor had a fleck of spittle on his lower lip.

"What good? Why, she has the blood of Shamans and Skalas in her. She is the last of the Aleksandrovs, the final root of the Romanovnas, and she must meet her grandfather. She must fulfill her destiny." He fiddled with his thumb, checking a bruise on his nail that had blossomed from a small grey-blue mark to cover the entire nail with black. "She is a brilliant, brave young woman. You must be very proud of her." Bitterness tinged his voice. Jealousy.

"I want no harm to come to her."

Roman looked at his twin, born the older by no more than one hundred seconds.

One hundred seconds that had haunted him all of his life. One hundred seconds that had driven every decision he'd ever made.

"Of course there will be no harm to her. Why would I harm the Heir of Gaia?"

TWENTY

Whether they were in Siberia or not, Marina didn't want to remain in the chamber any longer. She supposed GPS devices weren't incorrect very often, but she still found it hard to believe they could have traveled thousands of miles in three hours.

The pod they'd traveled in sat in its place, wedged into the metal-edged wall just as it had back in Canada. She brushed a hand over its smooth surface as if touching it would explain its mystery. But all remained silent. To her surprise, the metal wasn't hot. It was barely warm.

"Seems like if we'd been traveling so far so quickly, our spaceship would be burning with heat," she commented, walking toward Gabe, who held his gun like an extension of his long arm. Pointing down.

"You'd think. Maybe the satphone's got an error and we really didn't travel that far. We won't know until we get out of this underground launching pad."

"Let's go." Marina, suddenly antsy, started toward the far wall. She assumed there was an exit, just as there had been an entrance at the beginning of their journey.

"Hold up," Gabe ordered. "Let's wait a few to make sure that the arrival of this ping-pong ball didn't send some kind of alert."

"I'd rather not wait in here and be cornered if it did."

"So you'd rather rush out to meet whatever's coming?"

"Guess that's the difference between you and me." She grinned. "You the trained spook, and me—why, I'm just an ordinary girl." Marina continued her way to the wall she was sure contained a door.

"Ordinary's not a word I'd use."

The next thing she knew, the wall was rough and cold against her back, and Gabe was looking down at her, fingers curling around her arms. His eyes were very blue, and very serious. And very close. "You might be used to taking risks in rescue missions, but this is different. This is guns and terrorism and God knows what else—it's my expertise, Marina. You've got to take a step back."

She knew he was right. Even though his sudden proximity sent her mind spinning in a whole lot of different directions, she nodded. "All right."

He nodded back at her. And then he bent forward.

His mouth fit over hers and she lifted her chin to meet him head-on. Her eyes closed, and she settled her hands against his warm chest, curling her fingers over the tops of wide shoulders. He was good; *it* was good. A delicious warmth erupted under her skin, sending little shivers down her back and along her arms as they tasted and sampled and tested out the attraction between them. Hip to hip, thigh sliding between thigh, cold, rough wall scraping the back of her.

After a while, he pulled gently away and she opened her eyes when their mouths broke apart. His lips were full and they parted in a little smile. "I've been wanting to do that since you stepped out of the shower," he said. "At the hotel."

"I hadn't given it a thought…at least until I saw your face after that plane ride." She slid her hands down from his shoulders, feeling the solidness of his pecs, then pulled away. He was still smiling, his eyes glinting with humor at her comment.

Then, as if a switch had been turned on—or off, depending how she looked at it—he sobered. His expression tightened, his gaze sharpened, his muscles tensed against her. He was back in the game. "I don't know if we're really in Siberia or not, but either way, we're at a disadvantage."

"Yes, but if we find the Skaladeskas, I'll be the one they'll listen to," she reminded him. "I'm one of them." Marina felt along a groove in the wall and slipped her fingers in. Nothing happened when she pressed or pushed.

"If you're looking for the way out, it's over here."

Marina turned just in time to see the door open. She moved along the wall to stand next to Gabe, out of sight of whatever might lie beyond the opening.

She realized she was holding her breath when she was forced to expel it, several minutes later, after nothing happened. No sounds of alarms, no alerting cries, no booby traps springing up or open around them.

Just silence.

She started forward, but Gabe snatched her wrist and propelled her behind him. "I'm going first. I've got the weapon."

"Yeah. Okay. Hmm. Maybe I do need to learn how to fire one."

"A little late for that now, don't you think?"

"It's never too late." She followed him through the doorway into a passage of sorts. A man-made hall, not a cave chamber, of pure white. The ceiling was rounded and she felt like a hobbit stepping through a round door into a corridor illuminated by the glow of lights set into the ceiling every six or eight feet. "Guess we're not in Kansas anymore, huh, Toto?"

She wiped damp palms over her jeans, realizing her only tool was that small light slipped into her pocket. She wished she'd taken up Gabe's offer of a gun.

They walked about a mile in the white corridor without meeting anyone or hearing any sound but the dull pad of their own footsteps. The air and temperature remained constant, so Marina couldn't tell if they were still underground or heading further into the earth. When the passage dipped slightly downward at one point, it rounded back up at another.

The air was fresh, not stale or musty, as one might expect a long, uninterrupted hall to contain.

At last, they came to a door. The same pure white as the walls, it nevertheless differentiated itself by its smooth metal and a barely discernible line down the middle where it likely split open.

Marina looked at Gabe, who'd found the small niche that contained buttons and switches.

"The labels are in English," he told her. "Ready?"

She nodded, and he flipped a switch.

The doors peeled apart and they found themselves in a spacious room. *Room* wasn't quite the word, Marina considered, stepping through the door. It felt more like an airport. In particular, with its four-story ceiling, glass walls, and open stairways, the space reminded her of the terminal at Munich Airport.

They had entered at the highest of four levels and could look down from a shiny silver railing. Each floor had rubberlike flooring with flat circles raised no more than three or four millimeters, as if to provide traction on what would have been a smooth surface. One side of the building was a dark, solid wall, while the other, made of huge triangular pieces of glass fitted together with massive metal rods, allowed in a noontime-strength burst of sunshine. The railing at which Marina and Gabe stood was a mere eight feet wide, and behind them was the dark wall. In front of them was a drop clear down to the first level.

As soon as she'd stepped from the center-splitting door, Marina had registered the buzz of activity below and backed away. People moved about their business on the ground floor, and it was only good fortune no one had cause to look up in their direction. And a blessing they'd come out on the uppermost floor instead of any other.

Gabe nudged her with his elbow and raised his eyebrows. Did she want to go further?

Damn straight. She nodded back. She was in this up to her gills—and besides, if this was possibly a community of Skaladeskas, or at least people who knew them, she was bound to find out something about her father. And if they were responsible for the three earthquakes.

Marina looked down again, huddling behind one of the great steel columns that held up the ceiling, which was made of the same material as the walls as they curved up into a half-dome above them. There were about two dozen or so people visible at any given time.

Could she and Gabe blend in among them without being noticed? Certainly they'd have to change their clothing, as the people moving below were all wearing light-colored, loose pants and shirts. Not a uniform, exactly, at least as far as she could tell, but definitely not the jeans and flannel shirts she and Gabe had donned.

Was this a company? Some sort of business? Or simply a residential community? Despite its similarity to one, it wasn't an airport terminal. Would strangers stick out like the intruders they were?

Gabe had begun to move along the solid metal wall behind them, and Marina turned just as he opened a door that had previously been hidden. She hurried to his side and, when he slipped through the sliver of entrance, she followed without hesitation.

They were in an office.

The door closed behind them and they stepped into the room with perfect synchronization. Computers lined one half-moon wall made of glass, and chairs that reminded Marina of the stools in a beauty salon studded the long workspace that lined a blank wall.

After flipping a switch that appeared to lock the door behind her, Marina felt safe enough to wander over to one of the terminals and sit down at the chair. The monitor screen showed white fuzz, and its computer keyboard was tucked under the desk on a movable tray, just as ergonomically correct as her own workstation back at the University of Michigan.

When Marina pulled the tray out, she was slightly surprised to see that the characters were the standard QWERTY keyboard.

She'd half expected there to be the foreign characters of a non-Anglo language, most particularly, Skaladeska. But, having seen labels in English elsewhere in this strange place, she shouldn't be too surprised.

When she shifted the bullet-shaped mouse, the white snow evaporated from the monitor and she found herself looking at the very familiar Windows desktop screen.

That clinched it for her. Gabe's GPS phone was wrong. They had to still be in Canada—or perhaps they'd even shifted back to the States.

An idea perked in her mind, and on a whim, knowing it was a long shot, she clicked on the email program icon. Maybe, just maybe, there was something interesting in there. Like maybe an email from Victor to herself?

The email program popped open, but before she could begin to scroll through it, Gabe came up behind her and tossed a bundle of clothing into her lap. "Let's get out of our clothes and into something less obvious."

"All right, but cream is so not my color."

Gabe jabbed a thumb toward a half-open door at the end of the worktable. "I'll be the lookout while you change."

She slid off the chair, noticing he'd already made the switch. Gone were the jeans and green and rust plaid shirt. Replacing them were a pair of off-white linen-like trousers and a natural-fiber-colored top that buttoned down the front. However, his feet were still clad in the same hiking boots he'd been wearing since they'd been kidnapped back in L'Anse.

The fabric of the slacks was unlike anything Marina had ever felt before. Woven like fine linen, the cloth bore a silky sheen yet felt lightweight. It wasn't silk and it wasn't linen. It was something in between, and it didn't appear to be wrinkle-prone. Not quite as nice as stretchy matte jersey, Marina decided as she pulled them on, but pretty close.

When she stepped back out of her temporary dressing room, Gabe was clicking away on the computer. She walked up behind him and saw that he had opened a browser window and was surfing the internet.

"This is no time to be shopping at Amazon," she commented. "But I'd like to check my email if that's connected to the web. On the off chance Dad's been in touch again."

"I wanted to make sure there wasn't a firewall or anything that would keep us from browsing the web. But much as I'd like to check my messages, and possibly send an email to Bergstrom, we shouldn't. This machine could be monitored."

"Okay, then let's get out of here and see if we can figure out if Dad's here or not."

"Or at least where we are."

"Everything's in English. We can't be outside of North America, regardless of what your phone says."

"Split up or stay together?"

Marina considered, then replied, "I'm for staying together at this point. After all, you've got the gun."

"Right answer. Let's go."

Marina felt the tension that had begun to leave her shoulders seep back as Gabe unlocked the door. "What's the plan?"

"We look in every room we can for your father or something else of interest. We stay out of sight. If someone catches us, run like hell, and if we get separated, meet back here."

The hall was just as deserted as it had been when they came through the door from the cave travel. Marina glanced toward the entrance, which had opened in the middle like an elevator door, and she marked where it was and what it looked like in case a speedy escape was necessary.

"This must be a restricted floor," Gabe commented, looking down at the activity below. All three floors below them had at least two people moving about with purpose. "I hope there's no alarm that goes off when we go down."

"Let's check out that one there," Marina suggested, pointing to an entrance she had just noticed at the end of the hall at the opposite side from which they'd initially come. The door was set into a small alcove, and its boundary seams were nearly lost in the shadows.

He nodded in agreement, and they started off, silent-footed, down the hall.

The door opened with little effort. Marina was startled at how easily the panel slid to the side. If it was a restricted area, it was ridiculously easy to leave. Perhaps it would not be as simple to return, however.

Pushing around Gabe, Marina peered through. She felt strangely in her element here, as if she should be the one leading the way, making the decisions. It was something inside her, calm, yet nervy, that prompted her to step through the door and allow Gabe to follow.

He started, then stopped just before he stepped through. "Metal detector. Security screen." He jerked a thumb toward the walls. "I can't walk through with a gun."

"Go hide it by our clothes. We can't take the chance of setting any alarms off."

"Marina, I'm not going to walk around in here unarmed."

"Then it appears you're not going to walk around in here at all. I'm going to go on."

She started to walk through the screen, but he pulled her back. "Wait a minute—"

"Your gun didn't help you when we were attacked at the hotel, anyway. It's not a lifeline. We've only got another hour before we need to report in to Bergstrom. I'll just take a quick look and then we can leave."

"Wait."

Marina watched while he jogged back silently to the room where they'd changed.

But once he walked through the security screen, Gabe allowed her to set the pace, and as the door slid closed behind them, she chose their path: to the left, into the side of the building opposite the glass windows. This corridor was brief, the walls the same white, sloping into the same rounded ceiling. Marina realized how easily they could become confused in the endless, identical hallways, and she stopped.

"I'm going to mark this. The last thing we need is to get lost in here somewhere." She dug in her trousers and pulled out a plastic tube of lipstick. It was warm from being in there, which meant it would be soft, so she took care when she made a little dab on the base of one of the walls.

Gabe watched incredulously as she made sure the mark shifted into a sort of point, so they knew which way to go.

"What, you never saw a woman with lipstick in her pocket before?"

"Not only did I not figure you for a lipstick kind of woman, I sure as hell didn't expect you to transfer it when you changed clothes."

"My expertise." She shot him a look as she stuffed the tube back into her front pocket.

"I suppose that's what you use to mark your trails when you're caving," he said as she continued their walk down the hall.

"You never mark a trail when caving. That would be defacing the cave. You have to use a map and look behind as you're making your way through."

As they came around a corner, Marina nearly ran into a wall. Or, rather, when she looked closer, she realized it was another door. "How many of these halls are we going to be walking through that don't lead anywhere?" she grumbled.

"I don't know, but we're going to either have to turn around or find a way through this one."

Marina nodded, and moved toward the door, but just as she began to run her fingers around the edge of it, it moved. Open.

She whirled and slammed into Gabe, and they both turned and dashed around the corner from which they'd come. Keeping her footsteps light took effort, but Marina didn't want the pounding sound of her running to alert the person behind her.

Suddenly, a hand yanked her arm, and she felt herself pulled into a room. She landed in Gabe's arms, felt them come around her as if to steady her. Then he dropped his hands away and they moved together to the wall, pressing up against it behind the door in case it slid back open.

But then a noise behind her made her stiffen.

She grabbed blindly for Gabe's wrist, slowly turning.

They were not alone.

An elderly man stared at Gabe and Marina from across the room.

He sat at a large table, a cracked roll of thick, yellowing paper spread out in front of him. Even from a distance, she could tell it was ancient, and on the verge of deteriorating.

Something moved in her core as the man's eyes caught hers, delved into them, trying to read her innermost thoughts. A palpable *something* hung in the room; something that she could only describe as otherworldly, spiritual. Powerful.

The man blinked, and she could almost feel the dryness of his eyes as his lids scraped over them.

"You are hiding from someone," he said at last, and it was as if she were in a fog. The words, smooth and low, came as if from far away, and it took a moment for them to penetrate. She nodded.

Gabe shifted next to her, barely brushing against her arm, but enough that his movement reminded her that he was there.

"We wanted to be alone." She said the first thing that popped into her head, and just as the words came out of her mouth, she felt Gabe's arm spasm, his movement more startled than before.

Breaking her gaze with the elderly man, she looked up. Shock warped across Gabe's face and Marina realized what had happened.

The man had spoken in an unfamiliar language. And she'd replied in the same.

She looked back at him again, locking with his fathomless grey eyes, her mouth so dry she couldn't have spoken again if her life depended on it. And perhaps it did. Damn good thing she and Gabe had changed their clothing.

Maybe, perhaps, they would be able to get out of this.

The elderly man did not move. He stared at them as if considering. She felt the cool wall behind her, and skittered her gaze around the chamber, looking for a possible escape route. She wasn't in this alone, and the two of them would find a way out.

How much threat could an ancient man be?

The room was furnished simply, with seven chairs scattered about, including the one holding the frail man. Two large tables: one in front of him and a larger one nearer Marina and Gabe. Rolls of paper, a stack of what looked like ancient books, and in the corner, two beautiful drums. Crystals were piled on the table next to the old man.

"It has been long since I've seen young love," the man said, his voice smooth. "And I remember my own very well. But why must you hide? Deceit is not a strength one should embrace."

Marina felt her pent-up breath release. She managed to expel it slowly. The man believed her.

Gabe's hand convulsed next to hers and she felt his confusion, but she had no way to explain. She brushed her fingers against his in a request to let her handle this.

Somehow she knew this elderly man was an important person. That he was Skaladeska was clear, now that he had spoken the language. She guessed he was in his late eighties. His pale skin still covered his skull closely, without the sagging lines of one who'd overindulged in his long life. Indeed, he looked as though he'd lived a harsh life, full of tests and trials. Yet he had an aura of calmness, acceptance, and something spiritual. Otherworldly.

Suddenly Marina knew who he reminded her of. The Dalai Lama. Or Obi-Wan Kenobi. A Jain monk she'd once met in India, who had been able to heal with his touch.

He bore that same quiet strength, that same calm spirituality, the same *knowing*.

She wondered what the hell she was doing here. Why she felt so weirdly comfortable.

Here. Heaven knew where.

Thoughts popped randomly into her mind, as if something had been released from her unconscious. Why had she left her organized, self-directed life for this?

For duty.

For a heritage she'd thought lost.

"It is a"—Marina struggled to find the right word in a language she'd not heard or spoken for twenty-odd years—"secret."

Would he let them go?

It wasn't as if the man's frail muscles could stop them if they wanted to leave. But there was something else about him. He might, indeed, be a worthy adversary.

The man nodded. "I trust you have your reasons." He gestured with his wrinkled hand, the blue lines tracing skin as delicate as an elderly woman's. "Go, and live, then, with your deceit."

Just as she turned toward the door, it opened.

Marina froze and Gabe bumped into her from behind.

She looked up into her father's face.

TWENTY-ONE

H er father looked down at her, shock flooding his face,
Marina didn't move. Her breath filled her lungs and held
there, then expelled in a long, low, soft huff.

He looked healthier than she remembered. His face had filled
in; his skin had gone from gaunt and grey to creamy and smooth.
He'd shaved his head, and it gave him a whole different look. His
brows were trimmed and he was dressed neatly in clothing similar
to that which she and Gabe wore. When was the last time she'd
seen him so well groomed, his eyes so white instead of bloodshot?

He looked different. He had a different air about him.

It felt like minutes, but in reality, the mutual paralysis lasted
only a few seconds. Then Dad closed the door behind him and
stepped into the room, standing in front of it as if to block any
chance of escape.

Marina felt Gabe go tense behind her, but she gave a slight
backward thrust with her elbow as a signal not to make any rash
moves. She had no reason to fear her father. And the elderly man
obviously had no problem with them being here.

That Dad didn't react to their unexpected meeting didn't
strike her until he looked over at the old man. "What are they
doing in here?" he said in Skaladeska.

The old man's attention flickered toward Marina, but he
replied, "You might ask them yourself."

Her father didn't appear to embrace that idea. He stood, as if unsure what to do. His jaw moved, shifting from side to side in a broken rhythm.

Since he did not acknowledge her as his daughter, she assumed he didn't want the old man to know. Perhaps it had something to do with the email warning he'd sent.

Whatever the reason, she wanted out of there. The tension was too thick, and she felt smothered by an urgency she didn't understand. For the first time in a long time, she felt truly out of her element. Almost frightened.

Let the CIA take it from here.

"We were just leaving," she said in English, and started to push past her father. "I'll be in touch."

His face registered surprise, and he looked as though he wanted to stop her, but he didn't. She brushed past him, and he moved aside to let her reach the door. Gabe was behind her, and no sooner were they in the hall than he grabbed her hand and started running.

Marina's instinct was to run too, but she wasn't sure why. No one had tried to stop them. Her father was there.

She pulled her hand out of Gabe's and slowed to a quick walk. "No need to call attention to ourselves," she said.

Suddenly, they heard the sound of pounding feet. Many of them.

They looked at each other, and Gabe lunged for her arm, yanking her after him as he ducked into a room.

It was unlit, and once the door closed, she couldn't see her hand in front of her face. She felt Gabe bumping up against her, and she put her hands out in front to keep their foreheads from cracking into each other.

He hissed into her ear, "You lied to me." His breath was warm, but his words held ice. And the fingers around her upper arms weren't gentle.

"What?" It took her a moment before she realized what he meant. "The language? I didn't realize I could speak—"

The door burst open and a swarm of people poured into the room. Marina sprang away from Gabe and turned as a flood of light beamed into the darkness.

It blinded her, and she had no chance to move before strong arms grabbed at her, pulling her away from Gabe.

Soft, solid thuds mingling with grunts and groans told her he wasn't going wherever they were taking them easily, but despite the fact that Marina struggled like a fly wrapped in a web, no one punched her or kicked her. They just held on very tightly. One man at each arm, and one behind grasping her by the shoulders.

By now, the flood of light had diminished from a sudden, blinding one to something less invasive, and Marina noticed they were in what appeared to be an office. But she had no further chance to examine the room. By the time she got her bearings, she was being dragged toward the door, manhandled past a sagging Gabe and his machinelike attackers.

With a sudden burst of energy, Marina jerked her arm and managed to break the grip of the man next to her. She walloped him across the side of the head before she was subdued once again. She hoped his ear rang for an hour afterward.

"My father will not be happy," she gritted between her teeth as the two captors forced her arms, none too gently, behind her back. Something wrapped around them, from upper arm to down past her elbow, and she was trussed securely.

By that time, she'd stopped struggling. It was a waste of effort. She'd need it later. Instead, she spent her time and energy paying attention: to where they were, where they were going, and anything that was being said. She figured it was an ace in the hole that she somehow remembered her Skaladeska, and she was certain her captors—including her father—didn't realize that. Only the elderly man had heard her speak in the tribal language, for because of her distress, Marina had spoken in English when she threatened her captors.

Once the two men realized she was going to cooperate, they gentled their treatment of her. She was allowed to walk down the hall at her own pace, following their lead. Pretending to be subdued, she bowed her head slightly, but kept her eyes raised so that she could take in details of the hallways and their route.

Despite her submission, Marina's captors remained silent, giving her no information other than what she could see from the walk down the halls. They passed no one, and each passageway appeared the same as the one before.

Finally, they reached a door similar to the one with the old man. She watched with interest as they approached a blank wall with no opening other than a small panel at eye level. One of the men went to the wall next to it and opened the panel. As she watched, he took a finger-sized flat object and placed it on his tongue. Then he removed it and fed it into a small slot.

The wall in front of them split, folding into itself on either side like a theatre curtain.

Marina stared in wonder.

They stepped into a large open space that glittered with light shining through a faceted dome ceiling. Another huge atrium. Stepping inside was like being in one of her clear crystals, except that there were stairs and landings, hallways, and *trees*. Trees of all sizes and types grew everywhere, and they were peppered with birds. A few small buildings were scattered on one end of the atrium. And there were small vehicles that reminded her of golf carts but were shaped like little pods.

Unbelievable.

Like a little city under glass.

That was all she could think as they prodded her along. She walked agreeably, trying to keep her pace as slow as possible so she could absorb it all.

The realization stunned her. Not only were the Skaladeskas not extinct, they were as far from being an archaic, primitive tribe locked away in the mountains of Siberia as the US was.

Once he recovered from his enormous shock at recognizing Mariska Aleksandrov—or, as she was more commonly known,

Marina Alexander—in Lev's private study, Roman seized the opportunity to take control of the situation.

He was furious with Viktor for somehow bringing her here—for how else would she have done so?—and yet Roman was fascinated and terrified at the same time. What would this mean for him?

What would it mean to Lev?

Excusing himself from his father's presence, Roman stepped into the hall and ordered his men to apprehend her and her companion. And he took a moment to calm himself, stop his hands from trembling. When he returned to his father's library, Lev appeared to be deep in the study of the parchment paper before him.

Did he know?

He couldn't know. Surely he couldn't know.

Lev's eyesight was poor and he had no idea that Marina existed, let alone that she would find her way here.

Roman, of course, recognized her from photos and other surveillance footage he'd seen throughout the years. Aside from that, she bore a resemblance to his mother—could Lev have recognized her from that?

No, surely not. It had been too quick, and he was across the room from her. The old man's vision was poor...

Roman closed the door behind him and Lev looked up.

"That was my granddaughter."

Lev's cold voice drove all other thoughts from Roman's mind. What did he know? Did he know it *all*? Dare Roman continue the charade?

"Viktor has recently arrived, and somehow, after him has come his daughter, Father. I am just as shocked as you appear to be." Truths. Speak only the truth, and you will not be found out.

"Did you think I would not recognize my own flesh and blood?" Lev had lifted his eyes from the table and now stared at Roman, glinting like grey glass. "She has the eyes of my Irina. You would not withhold such information from me. Surely you were not aware of her presence, Roman." It was not a question. It was a demand for truth.

"Father, I cannot lie to you—but I did not expect her to come here, and she did not arrive with Viktor. I know very little about her. I am sure she knows nothing of us."

"But you knew she was my granddaughter. You knew she was the last of the Aleksandrovs. You knew she *existed*."

"While I have no proof that she is of our line, I suspected that." A lie. Such a lie. Roman kept his face impassive, and, more importantly, his mind blank.

"You have no *proof*? One look at her face will tell you so!"

"She is an Out-Worlder, Father. She will not understand us or our purpose. And her presence here puts us in danger."

"You will not harm her, Roman. You will not disappoint me again. And you will not lie to me ever again." Lev's voice was cold and forbidding, and his eyes flashed with fury. Power and knowledge vibrated from the frail man, and even Roman knew he'd stepped over too far.

"No, Father. Never again. I vow it."

"Leave me now."

Thus dismissed, Roman hurried from the study and rushed along the corridors to his private suite.

Stegnora was there, waiting for him.

As he came into the room, she rose, took two steps toward him, then stopped herself. They had been together for nearly thirty years, and she still moved instinctively to touch him whenever he entered the room, whether he wanted affection or not.

When he started toward her, she dropped her self-control and wrapped her arms around him. Aside from being beautiful, and the one woman to whom Roman always returned, Nora was a brilliant engineer. She was his partner, his support, his world.

"What is it?" she asked. Her eyes carried worry for him, and for them.

"Mariska—Marina. She is here."

"Marina? Here? But George and Bran—but I thought—"

Roman pulled away. "They are not with her. She is with a man, likely law enforcement. Perhaps the CIA, perhaps the FBI, perhaps merely her lover. I will find out." He stalked across the room, feeling Nora's concerned gaze upon him, but she would not move to touch him again until he signaled he wanted her. She had learned that too.

Roman passed a hand over his scalp, roaming over the base of his skull, and massaged the back of his neck. The tension there had tightened across his shoulders, pulling them taut and leaving a pounding between his scapulas. "They found us somehow, and now everything is in jeopardy. Thankfully, I expect Varden back any moment now. As soon as he returns, make certain he finds me. We're going to have to move more quickly—shift the Phase Two date to Friday."

"Three days from now?" Nora caught herself as Roman turned to look at her. He watched her face as she calculated silently, waiting for her confirmation.

He didn't care if she believed the change was possible. She'd find a way to do it. He could always count on her not wanting to disappoint him.

"But we'll need to… Roman, the explosives aren't completely ready. We only have two of them. And the detonators—"

"You'll have to get them done, Nora. We have to. This is our time. Our chance. I know you can manage it. You've never failed me before." He moved across the room and took her hand to draw her to her feet. Pulling her close, he rested his cheek on the top of her head and inhaled her scent. Comfort, steadiness, sexuality, all rolled into one piece.

One thing of which he was certain—and would always be certain—was Nora. She loved him.

And Nora… She would take whatever he gave her and make it work.

That was what she did.

Gabe swam to consciousness.

He didn't want to, but a gush of cold liquid and a brilliant white light forced him into reality. It took him longer than it should have to remember where he was and what had happened.

Where was Marina?

Where the hell was *he*?

A tall, bald man stood in front of him. Gabe recognized him as the one who'd interrupted their interaction with the old man. There was no one else in the room, but the man didn't appear to be concerned about facing Gabe on his own. They were about the same height, but Gabe was younger by at least two decades and had more bulk and muscle.

Still, the added strength wouldn't help him, as his wrists and ankles had been immobilized.

The man looked familiar.

"So glad you have awakened," he said to him in faintly accented English as he forced Gabe to sit up on the long, flat surface upon which he'd sprawled. "I'm Roman. I'll be your host."

"Why am I restrained?"

"I have a more pressing question. Why are you here? How did you get here, and who sent you?" The man's eyes were cold and determined, and Gabe knew his current discomfort was just beginning. He willed himself to calm, to grow cold, to turn off his neurons and go blank and numb.

"Ah. I see that you understand the situation." Roman smiled, and he looked, for a moment, rather benign. Almost kind.

Then the pain struck, suddenly, from nowhere. Gabe snatched in his breath and closed his eyes against the lightning pain. It shot down his left arm, culminating somehow in the curl of his palm.

It stopped.

"Perhaps if I'm a bit more persuasive you'll be more forthcoming."

Not bloody likely.

"Where am I?" Gabe forced his mouth to move and the words to come out clearly and smoothly.

The man merely smiled, and the pain zinged suddenly—this time from beneath Gabe's left ear.

Roman moved back and watched as Gabe pulled in a deep breath of relief. "Who sent you?"

"No one." He drew in a wavering gulp of air, dragged it in, and felt the oxygen flow through him. He relaxed his fingers from where they dug into his palms. "We found a cave and walked in. There was a vehicle. We got in and came here."

That was the truth, for the most part. Whether Roman would believe it was that simple was another question.

Indeed, when Roman pressed his handsome face near his, Gabe felt the disdain emanating from him like a wave. "Why did she bring you?"

Pain. Gabe jerked, and then spasmed again, harder, as the agony shocked him at the base of his neck. He couldn't suppress a cry, but stifled it as quickly as he could find the ability to take a breath.

Focus. *Focus.*

The room swam before him, and still the pain beaded through him in little shock waves.

"Accident," Gabe heard a voice groan, pitifully. It was his own.

The pain stopped. "We'll see if that's true. The rest of your tale leaves much to be desired."

Gasping for air, reeling it in, Gabe blinked rapidly as a drop of perspiration trickled onto his eyelid. "What do you want." He couldn't make it a question; it was all he could do to get the words out— to make his mouth and tongue move.

Good God.

What would they do to Marina? She was a civilian. She wasn't prepared for anything like this.

Focus. Draw in a breath. Let it out. Draw it in. Let it out.

"I want…" Roman stood suddenly, moving away from Gabe. Something long, thin, and silver flashed in his hand. "I want revenge. I want to be heard. I want to be accepted." An odd, quicksilver grin slashed across his angular face. "It's very simple. Not so much to ask."

Gabe's mind swam. He wanted to ask another question. He wanted to feed the man's starving ego, to get him to talk, to find out more. But his mouth wouldn't move. The ache in his bad leg screamed. And the points on his arm, and shoulder, and neck pinged with sharp pains, over and over. He couldn't focus on anything but the pain.

"What? Why?" was all he managed.

"Because I can." Roman, laughing, was the last thing he remembered before sliding into darkness. "Gaia wills it."

TWENTY-TWO

July 11, 2007
The Western Coast of Ireland

The ocean surged onto the pristine beach, washing over Junie's bare feet. Cold, but refreshing, and much more comfortable in this small dose than when she'd been hip deep in it after the sun went down.

Incredible that just over a week ago, this same gold-sanded stretch had been black with oil.

Her short-cropped hair—the same color, almost, as that poisonous liquid—buffeted around her face, leaving her ears uncovered in the brisk wind. She stared out over the grey-blue water as she pulled up her hood.

If she hadn't been here, wearing gloves slicked with residue, sudsing a seabird in hopes of saving another fragile life, she would never have believed it. A Tier Three oil spill suddenly gone, evaporated within hours.

Not to mention her own illness.

According to the medical professionals, she'd been very ill, unconscious for most of three days, and then she'd suddenly recovered. From what, they didn't know. They'd been unable to provide a diagnosis.

And then there was the faintest memory of a dream...of a green-eyed man who'd come to her in the hospital.

Junie shivered, but not because the wind from the ocean was cold.

Suddenly she became aware she wasn't alone on this lonely stretch of beach, this three-kilometer run of sand studded by harsh grey boulders, and edged with foaming sea.

A man walked toward her. He was dressed inappropriately for beachcombing in a dark business suit. His shirt beamed pristine white, topped by a dark jacket, a long black duster, and dark pants. A matching dark tie striped the shirt, bisecting the white with its mark. His hair—nipped short, along with the neat beard and mustache—was as black as her own, but his skin was several shades darker than her ivory complexion.

"Hello." He greeted her with a short bow, then thrust his hands into his pockets, winging the open edges of the duster behind them. "A bit chilly here today." Though his English was excellent, she heard the accent that told her he wasn't a native speaker.

"Yes, indeed." Though they were alone, she felt no sense of alarm, no instinctive heightening of the senses. "Though not so cold as it was during the evening hours last week, when I was trudging through that water."

The polite expression on his face morphed into one of interest. "You were here? Did you see the oil spill?"

"I was one of the people using liquid dish detergent to wash the gulls," she told him. "It's amazing that it suddenly"—she flapped her hands in vague explanation—"dried up."

The man nodded. "I find it hard to believe myself. Oil just doesn't dry up."

"It never has in my experience. And I've worked on three other spills." Sensing his interest hadn't waned, she added, "I'm a zoologist, and when something like this happens—well, I have to be here. It was very strange. I was working with the others all day, and into the night—well past midnight—and then we went to bed. But I couldn't sleep, and I came down here by myself. And the oil was *gone*. And then I became ill."

"You're the one, then. How fortunate I should meet you here. My name is Inspector Hamid al-Jubeir," he explained, and thrust out his hand. "I'm investigating the murder of the man who owned the ship that spilled, and the company that produced and sold the oil."

"Junie Peters," she replied as she shook his hand, wondering why he wanted to talk with her. "The man who owned the ship was killed?"

"In a most peculiar fashion," the inspector told her. "He was injected with oil. But it wasn't actually oil, which is why I am here. And pleased to speak with you."

Junie stared at him. "It wasn't oil?"

He shook his head gravely. "It was oil, and yet it wasn't. Our forensics laboratory tested it, and determined that it was indeed oil, but it wasn't aged. It was…well, the word they used was 'new.'"

"New?"

"As if it had just been created—as if the process had happened only days or weeks ago, instead of millions of years."

Junie had to pull up her hood again, for the wind had tugged it back. "How strange. I've never heard of new oil."

"Neither has anyone else I've spoken with. And so I came here. I thought there might be some residue left on this site we could analyze to see if it was the same substance. Since it has evaporated so quickly, it can't be the same oil on which we live. When you were ill. Pardon me for my curiosity, but it's my understanding the illness came when you visited this locale."

"Yes. When I came here alone and discovered the oil was gone. I became dizzy, and passed out." The vague image of the man in her hospital room swam abruptly into her memory. "He—there was a man, dressed in doctors' whites. He told me—he apologized and said I wasn't supposed to be around. No one was supposed to get hurt."

The inspector didn't seem confused by her staggering language. Nor did he seem impatient. He waited while Junie searched for what she wanted to say.

"I think...I think there was a man who visited me at the hospital. Who caused me to get better. He put something in my nose that I inhaled, like a nebulizer. And then he left. But he said they didn't mean to harm me, and that I would be well then."

Al-Jubeir pulled a folded paper from his pocket. "Was this the man you saw?"

She took the paper, opened it, and looked at the face. "No. No, it wasn't him. My visitor had green eyes. Brilliant green eyes."

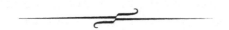

Siberia

Marina didn't know how long she was left in her room before the door finally slid open.

She remained seated in the large chair across from the entrance. Her father walked in.

"What's going on? Where's Gabe?" she demanded. And then she stopped, her words dying in her throat.

A second man walked in. It was her father.

Marina gripped the arms of her chair, and in her shock turned to look at the first man. The bald one.

"More lies, Dad?" she snapped.

How could she have mistaken that handsome, healthy man for her father? When the two stood next to each other, it was so obvious they bore only the faintest resemblance. Dad, frail and slightly hunched, with sallow skin that hugged gaunt cheekbones...thick, messy hair that needed a trim, brows just as dark as the other's, but scraggly and wiry, like spider legs.

And the other man—handsome, confident, almost youthful.

"Lies?" the first man repeated.

Marina glared at him, and an uneasy feeling settled in her stomach. "You must be brothers. Related somehow. That's the first lie."

"Viktor, you never told Marina that you had a brother? A twin?" False surprise cloaked his words.

"*Twins?* So you are my uncle." The shock colored her voice.

"My name is Roman."

"Marina…" Her father's voice was thready, pleading. "I warned you to stay away."

"By email! You sent me an email!" Now Marina stood, and she kept her voice steady and calm, though it threatened to crack. "If you had told me anything over the years, it might have prepared me to discover that our family hadn't died out, and that it's still alive and that I have an uncle—and perhaps other relatives. What is this place and what are you involved in? And how did I get here?"

"These are your roots, my dear," Roman told her. Easiness and a level of pride played in his words. "You have finally come home. I only wish we'd been able to bring you here in a more pleasant manner."

"You call kidnapping me and throwing me in the back of a truck pleasant? Breaking into my house with a gun?" Marina was much shorter than Roman, but she didn't let him intimidate her. She faced him, hands on hips, and let her fury show. What did she have to lose?

"A gun?" Roman's face showed its first authentic emotion since he'd walked into the room. "We don't use guns. Violence of that nature is forbidden."

"Well, someone tried to use it on me. And blew up my father's house—and nearly ran us off the road. If that's not violence, I don't know what is. What the hell do you want from me?"

"We disdain the use of firearms, but there are other methods to conduct our business. And as it turns out, you weren't actually brought here against your will, were you? You came on your own."

"Nevertheless, clearly you wanted me here. One of you did, at any rate. Was it you, Roman? Is part of this a way to manage my father?" As if it was going to be difficult to manage him without any leverage. The man was a mere shell. Standing next to his twin, Dad appeared even more frail and pathetic. Marina couldn't imagine they needed her presence in order to influence him.

She'd risked her life to come here. Because of him. Her skin crawled when she realized what a non-person he was. The vacancy and weakness that came and went from his eyes made her cold. She was swarmed by memories of his inability to care, to support, to listen, to be present to her in any way.

Roman spoke smoothly: "You needed to be here because you are a Skaladeska. You are of our blood and we wanted to make sure you remained safe."

"Safe from what?"

Roman looked at her, searched her face, steepling his fingers. "We are about to implement an operation that will capture the attention of the world, and secure its respect."

"For what purpose? To let them know the Skalas live and breathe?"

"That and more." He gestured to her chair. "Sit, please, my dear. There is no sense in stalking about the room when you can be comfortable. You aren't going anywhere."

She'd known that, of course, but hearing the words spoken so clearly was a blow. "Where's Gabe? What have you done with him?" She sounded too much like a deranged heroine from a gothic movie, but she didn't care if her words were panicked and clichéd.

"Gabe? So that's his name. He wasn't quite as forthcoming with that information as I would have liked." Roman smiled, his handsome face turning cold.

"You hurt him."

"One must do what one must."

"Am I to be tortured next, then?" she asked, standing again, pushing herself nose to nose with her uncle. Her *uncle*.

Roman laughed and turned to take her vacated seat. "Since you don't wish to sit… Of course you won't be tortured. You are one of us. You are an important piece in this whole puzzle, so you will be nothing but honored."

She didn't believe him. "Where is he? If I'm to be honored, I demand you allow me to see him."

"Is he your lover?" Roman asked idly.

"No. And even if he was, it's irrelevant."

"It's not irrelevant if you get with child."

Marina could hardly speak, she was so shocked and outraged by such a comment. "You must let him go. I demand that you release him. He's done no harm—"

"I beg to differ, Mariska." Roman stood, towering over her. Anger tightened his face. "He brought you here—or you brought him here. No matter. You are welcome; he is not. We do not allow outsiders unless they become part of our clan."

"So you're going to kill him?"

"Would it matter to you?"

"What a ridiculous question."

"That may be so, but your relationship with him does matter. It is in my interest to know how the last member of our line is procreating or continuing it."

"You have no control over my personal life—or any part of my life. Who the hell do you think you are?"

Her father spoke for the first time. "Marina, it's important for us—for Roman and myself—to know who will father your children and when that will happen."

"Is that what this is all about? Controlling my ability to procreate? Well, you've wasted a whole lot of time and energy, because I can't get pregnant. So you can release me—us—now and let us on our way."

The two men stared at her, then Roman said, gently, "I am sorry for that, Mariska. I see how it pains you."

"I have accepted it." She turned away, furious that her eyes had begun to sting. What kind of a fool was she? "Now that we've cleared that up, you can take me to Gabe."

Roman sighed. "Although that is an important one, Mariska, there are other issues to consider. I—"

He stopped suddenly and pulled a small device from a deep pocket. It resembled a cell phone, and Marina watched as he used his fingertips to pad through something on a small screen. Then he flipped it closed and looked up at her. "I apologize. We will have to finish this discussion at a later time. Viktor, you will accompany me."

Before Marina could react, Roman reached out his hand and smoothed it over her jaw in a sort of caress. "You will be well cared for. If you need anything, you've only to push that button." He gestured to a small oval indentation in the wall. She wouldn't have known it to be anything more than an unusual decoration, but when she touched it, a soft whirring opened a panel in the wall displaying a computer screen.

When she looked back, the two men were gone and she was alone with a menu-driven computer screen offering television, movies, games, food selections.

Forget that. She had to find a way out of this place.

TWENTY-THREE

Marina spent the better part of the next several hours exploring her room—or, rather, her suite of rooms. All the while she tried to digest what she'd learned about the family she thought had died off decades ago.

She'd come to the uncomfortable conclusion that they were, indeed, in Siberia. Somehow that egg-shaped transport had brought her and Gabe thousands of miles in little more than three or four hours.

Surprisingly, her accommodations were as comfortable as any hotel in which she'd stayed. The walls were the same white of the hallways and the other rooms she'd seen. They curved into the floor and ceiling in gentle arcs. Perhaps it was because of her caving experience, but the smooth connections reminded her of elongated tunnels and cave chambers.

There was one entrance to the suite, and the rooms themselves consisted of a main area with a sofa that slid into a flat bed and a separate room that offered a toilet, shower, sink, and tub.

A hotel room and nothing more.

A prison.

Damn.

And all the while, she was terrified for Gabe. What would they do to him? Would they really kill him? Would her father let them do that?

She shook her head. Her father didn't seem to have the strength to stop anyone from doing anything.

Marina, galvanized by concern and fired by anger, examined every iota of the crack around the door. There had to be a way to make it open. She couldn't remember how Roman had caused it to do so when he left with her father. She'd been distracted, as he no doubt intended, by the oval depression in the wall that turned on the computer screen.

She found nothing: no handle, no hinges, no little panel that opened to offer buttons or dials or even a slot to slip in the small pat as she'd seen her captors do. Nothing.

At last, weary and frustrated, she gave up and decided to try for some rest. If she was going to get out of here, she needed to have a clear head and strength—food would be nice too—and as difficult as it might be, she needed to sleep.

But before she succumbed to that, she poked around a little more in the area of the room far from the door. Since she'd spent the bulk of her time at the door, she'd missed the small cupboard and refrigerated chest tucked under a table.

There was food there. Dark, stringy meat she thought might be bison or elk, thick, hearty bread slices, bottles of water, apples, grapes, plums, carrots, and celery. Interesting. Had they compiled these supplies especially for her, or did they keep them on hand for other visitors—or victims?

Again she wondered about Gabe. Concern knotted her stomach. If she got out of the room, she'd need to have something for him to eat too, if she could find him. Not to mention something to patch up whatever injuries had been inflicted on him.

After eating, she took a quick, hot shower in an effort to get her body to relax, figured out how to turn the inset lights down to a bare glow, and curled up on the sofa. She had no idea when or if Roman would be back.

Surprisingly, it wasn't difficult to drift off to sleep.

It happened so easily that Marina only realized she'd been dozing because she awoke.

Someone was in the room.

It took a moment for her eyes to adjust to the dim light, but immediately she recognized the stooped figure of the old man.

She watched, still and silent, in the darkness. Ready but waiting.

He approached the sofa where she lay, and she had to focus all of her attention and willpower to not react. Her senses, her sharp instincts, weren't screaming "danger." Yet. But if he made one unexpected, quick move, she'd shoot off that sofa like a bullet.

But he didn't. He stood and stared down at her for a long time as she fought to keep her breathing steady and slow.

When he reached out toward her, she stiffened and caught her breath, but didn't move. He wasn't threatening.

His smooth, trembling fingers touched her cheek, pressing oh so gently against her skin, then drew away.

"You are awake," he said at last. In English.

"Who are you?" Marina asked, still unmoving. Shocked that he spoke so fluently.

"I am your grandfather. My name is Lev."

"Grandfather?"

"If you come with me, I would like to show you something. Your heritage. Will you come?"

She nodded against the pillow scrunched into the corner of the sofa, and slowly moved to sit up. She felt as though she were in a dream.

Perhaps she was.

Perhaps her food had been drugged.

But nevertheless, she dropped her feet to the floor and stood. She was of a height with Lev, her grandfather.

He grasped her arm, as much to keep her with him, she supposed, as to support his frail self. The door opened in front of them as if by magic, silent and smooth. She would have slept through it opening and closing if she hadn't felt his presence in the chamber with her.

Lev's fingers were strong, thin vises around her upper arm. Not uncomfortable, but firm. Marina could twist away from his frail strength and make a run for it, but she checked the urge to do so. She wouldn't get far—he'd alert the guards or whoever it was Roman had helping him, and she wouldn't have the time to search for Gabe. Plus, some big part of her wanted to know what he was going to show her.

He moved quickly for his age, and Marina tried to keep track of their route, but she feared her exhausted mind wouldn't remember all of the twists and turns. She wondered briefly why he'd chosen to visit her at night.

At last, after walking through a sliding door that required a tab moistened with Lev's saliva, they approached an entrance that was different from every other one she'd seen. This one had a door made not of white-painted metal, but of an iron-colored steel. Heavy, with riveted beams across it, it resembled the portcullis of a medieval castle.

Lev opened a small door next to it and pulled a lever. The heavy door rolled up, into the ceiling that Marina suddenly noticed was higher than the others.

Lev drew her in, and the door lowered closed behind them.

She looked around and gaped.

Cabinets—no, they were display tables with heavy glass tops—lined the room. Made from heavy wood, with strong, thick legs, the table-cabinets rose as high as Marina's waist. Low lights along the seams of ceiling and wall, and wall and floor, illuminated the chamber, bathing it in a delicate gold glow. She stepped in and looked down into one of the tables. What she saw made her gasp, then hiss in shock and wonder as she scanned the chamber, taking in the contents of the other cabinets and drawers, the items framed and mounted on the walls.

Marina left her grandfather behind as she moved from table to table, her eyes growing wider by the moment. Her mind was completely blown.

Ancient scrolls, books, papers, maps—everything one could imagine that was of the written variety was organized inside these cabinets. Each was properly protected and displayed like in the National Archives.

The writings were faded, but legible, and as Marina peered down into one of the display boxes, she saw the thick, neat font of an ancient language.

"Greek? Latin? Sumerian?" She looked up at Lev, who'd remained near the entrance, watching her. "What is it?"

"It is all of them." Rapture shone in his face —love for the secrets and the manuscripts protected in this room.

"Where did they come from?" Marina stared down at the book in front of her, walked a few paces, and found herself gaping at a cracked-edge scroll that lay half-unrolled. "My God…but this is incredible. Unbelievable. What is this? Why aren't they in a museum?" But she knew the answer. Because then it wouldn't be here, at the whim of the Skaladeskas.

This room made the Lam Pao Archive look like a tattered first edition of *Sense and Sensibility*.

"Come, sit." Lev gestured to two large chairs. The massive antlers of some animal created the frame, including armrests. The back and seat of each chair was upholstered with a thick, comfortable-looking cloth that reminded Marina of alpaca. "I'll tell you the story. You should know your family heritage."

She wanted to look at all of the manuscripts and scrolls, but she accepted the invitation. The historian in her could not fathom the value, the importance of this collection, so she had to hear the story.

"When Princess Sophia Palaeologa of Byzantium married Ivan the First of Russia, her father dowered her with, among other things, this library of ancient manuscripts. They were even ancient at that time, in fact—in the fifteenth century.

"She brought the books and manuscripts with her—there are nearly eight hundred pieces, most of which have never been translated or catalogued. In fact, throughout the ages no one has really been sure what is included in this selection. Sophia brought them to Russia and they were kept in a special chamber beneath the Kremlin. Moscow at that time was prone to fires, and no one wanted them destroyed, so a protective room was built especially for the library.

"Not many in Ivan's court knew about the library. Sophia herself was not an academic, and she saw little value in so many old books. But her father wished her to take them, and so she did. Ivan did not spend much time studying them either, and they languished, forgotten for decades, under the Kremlin." He took a sip from a cup nestled in a hollow in his chair's arm.

"Then, in 1560, Ivan the Fourth—whom you would know as Ivan the Terrible—became the heir at age three. He lived in the castle but was fairly left to himself. In fact, he was neglected for the most part—left to his own devices and dressed in rags, barely given enough food to eat.

"The courtiers subjected him to extreme and rampant violence, forcing or allowing him to watch them torture, punish, and execute political enemies. If there was a state affair, the men who acted for his mother, the regent, would dress him up in rich clothing and jewels and show him off like a puppet, and then afterward, banish him to roaming the halls, hungry and cold.

"Thus the poor boy was left to his own devices, but despite that—or perhaps because of it—he developed a great love of learning and reading. He found the lost library in its special chamber beneath the West Tower, and, fascinated by the books and appreciative of the solitude the library afforded him, spent as much time there as he could as he grew older.

"Of course, he could not read many—or perhaps any—of the books. As you have noticed, they were written in Greek—ancient Greek, Roman, Sumerian, Atlantean, and numerous others—"

Marina jerked upright, pulled out of the story. "Antlantean? As in Atlantis?"

"Oh, yes. Yes, that, and even other languages that have yet to be identified. The Vatican, among others, would kill to get its collective hands on this library and its contents."

She stared at him. Unbelievable. This had to be a dream. Or else the elderly man was demented. "Go on." She had to find out how the dream ended.

"When Ivan became tsar at age seventeen—Russia's first tsar, as you likely are aware—he immediately had a huge number of eligible women brought to him from which he intended to select a wife, and he did. He selected a woman named Anastasia Romanovna. Despite the way she was chosen—as one of many paraded in front of the tsar—it was a love match. Ivan almost immediately fell in love with her, and she with him, and they were truly happy together in the same way I was with my beloved Irina, your grandmother.

"Ivan shared with his Anastasia the secret of the library, and she urged him to set translators on it. She believed, and convinced him it was so, that the secrets in these books and manuscripts could unlock many mysteries, and unveil many things about this world that the ancient civilizations knew. Information, stories, histories that have been lost. Perhaps things that would turn civilization on its head." He shrugged his delicate shoulders.

"And? How did they come here? Did someone steal the library?" Even as she said it, Marina believed it an absurd idea. Wherever she was—whether it be Siberia or Canada—it was so far from Moscow that it boggled the mind to imagine how eight hundred ancient books could safely be transported that distance in the sixteenth century.

"No, they did not come, but, in fact, it was Anastasia who insisted the library be protected. She was very ill, and she and Ivan both recognized that she was dying. He believed she was being poisoned by his enemies in the court—and indeed, it was proven not so long ago that she was indeed poisoned with mercury—and he was overcome with grief. But there was little they could do to save her.

"As the story goes, one day near the end, Anastasia called him to her and extracted a promise from Ivan to protect the library. She urged him to hide it somewhere and keep it from the evil boyars at court.

"Although Ivan fairly fell apart after his tsarina's death—indeed, that is when the stories of him banging his head against the floor, and eventually murdering his own son in a fit of rage, came to pass—he did fulfill his promise to Anastasia. He had the library carefully packed away, and sent it off on a secret ship up the Moskva River, to the Kara Sea, to a new land he had recently added to Russia's vast acquisition: Siberia.

"Ivan always planned to come to this place where he had the library sent. In fact, he attempted to leave the throne several times during his reign, but he always returned. And he never saw the library again."

Lev grew quiet and took several long sips from his cup, draining it.

"May I get you some more?" Marina asked, fascinated and titillated by the story, unwilling to believe such a thing could happen—yet surrounded by the evidence, how could she not accept it?

"Thank you, my child." He smiled faintly. "I hope you do not mind that I call you that. I did not know of your existence until very recently."

"I don't mind." No matter what his sons were, Marina found she couldn't extend her anger or fear toward this man who seemed to exude spirituality and serenity like none other. And who was caretaker to a treasure that he appeared to love as much as she would.

Marina took his cup and moved to a small alcove he indicated, where she found a pitcher of the liquid he was drinking. She sniffed the dark concoction. It wasn't water. It smelled like some sort of earthy, spicy tea.

When she brought the cup back to him, he took it gratefully and smiled up at her. "Thank you."

She sat back in her chair, yet her attention wandered toward the cabinets. Marina could read some of those ancient languages. She wanted nothing more than to immerse herself in this room and study these texts. She desired it so badly that her fingers trembled and her insides churned.

Surely this was a dream.

"So Ivan never came back to his library? Is this where he had it sent?"

"It has moved several places in the last centuries, and in fact it may well move again. But when Ivan shipped it from Moskva, he sent several scholars with it, and some of his trusted friends. And it was one man he named responsible for the care of the library: a cousin of Anastasia Romanovna. His name was Leonid Aleksandrov."

"You—we—are his descendants?" Marina understood, then, what her heritage was. She felt light and faint with shock and disbelief.

Her family legacy was to protect this library. This priceless, miraculous, incredible library.

It was a treasure that could solidify her career. And keep her busy for decades.

It was a treasure with untold secrets and great mysteries and lost knowledge. Marina could hardly breathe. If what her grandfather said was true, was *actually* true...

"We are. And you, Mariska Aleksandrov, are the last of us."

"So I'm safe here, with you. But—"

Before Lev could reply, a soft *snick* behind her and the knowing look on his face drew her attention to the heavy metal door.

"I see you have found your grandfather."

It was Roman.

TWENTY-FOUR

Marina had terrifying dreams that night.

Water crashing down on her, its blackness smothering her as it had when she nearly drowned in a small pond as a child… Roman's angry face, livid and stark and threatening. Books, manuscripts, and scrolls crackling with age, and then blazing with uncontrollable fire, roaring hot and red…morphing into images of Repin's famous painting of Ivan the Terrible after he'd slaughtered his son. The tsar came to life and she backed away, enveloped in the scarlet of blood… Drums pounded, reverberating in a nonstop, hypnotic rhythm, thudding deep inside her…and all the while, she heard the groans and cries from beyond the door in her dreams…the sounds of Gabe being tortured.

When she finally awoke, Marina was drenched in sweat. She rolled off the sofa and staggered to the toilet. Still weak-kneed and nauseated, she splashed water over her face and wished for a mirror.

Then she decided she'd rather not see the hollow eyes and sunken cheeks that would look too much like her father's.

What had they done with Gabe?

How could she find him? He shouldn't have to pay for her family ties.

Her fingers curled over the side of the sink, which appeared to be made from some kind of shell-like material. She drew in a deep breath and cleared the last remnants of the dream from her mind, going over everything that had happened last night.

After Roman appeared in the library, interrupting her time with Roman, he'd quickly escorted her back to her chamber. That quashed any hope of her escaping while under Lev's watch.

Roman's anger and annoyance had been ill-concealed by his manner and stance, but he spoke only respectfully to his father. And he said nothing further to Marina, save, "So you have learned the family secret, have you." Then he took her back to her room.

Marina burned with questions she wanted to ask, but even stronger was the glittering desire to touch those old books and see each one of them. To study and pore over them, to translate and touch and dwell in the world of an ancient manuscript. It was a craving that grew ever more strongly within her even as she struggled for a way to find Gabe and get them both out of here.

It was a quandary with no simple answer. The scholar in her craved to revisit the library, to put all of her efforts into that outcome and find a way back to it, find the time to spend there. But the human in her, the woman and the American, knew she must focus all of her energy on finding Gabe and escaping.

Of course, that assumed he was still alive.

That dark thought numbed her obsession with the library, and Marina sank back onto her sofa bed to think. She had to find a way out of this room.

When Lev came in last night, she'd been dead asleep, but awake and aware when they left the room. How had he opened the door?

She thought hard, focused, pinpointed her memory, and came to the frustrating conclusion that the door had seemed to just *open* when it needed to.

Was there some kind of command? A sensor? A button—*in the floor?*

Marina launched herself off the sofa and began scrabbling about the thickly carpeted floor in the threshold area of the room. The floor covering reminded her of generous skeins of sheepskin, woven into a pattern rather than a carpet with pile threads.

Nothing. No slight indentation, no raised bump upon which one could step like one did on the automatic doors in supermarkets.

She used her nails to pick the carpet away from where it met the walls, trying to tear it up to see what was underneath.

And then the door slid open.

At first, Marina thought she'd somehow been successful, but then she saw the pair of feet in front of her.

She looked up into the amused, surprised face of an attractive older woman.

Her first instinct was to vault through the open door, right at the woman's feet, but her brain was still foggy and she wasn't quick enough. The door slid closed. The woman stood in her chamber.

"Looking for something?" she asked, not unkindly.

"My earring," Marina replied with sarcasm, cursing herself for not reacting more quickly. She could have been through the door and down the hall before the woman picked herself up from the ground.

"My name is Stegnora."

"What have they done with Gabe?"

Stegnora blinked as if surprised at her demand, her eyes showing a flicker of kindness. "He is alive, but not in the best of health."

"I want to see him. Take me. There's no reason for them to harm him."

Stegnora looked at her as if trying to read her face, and Marina stared her back down. If she could at least see Gabe, have a sense of where he was, if—*when*—she got out of here, she'd know where to go.

The woman drew in a long breath, then released it. "I came only to meet you, Mariska. Your appearance has both upset and delighted my Roman. I will have to get his permission to take you from your room. But I will tell you this. I will visit your friend myself and see if there is anything I can do to make him more comfortable. And if you want him to remain alive, do not anger

Roman. There is little chance that you might yet convince him to keep your companion alive."

Then it was true: Roman planned to kill Gabe. "I'll convince him. Tell me how."

"Roman does not like Out-Worlders, and he will not take the chance that someone might discern our location, or interrupt his plans. He will remove anyone or anything that stands in the way."

"*His plans.* He hasn't seen fit to divulge them to me, yet he indicated that I was somehow a part of it."

"You are a part of it because you belong to us. We are committed to doing what is necessary to—"

The door behind Stegnora slid open.

Marina looked up and braced herself, expecting to see Roman.

Instead, a tall man, very handsome and apparently very angry, strode into the room. He was well over six feet by her judgment, and his close-cropped dark blonde hair was brushed forward to frame a high, Slavic forehead. Piercing, unsettling green eyes scanned over her briefly then latched on to her companion.

"You have overstepped your bounds, Nora." His words matched the harsh expression on his angular face. "If you have any common sense in that scientific, love-sopped mind of yours, go now and do not come back."

Nora scrambled to her feet, and shot a look at him that smacked of fear. Without another word, or even a glance at Marina, she hurried from the room. The door swished closed, and left Marina alone with a man that in any other circumstance, she'd find utterly attractive.

"And who are you? A long-lost brother of mine?" Marina pulled to her feet and, though he towered over her, she refused to be cowed.

He looked her over, head to toe, slowly and arrogantly, as though waiting for her to turn and show him all sides. "So you are the infamous Mariska—or shall I call you Marina?"

"And you are?" She stood her ground, and gave him the same treatment, skating her gaze over his tanned face, broad chest, and well-formed legs hugged by battered jeans. He had a wide, sensual mouth that at this moment held the barest curve of an arrogant smile, and deeply cut dimples that might have made another man look soft or feminine, but merely made him more masculine.

"Rue Varden. And no, I am not your brother."

"How do you get that door open?" she asked suddenly.

He turned to look behind him. Apparently he saw the ripped-up rug, because he grinned sardonically. "Ah, I see you've been trying to find a way out of here. Well, a little hint for you: the only way to open the doors in these visitor chambers is through a radio key. Like this." He held out his hand, and the sleeve of his shirt slid back, revealing what looked like a wristwatch. A slim, brushed metal cuff of silver cupped his wrist, and the top sported a small screen and three buttons.

"I want one of those."

He laughed. "Guess you can't expect to get what you don't ask for, hmm?"

"I see no reason I should be a prisoner here, if I am, indeed, one of you."

"That is something you will need to take up with Roman." The gleam in his eyes told her it would be a fruitless endeavor.

"Well, now that you've come to view the family's latest freak, you can leave and give me some privacy."

"Of course. I'm sure we'll meet again, Marina."

She watched as he pressed onto his arm, through the sleeve of his shirt where the radio key was, and the door slid open.

How was she going to get one of those?

"By the way." He stopped in the entrance and pivoted to look back at her. "Your pleadings with Nora to care for your companion were for naught. Roman has placed the order for his execution tonight."

And then he was gone, leaving Marina to charge after him in futility, slamming into the door as it closed.

July 12, 2007
Langley, Virginia

This time, Colin had less than fifteen minutes' warning before Helen snagged him for a meeting, on her way back to Chicago from a briefing in DC. She'd made a detour to his second office at the Pentagon, where he'd been for another tedious budget meeting.

"We received this today," she told him without preamble, walking behind his desk as she dug in her briefcase. "We've got two days to figure this out, Colin. I hope your team's made some progress."

She pulled out a silver disk, reached behind him, slipped it into the drive on his computer, fumbled through a few buttons, and suddenly the screen opened up to show a man, vaguely familiar to Colin, sitting casually in an armchair. He was holding something in his hands that was not completely visible on-screen.

"I am Roman," the man said.

Colin stared. He'd thought never to see that man's face again; yet he'd longed for the opportunity. There had been a time when he'd wanted to destroy it with his bare hands.

He still did.

"I am a representative of Gaia, the earth on which we all live. The earth which we are all a part of. The decisions made by your people have damaged her beyond repair, and continue to eat away at her resources while the capitalists continue to consume more, dirty her more, and waste more.

"This is not acceptable to us, or to Gaia. This must stop. In an effort to persuade your government to take this warning seriously, we will be conducting Phase Two of our public relations program on Friday, July 14, at noon.

"You have already been exposed to Phase One of our program in the areas of Allentown, Pennsylvania, Terre Haute, Indiana, and Hays, Kansas. It was an elementary decision to put our attention on a company such as AvaChem that has no respect for our earth.

"Please be advised that Phase Two will be much more convincing and will have three big targets with more extensive damage. After we have executed our program, we will be in touch for discussions before scheduling a third phase. Depending upon the results of our discussions, perhaps there will be no need to move forward with Phase Three. But that will be up to you and your government." The screen went blank.

Colin blinked.

And so, the holy war had begun.

Rage and admiration warred within Colin. Roman Aleksandrov was mad...yet as brilliant and in control as ever.

Helen was speaking, and he dragged himself out of the past to tune into her. "One of the networks received the clip this morning via email, and they passed it on to me."

"What was he holding? I couldn't see."

"I've got Tech working on a clip of the video to see if we can enlarge it. Far as I can tell, it's a small metal object—but it could just as easily be a pen. So what does your officer have, Colin? He was due to report in four hours ago."

"He hasn't. I have been trying to raise him on his satphone since you and I met yesterday, but I can't get him. I did leave a voice mail to update him and Dr. Alexander on the status. He'll contact me as soon as he can."

"Let's hope the delay is because they're making progress and have found a way into the Skaladeska camp."

"Gabe's the best, and Dr. Alexander is no slouch."

"Gabe?" She looked sharply at him.

"MacNeil."

"Gabe MacNeil is your agent on this?"

"Yes. Is there a problem?" He didn't have time for female sensibilities.

"Of course not. I was merely surprised. I know him."

"Yes, he mentioned that. Now...three big targets."

Helen began pacing again, her blonde hair, loose today, swinging. Her face looked tired, and the gloss of her lipstick faded. "They're going to target another industry that is damaging the earth. But which one?"

"There are so many."

"That, I believe, is their point." She reached over to push a button on the computer. The disk slid out. "But which one this time? Oil? Air pollution? Manufacturing?"

"Noise? Light? Deforestation?"

They stared at each other. The potential target industries were endless.

Not to mention possible sites.

Colin had to shake his head, his stomach tight. "If Gabe doesn't contact us in time, we're on our own."

"We've got two days—I'd say we already are."

TWENTY-FIVE

July 13, 2007
Siberia

"The targets have been set, and the drilling has commenced." Roman paced the chamber he affectionately called the Green Room, despite the fact that its meaning was lost on everyone except perhaps Varden, who'd lived Out-World more than the others—for there wasn't a hint of green anywhere. "All three explosives should be deposited within the next twelve hours."

Lev, seated in a position of power at an oblong table, nodded slowly. "They are all in the same vicinity. And all are targeting automobile companies?"

Roman nodded. "Indeed. Three of the largest automobile companies in the world, all with headquarters situated within a fifty-mile radius, in or near the city of Detroit. The area will be devastated when those buildings fall, and because of the proximity, their suppliers will be affected as well. A chain reaction."

"I must agree then that your choice of three targets is appropriate. Automobiles are but one offender to Gaia, and the stink of their emissions but one poison in her world, the engorgement of oil and petrol, the waste of their metal... Still, the message will be clear and the devastation of the brains of the three companies will halt the production of those machines at least for a time. It will cripple the industry in one fell blow." Lev appeared to agree with the decision Roman had made, and for that, he was grateful.

Anticipation had kept him alert and focused since Nora notified him early that morning that the third explosive had been completed and was being delivered. She had sent it off before coming to advise him, so that it would already be en route to meet Dannen Fridkov and the others in Detroit. She knew Roman would be pleased with the progress.

She hadn't failed him.

Less than twenty-four hours, and he would have the world on the edge of its collective seat, listening for his very breath.

Roman resisted the desire to laugh, or even to smile. Not yet. He was not that careless. There was still opportunity for things to go wrong. Unlikely, impossible, truly—but Roman did not count the eggs in his basket as chickens until they were safely hatched.

Varden, who sat next to Lev, commented, "Surely the message you sent to Washington was taken seriously. They would be foolish not to."

"Yes, I am certain even now they are scrambling to determine where and how our Phase Two will be executed."

"Even if the targets were identified, they wouldn't be able to stop us," Varden continued. "Although they could possibly evacuate the buildings."

"That is true." Lev looked at Roman. "Have you considered providing them with further information? As you know, the loss of human life is inevitable, but not necessary to our cause. Crippling their industry and getting their attention is truly our goal."

"We could provide them with further information, but I'm not certain how timely it would be," Roman said. "I did provide enough of a hint—and if they cannot put the pieces together, then so be it. And there is always the outside chance that if they knew where our targets were, they could remove sensitive or important material in order to keep their businesses running as well as evacuate. Regardless, we detonate at midnight."

"That would be noon, local time in Detroit," Varden said blandly. "Which will give us a much higher rate of casualties than in Phase One."

"Precisely."

"And if we give them clear warning, we could enjoy seeing them scramble to prevent something they know will happen," Varden added with a quirk of his lips. "That would be amusing."

"There is value in that, too. Yes. It is worth considering for our next phase—"

"If there is one," Varden added.

"If there is one," Roman agreed.

Privately, he knew he would make sure there was. The world had not been kind to him. He saw no reason to hold back now that he was in control.

Desperation fueled her, yet Marina could only pace the room. Gabe was going to be executed within hours and she had no way to stop it.

She didn't have any means with which to summon anyone to her, to plead for his life. She was stuck in the room with no way to communicate.

To just wait.

And to Marina, death was almost preferable to waiting.

That was why she hadn't left Dennis Strand in the mine, even when the water was rushing in. She'd rather be doing something, anything, than sitting while things spun out of control.

Yet here she sat. For all she knew, Gabe could be dead already.

Frightened, frustrated, furious…she wandered the room, flipped through the menu options on the computer screen, and finally found herself at the small food cupboard.

She opened the tiny cooler, looked inside, and saw that it had been restocked. Water, juice, more meat, and cheese this time. She slammed the door shut and opened the cabinet next to it. Perhaps there'd be an apple.

Her heart stopped. Then started again as she gaped into the cupboard.

There was an apple. And a pear and some bananas—and a small silver wristwatch that looked exactly like the one Varden had showed her.

Marina snatched it out of the cupboard and stared at it, the pushed a button. What a joke it would be if it didn't work. What a gift if it did!

But who? And how?

She'd been in the room the whole time. She'd never left, except when Lev took her the night before, but she'd looked in there since then and the wristband hadn't been there.

But she'd taken a shower. Could someone have come in then? Restocked the food and left her the watch? Or maybe the cabinet opened from the rear, and that was how the food was restocked.

Marina slipped the band over her wrist, fastening it so that it fit closely, and turned toward the door. She had no idea what buttons to push, but damned if she wasn't going to try all of them.

Then she stopped. Plan. Make a plan.

She stuffed food and water into the generous pockets of her pants. The water bottles were heavy and made her trousers sag, so she limited it to two. She needed freedom of movement. And the meat and cheese—they fit into the pockets of her tunic. Gabe would need protein. Probably first aid, too, but she would figure that out later.

Anything she could use for a weapon?

She already knew the answer to that, but did a cursory search anyway. Nothing.

That was it. She pulled her sleeve back from her wrist and aimed the radio key at the door. She pushed a button and waited, hoping there wasn't some kind of alarm that would screech through the area.

Nothing happened. Silence reigned.

She pushed another button, the one in the middle, and to her amazement the door began to move.

Marina was out in the hall before the door fully opened, her head swiveling from side to side like a kindergartener checking both ways before crossing the street. The hall was empty. Turning back to face the open door, she pushed two buttons before finding the right one to close it.

Now. Which way to go.

The hall stretched in both directions without a break. Doors studded the passage, and Marina assumed Gabe was behind one of them. But which one?

And how long before she came upon someone else? Or until they realized she'd escaped her suite?

Marina started along the hall. She had no choice but to take the risk of being discovered. Gabe had no chance if she didn't take one.

And then there was an additional hurdle: would the wristband work for the other doors?

It had to. Varden hadn't been wearing more than one. Hopefully, the band worked like a radio. Tune in the right frequency, and push the button.

Marina didn't try the first few doors along the hall. Something told her she and Gabe would not be kept near each other. In fact, she suspected he would be kept in a less accommodating area, since he was dispensable.

She had walked about five yards down the hall when she heard voices from up ahead. Now or never.

She stopped in front of a door, pointed her wristwatch, and watched with curiosity as the digital numbers scrambled, racing through some calculations, then stopped. The door opened and Marina shot in, pushing the button to close it behind her.

At first she thought the room was empty, but as the door closed behind her, she saw a form sleeping on a sofa similar to hers.

It wasn't Gabe. The person wasn't big enough. But she approached, cautiously, curiously. Were there other prisoners here?

He mumbled and stirred in his sleep.

It was her father.

At last, a chance.

She reached for his thin shoulder and shook it gently. The stench of alcohol told her he was sleeping a chemically induced sleep, so she shook him again. Harder.

He rolled over, his grey-white face gaunt and stubbled with silver. His deep-sunken eyes fluttered, then opened, looking up at her vacantly.

"Dad!" she urged. "Wake up!"

At last her presence seemed to penetrate. He blinked several times, then opened his eyes to look at her. "Marina?"

"Dad! Wake up. I need your help." She was pulling him upright, and grateful to see that he was dressed in a t-shirt and boxer shorts.

"How did you get in here?" The putrid, stale odor of his breath made her reel.

"Dad, I have to know where Gabe is. The man who came with me. They're going to kill him. Where is he?"

He blinked, sat on the edge of the sofa, and scratched his balls. Marina's stomach turned when she looked at his spindly legs, still thick with dark hair, his trembling hand, and the way his shirt clung to a sunken chest. When had he become so pathetic? Could she have done anything to stop it?

"They have him in the Confining Area in the Family Segment."

"Where is it? The Family Segment?"

He seemed to be regaining his wits. "The area reserved for the family Aleksandrov. Your grandfather and his family live there. It's private, and no one can enter or exit unless they are Aleksandrovs."

"You have to take me there. I have to get him out of here."

He was shaking his head. "Marina, no. I can be of no help."

She pulled him to his feet. "You have to! For once in your goddamn life, you have to do something for someone else! I can't do this without your help."

He sank back onto the cushion. "Marina, you can't save him. Roman is determined in his course. He's about to destroy half the city of Detroit. One more life isn't going to matter—"

"Isn't going to matter? One more life *does* matter, you drunken sot. I can't believe I'm hearing you say this. Dad, *you have to help me.* Now." At that moment, Marina wished she had Gabe's gun. She would use it. She would jam it in his face and force him to get off his ass and help her.

Tears of frustration stung her eyes. "If you don't help me, it'll live with you for the rest of your pitiful life." She stuck her face right into his, and it struck her that this was the closest she'd physically been to her father in decades.

He looked away. "I'm not leaving this room. The last time I interfered with Roman—" He shook his head. "I will tell you how to get to where they are keeping the prisoner, but that is all."

Marina took a deep breath. Giving in to frustration and fear would only slow her down, make her sloppy, and lose whatever chance she had to save Gabe. She organized her thoughts and listened as he told her how to get to the Segment, and where to find Gabe.

"When are they going to kill him? And where?"

"Only an hour or two from now. And I don't know how."

Marina pulled to her feet and started toward the door. "I'll never forgive you for this."

"Marina, there's so much you haven't forgiven me for. This one more thing matters little."

She stopped. Turned. "Dad." And then she couldn't say anything. He was right. She had never forgiven him for not being a father in any way that mattered.

"You never hurt me physically, or even mentally. You just were a nonentity in my life. You were so wrapped up in yourself and your vodka that I meant nothing to you—or could mean nothing to you. I came to that realization long ago. It was neutral, really. Our relationship. But this is worlds different. You could do this. You could put yourself out and help me save a life. And that would mean so much more than not coming to my softball games, or my college graduation. Or having any idea what I was doing with my life."

She waited.

He closed his eyes and turned from her. "I can't," he said, as he lay down and curled into a ball, rolling away.

Marina left her anger and frustration behind as she hurried along the hall. She knew where Gabe was now. At least her father had given her that much, but she had no idea how she was going to get to him.

And then, as she was moving along, she remembered something that made her stop dead in her tracks.

Something Roman had said. Something that could help her.

"We don't use guns," he'd said when she mentioned the break-in at her house.

Gabe's gun.

If she had that…

Marina ducked into an alcove and tried to think. He'd hidden it where they'd left their clothes.

Did she take the chance of trying to find their clothes, hoping they were still where they'd been left—or get to Gabe first?

Her breaths were coming fast and hard, and she willed herself to concentrate, slow, think. Pretend she was flying and something had gone wrong with the plane. That water was pouring into a cave and she had to react.

And she decided. So far her instincts had been right on. She was going to trust them again.

Because of Dad, she had a better sense of the layout of the entire complex. Although he hadn't drawn a map or given her a complete overview, she was able to put together a mental picture of where she and Gabe had entered, and how they'd been moved.

Hoping she was on the right path, Marina hurried along the corridors. When she heard someone approaching, she ducked into a room and waited.

All along, her nerves were tense; she expected an alarm, or the sound of running feet to echo down the corridors.

But luck was with her. She made her way back to the area she and Gabe had first explored without being seen or heard. It took two tries before she found the office where they'd left their clothes.

She was conscious of a deep thudding in her middle, reverberating through her whole body, as she opened the cabinet where they'd stashed their belongings.

They were there. The clothes were there in a dark huddle in the middle of the shelf. She reached in, pulling them out, feeling for something hard and solid and heavy. Something clattered to the floor, and she jerked back, fearing it was the gun.

It wasn't, but it was Gabe's satphone. She jammed it into her pocket—it might come in handy if she could figure out how to turn it on—then she returned to digging through the clothes. Nothing but her little squeeze light. She stuffed the light in her pocket. The gun wasn't there.

A heavy feeling settled in her stomach, and Marina stood, ready to dash out of the room and try to make up the time she'd lost. Then something made her look back in that cabinet. She pulled the light from her pocket and shined it in there, back into the depths.

Something glinted.

Marina couldn't grab it fast enough. She dragged that heavy metal comfort from the very rear of the cupboard and looked down at it. Now she had a chance.

Not that she knew how to use it. But that had never stopped her before.

The first problem she encountered was getting through the security screen.

Marina paused at the doorway and considered. There appeared no way to get the weapon past without going through the sensitive screen. Was there a way to deactivate it?

She could always shoot the damn thing.

What more did she have to lose? If she didn't move quickly and boldly, she was going to lose Gabe anyway.

Marina looked over the gun gingerly. Was there a safety? Would she recognize it if she saw it? Did she have to cock it?

What the hell.

Taking a deep breath, she pointed it at the side of the security screen, aimed, and pulled tentatively on the trigger.

The trigger resisted at first, and she almost stopped—but then, suddenly, it snapped back and the shot kicked the gun in her hands. She almost dropped it, the jolt was so unexpected and her nerves were so strung out.

The screen sizzled, blackened, and Marina, her heart in her throat, ran through the archway. If someone heard the noise, they'd be there in record time.

More worried about haste than secrecy, she hurried back through the corridors with more speed and less care than she had the first time.

It didn't take more than fifteen minutes to get back to where she and Dad had been staying, now that she knew how to navigate the shiny white corridors and open the silent doors. It occurred to her at that point to wonder why her father didn't want to leave his room. After all, he seemed to be in the same kind of prison that she had been.

But she didn't dwell on that; he'd made his choice, she'd make hers.

Hurrying past his doorway, she continued along the hall and was just approaching hers when she heard the sound of voices. Male voices.

She had to hide.

Without conscious thought, she turned and jammed a button on her wristband, and the door of the suite in which she'd been imprisoned opened.

She closed the door none too soon, for just as she turned, the door began to open again.

The gun was in her hands. She looked down at it, instantly knowing it wasn't the time to use it. She threw herself on to the sofa bed and jammed it under a cushion just as the door was wide enough for her visitor to step in.

It was Varden.

"What do you want?" she snapped, hoping to hide her too-fast, too-deep breaths.

"I just came to be certain that you were still comfortable. And to let you know," he added, stepping closer, his green eyes scoring her as if trying to read what was going on in her mind, "that your friend is about to meet his end. So if you pray, you might send a few thoughts to your deity in his honor. Because nothing can save him now."

Marina wanted that gun in her hand. At that moment, she might have been capable of blowing the skin off his face, annihilating him for his arrogance and slyness. Instead, oh, it was difficult, but she resisted. She didn't move. She forced the fingers that itched to grab that heavy lethal piece of metal to stay still. Not to make not the slightest twitch to betray her emotions.

And she willed the bastard to leave so she could get out of there.

"Will you cry for him?" Varden asked, his face closer to hers. She felt overwhelmed, yet not precisely threatened, by his presence. Instead, she felt strength, tension—and attraction.

That realization almost made her reach for the gun.

Thankfully, he pulled back, looking down at her with an odd expression.

She met his gaze, mustering every iota of hatred she could. "Get out of here." She had to work to get the words from between her teeth.

He turned abruptly and turned toward the door. It was already opening, and he strode through without pause. And then he was gone.

Marina shook.

She dragged in five—count 'em, five—deep breaths, each one slower and longer than the last. The tingling in her stomach raced to the tips of her fingers. She was wasting time. But she had to get her emotions under control before charging out of there.

She knew where she had to go, and how to get there. But getting through the security would not be an easy feat.

And she wanted to make sure Varden was out of sight.

He was. The halls were empty again, and Marina wondered just how many Skaladeskas there were. Either there weren't more than twenty or thirty—which she found hard to imagine, based on the expansiveness of their compound—or she just happened to be in an area that was available to limited personnel.

Either way, she considered it a blessing that she hadn't been accosted yet by any random Skaladeskas.

Hurrying along the corridor, she found herself in a glassed-in walkway that actually appeared to let in natural light. It was the first time she'd experienced natural illumination since she and Gabe had arrived. This must be the connector between the Segment and the rest of the compound. Her father had mentioned it but gave it no further description. It was a tunnel, glassed in. Pale, golden-blue light filtered in from somewhere.

At last she reached the door to the Segment. This was where her real problem began.

In order to get through, the little tongue tab she'd seen the guards use had to be fed into a slot and "read."

Marina considered as the seconds ticked away. She could wait and hope they would bring Gabe through here. Then she could apprehend the group then, with the help of her gun.

But if they didn't bring him through, if they were going to execute him back in the private family area—she couldn't take that chance.

She opened the panel next to the door where the little tabs were, and thumbed one out. She hesitated. It was possible it would work for her. After all, she did have some of the Aleksandrov DNA. But if it didn't, what would happen? Would an alarm sound? Would the trespass attempt be somehow reported? Would she waste precious time?

She wouldn't take that chance. An idea caught her, and, holding the tab firmly between her thumb and forefinger, she ran back down the hall. There was one person who certainly had the right code.

When she burst into her father's room, he was sitting on the edge of the sofa, where she'd left him. He looked up as she ran over to him, grabbed his arm.

"You're coming with me. I can't get into the Segment without your help."

He pulled away from her with surprising force. "I'm not leaving this room, Marina. I do not have the will or the energy to interfere with anything ever again. I've paid my dues for my mistakes, and continue to pay."

Half expecting that reaction, Marina jabbed the tongue tab in his face. "Then spit on this, and give me your DNA one last damned time."

He hesitated, and she pulled out the gun. "Now, or I'll get it myself." Her hands were shaking and her stomach rolling, and she prayed he would cooperate. Because she knew she wouldn't pull the trigger. Dammit.

He did. He gathered the spittle in his mouth and let it drop onto the tab. Fighting back nausea, Marina turned and bulleted from the room, through the door she'd boldly left open, and clutched the dripping tab in her hand.

She ran back down the corridors, and was just coming around the corner when she heard it.

Voices. Lots of them. Coming from the Segment doorway.

Slamming herself against the wall, trying to fit inside a narrow indentation at an intersection of two halls, she waited. The gun, held pointing upward, her bent arm flush against the wall, the other hand gripping the tab.

This was it. She had to act.

Either they had Gabe or they were on their way to get him.

Or the deed was already done.

Please, no.

Deep breath. Voices coming closer. The tab in her hand, her key to entry, the gun growing heavy in her raised arm.

As they approached, she made her decision, tucking the tab safely into her pocket. At just the right moment, she stepped out into the hallway, grabbing the first and closest person in the group.

Roman.

"Don't move. Not a muscle." Marina felt a wave of satisfaction as she jammed the barrel of Gabe's gun into Roman's neck.

She felt him swallow, and the gun actually shifted with the wave of his terror.

The others froze, and she took that moment to let her attention blast over them.

Gabe!

He was there, hanging, quite literally hanging, from the arms of two men. As Marina stared, he managed to raise his head and look up.

His mouth moved; it could have been "fucking incredible" or "get the hell out of here"—she wasn't sure which. Either way, it didn't matter: he was alive, and conscious. Possibly even mobile.

"Release him." She didn't need to specify whom. Gabe stumbled toward her, holding on to the wall, and she saw the bruises on his face, along with cuts and other wounds she didn't care to define.

Varden and Nora were among the small group; Lev was not. There were three others, including the guards who'd carried Gabe. They all gaped at her, none daring to move as Roman trembled next to her.

The man was actually trembling. It amazed her.

By this time, Gabe had reached her side, and after a quick glance to ensure he wasn't going to drop to the floor, she refocused on Roman and the rest of the group.

"Everyone raise your arms—and remove your wristbands," she said when she saw Varden shift near the back. She should have done that immediately, but holding people at gunpoint was new to her, and she hadn't thought of it in her relief at seeing Gabe in one piece. So to speak. "Toss them up here." She gestured to the floor.

"Can you walk at all?" she murmured. Gabe nodded against her, and his blue eyes showed determination.

As the wristbands thumped to the floor next to her, she counted, and double counted. Even Roman complied when she jabbed him with the gun.

There was one for each person. But Marina wasn't satisfied. "Roll up your sleeves. Both arms. Everyone."

She found three more bands that way—one each on Roman, Varden, and Nora. That just confirmed who had the power and who didn't.

After kicking the bands into a small pile, she used her own to open a door and shove them inside with her foot, all the while holding Roman. When the door swished closed, she gave her uncle a shove toward his group.

He stumbled, fell against the wall, and stood there, chest heaving, face nearly as grey as her father's had been. Fascinating. Was he that terrified of firearms? Was that why the Skaladeskas didn't use them—at least, with his knowledge?

Marina started to back away, down the hall, one arm around Gabe, who was helping as much as he could, and the other holding the gun aimed at the group of people she left behind. Then she had an idea.

Stopping in front of a different door, she opened it and gestured for the group to move inside. "See how you like it," she muttered loud enough for Varden to hear as he walked by.

As soon as they were all in the room and she shut the door, she turned to Gabe.

He looked dead on his feet, but his eyes glowed with admiration. "Very well done."

"I didn't even have to fire the damn thing, except to get through the security screen," she said with a grin, which faded almost immediately. "I don't know how long we'll have until they get out of there, so let's get you the hell out of here."

Moving quickly down the hall, Gabe limping along and half leaning on Marina, they made good time navigating through the hallways.

But suddenly, no more than ten minutes later, their luck came to a screeching halt. A blast of an alarm blared through the halls, and the lights went out. Apparently, there was another way to get out of those rooms besides a radio key.

In pitch dark, in fairly unfamiliar territory and with a walking wounded on her arm, Marina was decidedly at a disadvantage.

She pulled out her tiny squeeze light, grateful once again for the little gadget, and continued trundling Gabe along with her. But she knew it would only be a matter of time before they were found.

Hobble, hobble, hobble...pause, turn left...hobble some more. Marina panted under Gabe's weight, and he seemed to sag more as they went further.

Finally, she veered into a room that was near the end of one of the halls. She wasn't sure where it was, for she'd lost her sense of direction during the last few minutes of mad rush. But perhaps a rest, maybe a little food, and some doctoring would help Gabe regain some strength. If they could remain hidden for a little while.

Inside the room, she propelled him toward a sofa—a real sofa, not like the one in hers and Dad's rooms. He protested weakly, but went.

She dug the water from her pocket and opened it, then shoved it at him and watched as he drank, taking slow sips. "No food, no water," he told her.

Marina pulled out the meat and cheese and offered that as well. While he ate, she scouted the room. This one didn't have an attached bathroom, but she did find some cloths that appeared to be laundry of some sort. Using some of the second bottle of water, she tried to wash away some of the sweat and blood that mottled his face. But when she tried to check the leg he favored, and the wound on his head, he pushed her hand away with surprising strength.

"No time for that now. We have to get out of here. I'm feeling better now that I have food and drink." He didn't look better, but his expression told Marina it was senseless to argue. "We have to stop them."

"What are they doing? It's something about Detroit."

"Earthquakes, I think. Like the one in Allentown. I don't know the details, but we have to find a way to stop them."

How could they stop them if they didn't know the details? And if the entire complex was looking for them? And if they were in Siberia?

Then Marina knew the answer. Dad. By God, she'd force him to tell her what he knew. "I'll be back. Gabe, you need to stay here and rest—"

His look stopped her. "I'm going with you. I'm feeling better now, and you've put yourself in enough danger. At least I know how to use that." He forced a feeble grin as he gestured to the gun. "It's a Smith & Wesson, in case you were wondering."

Marina hesitated only a moment; but two heads were better than one. And if Gabe were discovered, alone and weak, he'd be back in the same position from which she'd just rescued him. "All right. We're going back in there to find my father."

"Victor? He's here?"

"Oh yes, he's here." Marina took the time to tell him about Roman, Nora, Varden, and Lev, because she figured a few more minutes wouldn't hurt their cause and might help him regain a little more strength. She gave him the details of her confinement, and told him about everything except for Ivan the Terrible's secret library. She wanted to hold that to herself.

When she finished, Gabe said, "Marina. If you made it as far as my weapon, you were almost out of here. You didn't have to come back for me."

"I always go back. For anyone. Now, let's do what we have to do."

TWENTY-SIX

July 14, 2007

The halls were still dark when Gabe and Marina slipped out of the room. Not wanting to chance the full brightness of her light, Marina kept it cupped in her hand while Gabe managed the gun.

She was more than willing to give it up to him, and was also relieved that he seemed much steadier on his feet after the rest and nourishment.

It might have been the darkness, or the fact that no one would expect them to return to the place of their imprisonment, but Marina was able to lead Gabe back to Victor's room without incident.

"Only complete idiots would be coming back this way." Gabe's words echoed her thoughts as they stood before Victor's door.

Marina held her breath for a moment before pushing the button on her wristband. There was always the chance that Victor might sound the alarm when they entered.

Or that he would no longer be there.

And that, she found to her shock, was indeed the case.

The suite of rooms was empty.

"Now what?" Gabe asked.

"I want to go back into the private Segment. Maybe Lev's there. Maybe we can find out from him what's going on. He wasn't with the others."

"You're going to force an old man?" Gabe looked at her in the dim light of her flash, his bruised face appearing threatening in the shadows.

"Maybe he's being forced, and he'll be glad to help us." Marina didn't really believe it, but the way she saw it, there was no other choice.

"How are we going to get into the Segment, Marina?" Gabe whispered as they hurried back out into the hall.

"I still have the tongue tab from Dad. In my pocket. I'm hoping it will read the code even though it's long dried."

"And full of lint." Gabe's sarcasm was back, but he stayed with her on their walk down the hall. "Where the hell is everyone? You'd think they'd be scouring the place for us."

Marina could hear the effort in his voice. He was in pain. But she also recognized that he was built to keep going, regardless of personal discomfort. And saying anything wasn't going to make a difference. "I'm betting they're searching all of the exits—however many there are. They didn't expect us to be back in here, in the middle of everything. We're probably safer here than anywhere else." Then she remembered. "I have your satphone. Do you think—"

"My satphone? Are you—hell, give me the damn thing!" Gabe's voice shot through the darkness like a whip. "These things work everywhere!"

"I couldn't get it to work when I went and got the gun." She fished in her pocket as they hurried along. "Guess I have a lot to learn in the spook business, eh?"

"Well, you haven't gotten either of us killed yet, and you sure as hell know how to kiss...so I'm not complaining."

They'd reached the door of the Segment. Marina dug in her pocket and pulled out the tongue tab. "Cross your fingers."

She had to shine the light on the slot to feed the tab through it.

Then she held her breath.

And the door whirred, slowly opening.

Marina and Gabe hurried through, unsure how long the entrance would remain open, then paused to look around.

Unlike the rest of the compound, this hall was still illuminated. The pleasing yellow glow of lights studded the ceiling along the corridor, which was still the same rounded white walls Marina had noticed throughout. However, the floor was covered with a thick, padded carpet that looked like luxurious sheepskin.

It helped to muffle their footsteps as they hurried along.

"This look familiar?" It did to Marina. This was where Lev had brought her to show her the library.

Gabe grunted in reply as they paused at a T-intersection. "This way; they brought me this way. So let's go the other way."

She agreed, and followed him.

They'd gone only a few yards down the hall when Marina recognized exactly where she was. They turned a corner and suddenly a tall metal door loomed in front of them. And at that moment, they heard rapidly approaching voices.

"In here!" she hissed, and yanked Gabe after her.

The door opened when she pulled the hidden lever next to it—no DNA needed here, thank goodness, likely because she was already in the private section.

"Good grief. What the hell is this?" Gabe would have gaped if she hadn't pushed him down onto the floor while she frantically jammed the button to close the door. She pulled on the heavy metal closure, trying to help it move faster. "Hide!" she whispered to Gabe as the door clicked shut. She had a bad feeling.

She was right. She'd recognized Lev's voice. She sensed he'd want to check the safety of his library, knowing the prisoners had escaped.

Marina and Gabe scuttled along the floor behind the cabinets and tables and settled in a far corner of the room. The door opened again.

She recognized the voices right away. They were speaking English.

"They won't get far, *Sama* Lev. There are only three ways out, of course, and we have them all monitored." Varden. Marina mouthed his name silently for Gabe's benefit. The sound of his voice, smooth and cool, slid over Marina's taut nerves like the bow on a violin. It was much too soothing and calm.

"Yes. They won't harm her, will they?" Lev. Sounding more than a bit concerned for his granddaughter. Marina felt Gabe turn to look at her in the dim light, but she did not move. She wanted to hear more.

"You know Roman wouldn't do such a thing to the Heir of Gaia—however, that is not to say that there might be a skirmish of some sort and she could be injured. She was carrying a firearm."

"Where in Gaia's world did she get one of those? Roman has banned all forms of firearm here."

Marina imagined Varden's shrug, and had to keep herself from sliding to one side and try to watch them. She must be content with listening to the conversation, all the while knowing she was only inches away from priceless history. She wasn't sure which called to her more: the hidden secrets of this incredible treasure, or the need to stop Roman from carrying out his plan.

As if her thoughts had telegraphed themselves to the men in the room, Lev spoke. "How long until Roman's next phase is executed?"

"Two hours. Two hours and thirteen minutes," Varden replied after a short pause. "The detonators are in place. Fridkov is there, and has the controllers and is to set the timers at eleven thirty a.m. Detroit time. Then it will be inevitable."

Two hours and thirteen minutes.

Marina looked at Gabe, but he was already moving.

"Freeze." His voice cut through the room. "Raise your hands slowly. Both of you."

Marina didn't move for a moment. Then she pulled to her feet and faced the others.

Varden stood, managing to hold his surrender stance in such a manner that bellowed disinterest and unconcern, despite the fact that his position was one of vulnerability. Marina could feel the weight of his attention from across the room, and she returned his glare with a measured one of her own.

Lev's arms trembled with the effort of holding them upright, and when Marina transferred her attention to him, she saw worry and apprehension lining his face. It wasn't for their plans; it was for the contents of this room. She caught his eye and gave him a spare, meaningful look that she hoped conveyed…well, something. Her understanding, her empathy.

But Gabe was either unaware of the undercurrent, or didn't care. He'd started toward the two men, keeping the gun focused on them as he moved. "Thank you for your cooperation. It's not my intent to hurt anyone, but there will be consequences if you don't continue to cooperate. You may start by taking us to a room which will allow us to communicate with the colleague you mentioned was in Detroit."

He brandished the gun, and Varden, with one cool look at Marina, turned slowly, hands raised but cocked arrogantly to the sides of his body, and started toward the door. With a jerk of his head, Gabe indicated that Lev was to follow.

Marina fell into step, taking her time, desperate to have a moment—just a moment—alone with the documents in the room. She paused, running her splayed hands over the glass casing of a brown, cracked parchment.

This one was Sumerian. An unrolled scroll with some ancient secret that was only centimeters away.

Her fingers itched. Literally itched. To touch it. To study it.

But no. She couldn't.

She swallowed the lust and followed the three men out of the library, taking care to secure the door closed behind them.

She would find a way to come back.

Lev and Varden walked down the hall, further into the private area. Marina wondered where Roman was. And what Gabe's plan was for when they arrived in the control room.

As they walked along the hall, Marina marked the number of doors, for there weren't any hallway offshoots. She began to notice different patterns on the walls, along with some décor, shelving, and hangings. It began to look more like living quarters than a terrorist compound.

They rounded a corner, and everything happened very quickly: Varden ducked to one side, slamming into something on the wall that caused a shrill shrieking to blast her ears, then rolling into Gabe's feet. The force and his weakened leg caught him off guard, and Gabe was thrown off balance. He tumbled into the wall, and then onto the floor. The gun reported sharply in the small space, then skittered across and down the hall. And before Marina could react, a strong arm snaked out and yanked her back into a solid body.

Varden. Dammit, Varden.

He wasn't even breathing hard, and he held her easily, one arm around her neck and another looped through both of her arms, forced behind her back. "Leave it there," he commanded as Gabe started to reach for the weapon he'd dropped. "Lev. Please hand me the firearm."

Gabe pulled himself up, unable to stifle a groan as he slid up from the floor along the wall. The look he sent Marina was one of frustration and fury.

She could barely catch his eye, she was so completely aware of the man holding her. Furious, frustrated, and aware.

When Lev handed Varden the gun, she tensed, expecting to have the barrel jammed into her back and forced to walk along the hallway. But instead, Varden turned the gun toward Gabe and pulled the trigger.

TWENTY-SEVEN

July 14, 2007
Chicago, Illinois

It's got to be something related to oil," Helen growled, pacing again. Her feet hurt from being in heels since five a.m., but that didn't slow her down. The only way to keep her brain working was to keep her feet moving. "That's the biggest pollutant and the greatest harvester of natural resources. It makes sense."

Colin Bergstrom, loose-tied and weary-faced, sat slumped at the desk in her office in Chicago. His sparse hair tufted in awkward waves on the top of his head. "We've got Homeland Security and local authorities on alert all over Texas, Nevada, and Oklahoma. The plane's waiting—we should get down there ourselves. We've got no more than twelve hours, and no real clue where it's going to hit."

"And where's the plane going to take us? There's a lot of oil rigs down there. I haven't gone tearing down there because it doesn't feel right. Oil rigs? They aren't a powerful enough target. Big enough. They don't make a strong enough statement. If they were targeting oil, they'd be in Saudi Arabia or Iran. I'm thinking it's got to be plants or factories—they targeted the chemical plants last time. Or planes. Or cars. You haven't heard anything from MacNeil?" Frustration burned through her. And worry, though she tried to ignore it. Dammit, she *knew* the guy on the other side.

Knew him in every way.

Bergstrom shook his head. "No. I've called his satphone several times, and it's not turned on. I don't have a good feeling about this."

"You should have let me send my team up after them, Colin. One agent and a civilian's all we got, and right now, it's nothing!" Her biggest, most volatile assignment yet, and she'd bowed to the Good Old Boys Network and let a senior CIA director tell her how to run her operation.

Four older brothers and ten years in the Bureau and she'd learned diddly.

Damn her for a fool.

"You sent a team up there anyway."

"I did, but we couldn't find anything but their SUV. They're gone, and there's no trace of them." Her heels were clacking like her grandma's knitting needles working on a heavy woolen sweater. "If we could just figure out what he's holding... Let's watch that clip again."

She stalked over to her laptop, clicked the mouse buttons a few times, and stared at the screen. Waited for her fingers to begin their telltale tingling.

Roman's face filled the screen, and she watched, her eyes narrowing, staring, hoping for something to click.

"... Please be advised that Phase Two will be much more convincing and will have three big targets with more extensive damage—"

"Look! Did you see that?" Helen snatched up her wireless mouse—her one techie gadget, because she hated cords—and clicked. The picture froze, and she backed it up slowly. "'Will have three big targets'—did you see how he looked down? He's looking down at whatever he's holding."

Colin had pulled himself out of her chair and crowded next to her. He smelled like too much Old Spice and cigars. "Didn't your tech people ever get this clip enlarged? They couldn't figure out what it was?"

Helen grunted, impatient with herself for missing this important clue and focusing on oil rigs for too long. A few more clicks and she had another file open. "This is what Tech found for me—let's take a look."

She rolled the enlarged clip, which was fuzzy and dark, but the wrap of Roman's fingers around the object was clear. Peering closer to the screen, she tilted her head, trying various angles, repeating the message over and over. "Three big targets with more extensive damage. That's all he says. Three big targets with more—"

She slammed her hands down on the table so hard the laptop jolted. "Oh my God, that's it! Look, Colin, look—do you see? The edge of that metal thing? It looks like a bumper. And a red taillight He's holding a frigging Matchbox car. *Three big targets.* The Big Three...now known as the Detroit Three. The auto companies. Good Lord, how could we have missed it?"

He looked at her, amazement dawning. Then it fell. "Sure. And how many auto factories are there in this country? We'll have to get every Fed and cop in the country on call!"

"No, no, it's the *Big Three.* The Detroit Three. It's got to be— didn't Gabe and Marina disappear from Michigan? Isn't Alexander from Michigan? Detroit, Motown—Colin, the home of what used to be the Big Three auto company headquarters. He told us right out where and when!"

Bergstrom looked at her, nodding slowly. "Yes, that could be. That could be it."

Helen watched him, her adrenaline pumping...she knew she was right. She knew it. And she wasn't going to let Bergstrom sway her from what she needed to do again. Her fingers were tingling.

"I know I'm right. It feels right. It makes sense. We've got less than twelve hours to secure Detroit." Calm now, purposeful, Helen strode out the door of her office, already punching buttons on her cell phone.

Now that she knew what had to be done, it would be.

July 14, 2007
Siberia

"Why is he doing this?" Marina leaned close to Lev. He smelled like an old man. Clean, a little musky, and of age—something she couldn't define. It was strangely comforting to her.

Her grandfather looked at her with wise eyes. As before, she was struck by the peace and serenity that glowed there. "It is his calling, Mariska. It is our calling. Yours too."

They were sitting in a large room with a comma of a table along one side, studded with computer monitors like the crenellations on the top of a castle wall. Varden, Roman, and Nora clustered together around one of the glowing white screens, talking, gesturing, and alternately typing.

Command Central.

Victor had already been in the room with Roman when Varden brought Marina in, and now he sat in a chair near her and Lev, watching with apparent disinterest. He'd barely acknowledged his daughter's presence. No more than a brief flash of a glance and then, his mouth tightening, he had turned away.

Although she wasn't restrained, Marina felt as much a prisoner as if she had been. Varden had been clear enough when he propelled her toward the cluster of chairs and then turned to lock the door behind him. The sardonic grin he shot at her was the only warning she needed that she would be staying put.

Apparently, all the important people were now here.

While Gabe was left to bleed in the hallway.

Marina had seen him jerk when the bullet struck, but before she could break free of Varden's grip and rush to his side, Varden had yanked her off in an opposite direction. She had no idea where Gabe'd been hit, and what would become of him.

Her only solace, faint though it was, was that Gabe's would-be executioner, Roman, was otherwise occupied.

And here she was, in the heart of the Skaladeska compound, about to be witness to destruction in the name of Gaia. Unless she was able to find some way to stop them.

"My *calling*? It's no calling of mine to kill countless people and create massive destruction."

"Mariska, we are all a part of this earth. Slowly over the centuries and decades, She has been wasted. Irreparably harmed. Gaia is part of all of us, each of us a cell in her large body. If we do not protect Her, if we do not change the way we eat away at Her, there will be nothing left." Lev's passionate words bored deeply into her, and she felt a small click of response inside.

"I love this earth as much as you, as much as anyone. But to destroy people and their lives—that defeats the purpose."

"Does it? Marina, death and destruction and rebirth is a natural part of our world. Gaia has erupted with volcanoes. She's spewed *tsunamis* and hurricanes. She's burst with earthquakes, and roared with devastating fires. People, animals, plants, the earth—everything is destroyed by the natural way of things. This is how She responds to changes. This is how She controls."

"Lev—Grandfather." That the name came from her mouth shocked her as much as it did him; she saw it in his suddenly wide eyes. Why—how—could she feel any tenderness, any respect for this man? Yet she did. She did, dammit, in the same way she felt that irritating awareness of Rue Varden.

"Grandfather, that is the earth, yes, and we do have natural disasters—but to create them on our own…that's altering the natural course of things."

Lev's eyes crinkled slightly at the corners. Kindness and pride lit there, and his delicately wrinkled face pulled into a soft, weary smile. "The natural course of things has already been altered by man—since the beginning of time. He has taken over Gaia as though he is a god, as though he is somehow better than his fellow creatures. We all share the earth, as one, and when one species begins to thrust itself too dearly upon the others, the natural course must take place. Even if it is helped by man."

Marina lifted her eyes to look at the cluster of people around the computers. How soon were they going to detonate the bombs? Did anyone back in the US know what was going to happen? Could they stop if it they did? "What are they doing there?"

Lev placed his long, cold fingers over her hand. "Marina. Man has been helping—as well as hurting—Gaia since the beginning of history. Pompeii, for one. The sinking of Atlantis."

"Are you saying that somehow the volcanic activity of Pompeii was created by man? That's ludicrous. And Atlantis…" The legends of Atlantis were little more than that. Despite numerous theories, there was no real proof Atlantis existed, or if it had, where it was located. "Are you saying it's in the library? Atlantean writings?"

He nodded. His fingers still covered her hand. "It's there. I am ninety-nine years old, and I have been studying those manuscripts since I was fifteen. Thirteen, perhaps—it has been so long. There are many mysteries yet to be revealed—the languages are old and archaic, and difficult—but those are some of the things I've learned."

Marina wanted to believe he was delusional. She wanted to believe it with all of her heart.

"The Sacred, which I have long studied, and which reveals the ancient wisdom of Gaia, states: 'Gaia is one with us, and all living creatures are one with her, *and if there be a species of this earth that threatens the whole, it shall be expelled.*'" His look was steady, sure, serene. "Gaia has called us to act. And we shall. The time is ripe."

Marina pulled her gaze away from him. Like any other religious fanatic, he believed what he was doing was the right thing. And yet she often felt the same fear for the beauty of the earth and her resources. The dirt of auto emissions, the rape of the ground for natural energies, the stuffing of the landfills with waste…the puncturing of the ozone and the concern of greenhouse gases—all of it threatened their lives and, especially, their futures.

The old man sighed next to her. "You remind me so much of my Irina. She did not understand at first either—and you bear her resemblance so heavily. The same brown eyes, the same narrow, pointed chin."

Marina did not want to feel sentimental; she wanted to act. She pushed away the need to ask about the woman who must have been her grandmother. This couldn't become personal.

"Your grandmother did not understand that this is a battle, a movement; one that will not be won today, or tomorrow, regardless of the result of Roman's operations. We will be victorious. We will save Gaia, but it will not be an easy task. It will be a long-fought conflict. And that is something Roman does not comprehend." Those last words were spoken so quietly that they seemed meant for his own musings, instead of her ears.

Marina wanted to know more beyond his Obi-Wan philosophizing, and she asked, "Who's Rue Varden? He seems very close with Roman. Nora's son?"

"Not Stegnora's son. She is an Out-Worlder, one from the outside—like your grandmother was. It has been the Aleksandrovs' curse as well as our blessing to find love outside of our clan. Varden is Roman's nephew, I believe you would say—the son of Roman's wife's dead brother Brimar. He who died some years ago, and Roman and Nila took his son under their wing."

"Roman is married?"

"We say mated, but yes, he is. To Nila. But he has been obsessed with Nora since he met her at university in England, and eventually, he seduced her away—and brought her here. He will never leave her, nor she him. Varden is Roman's most trusted supporter, and it is fitting, as he is destined to be the next leader. He will take Roman's place when he is gone—unless an Aleksandrov shall take her rightful place."

"I would not."

Lev nodded once, then, as if satisfied, settled back in his chair and watched her. "And the library will come under Varden's control as well, then."

The temptation he dangled before her should be little more than a prickle of curiosity, when compared to the reality that simmered outside this room, in the city of Detroit. And, if Lev were to be believed, the world itself. Yet it was there. It burned in her belly, churned like white-hot lust.

To have those manuscripts.

He was offering her a lifelong dream—yet beyond anything she could have imagined, could have conceived.

Suddenly unable to sit, to listen any longer, Marina rose from her chair. She walked over to Roman, Varden, and Nora and thrust herself into their little group.

"Have you come to see what you're missing?" asked Varden with a cool look.

"I've come to learn what you're doing so I can find a way to stop you," she replied. Varden grinned suddenly, his eyes glinting, while Roman pulled his attention from the screen to look at her.

"Don't be foolish, Marina. It is too late to stop anything now, even if you knew how."

"Then why not let me in on the secret, since I am one of you."

She turned her attention to the screen. A man appeared on it. His pose was such that it reminded her of a newscaster—waist up, with a bit of scenery behind him: a sparkling river, five tall silver towers, a cityscape. She recognized him immediately.

"That's the man who tried to break into my house," she murmured. So he'd been working for Roman?

But instead of asking—what did it matter now, anyway?—Marina turned her attention to the screen and suddenly recognized the background. Behind him—the Renaissance Center, across the Detroit River. She knew where he was!

Excitement poured through her, then evaporated. So she knew where he was. What did that help? She already knew this was to go down in Detroit. It made sense that he would be one of the team that was there to detonate the underground bombs.

"He tried to kill me; guess he doesn't mind murdering a few hundred people in Detroit, eh?" Marina said.

"He tried to kill you?" Roman looked up. He looked stunned. "He was to bring you to me, unharmed."

"Tell that to the bullets he shot at me while chasing me up a tree," Marina snapped. "So now what? Does he flip a switch and everything goes boom?"

Varden was looking at her intently. "He sets a timer then walks away. Forty minutes later, the first of the bombs will detonate, resulting in the first earthquake. Ten minutes after that, the second will blow. And then the third." He made a show of looking at the clock on the wall. "And he will be setting the timer in less than sixty minutes. So ninety minutes, Marina. Only a little more than an hour is all that's left."

The lump filled her throat. Ninety minutes. What could she do? And why was he telling her all of this?

Why?

Marina wondered suddenly where Gabe's gun was. Did Varden have it? Maybe that would give her a chance. She tried to peer around to see if there was a bulge in his clothing. Nothing that she could see.

"And even if they found the box," Varden continued calmly, "there's nothing that can be done to stop the timer without the code. Which is written in Skaladeska. And it's right here, in this room. Nowhere near our associate in the US. He is powerless to stop the timer, even if he would wish to. Or be forced to."

"I'm going to be sick." Marina wasn't lying. No gun. She was helpless. The weapon she'd once disdained would have been a lifesaver in this situation.

"There's a toilet down the hall." Varden flashed her that nasty smile. "Victor, why don't you escort your daughter to the toilet. And keep her out of our way."

Roman had appeared to be uninterested in the repartee between Marina and Varden, but now he pulled his attention away from the screen where he'd been typing communications with his cohort. "Where is the code, then, Rue? You and Nora had tested it."

"It's here." Nora spoke for the first time and gestured to a green plastic sheet with writing on it. "I wanted it nearby in case there was need for it."

"No need. I just told Fridkov to set the timer." Roman pulled away from the controls with a satisfied smile on his face.

Varden looked as though he'd been slapped, but the expression was quickly subdued. "But that is twenty minutes early."

Roman looked at him. "I know. I could wait no longer. Why should I? I told them everything they needed to know—where it was, what the targets were—even the time—as you suggested. But I am impatient, and I see no reason to keep my word. I want to make certain they know we are in control."

Varden's lips were tight, and his face rigid. Obviously, he didn't like to be surprised—even by his boss. He didn't like to lose control. He looked up and saw Marina standing there. "I thought you were going to be sick. Take her to the toilet, Victor. We don't need her standing here looking like she's going to cry."

When her father gestured for her to follow him, Marina was too frozen to move. Forty minutes until the first bomb was detonated. At 11:40 instead of noon. And there was no way to warn them.

She followed Victor as if she'd just awakened from a deep sleep: numb, slow, heavy. When he led her toward the main door, out of the control room, into the hallway, she felt a minor blip of surprise. But then, what good would running away do? The place she needed to be was back in there, in control of the communication. And that wasn't going to happen.

Marina didn't speak to Victor as they walked down the hall; nor did he try to direct her or speak to her, other than to gesture toward what she assumed was the direction of the toilet. It was as if they'd both given up the pretense of anything remotely like a relationship.

As they rounded a corner, Marina saw a streak of dark blood on the white wall. Gabe! He wasn't there, but maybe she could follow his trail.

She didn't bother to explain to Victor; she just started off following the drops, splotches, and streaks that marked his route. She had no idea whether Victor noticed or cared that she'd gone on her own way, and she certainly didn't hear any shouts of outrage from him.

The bloody trail ended at the door to a room, and she pushed on it. If he'd gone in, he'd either had help or it didn't need a radio key. It opened.

"Gabe?" She dashed in, heedless that there might be others in with him. There was no time left to slink around. They were going to have to be bold if there was any chance of stopping Roman's plan.

"Marina?" a low voice called, and she found him near the back of the room, huddled, breathing heavily, clutching his satellite phone.

"Where are you hit?" Instead of embracing him, she started to lift his arm to assess the damage.

He pulled away. "Hardly more than a skim on my arm," he told her. "I'm okay. Been trying to stop the bleeding. I'm going to be okay, trying to figure out how to get in to where they took you. We—"

"We have to move quickly to stop them. We have less than forty minutes. Does that work in here?" She wanted to snatch the phone from him and start dialing herself.

"I was just going to try it. I just got in here; thought I could try to call Bergstrom and warn him, if the battery's not dead. It's been turned off since we got here, so it should be all right. Then I was coming after you."

"I followed your blood streaks. Victor—my dad—is probably right behind me." She was talking while he was pushing buttons on the phone. "I don't know if he's going to interfere or not—he seems so out of it."

"Colin?" Gabe was speaking into the phone. "Yes, it's me. I hope to God you're in Detroit." Marina could hear the voice squawking through the speaker. "It's going to blow in sixty minutes—" He looked at Marina, who was shaking her head. "Christ. No, they changed it. Forty minutes. Less. Less than forty—

"Damn!" Gabe looked up. "Lost the connection." He looked up and behind Marina, and she saw the expression on his face.

She whirled. Victor stood there, pointing Gabe's gun at them. "Roman might be terrified of guns, but I'm not."

"Where did you get that?" Marina demanded.

"I saw where Varden disposed of it."

Again Gabe moved before Marina expected. He shot up, knocked Victor's arms, and numerous shots blasted in the room above and around them. Victor fell back, and Gabe leapt on him, wrenching the firearm from his hands.

Once he held the Smith & Wesson firmly, he pointed it at Victor and ordered him to stand.

"I was going to give it to you," Victor said, his hands trembling. "Marina, Mina, I was bringing it to you."

Marina turned away. She didn't know whether he was lying, but she was past caring. Either way, it didn't matter. She would walk away and, if she got out of here alive, this man would play no further part in her life.

Gabe moved past Victor as if he hadn't spoken. His stride was awkward, and he held his arm against his chest, but he was mobile. He clutched the gun in one hand, and the phone in the hand curled against his ribs. "Come on, Marina. You lead the way."

She followed and left Victor staring after them: a shell of a man.

TWENTY-EIGHT

July 14, 2007
Detroit, Michigan

Helen had always pictured Detroit as a danger-infested urban location with murders on every street corner, but the downtown area where the General Motors Building was located looked peaceful, clean, and busy.

July 14 was a Friday morning, and the streets were packed with businesspeople and tourists alike; Comerica Park—where the Tigers played—was crowded with fans coming in for the first of a double-header, and the Fisher Theater was hosting a production of *Wicked* later that evening. Nearby, the MGM Grand Casino flashed lights, and gaudily dressed people hurried in to lose their hard-earned money.

And it wasn't even eleven o'clock.

The Detroit River gleamed gently in the low light, separating Detroit and the United States from Windsor and Canada. The five silver towers of the Renaissance Center, previously an office complex and now home to the largest automobile company in the world, loomed over the river and completed the skyline.

And if Helen didn't find a way to stop it, those towers would split and tip and collapse.

If she was right about the target.

Pray God her instincts were right.

"How big of a radius do we need to evacuate?" She had to be right. "We have two other sites to secure."

The Ford Motor Company World Headquarters was located twenty miles away in nearby Dearborn—an area, she'd learned, that contained a large shopping mall and the heavily traveled Ford Freeway, among other things, including the Henry Ford Museum and the Detroit area's only Ritz-Carlton.

The third site, the North American headquarters for the former Daimler-Chrysler, was situated thirty miles north of Detroit in the suburb of Auburn Hills—a mainly residential area, but also near the entertainment complex where the Detroit Pistons played and large entertainment events took place. It was also situated within half a mile of a busy freeway, appropriately named the Chrysler Freeway.

Detroit certainly loved its autos.

If any or all three—God forbid—of these planned explosions detonated, the damage would be so much more severe and widespread than the AvaChem factories. She could only assume the explosives would have been designed as larger and more powerful to be placed under such massive structures.

"Ten-mile radius, at least. We've already begun to give the orders," Detroit Police Chief Harold Benning told her. "But we can't evacuate the entire area; the traffic alone would be phenomenal. Instead, we're securing people in safe areas, and we can't do anything but hope our buildings are strong enough to withstand the force."

Since Detroit hadn't known many—perhaps any—earthquakes, Helen rather doubted the buildings had been built with that potential problem in mind.

Helen looked at her watch, willing the hands to stop turning. It was 10:55. Sixty-five minutes until the explosions would detonate, and they were powerless to stop them unless they found the person with the control box—which was like searching for a needle in a haystack.

Still. Helen wasn't about to give up.

Her fingers tingled. She had to be on track. And that was what she was counting on today. Little more than her instinct.

With the help of Dr. Everett, on-staff geologists had determined the controller must be within ten miles of the explosion detonation— yet he wouldn't want to be too close, or he'd be caught in the destruction. So the bomb experts and the geologists had done some rough calculating and pinpointed an outer radius of two miles where the searches were contained—at all three locations.

Three hundred law enforcement officials combed the areas: checking cars, buildings, shops, everywhere.

Someone had to find something.

The tingling in her fingers told Helen it was a matter of time.

She just hoped that time would come in the next hour.

At that moment, Colin Bergstrom ran up to her. "Helen!" he shouted. "I've got them! MacNeil!"

"*Tell me it's Detroit.*"

"It's Detroit."

She almost grinned, but there was no time. Hope, now, yes, but no time. "What else?"

"He called from his satphone. I could barely hear him, but he told me he and Marina Alexander were with the Skaladeskas."

"What else? Do they know how to stop this?"

"He said they moved up the time. Forty minutes from when we talked—which puts us at 11:40 for the detonation. We lost connection, but I know he'll try and call back."

"Forty minutes? Good God. Do they know how to stop this? Get him on the damned phone!"

Frustration crawled into her belly, gnawed there. It was close—so close. Gabe was still alive and on the job. And there was even someone who might be able to help them—*might*. But couldn't.

"Get him back on the phone! See if he knows anything!" She stalked away, ignoring the fact that she'd just snapped unnecessary orders to a senior CIA director.

She didn't care, because the tingling in her fingers was beginning to wane.

TWENTY-NINE

Siberia

As they hurried along the hall as quickly as Gabe could move, Marina felt the desperation crawling inside her. "Dial Bergstrom—try and get through again—and give me the phone. I have some information that will help—" She wanted to scream in frustration; it took too long to get the words out. "I hope to God he's in Detroit."

Gabe handed her the phone. The ring sounded tinny and far away, but when the voice boomed on the line, it came through loud and clear. "MacNeil?"

"This is Marina Alexander. Are you in Detroit?

"Yes."

"The man who is going to detonate the bombs—I can tell you where he is. You have to pick him up and get the box."

"Wait." There was silence, a scuffle, and then a female voice came on. "Helen Darrow speaking. Gabe? Am I to understand you're with the Skaladeskas?"

"This is Marina Alexander. Yes. The man you want, who has the control, is in Windsor. He's across the river from Detroit, directly across from the RenCen. You have about twenty minutes to apprehend him and for me to give you the code to stop it. If I can get to it."

"In Windsor? Jesus, God, we hardly have anyone over there—" Darrow's voice stopped abruptly, then Marina could hear her shouting orders, and the bumps as she moved herself, obviously running.

"Helen! Listen," she yelled into the phone. "Before we cut out again—he's got dark hair and he's wearing a blue shirt with green stripes, and he's right by the river. I couldn't see if there was a vehicle—"

The phone bleeped in her ear, and Marina knew it had cut out. She pulled it away and looked to see how many battery lines were left. One.

The next time she called, they had to have the man, and she had to have the code.

She turned to look at Gabe, who had a grim look on his face. "What is it?"

"We've only got one bullet left."

"Let's hope we don't even need that one."

They were at the door of Command Central. Marina looked at Gabe. His face was greyish; she wondered how much longer he could go on.

It might not be an issue.

He held up his fingers—three, two, one—and slammed his good shoulder into the door.

It didn't move.

"They've secured it somehow. How did they know?" Marina wanted to scream. She remembered Varden had insisted she go to the toilet. Maybe that had been his way of getting rid of her and Victor so there wouldn't be any interference.

How was it locked? None of the other doors were like this.

Then Marina saw the faint outline of a panel door. Jabbing at it with her poor fingernails, she managed to slide it open and display the now-familiar tongue tabs.

Holy crap.

The only way in was with Aleksandrov DNA.

Her heart thudding, she stared for a millisecond, then grabbed one of the tiny tabs.

Perhaps this would be the only time Marina was glad she carried those genes. She *hoped* that would be the case.

She stuck the tab on her tongue to moisten it, then fed it into the slot.

The little machine grabbed it, and Marina waited, clutching Gabe's wrist, hoping she had enough Aleksandrov genes that it would recognize her.

Then, miraculously, the door moved.

They were through the entrance before it was more than two feet wide, surprising the group at the computer table.

Gabe brandished the gun. "Freeze. Now move slowly to the right. Marina, get the code."

As soon as Varden and Roman were out of reaching distance, Marina sprinted into the room and snatched the green plastic sheet from the computer control area. She ran back to Gabe as he stood, holding the gun steadily on the group.

"You'll never make it in time," Varden told them. His words were general, but his eyes fastened on Marina. Again, she felt as if he were trying to tell her something—something subtle. He stared at her. Was that the slightest of nods? "Nice try, though. You've got brains and nerve, as well as good looks." Even now, his voice was mocking. But he'd given the barest incline of his head.

Gabe grabbed Marina's arm—partly, she thought, to help him stay on his feet, and partly to show their solidarity. "Wish we could stay and join your little victory party, but I don't think there's going to be one. I'm going to suggest that you not move for a moment while we make a phone call."

Marina took the phone and pushed the redial button while Gabe focused the gun on Roman, who, despite his supposed fear of firearms seemed ready to bolt. Which was greater, Marina thought, waiting for the phone to connect: his fear of guns or his fear of failure?

The phone connected and Helen Darrow's voice blared through. "We've got it. Do you have him?" Marina asked.

"Not yet. Ambassador Bridge was too crowded; almost there, though. You got the code?"

"Yes. Write this down," Marina said, starting to translate the code, which was written out in Skaladeska prose. "Green to the left—"

Roman and Varden moved at the same time, splitting, and Gabe fired reflexively at Varden as he shouted, "Run, Marina!" He whirled, slamming the gun at Roman's face when he threw himself toward them.

Marina didn't need to be told twice, but she yanked Gabe after her and pounded the button to close the door.

They tore down the hallway, and the sound of shouts blared after them.

Gabe wouldn't make it far; they needed to stop and finish the phone call—how much time did they have left?—and they'd never make it safely out of there.

The jumble of thoughts crammed in her head galvanized Marina to run faster, pulling Gabe along after her. Their pursuers couldn't be far behind.

As they rounded the corner, Victor appeared.

Marina readied herself to push past him, mow him down if she had to—but at the last minute, she changed her mind. Grabbed his arm. He was going to step up this time. "Get us out of here," she said, close to his face. "Or I will shoot you. I've got nothing to lose." She showed him the gun.

She looked at Gabe. He was fading fast.

Could she trust her father? Even with a gun pointing at him?

Victor blanched, but gave a short nod, his Adam's apple echoing it.

She looked at him, knowing she didn't have any time to waste, but what did her instincts say? Could she trust the man who'd lied to her for as long as she remembered? The man who'd never put anyone ahead of himself? The man who would have let Gabe die?

She had to.

"Help me with him," she told Victor, still pointing the gun at him. "How far?"

"It's not far." He gave her an enigmatic look. "I did mean to give you the gun."

"Come on. Get us out of here."

He looped one thin arm around Gabe, and it was ludicrous to think that he'd be of any help, but between him and Marina, they managed to move the three of them quickly down a passage that blended so well into the wall Marina would never have found it.

She felt the time ticking away, and she chafed. But they couldn't stop. The voices and pounding feet were too close behind—and getting closer.

They couldn't stop yet.

Suddenly, they were at a door, and Victor was pulling a tongue tab from a small panel. He licked it, and fed it into the machine, and the door opened.

Air. Fresh air. The grey light of midnight during an Arctic summer.

She became aware of a screaming alarm—a siren blaring a warning. One look at Victor—for she'd ceased to think of him as Dad—told her he was responsible.

He would not look at her. He merely stepped away from the lever he'd just pulled.

Marina yanked Gabe through the door and found herself on a small hill covered with tufts of brown-green grass. Four tall pines stood like sentinels overlooking the steppes below.

Marina grabbed Gabe's arm, trying not to think about what time it was back in Detroit, and ran. As if he, too, was spurred on by the fresh air, he picked up speed and kept up with her as they dashed over the uneven ground.

How much time?

As they came to the cleft of a hill, Marina heard their pursuers. She glanced behind and saw Victor, standing at the doorway, watching as a group of men dressed in pale Skaladeska clothing tramped through the door and after them.

Marina turned back to watch her own footsteps and stumbled to a halt seconds before Gabe did.

They stood at the top of a small hill, and down below them— ten feet or so—was blue-grey water, as far as the eye could see.

He'd led them into a trap.

THIRTY

July 14, 2007
Windsor, Ontario

Helen looked at her watch. Eleven fifteen.

They had twenty-five minutes to apprehend the bomber and reconnect with Gabe and Marina Alexander, who were God knew where, and have her translate the code—and hope that it worked.

Her underarms were soaking wet and her heart drummed so fast in her chest that she thought it was going to erupt from her body like in *Alien*.

First things first. She had to do her part.

"Did you get him yet?" she bellowed into her cell phone. Thank God she'd had some manpower near the tunnel that went under the Detroit River to Windsor, and sent them over immediately. Fortunately, the Windsor police were as dedicated to keeping the peace as she and her people were, and they didn't start any turf wars or jurisdiction games.

There was always the chance their target had moved, but he couldn't have gone far if he was keeping control of the bombs.

Could he?

"He's got a green and blue shirt on. Dark hair. He could be in a vehicle, or standing outside. Or in a nearby building." Stay calm. Follow the plan.

At last, the Taurus in which she rode blasted through the tunnel onto the Canadian side of the river and turned north. Her fingertips were tingling in earnest now; she knew she was close.

Urging Colin Bergstrom, who'd somehow commandeered driving her car, she pointed in the general direction she knew they needed to go. "Along the river! Go, go, go!"

She glanced at her watch. Eleven twenty. Jesus-petes, if she made this—

"Stop!" she screeched, flipping off her seatbelt so hard it smashed against the window. She was out of the vehicle before it came to a halt.

Yanking the Beretta from the holster at her waist, Helen streaked across the road, heedless of the oncoming cars. She'd seen a flash of green and blue near a streetlight, and, by God, she was going to get him.

"Stop! I have you covered!" she yelled, ignoring the surprised cries of bystanders.

Damn, it felt good to be moving, to be doing something. She ran onto the grass and bolted after the man who'd dashed off around the corner of a building.

She pelted up in his tracks and saw the wad of his green and blue jacket on the ground. Now she had no way to identify him… and he was gone.

But the man hadn't been carrying anything, so the box—the box she knew had to be at least twelve inches square, and that he had not been carrying—had to be around somewhere.

Bellowing into her cell phone, Helen ordered her men to look for the box. "It could be under a park bench. In a car. Anywhere! Grab anything you find that looks suspicious and bring it back." She sited and selected a landmark that was easily found, even with all the people around, and even to agents not familiar with the area, and started running back to the car.

She was almost there when she saw it. A faint gleam of metal under a park bench. Under a park bench, for crying out loud!

Helen veered to the side, shouting for Colin to follow her back to the car.

"Got it!" she shouted, recognizing the box as she ran up to it. She was already digging the phone from her pocket and stabbing at the keys to call back Marina Alexander.

Please let her answer. Please let this go through.

Green to the left. She remembered that one.

Eleven twenty-seven. She looked at Colin, who crouched next to her. His rugged face wore the same intensity, the same terror she knew her own did.

Good God.

Please connect. Please.

She looked at the box, already trying to tear into it. Colin's thick fingers, surprisingly nimble, pushed and shoved and poked at the box in her lap.

"Green to the left," she repeated aloud. What did that mean? "Green to the left."

She pulled the phone away from her ear to look at the screen. It was still trying to connect.

Come on. *Come on!*

Suddenly, on the bottom, a panel slid away from the box, falling into Colin's lap.

Buttons and dials. They were all there.

A green one.

She looked at Colin—their eyes locked. Holding her breath, Helen turned it to the left.

Nothing happened. That was good. She heard him expel his breath, heard him murmur, "Good girl." He looked at her again.

Please! Connect!

Then suddenly, it did. The phone was ringing.

"Green to the left," came a voice over the phone. She was running, moving; Helen could hear it in her breaths. "Blue down. Red…down." Marina was panting into the phone.

"Yes, yes, come on!" Helen said. "Blue down, red down."

"Black and white, cross over right—"

The phone went dead.

And Helen looked down. There was no black and white.

It was eleven twenty-eight.

THIRTY-ONE

M arina jammed the phone back into her pocket. She'd given as much as she could from memory of the code before the phone cut out.

She and Gabe were stumbling down a small hillock, toward the water that lapped trustingly below them, knowing their pursuers were on their heels. Hearing them.

A nippy breeze blasted her in the face as she pushed Gabe along the shore. There had to be something...somewhere.

The Skaladeskas had reached the top of the crest behind them, and Marina's back itched. She felt as though there should be gunfire raining down on them, but there was not.

Something else whizzed through the air and thunked into the ground an inch from where her foot had been. An arrow.

"Pick up the speed, Gabe!" she shouted between snagging breaths. "Toward those rocks over there. I can try to call Helen again then."

As they ran, she tried to look again at the green sheet in the dim light so she could spit out the code as soon as she had the chance.

Another arrow whizzed by, brushing the top of her hair, and Marina chanced a look back. The silhouettes of them were outlined where they stood on the top of the hill, firing, while another group chased them down the hill and along the shore.

Water splashed beneath her feet, cold and dark, and Marina veered away from it. Gabe was slowing down again. Bright red blood soaked his shirt and flung from his arm as he ran.

"Try Helen again," he said, gasping.

The rocks were only a few meters ahead, but what good would they do? A quick duck behind them and their pursuers would reach them in moments.

"Black and white cross right to green," Marina mumbled. The air she managed to drag in seared her mouth dry, and burned in her lungs. It was thin, and she suspected too late that they were at a high elevation.

And then she saw it.

A mirage? Good Lord, please don't let it be a mirage!

"A fucking boat!" Gabe shouted the words before Marina could reconcile it.

They kicked up their speed. The boat, a small cruiser, was sitting just beyond the boulders they'd been aiming for. Hidden. As if waiting for such an escape.

Had Victor known about the boat? The chance for escape?

Marina shoved Gabe the last few inches onto the boat and leapt on after. He was already untying its mooring, and she dashed over to the motor.

"Out of my way. This is mine," Gabe commanded, and before she could speak, he'd started the motor with a smooth purr. "Call Helen!"

Pushing buttons frantically, she placed the call.

Pulled the green sheet from her pocket again and started to reread it.

And realized she'd translated wrong.

Not black and white…orange and yellow. Cross right to left. She read the next line to be sure.

"Helen!" Marina yelled into the phone as the boat cruised into the lake. "It's not black and white. It's orange and yellow! Cross right to left!"

No one was on the phone.

"*Helen!*"

And as she waited, listening for that connection over the roar of the boat, she heard, somehow, the faint call of her name.

She looked up, out over the water. There was a dark shape. Victor.

How did he get there? What was he doing?

He was struggling, in the water, his arms raised as he went under. His face glowing white in the grey light above the dark water.

The Skaladeskas swarmed along the shore, arrows flying. A light beamed out over the water, scanning, searching. Except for that, Marina felt like she was in a medieval war zone.

"Gabe!" she shouted, still holding the phone to her ear, still waiting for Helen's voice, "Look!" She pointed. "Circle around!"

Victor was going to drown. Surely one of the Skaladeskas would pull him out.

"Marina!" Gabe shouted at her. "Talk to Helen. We have to get out of here!"

"Just one pass. I can't—"

The phone connected just as Marina felt the answering swerve of the boat. She shouted into the phone, "Helen! It's not black and white. It's orange and yellow. Hear me? Orange and yellow cross right to left." She looked up and saw Victor slide under the water.

None of the others appeared to notice or to care.

The boat wheeled around, and he didn't come up.

Marina's heart pounded. She looked at the phone, held it to her ear. Nothing. *Nothing!*

A shadow rose from the water again. Slower. Barely moving. Silent.

Marina's palms grew wet with sweat. She looked down into the black water—the cold, black, churning water that was waiting to swallow her. Smother her. She couldn't.

Please come up. Please don't make me do this. Dad!

She pushed the button on the phone, held it to her ear, listened to nothing. How much time had elapsed?

She looked down over the water again, ignoring Gabe's shout. It was as if everything stopped, slowed, dissolved away.

Dad or Helen?

Dad or Helen? One man, here, or many men, half a world away? And her own life…Gabe's life…

A hand moved in the water, reaching—she could barely see it—reaching from the inky liquid. Then slid back into the depths.

The powerful white light cut through the grey world, scanning over the water, glaring into her eyes. Arrows plopped into the lake, smooth and sleek, leaving only tiny splashes in their wake.

Why were they shooting at him?

Why weren't they helping him?

The phone remained silent. Marina's stomach tightened painfully. She pushed the button again, peering over the expanse of water, looking. Hoping.

Hoping for what?

He couldn't save himself.

"Gabe!" She turned, slapped the phone into his hand, and stripped off her shirt and pants. "Call her back!"

She heard his angry bellow as she dove over the side of the boat.

The cold water enveloped her like a heavy shroud, and Marina felt the shock through her body. Colder than Lake Superior.

Keep your mind blank. Keep it blank. Don't think. Just swim.

Stroke. Stroke. Breathe.

She focused on her strokes toward the last place she'd seen her father, tried not to think about the depths below…the blackness that settled far below her. She kicked, swam, breathed, counted…

And finally grasped the sodden clothing of her father.

His eyes were closed, and he didn't struggle. Marina wasn't a strong swimmer, but somehow she managed to hook her arm under his chin and cut strokes through the sparkling, cold water toward the boat.

The Skalas were close now. She could see the hair matted to the forehead of the closest one as he swam through the lake like an Olympic gold medalist, the light giving him a clear path to their boat.

How on earth had her father, such a frail man, made it this far?

How had she?

"Marina!" She heard her name and the roar of the boat over the buzzing in her ears.

Through a glaze, she looked up as the boat came near. She saw Gabe standing, holding the phone to his ear.

He didn't have to say more; she knew.

"Purple to left. Purple to left! That's it! That's all!" she screamed with what felt like her last breath.

The water closed over her. Her limbs wouldn't move.

The boat sluiced through the water next to her, and at last she felt the weight lifted from her arms. She let him go. She couldn't hold on anymore.

She'd saved her father. Somehow she'd saved him. Just as she'd saved Dennis Strand. And others.

And maybe, just maybe she'd saved Detroit…but herself? She couldn't move. Her arms were frozen, paralyzed…

Marina heard a shout behind her and she barely turned in the water. Then—someone was behind her, grabbing for her leg.

With a scream that came from nowhere, and a last burst of energy, she kicked, hard, caught something soft, and then suddenly she was lifted up and dragged over the harsh metal edge of the boat.

She tumbled onto the floor next to something else relatively warm, and as the roar of the motor filled her ears she looked over.

Somehow Gabe had pulled Victor up. And her.

They'd done it.

Had they?

Marina looked up and saw Gabe, grim-faced, staring into the wind that buffeted their watercraft.

"Gabe?" she cried, fearing the worst. That it had been for naught.

He looked down, surprised, and he nodded. A small smile curved his lips.

They had done it.

THIRTY-TWO

July 16, 2007

Later, when Marina recalled those next hours after their escape from the Skaladeskas, three things remained clear and burning in her mind.

There was the warmth and the solidness of Gabe as he pulled her close to him on the slippery deck of the boat. He surrounded her with his heat and arms and long legs, pushing the wet hair out of her face as he framed her jaw with his hands. The kisses were long and ferocious, slick and hot and frantic. And they promised much more.

When her heart settled and she was warm at last, cuddled against Gabe's chest, a realization suddenly crystallized in her mind.

It was the certainty, the innate understanding that, for some reason, Varden had deliberately given her everything she needed—the information, the opportunity, and, in his own arrogant way, the impetus—to stop the destruction in Detroit. He'd goaded her, poked at her, infuriated her—all of which served to urge her into action.

Her brain was frozen, but she mulled and reviewed and rewound, and it was the only explanation that made sense. Whenever Varden had lashed out with particularly nasty, inciting comments, they had come at a time when she'd believed all was lost. They served to anger her, as in the time he'd mocked her about Gabe's imminent execution—and renewed her determination to act.

And every bit of detail…he'd told her everything she needed to know to stop the bombs. He'd even given her the chance to leave the room, Command Central, when he sent her to the toilet to puke, and find Gabe and his gun.

But the most telling point was the fact that he'd had a point-blank shot at Gabe and had not killed him. How easy it would have been to put a bullet into his head.

Why not?

She wondered if it had even been Varden who'd put the wristband in her cupboard. It had appeared shortly after their conversation in which she'd asked for one.

Asked him, and hadn't mentioned it to anyone else.

And if so, why?

She didn't know—may never know. But she would be grateful to Varden for the role he'd played in her escape, regardless of his ulterior motive.

And then there was the other memory, which alternately horrified and mollified her.

When she recalled that last part of her adventure, Marina tried not to think about those later moments on the boat, with Victor huddled on the floor, coughing and shaking, trembling at her feet, but alive.

At one point, he looked up at her with gratitude and although Marina knew he would have liked it, she could not move herself to embrace him.

She couldn't touch him.

She'd saved his life, but she'd have done the same for anyone struggling, anyone at risk. That he was her father—the kind of father he'd been—didn't matter to her.

She couldn't cross that line.

Marina looked under the seats and found more blankets. She wrapped them around Victor and tried to make him as comfortable as possible, but her sympathy was impersonal. She couldn't help it. She felt nothing.

She'd done her duty—she'd helped him. But she'd never be his daughter. Just as he couldn't be the father she'd wanted.

It was the most they could give each other.

Perhaps she could have had some kind of relationship with him if he'd helped her when she begged for it—when she was trying to save Gabe.

But he'd turned away.

It wasn't until he had no choice, until he was faced with a gun, that he stepped forward to help them. And even then, had he really meant to help them escape?

"Marina." His voice was weak, and he began to cough with the effort. "Thank you."

She nodded, tried to smile, and pulled her own blanket around her. Gabe had moved away to drive the boat, and they were alone. "You're welcome." She tried to sound like she meant it. She really tried. Tears threatened her eyes.

She turned and sat watching Gabe as he navigated the boat while it sped through the choppy water.

And then, Victor started coughing uncontrollably. He couldn't catch his breath. He coughed, and spasmed, and coughed.

Marina, kneeling on the floor next to him, could do nothing but watch him struggle for breath as the boat thumped speedily through the water.

It was only because she was kneeling next to him that she heard his last words before he died.

There was no mistaking them; she heard them and they burned into her brain.

"Roman—is your father...I'm sorry. Not me...Roman is your father."

POSTLUDE

July 18, 2007
The Pentagon

The pod's been destroyed. The entire cave area that you traveled through has been devastated by some kind of explosion." Colin Bergstrom bore an expression that lined his face with stress. "There's no way to find our way back to the Skaladeska compound."

Bergstrom, Helen Darrow, Gabe MacNeil, and Marina sat around the small table in a conference room at Pentagon. Marina assumed this was what the professionals called a debrief. To her, it was more like the beginning of another chapter.

"The GPS readings from my satphone are long gone. If they were even accurate in the first place," Gabe said. His arm was wrapped in white bandages, and Marina knew from personal examination—and some intimate activity—that under his button-down shirt, more white wrappings hugged broken ribs and a nasty gash along one hip. "And when we left the compound, we were traveling in bad weather and at night. The boat had no navigational system, and I have no idea how long we traveled, or how far, or in what direction. Until we ran out of gas, then we floated for a while, made our way to shore and then walked for miles over rough terrain."

They'd had to leave Victor's body, for Marina and Gabe had barely been able to trudge along themselves, propped against each other.

"We've sent a crew over to the vicinity of where you were, from where you finally were able to contact us," Bergstrom said. Marina already knew that. She supposed that information was for Helen Darrow's benefit. "Radar isn't picking up anything. It's as if they didn't exist."

"But they did. They do." Helen's voice was firm and well modulated, and she never looked at Gabe unless she had to. "They're not going to go away, are they, Marina?"

No. They weren't. "Roman will be furious that things didn't happen according to plan. I'm sure he'll put some other plot into place as soon as he gets his bearings. They really believe—Lev does, for certain—that it's their responsibility to protect Gaia. To save her; save the world. For them, the end completely justifies the means. And according to Lev, Gaia, the earth, will work to expel any species that threatens the whole. They believe they are Gaia's instrument."

Around the table, an array of serious faces looked at her. "We're going to need your expertise, Dr. Alexander," Bergstrom said, unnecessarily.

Marina looked down at her hands—scarred, bruised, scraped. She thought of the mark on her foot, the genes that tied her to those people, and the same burning lust for the knowledge and the protection of the ancient teachings locked away somewhere in Siberia.

If she had to be truthful, there was a part of her, a large part—in fact, the majority of her—that was relieved the Skaladeska compound hadn't been located. Destroyed, it would have been, all of it. All of its brilliant technology and priceless antiquities would have been lost if the place had been stormed by US agents. In fact, she knew deep in her heart that if there was even a chance she could have helped them to find the location, she would not have.

Not yet. Not until they found her again.

And they would, for Marina had unfinished business there, with those people. With her family.

Her father.

Because, now that she knew the truth...Marina knew this wasn't the end.

It was just the beginning.

And her life was no longer her own.

Marina Alexander's
adventures continue with
Amazon Roulette

Now available!

Keweenaw Peninsula
Upper Michigan

Don't you think we ought to get back? The sun's getting pretty low," Kendra McElroy said to her companion. "Aren't there bears around here?"

The bottom of the orange ball of sun rested just where Lake Superior met the horizon, appearing eons of miles in the distance from the mountainous terrain over which they'd been hiking. Below, its blaze cut a matching path over the glistening expanse of water that stretched out past another small crop of mountains. The air was crisp and filled with the scent of pine, along with the screeches of crows and seagulls.

The last two days had been filled with furious thunderstorms, ragged lightning spearing into the forests, and torrents of rain— all of which caused the Sturgeon River to swell. But today, at last, had been a fine day for exploring the terrain where, for ages upon ages, massive amounts of copper had been mined. The Copper Country, as this northernmost jutting peninsula was called, had been the source of literally tons of its namesake metal extracted from the earth by man from prehistoric times through the mid-20th century.

"Don't you want to watch the sunset with me?" Matt Granger tightened his grip on her hand and wagged his eyebrows suggestively. "It'll be so romantic."

Kendra laughed. He was so cute! "You call black flies the size of bats romantic? And bears and wolves lurking about? Besides, it's getting cold." She paused to zip up her fleece vest and wished for a hat. What had started as a sunny Indian Summer day had turned into down right cold.

"I'll keep you warm."

"That's what you said when we went skiing…and I nearly froze to death!" But she was still smiling, and dropping his hand, moved closer so he could slip an arm around her waist. "It is a beautiful sunset, I'll grant you that. Your Copper Country is something, even with the flies."

"Let's just climb over this little hill, and we can sit and watch the sun go down…then we'll head back. I promise I won't let any bears get you."

"I'm going to hold you to that."

They sat on a rocky outcropping with the rippling waves of pines and fiery-leaved trees spanning the distance between them and the water. A golden moon hung behind them, and Kendra could see more stars dotting the twilight sky than she saw during the darkest part of night back in Columbus.

"I'm glad the storms ended and we had the chance to come out here before we had to leave," she said, tipping her head to rest on his shoulder. She was cold, and getting hungry, but there was no one else she'd rather be with. "It would have been a bummer if I'd had to go back without seeing this."

"There's nothing like the fall colors up here. The colors are so intense…well, take a look." He pointed. "Do you see that big fallen tree over there? Looks like it was hit by lightning, probably during these last few days of storms. Hey…maybe it's that cave that guy was talking about. He said he was going to come back and look inside tomorrow. " He hoisted to his feet. "I'm going to go take a gander. You never know what might be there."

Kendra watched Matt with an indulgent smile. That was her guy: an archeologist trapped in a computer programmer's life. He'd grown up here in the Upper Peninsula of Michigan, and they'd met at Ohio State two years ago. This was the first time he'd brought her home, but their sixteen-hour drive from Columbus to Houghton had been filled with tales of exploring copper mines and camping on Isle Royale so she felt as if she'd been here many times.

He'd taken her on the five-hour ferry ride to Isle Royale, a wild, uninhabited island in Lake Superior, on their first full day in Houghton in order to show her the prehistoric copper mines. To Kendra, they looked like little more than deep holes; they weren't anything like the cave mines she'd expected to see. And the hammers that had been used to chip away at the copper veins were shaped like large eggs. Sure, they were four thousand years old, but how anyone had recognized them as tools used by the cave men, she had no idea. But because Matt, who fancied himself the Indiana Jones of Northern Michigan, found it interesting, she found it interesting.

Or, at least, she acted like she did. True love required sacrifice.

"Hey, Ken, come here!" he called. His voice was high-pitched with excitement. "It does! It looks like there *is* a cave behind here."

She pulled to her feet, glancing at the sun, which had dipped a third of the way below the lake. "Is it a mine?" she asked, interested in spite of her freezing ears. It would be cool to be the first to find an old mine, and Matt would be in raptures for days. She pulled her hair out of its pony tail and shook it out, hoping it would help keep her ears warm.

"I don't know. It's pretty far from the other areas copper's been found; probably not a mine. But maybe a home site or burial place. It looks like it's been hidden behind these rocks for years… see the black smudge there? That guy was right—lightning must have struck here and tumbled some of these rocks out of the way. And the trees were growing in front of it? When this one fell, it moved them out of the way." He was beginning to sound excited. "Ken, this could be something!"

"We can come back tomorrow before we leave," she offered, looking unappreciatively at the narrow sliver of black. "I'm getting cold."

"I've got a flashlight in my bag…come on, let's go in."

"What about bears?"

He grabbed her hand. "No bears in here, Ken…the entrance has been closed off for years. Centuries probably—maybe even millennia! There could be prehistoric artifacts in there." His eyes were wild with excitement.

"Come on, hon. You're not going to find anything tonight."

"I just have a feeling about this place. What if there's something important in here? People have been arguing for years whether the cave men traded their copper with the Europeans, but there's not been one whit of evidence. What if there's something in there that proves it?" The words tumbled out of his mouth almost faster than he could form them.

Kendra tamped back her growing annoyance. Men needed to be taken firmly in hand and reminded of reality in a calm, logical manner. Even treasure hunters like Matt. Especially treasure hunters like Matt. "Honey, this is a cave. One of hundreds up in this never-ending forest. What makes you think it's any different from any other cave you've explored since you were ten? It's probably an old bear's den, in which case, I don't want to stick around and see if it comes back."

But Matt was already inside, and she saw the glow of his flashlight. Huffing angrily, she climbed over the broken tree trunk and stood in the doorway. "Come on Matt!"

"Kendy, look at this!" He poked his head out of the entrance, and even in the lowering light, she could see his the whites of his eyes, they were open so wide. "I think I've found something!" He was a five year old on Christmas morning.

Sighing, she started forward and slipped into the damp darkness of the cave. At least in here, the steady wind from the lake wasn't blasting into her ears. The interior was tall enough that she could stand easily. "What?"

"Look at this!" He was pointing to a small triangular pile of stones. The only thing keeping him from jumping around was the fact that his head brushed the ceiling.

"It's a pile of stones."

"Don't you remember me telling you about that lake in Wisconsin? Where they found those pyramids on the bottom?"

She didn't. "Yeah, I guess." She rubbed her hands together and wished for a pair of gloves. "Can we go now? We can come back tomorrow."

"I've seen pictures—this looks like a miniature version of those pyramids. Archeologists don't know where they came from—they weren't made by the Native Americans. Some people think they think they might have been from the Phoenicians! Oh my God, if this is true, I—" He took a deep breath and stopped. "Let me start from the beginning."

"Can't you tell me on the way home? I'm really getting cold, and I'm hungry, Matt!"

But he was in lecture-mode. Rapid-fire lecture-mode; one that nearly left her in the dust with the rattling off of dates and theories and numbers. "There've been people trying for centuries to prove there were other people here—from Europe or Asia—who either mined or traded for the copper. There was tons of copper taken from the earth here—4000 years ago, and we're not finding any remains of it. So where did it all go? Five hundred thousand tons of copper doesn't just disappear."

Kendra gave up and sat on a large boulder. "But you told me yourself, there's no evidence that much copper's missing—"

"But there's no proof that it *isn't!* No one knows how much copper was mined up here by the people with the stone hammers. I've done some of my own calculations, and I believe it's true— nearly five hundred thousand tons of copper taken out of those prehistoric mines."

"Honey, you told me, it's a legend! A myth! That there's no evidence any other culture lived here at that time—whenever it was—besides the natives. And you said yourself, all the experts say there's—"

"But what if it isn't? And what if this little stone pyramid was made by the same people who made the pyramids at the bottom of Rock Lake? What if there's another site in this area that's not under water!" He looked at her in the dim glow of the flashlight, his eyes pleading and at the same time, lit with an unholy flame. Was this how Howard Carter had talked to his wife while in search of Tutankhamon's tomb? (Had Howard Carter even been married? Poor woman.) "Just go in with me a little further, okay? It's warmer in here, isn't it?"

"Not really. But what if we get lost?"

"We won't. I've been exploring caves since I was ten; I know how to find my way out. Come on, sweetie, this could be really big! Just twenty minutes more, okay? If we don't find anything, we leave. I promise."

But it was only fifteen minutes later that Matt's dreams came true.

They rounded the corner of the tunnel they'd been walking through and found themselves in a chamber the size of half a football field.

"Oh my God..." he breathed. Kendra stopped behind him and felt her heart begin to race.

"Oh my God is an understatement," she said. "Wow!"

Two tall piles of smooth white rocks created neat pyramids, approximately ten feet tall, one at each end of the chamber.

"Mother Nature's amazing, but there's no way she did this."

Matt came unfrozen and started toward them, beaming his light around. "This is incredible, Kendy! There's no way the ancestors of the Ojibwa made these. No way. This has got to be from another culture."

"It's amazing, Matt! I can't believe it!" She really was excited, and had almost forgotten how cold she was. Almost. "Can we go now? We can come back tomorrow and spend more time, looking around."

He hesitated, beaming the light around the room a little more. Then, "All right. Let's go. It looks like the flash is getting a little dimmer anyway." He grinned and put an arm around her. "I can't believe it, Kendy! Just call me Indiana Jones!"

She had been. He just didn't know it.

"Or maybe it should be Keweenaw Jones!" he said gleefully.

They walked out of the chamber, and started back through the tunnel, hurrying now that they were on their way out. Kendra followed Matt when the area became too narrow for them to walk side by side, and she hurried along hardly paying any attention until she realized she was half-crouching for the first time.

The ceiling was too low.

"Matt, I don't think we're going the right way."

"Yes we are. Just keep following me, I'll get us out of here."

"Matt, I'm bending over. I didn't have to bend at all on the way in!"

He stopped and she bumped into him. "Maybe you're right. I'm feeling funny, too. Kind of light-headed."

"Let's turn around and go back this way." She tugged at his arm, realizing her head was starting to feel a bit muzzy too.

He pushed past her and she turned around to follow him. She noticed the flashlight beam, which had started off as a clean white light, was dirty now. A dingy yellow.

"Where are we?" she asked, panicked, ten minutes later when they had neither returned to the chamber nor found the tall, wide tunnel they'd come in through.

"I don't know, Kendra. Let's just go up around this corner, maybe the main tunnel is up here." But he didn't sound certain, and the note in his voice made her stomach squeeze painfully.

She was feeling dizzier now. Perhaps it was because she was hungry and tired…or perhaps it was because something bad was in the air.

When Matt rounded the corner, he tripped over a small stone and tumbled to the ground. As he fell, he slid against the side of the cave wall, and suddenly, stones and dirt and pebbles were raining down on them.

Kendra screamed his name, and more rubble fell in a loud rush, sending dust and pelting rocks onto her head and shoulders. The light was gone; either he'd dropped it or it had broken. It was dark, evilly dark; like she'd been dropped into a bottle of ink.

"Matt!" she cried. Then something heavy slammed into the back of her head and the darkness swamped her consciousness.

Colleen Gleason is an award-winning, *New York Times* and *USA Today* bestselling author who's written more than two dozen novels. Her books have been translated into more than seven languages, and she writes in a variety of genres, including steampunk, paranormal romance, and action adventure.

She loves to hear from readers, and can be found on the web at:
http://www.colleengleason.com
http://www.facebook.com/colleen.gleason.author

Sign up for her newsletter for updates, information, and contests!

CPSIA information can be obtained
at www.ICGtesting.com
Printed in the USA
BVOW08s1445180418
513720BV00009B/756/P